THE VANDALS

THE VANDALS

John A. Vikara

To order additional copies of this book, contact:

Xlibris Corporation
PO Box 2199
Princeton, NJ 08543-2199
USA

1-888-7-XLIBRIS
1-609-278-0075
www.Xlibris.com
Orders@Xlibris.com

CONTENTS

VIKA

TO THE FIFTIES AND ALL THOSE
WHO SHARED THEM WITH ME.

CHAPTER 1

PETE WILSON – OCTOBER, 1954

Pete Wilson looked thirteen years old. His baby face couldn't be compensated for by the black-dyed Eisenhower jacket with the crooked skull and cross bones patch on the right breast pocket. Not even the long slicked-back dirty blond hair and contrived hard expression could hide the pink cheeks and dimples that Dave Ryan said looked as smooth as a baby's ass. Dave Ryan would someday pay for that and other cracks he had made.

Three other teens stood behind him on the dark unpaved road; gangling Johnny Sadinski, Red Janek and Kelly Petrillo, the shortest and next youngest of the group. Kelly's black wavy hair was accented by a Tony Curtis curl that draped over his forehead. The three wore black leather motorcycle jackets, zippers secured against the cold, and collars turned up. Johnny and Red wore leather gloves. Kelly's hands were dug into his dungaree pockets.

The four lurked in silence, their streams of clouded breath piercing the air, moonlight their only source of illumination. They waited until the last three members of their fraternity ambled up the frozen road from Maurice Avenue, the closest paved street. Goggles Gaglione and the Ryan brothers, Dave and Timmy, offered their greetings. They could now start their nightly quest for action.

The dirt road ran adjacent to one of the many cemeteries that dominated the border of Queens and Brooklyn. It stretched for a quarter mile along an iron picket fence, disappearing into acres of woods and garbage-strewn vacant lots. The road was rarely used except for short cuts and by local couples as a lover's lane. There were only two cars parked on the road.

They stopped at the first car parked twenty yards from the intersection with Maurice Avenue. It was a new Cadillac sedan. Two silhouettes darkened the fogged windows. Kelly swept an open hand across the driver's window and peered through the clearing. The others stood a few feet behind, smiling in anticipation.

"What the hell do you want?" a muffled male voice asked from inside the car.

"You got the time?" Kelly asked.

"Time for little punks like you to be home in bed."

"Thanks for your help, lover boy. Doesn't look like you need a bed."

"Hey, what're you, a wise guy?" He threw the door open and sat up, dropping one leg outside the car.

Kelly sprang back into a crouch, ready to run.

"Go on, beat it before I give you a hop in the ass."

"Try it, scumbag," Dave shouted from behind.

The man leaped from the car and lunged for Kelly in one smooth motion. Kelly slipped on the hard surface and went down. The group scattered.

Pete headed for the side of the road, crashing through dried weeds and shrubbery. He turned back and saw a struggling Kelly being held by his collar. Pete caught a glimpse of Dave sneaking around the rear of the Cadillac. A howl of pain followed by a scream from inside the car echoed in the crisp air as Dave smashed a chunk of tree limb across the man's wrist. The limb snapped and bounced across the hood. Kelly pulled out of the loosened grip and they scurried off. Pete began running parallel to the road, hopping and dodging boulders and mounds of trash as he followed his companions onto Maurice Avenue and to a safe distance at the rear loading dock of a factory.

"Thanks a lot," Kelly said. "I thought I'd had it."

"It's the least I could do for a pal," Dave said. "Some friends let their buddies down when you need them."

Pete cursed to himself. *That no-good bragging rat bastard. Big deal. So he was in the right spot at the right time. Now he's a big hero.*

"Everyone split when it happened," Kelly said. "It's only natural. I would've been right behind if he hadn't grabbed me. But thanks to all of you for sticking close."

That's better. Don't single out that crud for anything special.

Headlights flashed to high beams and brightened the loading dock. Panic drove the teens toward any exit they could find along the sides of the factory. They knew the labyrinth of alleys and connecting vacant lots like the hallways and rooms of their homes. They could evade an army in the dark.

Even in retreat, now confident of their escape, they felt the urge to release their pent-up emotions. Pete kicked at an overstuffed metal garbage can, its lid balanced atop of protruding paper bags. It clattered onto the sidewalk and the paper bags ruptured spewing coffee grinds and fruit peels. A bottle broke and the lid scaled into the street. Garbage pails bounced and rolled as the group casually sprinted through the deserted streets like a soccer team moving downfield, leaving a sea of horizontal barrels and scattered trash in their path.

Kelly led and Pete was close behind. They had rounded a corner when Pete heard the shatter of breaking glass. He twisted as he ran and could see everyone behind, everyone but Dave. Then he appeared, his chunky body swinging wide and swaying into the street.

Kelly decided they were far enough from risk, turned down a slope into a vacant lot and ducked behind a row of thick barren hedges. They swooped in and scrambled to a halt one by one. Kelly counted them off as they arrived.

Everyone made it. Red was next to last and he and Goggles fell next to each other, gasping and blowing out billows of steam that glistened in the small amount of light filtering through the thickets. Dave brought up the rear, pounding down the slope and crashing into Pete.

"Watch it," Pete said, pushing Dave. A twinge of pain brought his hand to his shoulder.

"What's the matter, baby's ass, can't take a hit?"

"I can take anything from you," Pete said, dropping his hand instead of rubbing at the pain. He stared into Dave's freckled face, the round head cocked back from his beefy frame. Pete decided to back off. "What was that crash I heard when we were running?"

"I threw a can into somebody's storm door."

"Why?"

"I guess I felt like it. What's it to you anyway?"

"It might bring the cops around," Pete said.

"Cut the crap." Dave waved a fist in front of him. "We're the Vandals." He poked a thumb into his chest. "We gotta live up to our name."

"Can it, you two," Kelly said. "What's done is done."

"Fine with me," Dave said. The thumb flicked at Pete. "But this guy is still living in the past. Look at his jacket. We wore that patch last year when we had the bike club. He's too young to hang around with us."

Kelly stepped between Pete and Dave. He was a head shorter than Dave but his gaze was piercing. "We're the same age. You think I'm too young?"

Dave took a step back. "Come on. You know - I mean he acts too young. He's always complaining."

"Mostly about you." Kelly stepped into Dave's vacated spot.

"How about a smoke?" Johnny's gloved hand pushed a half-empty pack of Lucky Strikes between Kelly and Dave.

Johnny the diplomat, Pete thought. He was breaking the tension even though he wanted Kelly to kick Dave's ass, same as everyone.

Kelly blazed one last stare into Dave's eyes before he looked down at the crumpled white and red pack. He plucked out a cigarette. Johnny offered the rest around and everyone took one.

"I'm almost out," Johnny said. "Your turn to buy tomorrow, Pete."

"*Shit*. He always buys those fagot L&M filters," Dave said, having moved a few paces away from Kelly.

"My choice," Pete said, his thumb bouncing off his chest in an imitation of Dave.

"How do you guys hide yours?" Johnny asked. " My jailers caught me twice and raised all kinds of hell."

"They're all jailers," Goggles said, adjusting his black horn-rimmed frames on his large nose. His bushy black eyebrows and already thinning hair at age fourteen gave him an older studious appearance. "Whether they're Johnny's foster parents or our real families."

"Our stepfather says he don't give a damn," Dave said. "He says I can smoke all I want."

"Maybe Dave can take the butts home with him every night," Red said.

"Yeah, and smoke them all on us," Pete said. He was bolstered by Kelly's performance. It was time for payback.

"You got something to say about me?" Dave asked.

"Cool it, Pete," Kelly said. "Let's stop fighting among ourselves."

Everyone agreed and settled in quietly.

Timmy finally broke the stretch of silence. "So is that our official name?" He pulled the large turned-up collar of his Navy peacoat closer to his pale freckled face. "The Vandals?"

"What's the difference?" Red asked. "We can't get jackets or anything yet. The Comanches own this turf."

"Yeah, but they're getting old. How long can a gang last? They'll start going into the army and getting married," Kelly said. "Then it'll be our turf. We might as well agree on a name now."

"I kind of like the Vandals," Johnny said, brushing a gloved hand through his crew cut. "The grown-ups call us vandals when they talk about anyone like us. It's still their world so let's go with it. We're Vandals."

"Remember when Eddie from the Comanches told us how to be cool?" Goggles asked. "He knew we would take over some day and we had to act the part."

"Turn up your collar, swing your arms when you walk and look tough so the other guys will think twice about messing with you," Kelly said.

"Yeah, and listen to the Moondog. Cool music to be cool by," Pete said.

"I heard the guy who runs that show is changing the name to the Rock and Roll Party or something like that," Johnny said.

Everyone began talking at the same time. The low ground and thickets blocked the wind and it seemed warmer.

"Are we the Vandals?" Kelly shouted.

A cheer rose in agreement.

"Tomorrow is Halloween," Kelly said. "Then we'll really show them who we are."

"What's next on the agenda tonight?" Johnny asked.

"What's next on the agenda?" Dave mocked in a singsong tone. "What's with the fancy words? You trying to impress somebody?"

"You ought'a be in a sideshow with your corny cracks," Pete said.

"Who asked you for any comments?" Dave asked. "You should know a lot about sideshows since you still watch Howdy Doody. You probably sent your name in to ask if you can sit in the Peanut Gallery."

"Bullshit," Pete shouted above the laughter. None of them were fans of Dave's humor but he had struck a rare chord of delight. "I'm heading home."

"Come on," Timmy said. "The night's still young."

"Nah. I'll see ya tomorrow," Pete said, heading for the opening between the two hedgerows.

"What's the matter, baby..."

"Cool it, Dave," Kelly said. "See you tomorrow, Pete."

CHAPTER 2

Orange and black construction paper had been cut into shapes of witches, black cats, and pumpkins and scotch-taped to all the school room windows.

Pete sat in his normal relaxed posture, legs stretched around the seat in front of him, one arm draped over his backrest, his stare fixed on the store-bought paper skeleton tacked to the header of the front blackboard. He occupied the last seat in the last row. He had told his mother it was because his last name began with a W, but the truth was that seating was arranged by scholastic achievement, not alphabetically. He didn't consider himself dumb, and IQ tests proved that true, so effort had to be the reason. *Who needs this history, English, social studies crap. It ain't gonna get me a job when I grow up.*

"Peter Wilson."

Pete came out of his daydream. "What?"

"I called you three times. Are you with us?"

Pete cringed as a patter of giggles rose from the first two rows, occupied mostly by girls.

"Yeah. I didn't hear you."

"Perhaps a hearing test should be arranged for you. I said did you complete your homework?"

"No. I didn't get a chance."

"I should have realized that. Do you think it would help if your father and mother were asked by the principal to visit school?"

"I ain't got a father." Pete sat straight in his seat and pulled his legs under his desk. He had just spent an hour in Music Appreciation listening to Beethoven and those guys - at least they played

the Lone Ranger song - and he was in no mood for her crap, especially bringing up some son-of-a-bitch he never knew.

"Well then, your mother. Do you have one of them?"

"Yeah, I got a mother. What's that supposed to mean?"

The afternoon bell preempted the answer, the coming con-
frontation and the new round of giggles. It was only two o'clock
but this was Religious Instruction Day and everyone was required,
if registered, to visit their local parochial school for the final hour.

Pete didn't know his official religion. His mother never went
to church and he never saw any religious artifacts around their
apartment. Most of the guys were Catholic, so he had a forged
registration card filed to allow him the extra hour away from dear
old P.S. 78.

He scooped up his lone book; a loose-leaf stuffed with dog-
eared mimeographs and two comic books, and slid out of his seat.
He was out the rear door ahead of the crowd, ignoring the teacher's
final words. She was still saying something about his mother being called to school as he jumped down the metal ribbed steps
leading toward freedom.

Kelly and Timmy caught up with him at the side door leading
into the school courtyard.

"She's on your back again?" Timmy asked.

"What else is new?"

They pushed their way to the rear of the formation that was
being organized for the march to the local Catholic school.

"I was thinking about your problem," Kelly said to Pete. "I
don't think they would leave you back and have to send you to
another school after this one closes down next year. It wouldn't
look good for their reputation to push on a repeater."

Pete shrugged. "Yeah, I guess. You sure ain't got no problem.
You sit in the second row, front seat."

"So I pick up things quick. That still doesn't make me an apple
polisher. She still complains about the way my hair looks and crap
like that." Kelly twirled an index finger into his curl and pulled it
forward. "Nobody's perfect for her."

"If they pass Pete," Timmy said, "I shouldn't have a problem either since I already was left back once."

They all shrugged.

"Listen up." A tall teacher wearing a tweed sport jacket held a clipboard above his head. "Everyone line up in twos so the monitors can walk you to St. Mary's."

"What did you guys do after I left last night?" Pete asked as he paired off with Timmy.

"Nothing. We went for sodas and then headed home," Timmy said.

"I know he's your brother," Pete said, "But I'm really getting sick of Dave."

"Nobody likes him," Timmy said. He tapped his chest with an extended finger. "I can't even hack him most of the time. He always has to have someone to push around so he can feel like a big shot."

"And you take it easy," Kelly said poking Pete from behind. "Two years and twenty pounds is a lot to give away. He'd cream you in a fight."

"He doesn't scare *you*," Pete said.

"Nobody scares Kelly," Timmy said.

"Leave him to me," Kelly said. "I'll handle him."

"Okay, move out," the teacher said.

The parade of students followed two monitors through the flagstone-post gateway of the iron picket fence and onto the sidewalk for the ten-block walk. One monitor was on either side of the line and one bringing up the rear. It wasn't enough security to control fifty to sixty charges.

"I'm heading for home," Pete said. "I'll see ya tonight."

"Meet at my house at six," Kelly said.

Kelly and Timmy were properly registered and had to show themselves at the religion class or be reported for their absence.

Pete slipped behind a parked car. Kelly and Timmy would see that no one in line got talkative. Even the tongue-wagging girls from the first row respected Kelly.

Pete watched the formation until it disappeared from view. It reminded him of a prison movie where the cons were marched through the yard. *That's the way things were. March here. Sit there. Do this. Do that. Just like you were a con. You have no opinion unless they give you one. Who needs it?*

Pete pushed himself away from the trunk of the car he had used for cover and headed for home. The afternoon sun was warm. Maybe the mildness would carry into the night and it would be more comfortable than the previous evening. There were already preschoolers making their Halloween rounds, their mothers stopping on the sidewalk and allowing the ghosts and witches and pirates to toddle to the front doors, the tallest of the group elected to push the door bell button. Pete never remembered dressing in any costume. He didn't even know you could make money on Halloween until he started hanging around with the guys two years ago. *Get the bread, man. Screw the candy and junk.* That was their philosophy. Anyone who gives candy or fruit wins the trick part of trick or treat.

He cut through a series of vacant lots with overgrown bamboo-like stalks dubbed "beetle-bushes" by the kids who used the maze of paths and tramped-down clearings for games of ringaleevio and tag.

The last path left him on a sidewalk bordering Comanche Square. Three of the older gang members sat across the backrest of one of the weather-beaten wooden benches that circled a miniature Statue of Liberty. The other benches were empty. Everyone in the neighborhood knew that the area was off-limits. The neglected copper statue was green and it sat slightly turned on the cement pedestal. The story was that one of the Comanches - Pete didn't know his name but saw him and his bulging, tattooed arms around the neighborhood - had moved the statue by himself. Four Comanches working together had tried to move it back but could only budge it to where it now sat.

Pete didn't recognize any of the Comanches sitting on the

benches. They probably weren't in a harassing mood and let him pass as he skirted around the rear edge of the small park.

Someday we'll be sitting there and we'll rename it Vandal Square.

Two more blocks and Pete was home. The basement apartment; a kitchenette, bathroom, cramped living room and bedroom were stuffed into half of the floorage in the illegal three family house. The other half of the basement was used by the landlady for storage. As usual, there was a minimum of heat.

His mother was a waitress. He didn't know what shift she was working. No note on the refrigerator. He made a baloney sandwich and flicked on the nine-inch screen RCA on the living room coffee table. He spun the large plastic dial through the small selection of channels before turning it off.

Pete stuffed the last corner of sandwich into his mouth; leaned behind the couch that doubled as his bed, and lifted a boxy portable record player onto the table. He went into his mother's bedroom and took two 78 RPM records from under a pile of clothes in the bottom drawer of the dresser. The two bottom drawers of the tall, narrow dresser were assigned to him. He returned to the living room and slid one of the discs from its brown paper jacket.

The blue label read "Lily Maebelle" by the Valentines. He played the record, snapping his fingers to the beat behind the harmonizing group and then the inevitable saxophone bridge. He had embraced this music from the day he had heard Bo Diddley and a list of vocal groups on an R&B radio station. All of the guys were wild over this new sound and would turn on the Moondog or any station near the end of the dial that played it. The pop stations had ignored anything that didn't appeal to white adults only. *Well, screw those stations.*

Pete slipped the second disc onto the turntable. "At My Front Door", by the El Dorados. The grown-ups really hated this one because they thought the lyrics were dirty. Pete smiled, remembering some jerk in school asking him if his mother let him listen to that kind of music.

He turned the volume higher. The fingers snapped and he

sang along. "Crazy little mama come'a knockin'. Knockin' at my front door, door, door. Crazy little mama come..."

A heavy pounding on the entrance door interrupted the session. Pete turned down the volume.

"Who is it?"

"Is your mother home?" the landlady asked.

"No."

"Do you have anyone in there?"

"No. Why?"

"I don't want no bums in there playing that jungle music and ruining my house."

"I said there ain't no one else here."

"Open this door," she said.

"No way." Pete remembered the time that Red was visiting him and she pulled the same crap. He had opened the door that time and the old bitch had found his buddy hiding under his mother's bed. She had rousted Red from his hiding place and chased him from the apartment.

"I want to see who's in there. This is my house. Open the door."

"You gotta wait 'til my mother gets home. She says I don't have to let you in." Pete turned up the volume in time for the last two loud beats of the song.

"Turn that junk off and open this door," she said.

He wanted to tell her to go to hell. But then he'd get into another hassle with his mother. *They always win.*

Pete ignored the quacking demands until he finally heard the sloping of loose slippers move up the stairs. He was ready to fall into one of his frustrated moods when he realized the coincidence of the moment. Crazy little mama. He chuckled.

He spent the next two hours stretched out on the couch wearing down the grooves of the two records, the volume as low as possible, and reading the latest issue of Mad. Comic books were easy to swipe. Easier than large bulky records.

Pete was engrossed in the last few pages of Mad and didn't

hear his mother's approach until she jiggled her keys. He sat up and tossed the thin book onto the table next to the now dormant record player. She wore those white crape-sole shoes as part of her uniform. They were as silent as the sneakers he wore when stalking through the night.

Madge Wilson swung open the apartment door and stood in the opening about eight feet across the living room floor from Pete. Her brassy hair, pulled back into a bun, had a straw-like texture from years of constant color changes. Powder and rouge couldn't transform the angelic face that mirrored Pete's. She wore the standard black waitress uniform with white collar and pocket trim under an unbuttoned cloth coat. A black simulated leather bag hung from a strap around her shoulder.

"Guess who I just had a conversation with?" Madge asked as she closed the door.

"Who else?"

"Yep." She dropped the shoulder bag onto a chair in the kitchenette and slipped off her coat.

"What's her problem now?" Pete asked.

"The usual. She stopped me as soon as I hit the stoop. You're playing your music too loud. You have your friends in the apartment." She pointed at Pete in mock condemnation. "Probably that redheaded bastard again."

"Mom, such language." He was relieved that she was on his side this time.

"Language?" She opened and closed cabinet doors in the kitchenette. "I'd hate to be hiding behind a curtain listening to you and your friends holding a conversation."

"We had to hear it from some grown-ups to start with. We didn't invent it."

"Petie." She stepped into the living room.

He disliked being called Petie.

"You have to put up with what we have a little bit longer." Her voice was tender, yet firm. "I know we need a bigger apartment. You need a room of your own." It was the standard speech.

Not enough money. She could only afford the dump they were living in. They had to endure the landlady and her kind. But something was different. Her voice suggested it wasn't the usual hopeless thread-mill. "I've been seeing someone."

Pete stared blankly.

"A boy friend." She waved a flat hand back and forth as though breaking Pete out of a hypnotic trance. "Your mom isn't ready for a rocking chair. I can still date."

"But it sounds serious." Pete maintained his blank stare.

"Maybe. Hope so."

"He ain't like - you know - him."

"Your father?"

"I ain't got a father."

"You did. Maybe he turned into a boozer and a bum, but he was your father."

"I don't wanna talk about him."

"Neither do I." Madge stepped in front of the coffee table. "I'd rather talk about someone much nicer." She smiled and folded her arms in front of her. "He wants to take you and me out to dinner and a movie tonight. I worked a double shift so I'm off tonight and tomorrow."

Pete sat up. "Mom. It's Halloween."

"So?"

"So I gotta be with the guys tonight."

"The guys." She dropped her arms to her side. "You're always with them. How about me for a change? This is important to me."

He thought about it for a second. *No way*. I'm not ready for that. And tonight has got to be a wild one on the streets. Much wilder than meeting some sport who wants to take his mother out. "I promised," he lied. "If you'd told me sooner." He trailed off, and knew she wasn't buying it.

Madge glanced at the Mad cover on the coffee table. Alfred E. Neuman's sardonic face stared back at her. "Why are you reading that junk instead of your school books?"

"Here we go again," he said.

"Yes. Here we go again. You're not going to get into high school by reading comic books."

Pete stood. He was the same height as his mother. "I gotta go."

"Is it too much to ask you to be with me one night?" The tenderness was gone. Her voice was strained. "I said it's important to me."

Pete sidestepped her outstretched hand. "I gotta go," he repeated. "Maybe some other time. Not tonight." His jacket was on and he was at the door.

"Petie. Please. Did you eat?"

He was careful not to slam the door behind him as he usually did after one of their battles. He had to get out. It would be too much sitting around with some joker who was probably going to act as polite as hell to impress Pete while the Vandals were out there without him.

He thought he heard a sob from inside the apartment. He hesitated then drew away from the doorknob and quickly climbed the stairs. Why did she have to pick tonight? He felt a twinge of pressure in his chest. His throat was dry and he could feel tears welling up in his eyes.

You're a Vandal. You want Dave to see you like this? He'd rank you out for the rest of your life.

Pete rubbed at his eyes and quickly regained his composure as he hurried down the sidewalk. He'd have his night and apologize to mom in the morning. Then he'd meet her friend whenever she wanted. Who knew? Maybe something good was coming.

CHAPTER 3

It was twilight. Still too early for any action. Pete stopped at the corner grocery store and bought a pack of L&Ms with his last quarter. It was the same brand his mother smoked, and since the grocer knew his mother and that she sometimes sent Pete to buy a pack for her, there was no problem. He was given a Hershey Bar as a Halloween gift. It would be his dinner.

Four kids - nine and ten year-olds - were playing box ball against the side brick wall of the store. One of them slapped the pink Spalding into an opponent's box and it struck the wall at the base taking a deadened bounce before falling into a slow roll.

"Hindu. No good," the recipient of the shot said.

"It is so good," the slapper squealed.

"Hindus don't count." He turned to Pete who was munching on the Hershey Bar. "Ain't that right?"

"Wrong," Pete said, feeling a flush of power. "Hindus are good. If it hit the cellar door," he said and pointed at a set of double steel doors buried in the sidewalk that occupied the last chalk box, "and it took a fluke, then it's a do-over.

"You kids ever heard of the Vandals?" Pete asked.

"No," the closest boy said. "Who are they?"

"A new club. I'm one of them."

"The Comanches are the only club around here. Nobody would mess with them."

"Yeah, but they can't last forever. We'll be taking over some day. Watch for us."

The kid shrugged and went back to the game.

Pete started down the sidewalk again, feeling an air of confidence. It would be a good night.

The sun was just dropping behind the apartment buildings in the distance when Pete reached Kelly's house. Kelly, Goggles and Timmy were sitting on the stoop of the two story brick building.

"What's happening?" Pete asked.

"We're going to meet Johnny and Red at '78," Kelly said. "They're bringing a guy they met in high school - I think his name is Sonny - and some of his guys from across Queens Boulevard."

"Cool." Pete was reluctant to ask but curiosity won. "Where's Dave?"

"I don't know," Timmy said. "He wasn't home when I left."

"Let's get going," Goggles said.

Yeah, Pete thought. *Before the crud shows up.*

Throngs of Halloween merrymakers were taking advantage of the sudden mild weather. They ran and skipped along the Vandals' route, the younger ones rustling their multi-colored shopping bags and asking for goodies. Pete and Timmy rang a few doorbells along their trek. They made twelve cents between them and a list of addresses to visit for revenge.

"People are becoming a bunch of cheapskates," Pete said. "My mom says everyone is becoming lousy tippers."

Madge Wilson's face flashed into her son's mind. He saw it as it was when he walked out. The dark circles under her eyes. The sad bowed mouth that had tried to smile for a rare moment. She usually came home from a double shift in a bad mood. She would complain about how tired she was, take off her shoes and rub her feet. But tonight she finally came home happy. She had something to be excited about. And he let her down. He shouldn't have a mother like her.

He tried to shake off the thoughts, and promised he would make it up to his mom, when his thoughts were suddenly scrambled and his mood dropped a notch. Dave stood under the street light on the next corner.

"What kept ya?" Dave asked, falling in step with the group.

"We were waiting for you," Timmy said. "How come you didn't

come home?"

"I was making some kids hustle for me. I had them go door to door and then grabbed their loot."

"What a hero," Pete said.

"You say something?" Dave asked, craning his neck toward Pete.

"What'd you make, twelve cents?" Pete asked.

"Three-sixty," Dave said. "I let them keep the candy and other crap."

"Three dollars and sixty cents?" Timmy asked. He turned to Pete and they both fell silent from embarrassment.

"Wonder what time it is," Goggles said.

"Probably about six-thirty, seven," Timmy said.

"It ain't that late," Dave said.

"Okay, Mr. know-it-all," Pete said. "What time is it?"

"What'a you got against me? I asked you before and you clamed up," Dave said. He stopped in front of Pete and turned.

Pete bumped into Dave, then stepped back. "I had all I can take of you." His voice cracked. "You think you're a big wheel."

Dave reached out and straight-armed Pete. "You wanna do something about it?"

Pete stood his ground.

"Come on," Dave said. "Do something. I'm waiting."

Pete stepped forward, and his fist started up from his side.

Kelly and Goggles jumped between them. Goggles grabbed Pete's arm.

"Knock it off," Kelly yelled at Dave.

"He's the one that wants to start something," Dave said pointing at Pete.

"He isn't starting anything," Kelly said.

"Let us get it over with," Dave said. "He needs his ass kicked."

"No, I think you need your ass kicked."

"What'a you mean, Kelly?"

"Everyone is fed up with your crap. Maybe we should take a

vote about kicking you out of the club. You know you'd loose. I doubt if your brother would even vote for you."

"You'd vote me out after what I did for you last night?" Dave asked.

"You bet," Kelly said. "You did it to have something to brag about, not for me."

"That ain't so. I saw you in trouble and I stayed to help."

"You're full of shit. Shut up and keep walking."

Pete couldn't believe his eyes. Dave turned and started walking as ordered. He knew Dave never argued with Kelly, and just like the night before, a thirteen-year-old kid had backed down high and mighty Dave. What a sight.

"Let's have a smoke now so we don't have to share them with all the new guys we're meeting," Kelly said in his usual calm voice.

Pete produced the full pack of L&Ms, opened it, took one and handed the rest to Goggles who walked next to him. The pack went around the group and back to Pete.

Pete smiled as he sucked on the cigarette that Goggles had lit for him. Dave was silent. - No complaints about the L&Ms.

The school was five blocks from Kelly's house. Its old-style concrete buttresses, wide slab ledges and roof parapets stood imposing against the moonlit sky. The three massive stories towered over the surrounding houses. It was rumored that the building was originally a mansion that had once stood alone on the acres of land that now comprised their neighborhood.

Johnny, Red and eight new faces crowded the corner, some leaning against the iron picket fence; the others bunched along the curb. Most of the group had a white powder embedded in their jackets and dungarees, the aftermath of a battle with flower packed stockings knotted into soft blackjacks. Johnny and Red stepped out of the crowd.

"You guys are late," Johnny said. "We thought you weren't coming."

"We got delayed," Kelly said. "Tell you about it later."

Introductions passed between the groups. Sonny was a pretty

muscular guy for his age, Pete noted. He seemed friendly and out-going. One of his boys, Blackie Chase, was the troublemaker of the group. He was loud and pushy. His hair was the color and texture of a Halloween cat. His attitude reminded Pete of Dave, and like Dave, he was fifteen.

"There's a dance in the basement tonight." Johnny jerked his thumb over his shoulder.

"What for?"

"Halloween, I guess."

"So what?" Dave asked.

"So let's go in and screw around," Red said.

"I ain't going to no stupid school dance," Dave said. "Especially a joint that kicked me out two years ago."

"We don't have to go in," Johnny said. "They should be getting out soon."

"Let's stick around and see who went. We can razz them."

"Nix. Count me out," Dave said. "Who gives a damn who went? Squares. I'm gonna drift up toward the boulevard. I'll meet ya at the diner. Anybody with me?"

Timmy, Sonny and three of his group joined Dave. Dave made sure everyone knew he was treating his brother to a hamburger with his swindled money.

The remaining mixed group moved into the school courtyard. The Vandals crouched at the school wall and peered through the basement windows.

"Let's go in," Blackie said.

"Yeah, why not," Red said. "I'm for it."

"Sure you're for it," Kelly said. "You graduated already. Pete and me could be spotted by one of the teachers."

"You and Pete wait out here. It'll probably be over in a couple of minutes. We'll just bust chops a little and be right out," Red said.

"They won't let us in," Johnny said.

"Come on," Blackie said. "We'll get in."

They stood and entered the building through the heavy metal

door. Blackie pushed his way to the front. Pete and Kelly waited on the entrance landing just inside the door while the others stamped down the stairs to the basement.

The teacher in the tweed sport jacket halted their advance. He stood at the foot of the stairs, his clipboard tucked under his arm. "You boys going somewhere?" he asked.

"Inside," Blackie said.

"Sorry, but the dance will be over in a few minutes. And it's only for our students."

"Tough luck, man. We wanna go in."

"Sorry, boys. I said I can't let you in."

"Come on, Blackie," Johnny said. "It's a drag anyhow."

"Look, man, I wanna go in and nobody's gonna stop me."

"Don't start no trouble." Johnny tugged on Blackie's sleeve. "Not in here. We'll wait outside for them. What's the difference."

Blackie hesitated for a moment then turned and started up the stairs. The others followed.

"Stinkin' teach," Blackie said as he pushed passed Pete and Kelly. "I see him outside and I'll rap him in the head."

"This guy is a real wild man," Johnny said to Kelly as they left the school.

"You handled him okay. It looks like he listens to reason," Kelly said.

The Vandals and their allies waited quietly until they heard the thunder of feet on the basement stairs. The side door swung open and scores of boys and girls poured into the courtyard. Blackie slowly approached them.

"What'a ya say, pal," Blackie said to a tall, pimple-faced boy named Preston. Sandra, a classmate, stood next to Preston.

"Who are you?" Preston asked.

"Never mind the details, punk. Just let go of my girl."

"Your girl?" Sandra asked. "Who is this person, Preston?"

"Keep out'a this, sister." Blackie pushed Sandra aside. "I don't like your looks, Preston." He laughed. "Preston?"

"Hey, look, I'm not bothering you," Preston said.

"Everything about you bothers me, pal."

Pete and the others gathered behind Blackie. Neither Pete nor Kelly moved to save their classmate, who they knew was the worst fighter in school, regardless of his height.

"Pete," Preston said. "Do you know this guy?"

"Never saw him before in my life," Pete said. *Who cares about him? Who cares if he gets his head beat in. Too bad he's not Dave.*

"What's the matter, punk?" Blackie pushed Preston against the side of the building. "You scared or something?"

"Not of you," Preston said.

Blackie threw a punch to Preston's stomach, doubling him in pain.

"You ain't, hah?" Another punch to the stomach sent the taller boy to his knees. "Fight back," Blackie said. "You said you ain't scared."

Some of the dance patrons had flocked to the scene but were silent during the beating. Sandra had inched her way to the rear of the crowd.

"Leave me alone," Preston said.

"You tellin' me what to do?" Blackie grabbed Preston by the hair. With a yank, he pulled Preston to his feet. He shouted in pain as Blackie landed a third punch to his stomach. Tears appeared in his eyes.

"He cries easy," Blackie said turning to his companions. With a quick swing back, a fourth blow was thrown and Preston burst into a fit of crying.

"Get your filthy hands off that boy," the teacher said from behind the crowd.

"Okay, teach." Blackie threw Preston to the ground.

The teacher rushed through the parted crowd. A sneaker poked into his path and he sprawled across the cement yard, his clipboard rattling in front of him.

"Run, Blackie," Kelly said.

"Not me. I ain't scared of that crumb."

"Run, you dope," Johnny said and grabbed Blackie by his

arm. Blackie finally decided to make his escape but not before delivering a sharp kick at Preston who was still doubled in pain next to the stunned teacher.

Pete cursed to himself at Blackie's actions. *This was too big. Somebody would squeal and put them all in Dutch.* Pete started into a trot, joining the stampede fleeing the scene. *This is really gonna screw things up. I'll never graduate now.* Pete didn't notice the car was green and white at first. It had rolled to a stop at the curb outside the flagstone gateway. He swerved into the street to avoid slamming into the fender and was caught in the headlights of the police car.

"Cheez it. The cops," someone yelled.

The mob scattered, heading for alleys and backyards. After running for five blocks, and overcome by exhaustion, Pete dove over a low hedge and crawled to the side of a dark house. Red and Johnny were a few steps behind.

"The cops grabbed Blackie and Kelly," Red said in quick breathes.

"Kelly's old man will blow his stack," Pete said.

"He'll be okay," Johnny said. "Blackie's the only one they can do anything to. Kelly can say he was at the dance. He can prove he goes to school there. Nobody would know or say he wasn't inside."

"We better head for the diner," Red said. "We gotta warn Dave and the other guys."

"Screw Dave," Pete said.

"Why don't you ignore him like the rest of us," Johnny said. "Maybe if he doesn't get a reaction, he won't bug you so much."

"I doubt it," Pete said.

"I mean, no matter what Dave is like, he's still one of us. We can't fight among ourselves," Red said.

"Everything'll work out," Johnny said. "Come on, the cops are probably gone by now."

CHAPTER 4

Pete, Johnny and Red wouldn't arouse suspicions if they behaved themselves. They traveled openly along main streets. A police car passed, slowed and observed them for a few seconds, then continued on patrol.

The diner was in the middle of the block. They cut through a corner gas station and stopped in the brightly-lit parking lot.

The shape of the building resembled a sleek railroad car. A string of continuous windows showcased the interior booths and counter. None of the customers were familiar. Pete could see the waitress, dressed in the same black and white uniform his mother wore. He remembered his mother's face again. *He would have to make it up to her. He would...*

"Yo," Dave called.

They turned to the rear of the lot and saw Dave, Timmy and Sonny on the edge of the shadows. Timmy beckoned for the trio to join them.

"The fucking owner threw us out," Dave said.

"How come?"

"We put sugar in a salt shaker on the table next to us," Timmy said. "And left the top loose on the shaker."

"Some guy sat there and ordered a hamburger," Dave continued. "He got a pile of sugar in the middle of his burger."

They laughed.

"Keep it down," Sonny said. "They might hear us."

"I thought you guys were going to that school dance," Dave said.

"Big-mouth's back," Pete said.

"You got something to say?" Dave asked.

"Knock it off," Johnny said. "Pete, you started this one. What'd I say before?" He took Pete a few steps back into the parking lot. "Ignore him," he said just above a whisper.

"It's *the way* he says things that gets under my skin."

"Tomorrow we'll get together with Kelly and talk about it. Maybe Kelly can do more to shut him up. Or maybe we'll kick him out of the club."

Pete shrugged.

"Okay?"

"Yeah, I guess so."

Pete and Johnny moved back into the rear of the parking lot.

"Let's bug out'a here," Timmy said.

"Yeah, before some cops spot us," Red said.

"Wait a minute," Dave said. "We got some unfinished business first."

Pete stiffened. *Did he mean him? Was this it?* "What'a you mean?" Pete asked.

"The Greek." Dave pointed at the diner. "We owe him one."

"What'a you mean, we?" Johnny asked.

"He screwed over some of your guys. That means he screwed over all of us."

"So what do you wanna do?" Red asked.

Dave turned and strutted to the rear of the building. He lifted an empty garbage can over his head. "Ready?"

"Oh shit," Red said.

"Out the back," Johnny shouted. "Over the tracks."

Dave released the can as the group reached the rear of the lot. They scrambled up a gravel and coal grading. The familiar sound of shattering glass and splintering wood was followed by a series of hollow thuds as the can bounced from its target.

They stumbled and clawed up the steep embankment, unable to gain traction on the covering. They reached the top and started across the double set of railroad tracks.

Dave stopped between the tracks and turned back toward the

diner. Someone was shouting from somewhere below the embankment.

"Vandals," Dave shouted, throwing his fists above his head.
"Don't fuck with the Vandals."

Dave spun around just as Sonny tripped over the wooden beam
that protected the third rail. Sonny tumbled forward and down
the far slope. An avalanche of pebbles cascaded around everyone as
they followed Sonny down the second embankment, feeling like
they were surrounded by thousands of marbles bouncing down a
tile floor. Red helped Sonny turn himself upright. They slid on
the seats of their pants to the flat ground below, finding a ten-foot
cyclone fence blocking their escape. They headed for the lights
about fifty feet away. Johnny found a breach in the fence just before the ground began to rise near a trestle above the next street.

Everyone managed to squeeze through the separation. Pete's
skull and crossbones patch caught on a jagged wire and tore to
within a few threads, flapping as he jogged after the others through
the storage area of a coal yard.

The gate to the yard was open and they were back on the
street. Pete looked toward the gas station a block away. A car pulled
out of the station but headed in the opposite direction. A man in
a white apron appeared. He saw them and broke into a sprint.

"It's the guy from the diner," Pete yelled.

They scattered, some down a side street, the others spread out
through a vacant lot. They were too busy with their flight from
him that they didn't notice the man stop after two blocks, unable
to keep up with their youthful speed.

Pete had traveled six or seven blocks before he charged out of
the darkness of one of the many vacant lots along his escape route.
He saw the car and managed to pull to a halt, sliding into the
street like it was second base, his feet inches away from the tires of
the speeding, swerving vehicle.

Pete rolled to his feet, about to curse the driver, when he saw
the second car with the red flashing dome light on its roof. There
was no siren. He turned back and scurried into the brittle weeds as

the police car roared passed him. By the time Pete returned his attention to the street, both vehicles were out of sight, and only the fading red blinks of the patrol car were evident in the distance. *What the hell was that all about? Maybe it was a stick-up.*

Pete brushed himself off and started down the sidewalk. Three boys stepped out of the continuous vacant lot a block ahead. He couldn't make out who they were. They stopped under another of the many railroad trestles that crossed over the neighborhood streets. They were probably some of his group.

He reached the trestle and leaned against the concrete retaining wall, gulping in cold air, his undershirt soaked with sweat. The sides of his hair hung over his ears like the wings of a bird at rest. He ran his hands along the sides of his head brushing the hair back into place.

"That goddamn idiot." Pete puffed out short breaths, thinking of what Dave had done at the diner. The dark escape route had made it impossible to tell who was in the group. Pete realized he had spoken without thinking. He looked at the others. The only light came from a gooseneck lamp attached to a supporting I beam under the far end of the trestle. Timmy. Sonny. *And Dave.*

"Who's a goddamn idiot?" Dave asked.

"The guy in that car that the cops were chasing. He almost hit me."

"What car? I didn't see no car. You sure you weren't talking about me?" Dave pushed off the wall and stood in front of Pete.

Pete stared back at Dave.

"Come on, punk. You've been asking for trouble. Admit it. You were talking about me."

Pete continued to stare at Dave's twisted face.

"What's the matter? You ain't got Kelly or Johnny to bail you out this time?" Dave grasped the hanging patch on Pete's jacket and tore it from its last threads.

"Gimme that." Pete reached for the patch.

Dave flipped the cloth skull and crossbones into the gutter.

"Stop it," Timmy said.

"Stay out'a this, little brother." Dave shoved Timmy against the wall, then turned to Sonny.

"Hey, I just met you guys," Sonny said. "If you got a beef going, it's none of my business."

Pete slipped off the wall and began walking away.

Dave started after him. "I ain't through with you." He snapped his middle finger across the tip of Pete's ear. "Come on, baby ass. You got a face like a baby's ass."

The physical and emotional sting released a surge of adrenaline. *You gotta do it!* Pete stopped.

"My stepfather said he saw your old lady in a bar," Dave said. "He says she looks like a whore."

Pete spun and threw a glancing blow off the side of Dave's head. Dave retaliated with a flurry of punches, whacking into Pete's body and face. Pete landed another shot to Dave's jaw before sinking to his knees. He folded his arms around his head as Dave pummeled him.

"Enough." Timmy leaped on Dave's back and secured a headlock. The two brothers fell into the street, the headlock still intact. "Get out'a here, Pete," Timmy said.

Pete spat blood. "I ain't running from him."

"Come on." Sonny grabbed Pete's sleeve and pulled him to his feet. "Let's get going." He tightened his grip on Pete's jacket and began leading him. "We'll find the rest of your guys. Come on."

As they cleared the far end of the trestle they could hear Dave yelling threats as he struggled to break free of his brother's stranglehold. Pete and Sonny were two blocks away before the sounds of the conflict faded.

The progressively cooling air cleared Pete's head. He and Sonny slowed their pace.

"You okay?" Sonny asked.

"Yeah." Pete jiggled a loose tooth. "Nobody says nothing like that about my mother. Especially not a shithead like him."

"I'm with you on that."

Pete kicked at a stone and sent it skipping down the sidewalk.

A tin can was next. It clanged off a fire hydrant. He was kicking Dave's head. *He'd face off with the crud again. Everyone would side with him this time. They'd all get Dave.* Pete veered into the weeds and kicked at a brown shopping bag lying on its side. The bag lifted into the air with a dull clunk. A flutter of paper strips spurted from the bag and hung suspended as the bag crashed into the middle of the street.

"It's money," Sonny said, snatching one of the bills before it floated to the ground.

Pete reached the shopping bag and turned it upright. "A piece," he yelled. He pulled a pistol from among the crumpled bills still in the bag.

"What?"

"Look," Pete said, holding up the pistol. He looked at the snub-nosed revolver. "It must have been those guys the cops were chasing. They had to get rid of the bag so the cops wouldn't find it on them if they got caught. "It's real," he said.

"You're dead, baby's ass!" Dave was a few steps behind Sonny, lumbering along the sidewalk like a linebacker after a quarterback.

Sonny twisted in surprise just as Dave's weight and momentum struck him. Sonny hit the ground in pain, his strained rib muscles tearing from the double impacts.

Pete came out of his fixation on the revolver as Dave veered off from his collision with Sonny and stumbled to a halt facing Pete.

"Get away from me," Pete screamed. He stepped back and his hand shook as he pointed the revolver at Dave. "I'll kill you, ya bastard."

"You wouldn't know how," Dave said. "Let me see it." He leaped forward.

"Get out'a here." Pete pulled the gun out of Dave's reach.

"Gimme it." Dave clutched Pete in a bear hug and they toppled to the pavement.

"You'll get it," Pete said through clenched teeth.

Dave squeezed Pete's wrist, trying to twist the barrel away

from them. Pete strained against Dave's strength until he lost the feeling and control of his hand.

A loud explosion ripped apart the still night, its thunder echoing for blocks. The smoking pistol pulled to the ground like a magnet had been placed between the two still figures. Dave lay dead, the side of his head blown apart, fragments of bone and brain splattered across them both.

Pete stared at the sky. A piercing ring deafened him. Red's face appeared. *Where did he come from?* Then Kelly, who was saying something Pete couldn't hear. There were other blurred faces, all staring at him, all with the same fuzzy expression. He felt no pain but there was blood on the hand that he lifted into sight. Then he knew what had happened. His stomach churned as the shrill noise in his ears began to subside.

"You killed him," Timmy said as he appeared in the sea of faces. "You didn't have to. He wasn't going to kill you."

Why did he say it like that? Pete tried to sit up but his body was frozen to the street. "I didn't mean it," he said. "It was an accident." It was all he could think of saying.

"Hell of a baptism," Kelly said stoically. "What a stinking way for the Vandals to begin."

CHAPTER 5

KELLY PETRILLO – SEPTEMBER, 1955

Kelly Petrillo sat in the president's chair behind the long oak table. Johnny Sadinski, the vice-president, sat to his right. Red Janek, the war counselor, was at the far right. To Kelly's left was Blackie Chase, sergeant at arms, Sonny Kraus, secretary, and Shades Gaglione, treasurer.

There were thirty Vandals at the meeting. The three-car garage was cramped and stuffy. They sat on folding chairs, boxes, two broken sofas and the floor. A cloud of smoke hung below the ceiling.

"We've got to war on the Madhatters if we're going to expand," Kelly was saying. "We beat the Eighty-Second Street Bops. Maybe it was just a few of us duking it out but we still sent them back to their own turf with their asses in a sling. They're not pushovers but we took them."

"But the Madhatters are a tougher crew," Jimmy Yadenik said.

"Bull," Kelly said. "All they got is a name. You don't see them picking on any big cliques. They jump our guys who have to pass through their turf to get to the subway. They jump us when they got the odds on their side. They hold us in check because they think we're nothing. We can take them. I know we can."

"Look, fellas," Johnny said.

As the pros and cons bounced around the room, Kelly took a moment to reflect on his desire to bring down the president of the Madhatters. Charlie Malloy was his second cousin and they had been rivals for as long as he could remember.

Kelly was seven years old when he first met Charlie. Their mothers were first cousins and would visit often. They encouraged their boys to play together. Charlie was three years older than Kelly and would be charged with watching over him when they were out of sight. Charlie began bullying Kelly. Money for ice cream or candy intended for sharing would end up in Charlie's pocket or the goodies would be split 75-25 in Charlie's favor if Charlie was in a generous mood.

This lasted for two years before Kelly finally began to stand up to Charlie. The feud intensified, Charlie lying his way out of accusations and trying to blame Kelly for the bickering. It affected their mothers' relationship and soon the visits stopped, each woman sure the other child was the problem.

Kelly's personality was influenced both by learning how Charlie dominated and manipulated and by his own feelings of helplessness over being tyrannized. He had been molded into a benevolent dictator.

They met a few times after the family break-up, each time resulting in a shouting match that carried to the brink of a fistfight. The quarrel would always be defused before it became physical. The last incident occurred on Kelly's first day as a freshman at Bryant High School. Charlie said that he didn't want to waste his time on the young punk and sent three of his Madhatters as a welcoming committee. Kelly was caught alone and astonished the gathered crowd by decking two of the older attackers before being overwhelmed. The three had disappeared into the crowd by the time a contingent of Vandals showed. Kelly had made a quick reputation and it would have to be protected. Charlie would have to be embarrassed and the only way was by beating him and taking away his power.

"We can't let the 'Hatters claim the old Comanche turf," Kelly said. "It's ours and we have to fight for it. We need a candy store to hang out in. We have to show ourselves. We need color. A place we can say '*that's* our headquarters and it's a swinging place.' There's no places like that on this side of Queens Boulevard. Across it, there's plenty of joints we can take over. But the 'Hatters won't let us.

"Think of our pride. If we declare war and beat them, we'll have a turf. We'll keep this side of the boulevard, which is right-fully ours, plus we'll take a chunk of their turf. We'll have a bigger name. We'd be on our way."

The club officers had been assigned four members each to buttonhole for the meeting. Kelly had made it clear that the meeting was very important to him, and the officers could use whatever means necessary to get their charges there.

All of the officers and some of the rank-and-file wore the new club jackets. If Red Janek had his way, they would be wearing military style jackets with epaulets showing officers ranks and rib-bons over the breast pocket. His obsession with military history had earned him his present job and title. But Red's idea was not only expensive but considered 'kid shit' by most of the members.

The selected jackets were the style worn by most of the New York City gangs, single ply black felt with no lining. An aqua stripe ran down each sleeve and the members' first name was scrolled on the left breast. VANDALS, in bright aqua, flared in script across the back, the S tailing off to underline the name. The tail widened at the end and contained the block letters S.A.C. - social athletic club - used by most gangs as a cloak of respectability.

It was six months after Dave's death before the original group had drifted back together. Then the spring and summer months drew individuals and small groups from other areas of the neigh-borhood, increasing their ranks until the organization was offi-cially formed.

They were all high school students; some undeserving and who would last until they were sixteen and be allowed by law to drop out. Those looking for a future were intelligent. Some of those still needed a guiding hand or a kick in the butt to shake loose the intelligence. It was primarily their appearance that por-trayed a change. Sneakers had been mostly replaced by engineer boots or French-toed and featherweight dress shoes. Dungarees were still prevalent but some of the cooler members had them pegged. Dress pants with a two inch rise above the belt loops, saddle-stitched sides and pegged, cuffed bottoms that fell into a drape at the shoe tops was also popular. Some pegs were so tight at the ankles that a zipper was needed to remove the pants.

Kelly's appearance was much the same as a year ago. Johnny Sadinski's crew cut had grown into a Detroit, the top still relatively short with long sides combed into a DA. Most members wore the DA - duck's ass - hair comb. Anthony 'Goggles' Gaglione had converted to prescription tinted horn-rimmed glasses and with it a change in his nickname to Shades. His hair had continued to thin which prompted one of the members to an observation that the Vandals' treasurer resembled some of the group of adult mob bosses whose pictures appeared in the newspapers all the time.

"What's it going to be, guys?" Kelly asked.

The members were stirring restlessly in their seats.

"I'm with Kelly," Johnny said.

"Me too," Red said.

A few of the others shouted their opinions. Soon the meeting was in chaos.

"Okay, quiet," Kelly said. "We'll take a vote. I'm sure you guys know what you want and I know it's the same as me. The Vandals are going to be somebody. All in favor of bopping with the Madhatters raise your hand."

Sonny counted the raised hands. "Twenty-three in favor," he said.

Kelly smiled. "That's over two thirds majority," he said.

"Make that unanimous," Sonny said as seven more hands punctured the cloud of smoke.

"The Vandals S.A.C. hereby declare war on the Madhatters S.A.C.," Kelly said.

A cheer rose from the crowd. It took Kelly and the other officers a few minutes to quiet them.

"Alright, when can the war council go into 'Hatter turf to declare war?" Kelly asked Red.

"We'll go tonight if you want. I'll try to set up the rumble for tomorrow night."

"The sooner the better."

"On our way."

"Wait a couple of minutes," Kelly said. "Meeting adjourned. We'll meet here tomorrow at noon to find out when the bop is coming off."

Johnny turned on the cathedral radio that sat on a packing crate in a corner of the garage. Little Richard screamed out "Tutti Fruitti." Some of the Vandals scrambled for the two side exits, and the once crowded cinder block garage seemed to shrink. Ten Vandals remained.

"You tell my ever-loving cousin we want a fight," Kelly told Red. "I'd like to make it one on one. But it's better to get everyone in there so we can say it was the Vandals that beat them. We're going to have to face a full-fledged rumble someday. It might as well be now. Better make it twenty-five guys apiece in case some of ours don't show. You and the council can figure out the place and weapons with him. I don't want any knives. I'd rather keep it at fists and belts, but get the best deal you can."

"I'll give you the details in the morning," Red said.

Red, Blackie and the three members of the war council filed out the side door. Kelly, Johnny, Sonny, Shades and Jimmy Yadenik, a new member, settled into the most comfortable seats as "Pledging My Love" by Johnny Ace drifted out of the radio speaker.

"How do you think we'll make out," Kelly asked, addressing everyone.

"Don't know," Johnny said. "Some of the guys are probably scared."

"That's natural," Kelly said. "I'm kind of scared."

"You?" Shades said. "You'd be the last one who'd scare."

"You never know what's going to happen. I'm mostly scared that we may not make a good showing. That would end everything."

"We'll stay together no matter what," Sonny said. "I saw a big rumble when I lived in Hell's Kitchen. Zip guns. Malatov cock-tails. I was on a roof watching and it was some sight. No one ran. Once it started, they were in it and part of it until one side or the other showed more balls or the cops broke it up.

"We'll hold our own," Shades said. "We got a lot of solid guys."

"I think so, too," Kelly said. "The 'Hatters will fold when they see us standing up to them. The rumble doesn't mean as much to them as it does to us."

"You think they might bring a gun?" Jimmy asked.

"I'm pretty sure they don't own one. Besides, I even called for no blades," Kelly said. "No way I'd agree to guns. I still remember what happened to Dave."

The conversation came to an abrupt halt. "Sunday Kind Of Love" by the Harptones played in its entirety before someone spoke again.

"I saw Pete's mother yesterday," Johnny said. "She didn't look too good. Almost as bad as she looked at the trial."

"The stinking law sucks," Sonny said. "It's not only out to screw over us but they hurt her, too, by taking away her only kid. It doesn't matter if you're young or old. If you ain't got the bread to pay somebody off, you're out'a luck."

"Anybody ever heard from Timmy?" Jimmy asked.

Everyone shook their heads.

"He's probably still in Vermont or someplace like that where his stepfather sent him," Johnny said.

"Tough times," Sonny said.

"Yeah," Johnny said. "The Vandals were almost out of busi-ness before we even started. But tomorrow we'll really be back in action."

"If we impress the Madhatters," Shades said.

"We will," Kelly said. "Charlie controls them completely. Most of them can't think for themselves. Charlie tells them what to be-lieve. If I can take him out of the fight early, the rest of them won't know what to do."

A newsbreak came through the radio speaker "Popular actor

James Dean was killed today when the Porsche he was driving collided with another vehicle."

"Jeez, that's something, hah?" Jimmy said. "I wonder how Red and the guys are doing?"

It was a balmy Indian summer day. An occasional car passed, their buzzing tires the only disturbance to an otherwise peaceful morning.

"With the hub caps we swiped last week," Shades said, "It should bring the total of the treasury to about forty-two bucks. We're gonna need eight more bucks just to pay the rent for the next couple of months."

"We may not need the garage after tonight," Kelly said. His thoughts weren't on the treasury. *What happened at the meeting last night? Was the rumble on?* Everything hinged on this day. "I wonder if Red's up yet," Kelly said before Shades could start another report.

"Probably," Shades said.

"Let's take a walk over to his house."

Red's house was a block away. As they approached, they spotted Red in the backyard carrying two loose-leaf books.

"Hey Red," Kelly yelled, still a half-block from his friend.

Red turned to the two boys and waved a greeting. "Come on in," he said. "I'll be right with ya." He disappeared into a wooden garage that stood in a corner of the small yard.

They entered the yard through an open gate and leaned on the wooden fence.

Kelly restlessly fumbled with the zipper on his jacket. *Come on, Red.* "Damn it," he said. "That guy's as slow as my grandmother."

Shades nodded and was about to comment when Red appeared in the garage doorway, his Vandal jacket hanging over his arm.

"Sorry to keep ya waiting," Red said. "I keep my jacket and club stuff in the garage so my folks won't find them."

"What happened?" Kelly asked.

"It's all set. Tonight at eight. Twenty-five guys each. No blades. I couldn't get a deal on other weapons. Your cousin is a real ball buster."

"I know." Kelly smiled. "Good job, Red." He patted the war counselor's back.

"You know what he said when I called for no knives," Red said. "You're probably scared you'll cut yourselves. So I said we don't want any bad cutting for the cops to trace."

"Smart," Kelly said. "Makes us look like we got some brains."

"Then he gives me a real dig," Red said. "He says he's glad we didn't call for guns; that from our past reputation, we'd probably wind up shooting each other before his boys could get a crack at us."

"Nasty bastard," Kelly said.

"One other thing I found out," Red said. "I met one of the 'Hatters a couple of blocks from their candy store. His name's Freddy. Nice guy. I know him from before. Freddy says that he doesn't think Charlie can muster twenty-five guys on short notice. They're beginning to break up and Charlie's loosing control."

"That's very interesting," Kelly said. "Charlie probably agreed to that many guys so he wouldn't tip his hand. Great work. I hope this guy Freddy doesn't get messed up tonight."

"He says he's one of the guys that won't be there," Red said.

"Let's get the guys together," Kelly said.

The trio shuffled out the gate. They kicked up a cloud of dust that drifted into adjoining yards and settled on clean laundry hanging from a network of clotheslines.

CHAPTER 6

Kelly pulled back the sleeve of his jacket and looked at his watch. Five minutes to eight. He slipped off the watch and stuffed it into his pocket. It was a graduation gift and the way his father had moaned about the cost, he would have to protect it or answer to his family's wrath. Kelly stood a few feet from the iron picket fence that surrounded Mt. Zion Cemetery. Johnny, Shades and nine other Vandals flanked him at equal intervals across the wide pebble and rock covered dirt road.

Red had worked out a plan based on some Revolutionary War battle. Kelly, although unfamiliar with military history, had patiently listened to Red's detailed plan and thought it was sound. The Vandals were briefed on what they had to know to make the plan work, and here they were, ready for their moment of truth.

Charlie and the Madhatters would approach from Queens Boulevard and would come into sight only as they rounded a bend ahead of the Vandals. There was a sudden flash of light from the top of a cliff at the bend. It was Red's signal. The Madhatters were there.

"This is it, guys. Let's go," Kelly said tightening his garrison belt around his wrist and hand.

Shades folded his glasses and placed them in his shirt pocket, protecting them by his quilted jacket and two heavy sweaters, extra padding to deaden the effects of expected blows. The blurred images around him knew to stay far enough away or catch an accidental sting from the bicycle chain that swung at his side.

The small band of Vandals started up the road.

The Madhatters came into view. Kelly counted eighteen.

"Where's the rest of them?" Johnny asked.

"It looks like that guy Freddy was telling the truth," Kelly said.

"I hope they're not pulling the same shit we are," Johnny said.

"No, we were here first. They wouldn't have time to set anything up."

"What'll we do?"

"Go through with the plan. Back off." Kelly raised his voice so the others would hear. "Back off."

The dozen Vandals stopped, acting confused and scared, slowly reversing their steps and spreading their battle line into the adjacent lot.

"They're following," Kelly said to his two officers. "Keep backing off."

"Where you going, chickens?" Charlie yelled. He wore a pork pie hat and a leather bomber jacket with the symbol of the gang, Alice in Wonderland's Madhatter, painted along the length of the left front. He was a few steps in front with a baseball bat in his hand. "What happened to the rest of your punks? Gotcha outnumbered, don't we?"

The Madhatters laughed and began making clucking sounds.

Kelly studied them as he paced off his retreat. They always wore hats when they rumbled - fedoras, derbies, chauffeur caps, a civil war kepi - two of them even wore helmets.

Kelly rammed two fingers between his lips and blew a loud shrill whistle. A hail of rocks, pieces of furniture and garbage rained down on the Madhatters from the cliff behind them. Two of them fell. The others turned their attention to the cliff just as Blackie and seven Vandals charged at them from a grove of trees at the side of the road.

"Let's get 'em," Kelly yelled. "Hit 'em hard."

Kelly's division broke into a sprint, their belts, car antennas and other weapons viciously poised. Their piercing yells had a ring of confidence. The plan would work.

A moment before the dozen met the mass of floundering Madhatters, Red and his five troops assaulted from the cliff. There were Vandals everywhere. There were no other Madhatters coming.

Charlie turned to face Kelly's group. He tightened his grip on the bat like he was waiting for a fast ball.

"What kind'a punk way of fighting is this?" Charlie shouted in frustration. "We're supposed to face off and swing out. This fight don't count."

"Your rules, pal. You told us anything goes," Kelly said.

"Your ass is mine."

"Then come on and get it." Kelly swung his belt in a sweeping arc as he pushed off his back foot. The rocky surface of the road crunched and gave way. The buckle sailed passed Charlie and bounced off the cragged road in a shower of sparks.

Charlie golfed the bat, glancing it off Kelly's knee. Kelly screamed as his leg collapsed, twisting under him and driving him to the ground. Charlie became tangled and uncoordinated in his haste to finish off Kelly, kicking at the injured knee while pulling the bat over his shoulder for another swing.

"Get up, Kelly." The sharp whip of Johnny's antenna slashed across Charlie's leathery face and opened a gash on his hollow cheek.

"No, Johnny." Kelly scrambled to his feet. "Leave him to me."

"I'll get you later," Charlie roared at Johnny, who had moved back toward the main battle when he saw Kelly was mobile.

Charlie brushed his hand across his injured cheek and glared at the blood smear on his fingertips.

"Come on, man. You gotta get me first," Kelly said.

Charlie aimed the bat at Kelly's ribs. Kelly leaped back, pressing off with his good leg but cringing as a sharp twinge of pain shot through him when he landed on the injured leg. The bat slipped from Charlie's hands and flew across the road, bouncing wildly off a tree.

"Tough luck, cous'." Kelly shifted his weight to ease the pain and chopped down with his belt. It caught the brim of the pork pie hat and smashed it to the ground. Charlie scrambled backward and reached into his jacket pocket. There was the sound of a sharp click and a knife in his hand.

"We agreed on no blades." Kelly dragged his throbbing leg as he moved away.

"Tough luck, cous'." Charlie moved in, tossing the knife from hand to hand. "I'm gonna cut you from ear to ear, and everybody'll know who scarred you." Charlie's cold gray eyes glared. He lunged at Kelly.

Kelly sidestepped and threw an uppercut with the belt and the razor sharp buckle tore open the armpit of Charlie's jacket. The knife thrust forward again and missed Kelly.

They were both wearing down and paced in a circle, trying to regain their senses, looking for an opening.

"Cops." Two Madhatters ran passed them. "Cut out."

Charlie's attention was diverted and Kelly took advantage. He rammed his good knee into Charlie's groin. A dull grunt rolled from Charlie's mouth as he doubled in pain and sank to the ground.

"Beat it, Kelly," Johnny said as he scurried passed. "Cops coming from both directions."

"Take it easy, cous'," Kelly said. Charlie was rolled into a ball, his knife lost along the rocky surface. Kelly turned away and started for the trees. His limp slowed him and he hoped he could reach cover before the cops spotted him. He turned to check the approaching police cars. He could see one car in the distance, at the Queens Boulevard end, trying to block that exit. Most of those caught in the glare of the headlights wore hats. They didn't know the terrain and were clumsily using the only route they knew back to their territory. Kelly's eyes dropped to Charlie who was trying to struggle to his feet.

"I beat you," he yelled at Charlie. He limped toward the tree line, but stopped after a few feet, and turned back. "Admit it. The Vandals won!"

"Get out'a here, punk." Pain had replaced the sneer in Charlie's voice.

"Can you walk?" Kelly asked, hobbling back toward Charlie.

"No. *You little bastard.*" Charlie was on one knee.

"Shut up and give me your hand."

The two stared at each other for a moment. Then Charlie grasped Kelly's hand.

"Tell me who won," Kelly said.

"Fuck you."

Kelly loosened his grip. "Then tell it to the cops."

"I can't afford another bust," Charlie said.

"They're getting closer."

"They'll get you, too."

"I'll risk it."

Charlie tightened his grip. "It was a tie."

Kelly yanked his cousin to his feet and, supporting each other, they started for the woods. "We'll see about that tomorrow," Kelly said.

"What'a ya mean?"

"You didn't have enough guys tonight. You'll probably have less tomorrow."

Charlie didn't answer.

"I don't think the cops spotted us," Kelly said. "We'll loose them in the trees and then hide in the cemetery."

"What the hell did you come back for?"

"You wouldn't be able to negotiate with me if you're in the can."

Charlie's expression was still hard, but Kelly knew he had won. And there was no need to start up a friendship. Charlie's ego wouldn't allow it and Kelly's victory didn't need it. Kelly would have one final sit-down about their business, providing Charlie still had any means to conduct business. Kelly was sure that he didn't. The spoils would pass to the Vandals.

The two limping figures disappeared among the trees. Behind them, the police cars, filled with members of the two gangs, started their journey to the local station house.

CHAPTER 7

JOHNNY SADINSKI – MARCH, 1956

Johnny, Red and Sonny cut out of school after the second period. It wasn't something they normally did. They were smart enough to know they needed an education to survive. But they also needed a break and an extended weekend was in order. After bribing a door monitor at Haaren High School in Manhattan, they wandered through the arcades in Times Square, had lunch at Nedicks and headed for their home turf.

They took the Flushing el train to Seventy-Forth Street in Jackson Heights, proceeded to the passageway behind Bickford's restaurant, and down a second staircase to the underground mini mall that spread in front of the turnstiles of the connecting subway line.

A newspaper stand, an adult bookstore, a notions shop and a record store lined the corridor. A small alcove before the subway steps housed a handful of coin operated lockers. The boys stuffed their books into one of the lockers and Johnny pocketed the key.

Johnny had started the day depressed and tired. His frame was lanky and his face drawn. The hot dog and orange soda he had earlier was the only food he enjoyed in the last two days. Nourishment doesn't prevail when you live with six other foster kids that mean nothing more than competitors at dinnertime. His foster parents ran a business and food cut into their profits.

They walked to the front of the record store. The windows were bare and overlooked rows of plain racks in unpainted wooden stands. Thousands of black vinyl semi-circles peeked from the tops of dull brown or faded gray paper jackets.

"So, we're here. We look at some records and then what?" Red asked.

"When we're done, we'll have some laughs with these," Sonny said, exposing the top of a transparent bag of multi-colored balloons from his dungaree pocket. "We can go back up on the el steps and bombs away."

"Yeah, cool," Johnny said. He had slowly come out of his doldrums during the afternoon.

They entered the shop and began browsing through the many racks of 45's. There were two smaller stands of older 78RPM's, and albums, which were beginning to gain in popularity.

The records were divided alphabetically by artist. Johnny took the beginning of the alphabet. He flipped through the heavy brown paper jackets, recognizing the record titles from their play on Alan Freed's radio show, or Jocko or Dr. Jive. The Avons. Chuck Berry. Bo Diddley - out of order, he commented to himself. The Bop Chords. *Pat Boone?* How the hell did he get in there? Johnny flipped through the next five records. Look at that crap, he thought in disgust, being a staunch purest when it came to R&B and rock and roll. At My Front Door - he stole that from the El Dorados. Tutti Fruitti - he stole that from Little Richard. Ain't That A Shame - from Fats Domino. *The carbon copy kid.* In his fruity white buck shoes.

What kind of jerks would buy his records? Well, they aren't buying these. Johnny stuffed the five Pat Boone records into the back of his dungarees, tucking his shirt over them and hitching his garrison belt up for support. *But what if he got caught stealing Pat Boone records?* He would never be able to explain himself. This was a special mission. He would have to chance it.

It would be less suspicious if he bought something; so he picked out two fifty-cent records he liked and brought them to the check-out counter.

"'My Girl Awaits Me' by the Castelles," the balding, bushy

eye-browed clerk read off one of the labels. "That's a Philly group, isn't it?"

"I don't know," Johnny said. "I just like their sound."

"They're good." The clerk punched the totals into the register. "One dollar and two cents."

Johnny handed him a five-dollar bill that he had borrowed from Sonny.

"You got two cents?" the clerk asked.

"No. That's it." Johnny pointed to the five-dollar bill.

"I trust you. Give it to me the next time you're in." He slipped the two records into an oversized paper bag and handed it to Johnny with four single dollars change.

He trusts me, Johnny thought. *And I'm stealing records from him.* Records I don't even want. Johnny froze for a minute, ready to confess his deed. He made a vow to return there and pay off his two-cent debt. Pat Boone and his record company would be the only people Johnny would impose a financial loss on.

Sonny and Red had each bought a record and Johnny waited outside while they rang through.

"You got a new friend, hah?" Sonny said when he met Johnny outside the store.

"What'a you mean?" Johnny asked.

"He was looking at you like he was your mother."

"He was just a nice guy. Some adults are like that."

"Not really. An adult ain't friendly unless they want something from you," Sonny said. "That goes for parents, family, whoever."

"I don't know much about family and parents, but you're wrong. You just take family for granted. I don't have that luxury."

"What's next? Water balloons?" Red asked as he stepped into the corridor.

"You remembered," Sonny said in mock surprise. "What a mind. Like a steel trap."

"Fuck you."

"There's a john near the back steps," Sonny said. "Let's load up."

They put the records in the locker with their books - all except the Pat Boone collection that Johnny kept hidden. The men's room was at the opposite end of the mall. They filled the balloons with water. They had a half dozen filled and tied off when Sonny glanced at the pair of stalls in the corner of the yellowing tiled room. The closest cubical was occupied, the feet and lowered pants of the user exposed through the gap between the bottom edge of the gun metal gray side panel and off-white tile floor.

Sonny motioned with his head toward the stall. Johnny and Red smiled. They each lifted a pair of balloons, the flexibility of the mounds overflowing around their hands.

Sonny silently counted with his head. One nod. Two. Threeee - All six missiles were on target, landing inside the small enclosure, bouncing off walls or finding direct hits, flooding the tiny cubical with at least a gallon of water. They had been out the door before the last water bomb had burst and the garbled shout came from the stall.

They wanted to have a fun day, and so far it was turning out that way. Never mind whose expense the fun would tax. They bounced down the street in glee and youthful abandonment.

Somewhere between Seventy-Forth Street and Bill's candy store, their next destination, Johnny pulled the Pat Boone records from the back of his dungarees.

"Anybody here like Pat Boone?" Johnny asked.

"Hell no," Red said.

"What're you kidding?" Sonny asked.

"Well, let's see how far he can travel in our turf before he cracks up," Johnny said, handing records to Red and Sonny. He scaled one of them across the street into a concrete railroad embankment. The record hit edge first and shattered.

"Good shot." Sonny spun his record toward the embankment but it lazily bounced off, only chipping the edge.

Red's disc broke into three pieces. Johnny plunged the two

remaining records into the sidewalk at his feet. They shattered and he jumped on the pieces.

Johnny felt like he had just beat the hell out of someone and stomped on their head, and yet no one was hurt. *Too bad it couldn't be like that all the time.*

"I guess you hate him more than we do," Red said.

Johnny looked up, feeling a rush of embarrassment. He had overreacted. "How can you hate someone you don't know."

They walked the last four blocks to Bill's in silence. Sonny opened the door and poked his head into the store. He pulled back and closed the door.

"It's like a tomb. Still nobody else around," Sonny said. "I'm getting hungry. You guys wanna get a sandwich here?"

"Nah. Let's get some White Castles," Red said.

"Good idea," Sonny said.

They walked down Sixty-Ninth Street to Roosevelt Avenue, and Johnny paid for the bag of twelve-cent mini-burgers. They sat on the retaining wall of the parking lot, tossing the empty castle-shaped white and blue boxes into a red steel barrel as they finished each burger.

Johnny tried to analyze his mood swings as they ate in silence, an occasional belch from the onion-laded patties the only sound from the trio. He knew it had to do with Sonny's words about family and mistrust. He had learned to trust only the Vandals, because they were the adopted family of his choosing. But he was also sure a true family relationship went deeper and was something special.

A lot of the guys had only one parent, but at least they had half a family. They had someone that maybe cared or showed a spark of compassion or understanding. He would give anything to sit and talk with his mother or father, who he had no idea of what they looked like, no less how they acted or thought. All Johnny had from them was his name. Everyone else had someone to remember, even if to remember them as being a bastard.

There was someone, though. He had seen her many times in

the neighborhood and had thought about talking to her. The idea had dropped into his thoughts like a piece into a puzzle. *Yeah, why not?* He pushed the idea into the back of his mind to be mulled over later.

"You guys ready for some action?" Johnny leaped to his feet and arced his last paper box from a jump shot into the red barrel.

"Hey, he's back among the living," Red said.

"Let's go," Sonny said.

They crossed the street, passed a row of stores, and turned the next corner. The two blocks that stretched out before them had been the home neighborhood of some of the Vandals until the city or state or some politician decided that the neighborhood would no longer exist because they wanted to run a highway through.

They stopped in the middle of the block of deserted houses, the closest they would come to an old west ghost town in the middle of New York City, and scanned one of the two story frame houses that was deteriorating from neglect. The windows were boarded over and the surrounding grounds were overgrown with tall weeds.

"I think Pickles used to live here," Sonny said. "Let's look inside."

The front door was nailed shut. They made their way down the narrow driveway between the buildings and found an entrance through a screen door that swung open to an overlooked and unsecured solid door. They explored the house; the outside light beaming through staggered window boards, and found that there were scattered pieces of old furniture in the living room and upstairs bedroom. There was even flatware and a half-empty bottle of catsup and other condiments in the kitchen cabinets.

"This would be a great make-out spot," Sonny said. "Even to come to when the cops kick us out'a the school yard. We can get some candles or lanterns and play cards or hang out when Bill's closes down at night. Kind of like an after hours joint."

"Yeah," Red said. "I can use one of the rooms for my council meetings, even set it up as my own war room with maps."

VIKA

Johnny and Sonny stared at Red in disbelief.

"Okay," Red said. "Maybe I'm getting off-beat, but at least I got a hobby that's different. If it wasn't for the way I think, we wouldn't have beaten the Madhatters and we wouldn't be where we are now."

"You're right, buddy." Johnny patted Red on the arm, patronizing the Vandal war counselor. Red's addiction to anything military was beginning to block out reality. He had devised his own war games that he played alone because he was the only one who understood their complexity. Most of the Vandals already had their doubts about Red's sanity and were betting on when he would completely flip out. Johnny also knew that Sonny had mixed emotions about Red. Sonny would be the next choice to step into the war counselor slot and be the third ranking officer of the club. But he also knew that Sonny's ambition was tempered by the friendship they shared. He knew the friendship was stronger, and until the time something actually happened to Red, things would stay the way they were.

"I got an idea," Johnny said. "With all the junk laying around, we can make a dummy and have it laying in the bed upstairs. We can bring the girls here and scare the shit out'a them."

"Yeah," Sonny said. He grabbed the bottle of catsup and a wooden handled steak knife. "A little added touch," he said.

They climbed to the second story and entered the front bedroom at the head of the stairs. A rusted metal bed frame held a bare, torn mattress. It stood in the corner to the left of the open entrance. They rummaged through a pile of clothes and remnants in the bedroom's closet and had no trouble constructing an image lying on the bed. A blanket covered stuffing of clothes and rags with a crumpled fedora at the head tilted as though a head was facing the wall. A pair of shoes, stacked side on side, peeked from under the foot of the blanket.

"A little horror for effect," Sonny said. He plunged the knife into the upper body of the dummy and then flicked the catsup bottle, splattering the blanket around the knife. He pulled his arm back and hurled a shower of catsup against the wall, the bed frame and the floor.

"Looks great," Johnny said. "Edgar Allen Poe would be proud of you."

"Thanks. Let's go get some victims."

The trio returned to the schoolyard. To their surprise, three more Vandals were there, sprawled across the concrete steps on the far side of the yard next to the fenced, weed covered area that was supposed to have been a garden for the kids in the elementary school. The Vandals had named the weed patch "The Beer Garden" from the empty cans they tossed over its fence after weekend parties.

"When did you guys get here?" Sonny asked Blackie, Jimmy and Speedo after cutting across the block-wide yard.

"About ten minutes ago," Speedo said. "You guys cut out'a school, too?"

"Yeah. We've been having a ball," Johnny said. He gave a quick rundown on the deserted house and their plan with the dummy. They liked the idea and Jimmy and Speedo wanted to visit the house to see the set-up. Red volunteered to lead the pair back to the building. The others would wait for some patsies.

"How'd it go last night after the cops nailed you kicking the shit out'a that Assassin?" Johnny asked Blackie.

"No sweat. I spent the night at the precinct and went to court this morning with a couple'a the other guys." Blackie ran his hand through his thick raven hair. "My old lady bailed me out and I'm supposed to go back to court in a couple'a weeks."

"Someday those Assassin punks are gonna learn to keep the hell away from our turf," Sonny said.

"Did you see the Long Island Star Journal today?" Johnny asked.

"I just got up," Blackie said. "I ain't seen shit."

"They had your name and Freddy The Hat and Eddie Comanche on the front page. They made it sound like a full scale bop."

"The papers always do that shit," Blackie said.

"The main thing is they mentioned the Vandals," Sonny said. "And we were named first this time." Sonny punched the air. "Top billing from now on."

"Since I helped heap all this glory on us," Blackie said. "I think the treasury should kick in for some of my bail money."

"Sure, why not?" Johnny and Sonny nodded. "That's what it's there for, emergency situations. We'll talk to Shades later."

Blackie jumped to his feet. "I been lookin' for that kid." He pointed to two younger boys who had appeared from the rear of the school and were inching their way along the fence line.

The boys were concentrating on the school building and didn't notice the Vandals. They turned the corner of The Beer Garden and came face to face with Blackie, who had silently crept forward.

"Come'er, you." Blackie pointed at the shorter boy, who had a round face accented by a ruddy complexion and pimples. He froze and Blackie clamped his hand on the boy's shoulder. Blackie pulled him back into the alcove formed by the steps and The Beer Garden. The boy's partner escaped through the distant gateway.

"What's up?" Johnny asked.

"This punk's been botherin' my kid sister," Blackie said, snapping his finger into the side of the boy's nose.

"Ow! I didn't do nothing," the boy said.

"You callin' my sister a liar? She pointed you out to me. There's no mistakin' your puss. It looks like a friggen pizza pie." He shoved the boy into the corner. The back of his head bounced off the iron post with a ring. "I'm gonna kick your fat little ass."

"Blackie, wait a minute," Johnny said.

"What?"

"Come over here." Johnny beckoned with his index finger. "Keep an eye on the kid, Sonny."

Sonny spread his arms across the corner, holding onto the chain link diamonds of both fences, enclosing the boy in front of him.

"Why ain't you in school?" Sonny began to interrogate. "You know who we are?"

"Blackie, listen," Johnny said out of hearing range. "This kid would be great for the deserted house. If we scare the shit out of him, he'll remember that more than you smacking him around."

"I don't know, man. I gotta teach him a lesson."

"Come on. It'll be a blast. If it doesn't work, you can always find him again."

Blackie stared at his shoes. "Alright. But I lay down the law with him about my sister."

"Sure. You have to do that. It's expected. Come on."

They moved back to Sonny and the boy.

"Listen, kid," Johnny said. "I wasn't sure at first, but I think it was your uncle who we saw going into one of the old houses down the block. We thought we heard a yell, and he never came out."

"Yeah," Blackie said. "I'm sorry, I didn't know it was your uncle. Johnny, here, just reminded me. Your uncle could be hurt bad or somethin'. We'll help you find him."

"My uncle? My uncle's working."

"No, it was him," Johnny said. "We've seen him around the neighborhood. We know what he looks like."

"Come on, we'll try to find him." Sonny picked up the scheme and, ushering the boy between him and Blackie, began marching him across the schoolyard. Johnny closed up the rear, plugging any escape gaps.

"I really don't think it was my uncle, fellas. Maybe I ought'a get my father."

"Nah. That'd take too long. This is an emergency."

Blackie scolded the boy and counseled him on the proper manner when dealing with girls, especially his sister, as they walked to the house.

They opened the screen door and pushed the boy through the rear entrance into the kitchen. There was no sign of the other Vandals. The rooms were empty and quiet.

"Hello. Anybody here?" Johnny yelled. *Red and the other guys must have seen us coming. They're probably hiding.*

"There's nobody down here," Sonny said. "Let's look upstairs."

"Come on, fellas," the boy said. Fear began to grip his words. "I don't wanna be here. I wanna go home."

"You gotta be brave," Blackie said, pushing the boy ahead of him. "It's for your uncle."

They climbed the creaking stairs, jostling him, prodding him into taking each step. He was maneuvered passed the head of the stairs and to the front room. Blackie gave the final shove and the boy stumbled through the doorway, gaining his balance in the center of the room. He stared at the bed and his jaw went slack.

Johnny stepped into the room and looked at the bed. *What the hell?* The dummy had been replaced by Speedo. He faced the wall, partially covered with the catsup splattered blanket, pants legs rolled to the knees, the knife still positioned like it had been plunged into his body. The fedora was pulled down to his ears.

The boy screamed and charged forward, slamming into the three bodies blocking the doorway.

Speedo rolled over, his arm falling limp against the side of the bed. He moaned through missing front teeth, his dentures hanging along his lower lip. "Help me," he said, the false teeth resembling the lower jaw of a ventriloquist dummy.

"Oh shit," Blackie yelled. "He's still alive. We're gonna have to kill him again."

"No." The boy desperately tried to smash through the line of older boys.

"Somebody's gotta die," Sonny shouted, pushing against the rush of the boy. "If we don't kill him, he'll kill us."

The closet door opposite the bed swung open and slammed into the plaster wall. Jimmy stepped out of the closet. The green bathrobe he had found was worn backward, the collar turned up against his chin. His long, straight hair was mussed and hanging in front of his eyes, his arms outstretched as he walked stiff-legged like a movie monster.

"You killed my friend," Jimmy bellowed, his finger pointing at the boy.

Jimmy surprised everyone in the room. The blockers' guard

dropped for a moment and, seeing his chance, the boy ran. He hurdled down the stairs, leaping the last four in one bound, and bounced off the retaining wall.

The escape was so swift that no one could recover in time to give chase. Most of the Vandals collapsed in laughter. But Blackie's inbred viciousness wouldn't allow him to simply enjoy the situation. *The kid was getting off too easy*.

"He's after us," Blackie yelled, pursuing the boy. "He's gonna kill you."

The kid shook off the momentary stun of hitting the wall and headed for the only exit out of the house. The rear door had been left open, leaving only the tattered screen door as a barrier. He plowed through the netting, pulling the side moldings with him as he leaped down the one step to the ground.

Blackie snatched a purple stained, unlabeled jar from the kitchen counter before he crashed through the shattered screen. He wheeled around the rear corner of the house and caught sight of the boy streaking down the driveway, stomping out a path through the overgrown weeds.

"Keep away from my sister," he shouted, hurling the jar. "The next time, you're dead."

The jar sailed high and smashed against the front corner of the building, shattering shards of glass and purple slime across the sidewalk. The boy had turned the corner when the jar hit and was out of range. Blackie slowed to a trot and was joined by Johnny and Sonny at the sidewalk. The kid was out of sight.

Red Janek appeared two houses away. He was carrying a paper bag.

"Where the hell were you?" Sonny asked.

"We got tired of waiting for you guys so I went to the store to get some sodas," Red said.

"You missed the best action of the day," Johnny said. "We were laughing so much we almost pissed in our pants."

"Some kid came flying down the street like his ass was on fire,"

Red said. "He looked like he was gonna piss in his pants when he saw me."

They all broke up in laughter as Speedo and Jimmy joined the group, Speedo still wearing the battered fedora pulled down over his ears. The joke had worked and they would have more fun pulling it again. Red wanted to be in on the second act.

They split the sodas and returned to the schoolyard. Speedo stayed behind to recreate his murder victim role, and Red to keep him company. The concrete rectangle was full of life. A stickball game occupied the heart of the yard. Most of the players were a few years younger but a few of the Vandals took part. The steps next to The Beer Garden were packed with Vandals and Vandal Debs. It was Friday night and things would be popping.

Sonny made a pitch about noises they had heard coming from the deserted house and sold two of the girls along with a quartet of Vandals into checking out the place. The second performance of their play was about to unfold.

Johnny, Blackie and Jimmy stayed behind. Johnny began to sink into his normal depression. The day had gone too fast. Sure, there was more to come, but it would probably be the normal hanging out; bragging about how great the Vandals were, and somebody trying to make one of the girls, and maybe a good suggestion that would eventually fizzle.

How much more could be piled on to surpass what had just taken place? It was like that time he experimented with the marijuana joint outside school. He had his high from the day and now he was coming down. It didn't last. He was still Johnny Sadinski. He needed something more.

The normal crowd began to drift off. They were going home to eat dinner or check in. They had a *normal* family life but were also fortunate enough not to be derailed from their social life. Their parents either had no idea what that social life was about, or didn't have the patience or time to control it.

Johnny thought about the woman again. It seemed like a logical solution. He needed someone. She needed someone.

Jimmy Yadenik started down the sloped street that bordered the schoolyard steps. Johnny called for him to wait-up. Blackie and a few of the crazies, members who also had no family life and liked it that way, remained glued to the steps to protect the turf until the others returned.

Johnny had a good relationship with Jimmy. He took the time to talk with the guy and listen to his problems. He didn't condemn Jimmy as "The Mad Russian" - a title bestowed upon him for his erratic behavior - like the others. He found out what bugged the guy and why he acted the way he did.

Johnny and Jimmy had a bond because of their similar situations. Jimmy had been a foster-kid for seven years before his parents had reclaimed him. He felt that it was more difficult being in that situation than in Johnny's because Johnny knew his parents had abandoned him. Johnny had learned to make peace with himself. Jimmy had told Johnny that he came back to strangers after seven years. Both he and Johnny lived with strangers, but it was worse for Jimmy because he had known someone was there those seven years and they had done nothing to end his exile. Johnny became attached to the Mad Russian after that revelation about themselves and they shared most of their thoughts, and at times, their depression.

They crossed Queens Boulevard back into original Vandal turf. Jimmy broke off at his block and they agreed to meet later. Johnny made a U-turn and headed back along their route. They had spoke of Pete's mother when they passed the house, agreed that it had been a bad deal suffered for everyone involved, but Johnny made no indication of what he had planned. This was his secret and he wouldn't even share it with Jimmy. After all, it might not happen the way he hoped it would.

Unconsciously, Johnny had tracked her moves. He saw her in the neighborhood and each time he, unknowingly, would record the time and movement of her life. Now, the pent-up facts came to the surface and he knew that she was home.

He walked to the rear of the house and, having been there in the past, easily found his way to the apartment door. He lifted a shaking fist and knocked, at first lightly and then with more force.

"Who's there?" Mrs. Wilson asked from inside.

"Johnny Sadinski. I'm a friend of Pete's. We met before. I'd like to talk to you."

CHAPTER 8

RED JANEK – THAT SAME EVENING

Red Janek sat on the bottom mattress of the double-decker bunk bed. He had slept on the upper bunk for most of his childhood, inheriting the more coveted lower level a year ago when his older brother was drafted. The walls of the small room were decorated with military unit patches and other memorabilia sent home by his brother. Hand-painted model soldiers and armored vehicles lined the rear edge of a table that doubled for a writing desk.

Red was reading the final pages of a book on Custer's Last Stand. He had read the last two chapters several times trying to analyze how he would have handled the battle. What a set of brass balls, Red concluded. I hope I never get that arrogant. Screw up, blow a fight and get killed all in one shot. It's important to know what you're up against and handle the situation accordingly.

Red was confident that he someday would be a military officer. He was still undecided whether to follow his brother into the army or be a Marine. Most of the old Comanches had become Marines. Either way, he would still have to finish high school and get his parent's permission because he would still be only seventeen after graduation, and seventeen was the minimum age of enlistment with parental consent. His mother already made it clear that she would never approve of two sons in the military at the same time. There was still time for a plan. Red wouldn't be seventeen for four more months and graduation was still a year away.

"Richie. Dinner."

Red never recognized his given name on the first call. It took a minute to sink through the layers of habit answering to his colorful nickname and the intense involvement in Colonel Custer's dilemma.

His mother called a second time.

"Be right there." Red finished the final paragraphs, closed the book and headed for the kitchen. The railroad style apartment was typical of the older buildings in the area. There was no hallway; each room led to the next through the center of the apartment with the exception of the two rear bedrooms and bathroom. The kitchen was the second room from the front of the house.

His mother was at the stove, her back to him. Her salt and pepper hair was shoulder length. She jokingly complained that the white and gray hairs were from anxiety caused by bringing up Red and his brother. Actually, her hair hadn't changed in eighteen years. The anxiety was from when she and her husband had escaped from Czechoslovakia, a few steps ahead of Hitler's army.

"Go call dad," Harriet Janek said, still facing the stove. Her words were toned by a slight accent.

"Hey dad," Red yelled over his shoulder.

"Don't get smart, young man."

Red snickered. "Okay lady." He shuffled across the kitchen to the window overlooking the back yard. He leaned on the sill and stared at the wooden garage that took up most of the dirt yard.

He had slept there the night Dave was killed. He couldn't tell his parents what had happened. They'd have been as sick as *him*. He sat there in the dark and vomited before he had gained his composure and realized that what he had seen was something he would have to get used to if he expected to have a military career. But no matter what he told himself, he couldn't shake the picture. Somehow, he felt a share of responsibility for Dave's death. He felt haunted. The specter of Dave and that night would always be lurking in his unconscious, ready to spring into his thoughts like the scene from some horror movie.

Red constantly filled his mind with details to help squeeze out that night. He read. He studied. He made sure that everything he knew about was correct to the last detail. And, of course, he had two families to fall back on.

"Dad." A minute passed. "Hey dad. Dinner's ready."

A short stocky man in his early forties appeared in the garage doorway. He was wiping his grease-laden hands with an equally greasy rag.

"Be right in." The man's voice was soft and low and accented as his wife's. Red never knew his father to raise his voice. He was a good ol' guy, Red thought. He and mom were the best parents in the world.

Red considered himself twice as lucky as most of the Vandals. He had a family at home and a family on the street. But having two families was difficult in itself. Trying to satisfy both took an emotional juggling act. He wasn't aware of it on the surface but everything in his life was pushing him to the brink of self-destruction.

He turned from the window and walked to the oilcloth-covered table. His mother was placing a steaming bowl of pierogis in the center of three plates.

"He'll be right in," Red said.

"Did you wash up?"

"I ain't dirty," Red said as he straddled one of the chairs.

"Come on." She grabbed Red by his ear and twisted it gently.

"Ow! Stop, hah." Red stood. He was much taller than his mother was. He was six-foot and still growing. He had been a decent basketball player during his first year of high school, but slowly slipped away from the sport when his duties of war counselor were becoming neglected.

After washing his hands, he returned to the kitchen and resumed his spread legged position at the table. His father had entered the bathroom after him and was using a solvent to clean his hands.

"What are you going to do after dinner?" Red's mother asked.

"I don't know," Red said with a shrug. "Go out, I guess."

"Where?"

"No place. With the guys. Just out."

"Why don't you stay home one night and watch television with dad and me? Milton Berle is going to have that rock and roll guy on. Elvis something."

"Presley. Elvis Presley. Nah. Watching TV is a drag."

"Drag. Where do you get this language from?"

"Here and there."

"Here and there? Didn't you have enough when that boy Dave was-"

"Murdered? That's what you always call it. Murder. How can you think Pete was a murderer? It was an accident." Red felt sick to his stomach. He wanted to forget it but she always seemed to bring it back to life.

"They sent away the boy who did it, didn't they? They didn't think it was an accident."

"Stop it, ma." Red jumped to his feet. "He was thirteen years old. He wasn't a killer."

"Sit down." His father stood in the doorway of the kitchen. He always had a sullen expression. He never smiled and never showed anger.

"I ain't hungry," Red said, his head bent, his gaze on the floor.

"Well, I am. Sit down and stop arguing with your mother."

"She started it." Red's voice was soft.

"Sit down," his father said. He was a short but solid man with large beefy hands that were constantly busy.

"I'm going out." Red strode quickly toward the front of the house, avoiding the side door closest to his father.

"Now, come back here," Mrs. Janek called, a touch of apology in her tone.

"Let him go." His father moved toward the table as slowly as he spoke. "Let him cool off."

"But dinner."

"He'll come back when he gets hungry."

She began sobbing. "I don't want him to get into any trouble or end up like that boy, Dave. Richie is a good boy."

"Stop beating your head against a wall." Henry Janek moved to his wife's side, trying to comfort her. "He knows what's right and wrong. He's smart. Someday he'll be off to college. Maybe West Point like he's dreaming about. We'll have a son to be proud of. Two sons to be proud of. Who could ask for more?"

"I am proud of him."

"Then smile for me."

She smiled and so did Henry.

Red had circled the block, changing his mind twice about returning home. He decided he wasn't in the mood for another conflict. Dave had flashed through his thoughts again, and he just couldn't go back and have that night come up as a topic. He would let things cool off and face his parents the following day. The sun was still an hour away from disappearing. Red would have to wait to retrieve his Vandal jacket from its hiding place in the garage.

He began wandering the neighborhood, trying to walk off the image that his mother had brought back to the surface. When he came out of his thoughts, Red found he was a block from where it had happened. An urge started him into a slow trot just as they had done that night. Then faster as they realized the intensity of the fight. Then came the crash of a gunshot, with a quick flash and blood spraying. He stopped and froze in place at the curb overlooking a patch of blacktop. There was still a stain. Maybe it was an oil smudge. *It looked very much like a bloodstain.*

He had to put that Halloween night to rest. He couldn't let it eat at him. The future was too important. The past would have to be as pedestrian as when he slammed shut the Custer book. *Go away, Dave. It's over. You brought it on. You were to blame as much as anyone. You ruined too many lives that night.*

"Come on, Dave," he said. "We're not bothering you. We're sorry, okay? We're sorry it happened. So go away and rest in peace already."

"You loose something, kid?"

"What?" Red looked to the sound of the voice. A van was

stopped passed the intersection, and the driver leaned out his window.

"You're standing there talking to yourself. I thought you lost something."

"Yeah, I think I finally did." Red spun around on the balls of his soles like a soldier doing an about-face. "Everything's okay. Thanks for asking." He started back toward his home. The van continued on its way.

The sun had set when Red climbed over the back fence out of the view of anyone who might glance out a rear window. He slipped into the garage, stood on a wooden box and lifted his folded jacket from a stack of boards resting between the rafters. He was the only person in his family tall enough to reach the spot. He was over the back fence again and on his way.

CHAPTER 9

Red reached the corner of Woodside Avenue and Sixty-Ninth Street. He waited until a Bungalow Bar ice cream truck rolled passed before scooting across to the curb in front of Bill's candy store. The scene along the sidewalk had a circus atmosphere.

A small public library annex occupied the corner storefront next to Bill's. The library was closed for the night, its outer enclosed entranceway being used as an echo chamber by five Vandals harmonizing in accappella to the Cadillacs' "Gloria". The book-lined plate glass windows bounced the sound of their voices into the street. They called themselves the Emeral-tones. The bass singer, Speedo Moran, had earned his nickname from the bass part of another Cadillacs tune he constantly bellowed. Three of the Vandal Debs, named as the female auxiliary, slouched against the front windows of the library swooning over the lead singer, Val McKay. The girls wore dungarees that hugged their young hips and bright chartreuse or fuchsia blouses. Two brunettes flanked a blond pony-tailed girl; their hair bobby-pinned and covered with kerchiefs.

Chico Perone and his girl, Roxie, were under the street light grinding out a slow dance to the group's rhythm. Roxie wore Chico's Vandal jacket. Sonny and Blackie were sitting on the sidewalk in front of the candy store, leaning against the footing of the window that displayed cardboard Coke and Chesterfield signs. The Mad Russian was lying under the window on the opposite side of the front door, his body stretched halfway across the sidewalk, his head cradled into cupped hands behind him. Red headed for the glass, silver-strip rimmed front door.

"What'a ya say, Red?"

"What's happening, guys?" Red stopped before opening the

door.

"The Sunnyside Loews is showing Blackboard Jungle and The Wild One again. Most of us are going to see them," Sonny said.

"That's cool. Remember when they came around to our school looking for extras to be in Blackboard Jungle?" Red asked.

"Yeah," Sonny said. "I wish I would'a known about it. I would've bugged the hell out'a them to pick me. I could've found fortune and fame in sunny California."

"Yeah, sure. Your puss would'a broken the camera," Blackie said.

"Who's going?" Red asked.

"I don't know. Ten or twelve guys." Blackie motioned with his head toward the glass door. "Kelly and some more guys are inside."

"What's his problem?" Red asked, pointing at Jimmy with a steel-tapped engineer boot.

"Hey Jimmy. What's your problem, Red wants to know?" Blackie yelled at the seemingly sleeping Vandal.

"No problem, man. Just resting," Jimmy said.

"Why don't you bring your bed with you?" Red asked with a laugh.

"My bed is too hard." Jimmy patted the concrete, his eyes still closed. "This is just right."

"You ain't gonna believe what I just did," Red said.

"What?" Sonny asked.

"My mother started that noise about Dave again."

"Christ, when is everybody gonna let us forget it?" Sonny said.

"That's what I want to know," Red said. "But, anyway, I walked out and went to where it happened".

"What for?"

"I don't know if something inside led me or I just happened to wind up there, but I think it helped me clear everything from my mind. At first I thought I was flipping out. I started talking to Dave like I was at his grave or something, and telling him to let us forget it already. In the end, I just wiped it all clean. I put it to rest."

"Jeez," Sonny said. "Don't tell Kelly about flipping out. I'd hate to get your job because he thinks you're going nuts like the Mad Russian."

"I told you I ain't Russian." Jimmy pushed himself into a sitting position and leaned against the storefront. "My family is Ukrainian. They hate being called Russian."

"What's the difference?" Blackie said. "You're all a bunch of Polacks like ol' Johnny boy."

"By the way, where is Johnny?" Red asked. "He's usually here by now."

"I don't know," Jimmy said. "I was supposed to meet him on the way back here, but he wasn't home."

"He'll probably show later."

"And who's nuts?" Jimmy said. "I'm keeping track of everything. I'm writing it down, and when I write my book about us and make a million bucks, you'll see who's crazy."

"Yeah, sure. More like two bucks," Sonny said. "And that's all we need, a permanent record so they'll never let us forget."

"We have to forget about it," Red said. "It's the smart thing to do."

The beat cop rounded the corner and rousted everyone away from the storefronts. Those who were going to the movie slowly shuffled inside. The others headed for the school yard a block away where they could hide in the many dark corners of the odd shaped area. They might play a game of knuckles or pitch quarters under the street lamp outside the back gate of the schoolyard, a side street the cops rarely patrolled. One of them would find an older person or use a phony ID to buy a couple of six packs. They would pass the early hours of Friday night amusing themselves.

Ten minutes later, the group at bill's decided to leave. Red spun two of the round stool seats as he followed everyone passed the counter. A loud squeal from one of the spinning red cushions jerked Bill's wrinkled face up from a copy of the Daily Mirror. He mumbled something about his nerves. They chuckled as they stepped from the store into the warm night.

The cop had left the block, but it was still better judgement to split into smaller groups and travel different routes. The cops had their special rules. Any group over three could be stopped for unlawful assembly, and anyone wearing a garrison belt outside of at least three belt loops could be picked up for carrying a weapon.

Kelly, Red, Sonny and Blackie were decked out in their aqua and black Vandal jackets. Jimmy, the odd ball as usual, wore a black motorcycle jacket. The movie theater was a little over a mile from Bill's, in an area that was considered neutral. Unlike international boundaries, no one would be in danger of provoking a war if they crossed a corner of a neighboring territory, as long as someone didn't get paranoid and create a situation.

Blackie was jittery as they walked under the el structure on Roosevelt Avenue. The sudden arrival of the cops the night before had prevented him from finishing off the Assassin he had been battling and he felt cheated. The three baby-faced youngsters who now happened into his path might satisfy that urge.

"Yo, guys," Blackie shouted in a feigned happy greeting to the trio as he crossed the street toward them. "Wait up."

Blackie walked quickly - He never ran because it was uncool. He mumbled something out of the other Vandals' earshot. The scrubbed trio, dressed in crisp clean clothes, suggesting they were headed for a chaperoned affair, stopped.

"What money?" the middle one asked before he caught a sharp kick to the groin and went down in a heap.

His two friends were slammed with consecutive right and left hooks, dropping them to the sidewalk. Blackie danced over them in a boxer's crouch, throwing jabs into the air.

"Come on, get up." He kicked one of them. "Three to one. Fight."

The Vandals crossed the street.

"Come on, man," Kelly said. "You got them good. Three to one. You dumped them all."

"Yeah," Blackie said. "Little punks from some rich-bitch neighborhood. Go back and tell them who the Vandals are."

"Okay, man." Kelly put his arm around Blackie's shoulders. "Let's get to that flick. Fuck these punks."

"Yeah." Blackie broke from Kelly's loose hold and started forward, his foot pressing deeply into the closest supine stomach. A muffled scream was left in his wake as Blackie started up the street like he had stomped over nothing more than a pile of garbage.

"Be cool, fellas," Red said, staying behind to make some retribution of the situation. He felt slightly nauseated but couldn't let his feelings show. "The guy's not all there," Red said, spinning his index finger next to his temple. "Go do what you were doing. Just don't come back this way."

Red spun around and caught up with his group, suppressing his feelings about the ugly, unnecessary interlude in their journey. Blackie's type was needed in the Vandal ranks. It was too bad but semi-psychos like him were needed to keep them were they were.

Red couldn't help but think of Dave again, comparing him with Blackie. Why the hell were they so alike? *Forget it, man. Just forget it.*

They reached the theater and passed under the marquee with one of the attractions misspelled: BLACKBORD JUNGLE.

"What a bunch of schnooks," Red said. "You'd think that they'd be embarrassed about putting something like that in public."

"The picture should be starting soon," said a cute redhead girl collecting tickets at the one open space in a bank of five padded and tufted doors.

"You mean you don't care that your sign is misspelled?" Red asked for a second time.

"Please move in," she said. "The picture should be starting soon."

"Hey, trying to make that babe?" Sonny asked as they stepped into the inner lobby. "Two redheads. Real hot."

"Miss Iron Drawers? Yeah, *sure.*"

Kelly and Jimmy stopped at the refreshment stand to buy

popcorn and sodas. The others entered the theater area, stopping momentarily to adjust their eyes to the darkness. They were in their seats only a minute when the scene of a New York City schoolyard filled the front of the theater and "Rock Around The Clock" by Bill Haley and the Comets blasted through the huge speakers at both ends of the stage.

The other groups of Vandals had arrived earlier. They occupied all but two seats in the last row, center of the theater. Red's group sat in front of them. They greeted the larger group loudly, drawing grumbles from the scattered audience. Blackie jumped into the aisle as soon as the music started and went into a victory dance. He was joined by Speedo, and Blackie flipped Speedo from hip to hip, prompting more complaints and a few laughs from the patrons. An usher finally convinced them to sit, and they took the two vacant seats in the last row.

Red looked over his shoulder. He counted fourteen Vandals, plus Roxie. She was in a clinch with Chico at the far end of the last row. Johnny wasn't in the group. Red figured that he must have made it to the schoolyard after they had left for the movies.

"Kelly," Vinny said.

Kelly turned. "Yeah?"

"There's a bunch of the Imperials here tonight," Vinny said, pointing toward the front of the theater.

"So?"

"So, they been throwing hard looks at us. One of them said something to Chico's girl."

"Come on," Red said. "The Imperials are only number one in North Queens."

"Red's right," Kelly said. "They're too big for us yet."

"I know," Vinny said. "But, you know we can't let them think we're punk or anything."

"They probably never heard of us. Just let it pass. Nothing'll happen."

Vinny settled back into his seat and Kelly and Red turned their attention to the screen. Everyone began commenting about the movie, growing loud at intervals until the shhshing summoned the usher to continually remind them of where they were. Red and Sonny kept talking about how they could have been discovered by the movie scouts that had visited their high school until they were shhshed by their own crowd.

CHAPTER 10

Red began to think of the argument with his mother and how he had walked out. *Mom's probably pacing the floor.* "I'll be right back. I wanna make a phone call."

"I'll go with you," Kelly said. "I can use something to munch on."

"Wait," Sonny said. "Never mind. This ain't the good part." The second feature, The Wild One, was in progress and Marlon Brando was engaged in a conversation with Mary Murphy. "They don't start wrecking the place for another couple'a minutes." Sonny pushed himself out of his seat and followed Red and Kelly through the padded double doors into the lobby.

Red spotted the telephone booth in a corner of the lobby and started for it. His attention to detail wasn't functioning. He didn't consider the group of five older youths standing to the side of the open folded door. Two of them wore the same black cloth jackets. One stood with his back to Red and he noted the script lettering. They were Imperials. His mind jammed back into gear, but too late. He was right on top of them and walking with the arrogant strut of someone about to bully their way to where they were going. He drew in a deep breath, released it, and continued on his straight line for the booth. He tried to detour around them but bumped into the closest.

"Excuse me, man," he apologized meekly, pushing passed the older boy.

Red felt a tight grip on his arm and turned to face them.

"I'm expecting a call on this phone," the Imperial said.

Red regained his composure and flashed a quick look into the shorter boy's face. He couldn't help but stare momentarily at the curved scar running from the ear lobe, across an unshaven cheek to the thin-lipped mouth.

"How long's it gonna take?" Red asked.

"What's it to ya?" another of the Imperials asked.

"Nothing. I just got a call to make."

"We'll tell ya when you can make your call."

Kelly and Sonny, seeing their friend in trouble, moved to his side.

"What'a you guys want?" the Imperial holding Red's arm asked.

Another of the group snickered before an answer came. "The Vandals? Who the hell are they?"

"Just a bunch of guys trying to get along," Kelly said, wishing Johnny was by his side for his diplomatic aide. "We ain't looking for no beef."

"Ain't you guys from the old Comanche and Madhatter turf?" the scar-faced Imperial asked. He released Red's arm.

"Yeah," Kelly said.

"Big men now, hah? You think you can take us? You like to raise hell in a place in our turf and disturb everyone like you own the place?"

"We heard this was neutral turf. If you guys say you own it, then so be it. Come on, Red, let's make it back to the seats."

"Wait." The Imperial grabbed Kelly by his jacket. "We ain't done talking."

"Well, I am." Kelly pulled away from the grip, turned and walked back into the main theater without looking back.

Red and Sonny followed. They shuffled down the aisle, found their seats and sat as though nothing had happened. The Imperials didn't follow.

"Think they'll give us any more trouble?" Red asked Kelly.

"I don't know."

Five minutes later, a detachment of ten Imperials swarmed around the four Vandals in the forward row. Some of the Vandals jumped to their feet behind the assumed outnumbered four. The Imperials hesitated.

"What's happenin'?" Blackie asked, looking up at the Imperials blocking his view of the screen.

"That's what we wanna know," a short muscular Imperial said.

"Tell your boys to sit down," the one that had stopped Red at the phone booth told Kelly.

"Okay, guys," Kelly said over his shoulder. "Grab a seat."

The Vandals sat as quickly as they had risen. The lead Imperial glared at the back row of Vandals before he turned his attention to Kelly.

"I don't like the way you and your people left so fast back there." He motioned with his head toward the rear of the seats. "I'm thinkin'a taking you outside and kicking your ass." He leaned forward, shifting his weight to the bent knee pressing against a backrest.

Kelly was silent, a thin provoking smile frozen on his face.

"I can't see the picture," Blackie said.

"You wanna fight me, leader?" the Imperial asked Kelly.

"You're a little older than me," Kelly said. "I heard you guys are tough. You get your rep from beating on guys two, three years younger than you?"

"Okay, I'll fight you and one'a your buddies. Even two of them. Come on."

"Not interested."

"Well, I am." The older boy reached down, grabbed Kelly by his jacket and shirt and yanked him to his feet.

Blackie sprang from his seat and landed a fist to the temple of the closest Imperial. The blow drove him into the Imperial holding Kelly and they all tumbled back, arms stretched or grasping for support, Kelly a part of their mass.

The two dazed Imperials bounced off the backs of seats, sandwiching Kelly between them. Kelly swung wildly and smashed free.

The Vandals climbed over backrests or streamed into the aisle. They surrounded the Imperials and crushed in on them from all

angles. The whack of knuckles ripped apart the once relaxed atmosphere of the theater.

"Get out'a here," Chico yelled to Roxie before he was hit in
the face by an armrest ripped from a broken seat.

Red was the only one still seated. *Everything happened too fast.*
There wasn't enough time to formulate a plan. The best plan was to
withdraw and reassemble so he could access their situation. Two fighters rolling over him were crushing his head against the top lip of
the seat. He needed breathing room and with a violent push, he
managed to eject the struggling bodies.

Red continued upward until he was on his feet, fists and el-
bows flying, trying to establish swinging room. He felt his fists
connect again and again with the scar-faced Imperial trapped in
front of him, pinned between a set of constrictive seats. His face
was bloody; his jacket pulled down across his arms. Red continued pounding away, smashing his knuckles into the bloody face
until the head bobbed, the still figure wedged between a combination of folded and recessed seat cushions.

Marlon Brando was being beaten by the outraged town-folk
on the screen. Then it suddenly went blank and the theater lights
glared on, bringing the spectacle of the real-life fight into view. For
a brief moment it seemed that the fight had ended. But the surprise of the lights only lasted a pulse beat.

Some of the youths pushed aside the regular audience along
the front aisles as they scurried for exits. They knew the cops would
soon be there.

Most of the groups were still struggling, unable to break free,
either because they were willing to fight to the end or because
they couldn't stand the stigma of desertion. Anyone who came out
of this without a wound or an arrest would have to have a very
good reason.

Red had found a new enemy. His mind had started to clear
and he was aware of the nine-inch switchblade in the Imperials'
hand. He had heard the sharp snap of the blade and saw it spring
from the side of the handle. Then he saw it again in slow motion,

an instant replay that his mind used as a respite. *Something was wrong. He couldn't think straight again.* The Imperial stood in front of him, his apish mouth dribbling blood from an unseen wound.

Red slowly backed toward the rear doors. The Imperial followed, his gaze focused on Red's face. It was a blank gaze, but full of hate. Red stared at the blade and visualized his own blood dripping from the sharp surface. *This is what his mother always worried about.* He smiled, wondering why he had such a thought. *Was she thinking about him? Praying for him?*

"What the fuck's so funny?" the Imperial asked.

Funny? Nothing's funny. Did Custer think it was funny? Plan ahead. Plan, damn it. There was Crazy Horse and Sitting Bull and all their braves ready to cut him into little pieces. There could be no more plans. He would have to take out as many as he could. Wait a minute. It wasn't Crazy Horse. It was Dave. What the hell was he doing here? Dave was holding a knife. And he was stalking Red. He wanted revenge. Dave was going to kill Red to avenge his death.

It was that Halloween night again. It hadn't been put to rest like he had hoped. It was still there, inside his head. Red struggled for his sanity. He was back in the theater, and the guy in front of him was an Imperial, not Dave. And something had to be done before this guy started slicing him up. Dave flashed into his mind again. *What the hell was happening?*

"Come on, Dave. Didn't I ask you to let it go?"

"What?" The switchblade stopped its circling motion.

"You can't get us all, Dave. Maybe you'll get me, but there's lots more guys that were there that night. You can't get everybody."

"What the fuck're ya talkin' about?"

"I told you before that it was time to put things to rest."

Red dove into the air and descended on the Imperial. He struck his wider, shorter adversary so hard that the momentum carried them to the floor. Red's chin struck the hard concrete that was under the thin carpeting while the rest of his body was cushioned by the mass of flesh beneath him.

"Is he home yet?" Harriet asked, knowing the answer.

Henry turned away. He looked out the window at the garage in a vain, pessimistic attempt to see if his son was heading for the side door.

"No," he said very softly. "I'm beginning to worry, too."

The telephone rang.

"Oh God," Harriet said.

"I'll get it."

"No. Let me. I want to know. I want to be the first to know."

She slowly pushed up, stood beside her husband for an instant, and walked toward the front room. The telephone rang twice more before she reached it and lifted the receiver from its cradle. Henry had followed her and stood in his solemn but tense demeanor behind his wife.

"Hello."

"Mrs. Harriet Janek?" The voice was heavy and gruff.

"Yes."

"You have a son, Richard?"

"Yes." Tears began welling in her eyes. "What's wrong?"

"This is Sergeant Preston, hundred and tenth precinct. I'm afraid I have some bad news for you."

The tears started down her cheeks. "What happened? Is my boy alright?"

"I'm afraid he's not alright."

"He's alive? Please tell me he's alive."

"Yeah, he's alive. A little banged up. I'm afraid I can't tell that to the boy's mother who your son stabbed tonight."

"Stabbed?"

"That's right. The other boy is out of danger, but your son will have to face charges."

"He's alright. Thank God. Henry, our boy's alright."

"If you call assault with a deadly weapon alright, lady..."

"I don't care, sergeant. My boy's alive."

Henry moved to his wife's side and took the receiver from her trembling hand.

"Now, if you want to see your kid..."

CHAPTER 11

The month of October, 1956 had witnessed uprisings behind the Iron Curtain and the crushing of the Hungarian Freedom Fighters by Russian tanks; the return of the New York Yankees as world champions of baseball, ending the one year reign of the Brooklyn Dodgers; another Halloween, and with it, the unofficial second anniversary of the founding of the Vandals.

As November made its entrance, one of the Vandals experienced an adventure that he turned into his first completed work:

WALK AMONG THE BLIND

by
James Anton Yadenik

A stiff breeze pushed me to the oak door of Pat's Tavern. I tugged at the brass handle and stepped into a gray cloud of cigar smoke, its pungency accented by the stench of stale beer and cat urine.

Mom and dad occupied a corner of the mahogany bar with a gaunt, white-haired lush named Willie.

"Mom."

She turned to me. Her eyelids were drooped and hazel eyes dull from the boredom of a Saturday afternoon-into-evening sharing dad's pastime at the bar.

"Hi, Jimmy." She yawned. "I thought you were staying home."

"I wasted a whole summer staying home. I gotta talk to someone."

"You're not going back to that hangout, are you?"

"Maybe."

"You know you were told to stay away from there after that trouble." Her tone was neutral, rather than authoritative as she intended. "We don't want anymore problems."

"I'm bored, mom. I gotta talk to someone before I flip out. You never talk to me anymore." I glanced at dad's back. He didn't even know I was there. "And he's never even made an effort to say two words other than to put me down."

"That's not right to say. You know he works hard in that lousy factory. He doesn't have time to sit and talk. He hardly talks to me. It's the way he is."

"But he's got time to come to this dump? And talk to *his friends?* "

She shrugged. "And you were told not to hang around with those bums. I'm not going to no police station to try to get you out again."

"That was five months ago. I told you we didn't start that fight at the movies. It was some older guys."

"Have a coke," she said.

"Why do you keep changing the subject?" I wheeled around and straight-armed the door.

"What's the matter with him?" I heard dad say; finally realizing I was there.

"Oh, let him go. He's in one of his moods," mom said.

I turned up the collar of my motorcycle jacket and started down the sidewalk as dad roared, "Hey, Willie, we should'a beat them Yankees again this year."

Yeah, should'a, I thought. That's their whole life. They'd rather complain about what *should'a been* instead of doing something to change it.

I cursed myself as I turned the corner heading for home. *Where are you going?* I did an about-face and let my slightly rusty but instinctive compass steer me toward Bill's candy store. My life was there, not in the confines of my room. I had used some of the five months to read and to write a few unfinished stories, but now it was time to be with people again.

It had been hard to avoid going to Bill's. But I had promised not to go back, and if anything, I kept my promises. Maybe I thought it would help change things at home. I was wrong. It was still the same rut.

As I crossed Queens Boulevard, I thought about the paradox of suddenly wanting to be with people. I was a loner. I had become that way from living in solitude when I was growing up.

Yet, even when I embarrassed myself, it seemed that the need for attention always outweighed the embarrassment. Maybe they were right in calling me the Mad Russian. I had no emotional or internal equipment to judge my actions as right or wrong. If that was madness, then so be it.

I thought about Red and how he flipped out at the movie house fight. Everyone knew it would happen to him sooner or later. But after it happened, it was done with. He was back to normal. Sure, it brought him trouble, but he was over and done with what was bugging him.

The things that bugged me were constant and not something that could be resolved in one quick explosion of emotions. They would only dissolve with time. *But how much time?*

I wondered why I had to be a Vandal. Protection? Maybe. To hide? Become a face in the crowd. That's great, a coward hiding out on the battlefield. I wasn't a fighter. Nor a lover. No. That damn shyness saw to that. What drew me to them?

I remembered the first time I had met them. I was fourteen and a nobody on my block. No matter how hard I had tried to improve my skills in stickball, baseball, basketball, whatever, I was only mediocre and the brunt of continuous harassment from the jocks on the block.

One day a mob of Vandals swept down my street, breaking up the stickball game. I knew a couple of them from elementary school and they asked me to join them. It was like they had busted me out of jail. The jocks were surprised as I entered the Vandal ranks and was swept away. By the end of that day I knew that I had entered into new and lasting friendships that respected me because I was me, not for my athletic abilities or something else superficial.

I stopped for an instant when I reached the corner opposite Bill's candy store. It was only five o'clock but the sky was darkening. The storefront looked the same as when I had last seen it. Only now, the tattered valance of the green and white striped awning was flapping in the wind. There was no one in front of the store.

I crossed the street and as I reached the front door, Johnny Sadinski opened the glass panel from inside.

"Johnny. How are you?"

"How am I? How are you, stranger?'

He stepped out and let the door swing closed behind him. He put an arm around my shoulder and hugged me. "Jeez, it's good to see you."

"You, too, man." I let him lead me to the closed library annex next door. "I missed our talks."

"Me, too. I haven't been around much myself."

"How come?"

He glanced over my shoulder. "I gotta tell somebody. I'm busting to say it."

"What?"

"You're the only one I could tell this to. Remember the day we cut out of school and you guys had the fight with the Imperials?"

"Do I? It's the reason I haven't been around until now."

"The reason I didn't come back that night was I found something I've been looking for all my life." He stared into my eyes. I usually couldn't look people directly in the eyes for more than a second, but he mesmerized me with his expression. "I found a mother."

"Your mother? That's great."

"No, man. Not my real mother. A replacement." He let out a long breath. "This is hard for me to say."

"Don't worry. Say it."

He shifted his weight to his other foot. "I'm seeing Pete's mother. Pete Wilson." He bowed his head, then quickly looked back into my eyes. "I knew I'd say it wrong. I mean, I'm seeing her like she was my real mother. She's really a good person. She understands. She *is* like a mother to me."

I smiled. "That's great. I know what you mean."

"I knew you would. One of the other guys would say something stupid like - " His expression changed to anger for an instant. "Like I was shacking up with her. Taking advantage of her while Pete was away."

"Screw what they'd think. It's our secret and I'm happy for you." I stepped back. "You even look better. You gained a few pounds."

"Thanks, buddy." He clasped my shoulder. "I just had to tell somebody before I exploded. We've been sneaking around and trying to arrange our free times together. She misses Pete a lot and I'm glad I did what I did. It helped us both."

"Does Pete know?"

"No. She thinks he might get the wrong idea. No sense making him more crazy while he's up there."

"When's he getting out?"

"A couple more years, if he's lucky. The guy she was going out with turned out to be a scumbag. He dumped her when he found out the trouble Pete was in. She needed me and I needed her. It really worked out good."

I smiled again. I could see the relief on Johnny's face. *Still the same old Johnny with an added spark.* I felt good that I was the one he trusted. At least there was some purpose in my return.

"What about yourself?" he asked. "How's it been going?"

"Terrible, as usual. The normal crap. They can't see passed their noses."

"Look, man, you're like a brother to me. I'm glad you're back, and I'm sorry I didn't see you all those months. I've been trying to get a new life for myself. I didn't think of much else."

"I know. No sweat."

"The thing to do is find someone. When we talk, we can only kick things around just so much before we wind up with the same conclusions. You gotta find someone who thinks like us but maybe with a better outlook. Someone to give you a reason to be alive."

"Easier said than done."

"Agreed. But you've got to make the effort to find it. Get out of your rut. Be you. You're not James Dean or some character from a story. You're you."

"What're you saying, I'm always fantasizing or something?"

"Relax, hah." He snapped his finger against the lapel of my jacket. "I'm saying that it's your life. Nobody else's. It's up to you to make it work for you." He glanced at the right breast of my motorcycle jacket. "Isn't that a Polish flag?"

"Yeah." I felt a flush of embarrassment. I had painted an American flag above two smaller flags of Poland and Hungary over the zippered breast pocket of my jacket. "And Hungary. For the Freedom Fighters."

"See, man, that's you. Nobody else would have dreamed of doing anything like that. Except maybe Red."

"I heard he was allowed to join the army instead of going to the can."

"Yeah. What a deal. His parents agreed to let him join when he became seventeen, and his lawyer worked it out with the D.A. and the judge. He got strict probation until he turned seventeen last month and then got shipped out to boot camp. It's as though he arranged the whole thing himself."

"Too bad things couldn't fall into place like that for everyone."

"They can," Johnny said. "That's what I was trying to tell you. You've just got to work at it and look for opportunities. It can happen, believe me."

"Okay." I shrugged. I knew he meant well, but my make-up told me things just didn't change so easily for me. It was great to talk to Johnny again, and maybe some of the things he was trying to impress on me would eventually sink in. He was right about one thing. I was me. And, unfortunately, me didn't have a hell of a lot of confidence to try to make the changes he did.

"I gotta go," Johnny said. "Mom gets off work in a half hour. Mom. Jesus, I can't believe I call her that. Or that she accepts it, too." I thought I sensed him shudder. "I gotta meet her and walk her home."

"You coming back?"

"Maybe. Depends on what she wants to do." He smiled. "Check out the store. The guys'll be happy to see you. They're going to a free rock and roll show at a park over by Northern Boulevard. Should be a good time."

"Come on back, man. I'd like to talk some more. Bring her with you to the show."

"I can't. You know that."

"Yeah, you're right. I guess I just wanted to see you and her together. Okay. Let's make sure we see each other more often." I slapped him on the arm. "Take it cool, man."

"You got it." And he was gone in an instant. It was like his excitement couldn't hold him in place any longer. He disappeared behind a swirl of dust and discarded papers as he started down the hill toward Queens Boulevard.

I entered Bill's. The door opened onto a floor of small white octagon tiles - thousands of them. I tried to count how many there were when I was in one of my bored moods. A stool-lined marble soda fountain and a long glass confectionery display case flanked either side of the tiled aisle. Bill and his wife had a thriving, respectable neighborhood business. The display cases would be colorfully decorated and appointed with handmade chocolate figures depicting the holiday season. Turkeys and pilgrims were displacing pumpkins and witches. They were good people and presented yet another paradox in our lives, allowing a bunch of kids who could very well explode in anger one day and destroy what the owners had spent a lifetime to build, hang out there. Maybe it was that show of respect and trust we saw each day that kept things calm.

It was as though I had never left. I was part of the scene as soon as I stepped through the doorway. Bill was rinsing out glasses behind the gray marble counter. He dipped his head in greeting when he saw me. He probably didn't know my name from the months of exile and that I rarely displayed my mood shifts in his presence when I was there. His wife was usually on duty when I had gone bananas and was asked to leave.

"Crazy For You" by the Heartbeats was playing on the juke box. My appreciation for the song shifted my attention passed the throngs of people sitting at the white marble tables in the rear, main area of the store. The juke box was a low profile, clear plastic machine. I had expected to see the tall, brightly colored majestic Wurlitzer that was sitting in the rear of the room the last time I was there.

I slipped into an empty seat behind Speedo and Val. They welcomed me with pats on my back. I acknowledged and turned back to the group at my table. Surprisingly, it was three of the Vandal Debs. Sheila and Dolores sat across the table and Karen in the chair next to me. They smiled and told me how much I was missed. I thanked them and then Bill showed up to take my order.

"Coke, please."

Bill returned to the counter.

"Is it still fifteen cents?" I asked the girls as I lit up a Marlboro. The rule for admission into Bill's was that you bought an obligatory fifteen-cent soda when you arrived and you could stay the night.

Sheila nodded. Dolores and Karen stood to leave.

"What'd I say?" I held my hands out in exaggerated surprise.

Dolores and Karen laughed. "We were leaving before you came in," Karen said looking down at me. "We stayed to say hello."

"We'll see you tomorrow," Dolores said to Sheila. "'Night, Jimmy."

"Bye." I turned to Sheila. "You're looking as lovely as ever."

She made a quick sideward tilt of her head tossing the bottom of her auburn hair into place at her shoulders. "Thanks." She wrinkled her sharp, straight nose. "You, too."

Bill returned with my coke and I dug a nickel and dime from my pocket. "In The Still Of The Night" by the Five Satins began. Bill left.

"New box, I see." I motioned toward the rear of the store with my head. "Still got the good sounds though."

"Yes." She looked down. I expected her to raise her head again, but it seemed as though she had nodded off to sleep.

"You okay?" I asked.

She raised her head and her almond-shaped eyes were glistening. "I'm sorry, Jimmy."

"What's up?"

"This was Tony and my song when we were going out."

"You broke up?"

I thought of the first time that I had seen her. She and Karen had been invited by one of the Debs to visit Bill's. New girls were instant celebrities, surrounded and questioned by hoards of Vandals trying to impress them. I was never part of the wolf packs that formed when new chicks showed up. That particular night, though, as I sat leaning against the corner light post observing the guys falling all over themselves, I took notice of her demeanor. I had liked her quiet ways and hint of innocence. I found out that night that whoever said that time waits for no man was right. Tony Vellari was a fast worker and within a week of her arrival had asked her to go steady while I was still preparing my opening speech.

"I'm sorry. I like Tony," I said. "But I like you better. I always liked you. Maybe it's best what happened. Tony's a little pushy. You're sweet and gentle." I began rambling and decided it was time to shut up. "I'm sorry. Forget it."

I shouldn't have opened my mouth. I could never finish what I started in the past. I had that uneasy feeling of vulnerability surge through my body.

"No, I won't forget it," she said. "You said it and you're stuck with it."

"What'a you mean?" I looked into her brown eyes. I realized it might have been the first time I noticed the color of any girl's eyes.

"You're right." A thin smile helped to break the anxiety in me. "I don't mean the sweet and gentle part. I mean, Tony and I weren't compatible. And I finally realized that."

Even though the old feelings I had for her were beginning to come to the surface, I still couldn't put them into words. But this was something I should have started a long time ago; something that I now realized had been put on hold. What did Johnny say, look for opportunities?

"Would you go out with me?" I asked.

"Not right now," she said. Her words seemed final. "I need time to think."

"Sorry again," I said. "I guess I'm the sorriest cat around tonight."

"Don't be, Jimmy. I appreciate your feelings. You have a different attitude than most of the guys. And those sad blue eyes." She smiled and her almond eyes stretched into thin slits. "Most of the Vandals are always talking about rumbling and sharp cars, but you're talking about James Dean movies and books and what's going on in the rest of the world."

My spirits lifted. Someone had actually been listening to what most of the crowd considered my raving lunacies. "Hell, I figure there's more to life than a ride in a cool car, drinking beer and acting tough. There has to be."

"There is."

"So find it with me."

"Give me some time, Jimmy. Please." She stood up. "I'm going on an important trip with my family for a month or so." She shrugged. "I had to get special permission to skip school. We're leaving the day after tomorrow." Her eyebrows raised in mock astonishment. "Imagine me, a privileged character."

"I know you are. You could probably skip a full semester and still come out ahead of your class." This was one of my true heartfelt compliments that I rarely gave to girls. "You sure I can't see you before you leave? I mean, in case you change your mind."

"I don't know. I'll see. I have to go." She turned and hurried for the front door.

My cigarette slammed against the half-mirrored wall in a shower of sparks. *"Why can't anyone talk with me?"*

Val let out a horselaugh. I didn't realize he had heard me. "What'a ya wanna talk about, sweetheart?" he shouted.

Bill saw the cigarette as it ricocheted behind the counter and yelled about how things like that could start a fire.

I heard someone shout, "The Mad Russian is back in town."

II

I stood up and walked to the cigarette. I didn't want to set a new record and be thrown out fifteen minutes after walking through the door.

"Hey, sorry, Bill." I half-bowed in apology. "It slipped out of my hand while I was swatting at a fly."

"We have no flies in here."

"Maybe it was my imagination."

I picked up the broken cigarette and crushed it into an ashtray at the closest table, occupied by Sonny, Blackie and Eddie Comanche.

"You're still a pisser," Sonny said chuckling. "Glad you're back."

"Thanks." I sat. "What's going on? I hear you're making it to a show or something."

"Yeah," Sonny said. "It's gonna be held at a park in Jackson Heights. It's for nothing so the price is right. I think they're gonna have 'Sam the Man' Taylor's band and the Harptones and some other groups. Kelly's cousin, Benny, from the heights wants to merge his boys with us. We're gonna meet them there so we can discuss things."

"Kelly's got more cousins than Carter's got little liver pills." I lit another cigarette. "How many guys do they have?"

"About thirty, I heard." Sonny pulled my hand with the match to him to light his cigarette. "With our thirty or forty we should be one of the biggest around," he said between puffs.

I was back in time to see an event that I could store in my Vandal history files. I always seemed to be at some major happening. I considered myself to be the unofficial historian of the club. The only show I had missed, and thankfully, was the Pete and Dave thing, but through the years I had heard all the gory details from anyone who had been there.

"Welcome back, Jimmy." Kelly grasped my shoulders from behind.

I strained back my neck and looked at him. "Hi'ya, prez. What's happening?"

"We're splitting. You hear about the rock and roll show at the park?"

"I'm ready."

Kelly stepped to the side of the table and stroked his Tony Curtis curl until it fell across his forehead exactly where he wanted it. He began to make last minute arrangements for the trip to Jackson Heights with Sonny, Blackie, Eddie and Shades Gaglione, who had followed him over from what was probably one of their state-of-the-treasury meetings.

Eddie, who at twenty, was a leftover from the old Comanches, owned a car and could transport seven or eight of the group. Eddie was one of those guys who couldn't stop being a gang member. He had been a minor figure on the Comanches and, despite his age, was no threat to the leadership of the Vandals.

Eddie was considered an unofficial advisor to Kelly in order to satisfy his ego, but in reality was welcomed as one of the boys for the use of his car. No one could ever remember seeing Eddie light up a fresh cigarette. It just seemed that a roach was constantly pinched between his thin lips, the smoke floating up into his squinting eyes.

I was teamed with Speedo, Val and Freddy The Hat, another ex-member of a defunct gang, the Madhatters. Bill watched us parade passed him as he stood half-smiling behind the counter. His store became a vacant cavern, as the sounds of "Come Go With Me" by the Del Vikings bounced off the solid walls and followed us out the door.

Kelly started off three groups at five-minute intervals before allowing his motorized unit to leave. He wanted a decent show of bodies to support his meeting with Benny and the proposed Heights Vandals, and this temporary division would keep trouble with the cops away from our door until we could regroup at the park.

My group was the second to leave. We took a route along Woodside Avenue before turning north at Seventy-Ninth Street. The wind pushed pearl gray clouds swiftly along the black sky and whipped our hair. I tried to comb mine into its normal style during lulls before finally giving up and allowing it to snap against my ears or hang in strings over my eyes. Freddy The Hat, after three sprints to retrieve his crumpled fedora, became just Freddy for the rest of the trek, stuffing the hat inside his jacket.

We spotted the three couples of the vanguard group only a block ahead when we crossed Roosevelt Avenue into Sinner's turf.

"Kelly should'a let them leave last," Val said. "Every time you put two or more broads together they gotta stop and look in every store window they pass."

"We better slow down or we'll bunch up," Speedo said. "The Sinners will think we're invading their turf."

I spotted Eddie Comanche's black Oldsmobile sedan slow down along the curb next to us. Kelly leaned out the shotgun window to hail us. I could see a mass of heads and arms behind him like a cartoon in Mad.

"Cross the street and pass them up," Kelly said. "I sent Chico's group down Eighty-Second Street."

We waved an okay to Kelly and the Olds pulled ahead, stopping alongside the lead group. We crossed the street and increased our pace.

"So, tell us what they did to you," Speedo said to me.

"Who?"

"The cops. You know, when you got nabbed at the fight." He held out his hand, his thumb pointed at me. "I saw Jimmy deck a guy real good. He was in the middle of the main swing out and all of a sudden I see Jimmy throw a left hook and this guy comes flyin' out and sprawls all over the floor right in front of me."

"I was just swinging wild," I said. "Lucky punch. I got creamed right after that. I was at the bottom of a pile when the cops got there. No chance to get away."

"Yeah, they were there quick. Lucky for some of us they didn't stake out the emergency exit."

"When the judge found out we were Vandals, he hit the ceiling. Thanks to you guys." I pushed Freddy and he stumbled into the street. "He was the same judge that you guys had the night before."

Freddy, his hat again in place, moved back onto the sidewalk. "Shit, yeah, he was a mean bastard," Freddy said.

"He slapped us with bail of two grand each," I said. "It could have been a million bucks for that kind of bread. He said he was tired of seeing this kind of display of disregard for the law, blah, blah, blah. So most of us spent the next four days sitting in the Long Island City Tombs until the hearing.

"That was fun," I said sarcastically. "First a strip search and a lot of crap from the guards." I chuckled. "When they told us to bend over and spread the cheeks of our ass - no, shit, this really happened - Billy Ryan only heard cheeks so he put his fingers in his mouth and pulled the corners of his mouth apart."

Everyone laughed.

"Then they gave us some cruddy World War One uniforms that didn't fit and a moldy liverwurst sandwich. I didn't have anything to eat since dinner the night before but when I saw the liverwurst on green molded bread, I could've puked. When we got into the main cellblock, I had guys begging me for the sandwich, so I gave it away. I knew why they wanted the sandwich when I saw the crap we got served for meals. Most of the guys I met were there for burglaries or stick-ups or something they did for money. They called us crazy for taking a chance at getting nailed for no profit. I felt like I was getting a sermon from Shades. One of the Puerto Rican guys called us *'the gangistas'.*"

"Your folks couldn't raise the bail?" Val asked.

"Two grand? My uncle wanted to lend it to them, but I told them I'd be okay. I guess I knew my old man would get pissed off if I made him feel obligated to someone. Anyway, when we went back to court the next time, we had a different judge and he threw the case out for insufficient evidence. Red had a separate trial because of his assault charge."

"Yeah, and it worked out good for him," Val said. "He's doing what he wanted. He would've wound up in the army sooner or later."

"Yeah," I said. "Who else could say they're doing what they wanted? Mostly we wind up doing what we're told to do."

The conversation dropped off as we approached Northern Boulevard. The wind picked up again as we started along the last block of apartment buildings. The block was like the bottleneck of a funnel. The wind swept from Flushing Bay and La Guardia Airport across the low, undeveloped lands above Northern Boulevard and then channeled into the canyon of streets with the force of a flash flood. Freddy's hat sailed back along our completed route and it took him a block to catch it. By the time he had stuffed it into his jacket again and rejoined us, we were standing across the street from our destination.

The park was two square blocks of concrete and blacktop surrounded by a chain link fence. Two softball diamonds were painted on the blacktop and were finished off with chain link backstops sitting catty-cornered over the home plates at opposite ends of the fields. It was an expanded version of our schoolyard hangout with twenty-foot poles supporting rectangular lights that ran along the fence line. The lighting turned the concrete and black square into a bright shining contrast to the dark streets along its border. It reminded me of the times I had been to a night game at Ebbet's

Field or Yankee Stadium. Hundreds of people milled about in the fenced oasis.

I could see the far end of the park in the splash of light. It looked like there was a playground, trees, probably some grass and a long brick building that housed the *parkies*, - park workers - their equipment and the rest rooms.

My attention was quickly drawn back to the festivities in the lighted area. There must have been five hundred people spread out through the spacious outdoor arena. A stage was prominent at the far edge of light, flanked by two white trailers, their sides decorated with an oak leaf logo and N.Y.C. PARKS DEPARTMENT painted in green.

The stage was bare. The wind whipped the exposed park and the light fixtures shook atop the stanchions. I could hear a clanging of rope hasps against metal flagpoles in the distance.

We crossed the street just as Chico's group reached us and we all stopped at the closest entrance to the park. We'd been told by Kelly to use that landmark for a marshalling point.

Eddie's black Olds turned the corner followed by a police car, its red dome light flashing. The Olds pulled to the curb in front of us and the police car stopped behind. The cop on the passenger side stepped out and walked to the driver's window of Eddie's car.

"You passed a red light," I heard the cop say.

"Where?" Eddie asked.

"On Seventy-Eighth Street while traveling along Northern Boulevard."

"There ain't no light there."

"Then it was on Seventy-Seventh."

"Can't you make up your mind?" Eddie asked.

"You passed a red light." He looked like he was changing the street location on the ticket as he spoke with Eddie. He glanced back to his partner in the patrol car, who gave him an okay sign with his fingers. The partner must have run a check on Eddie's plate.

The rear door of the Oldsmobile opened and Sonny, Blackie

and three Debs piled out just as the cop finished altering the ticket.

"That's bullshit," Eddie said, pulling the short cigarette stub from his lips and flipping it passed the cop into the street.

"Watch your language, pal, or you'll get another summons for transporting more than the legal limit," the cop said.

"Yeah, alright." Eddie waved his hand in disgust.

Kelly and Shades slid out of the front seat as our last contingent crossed the street and inquired in low, muffled tones as to what had happened.

The cop glanced at us as he handed Eddie the ticket. "You might as well go home," he said. "There's a hurricane coming and they'll probably cancel the show."

He strutted back to his patrol car. The flashing light flicked off and the car pulled away. It headed back toward Northern Boulevard to trap some other poor slob.

I thought of a couple of the beat cops in our neighborhood for comparison. They were decent guys that talked to us and gave us as many breaks as they could without going too far. They remembered that they were kids once and may have been in the same boat as we were.

Kelly and Shades consoled Eddie and I thought I heard them say they would help him pay the ticket from the treasury. I turned toward the park and saw that a crowd had gathered. About fifty guys and girls were bunched along the wide entrance in the fence. Some of them were asking our guys what had happened and began cursing when they were told.

"Cops suck. Cops suck." A chant went up as the group turned and started back toward the main body. We followed, letting Kelly lead our way.

I saw all kinds of names on jackets. Dukes, Gents, Sinners, Gaylords and Barons among the many. There were a host of rivalries massed together. The gathering certainly had an unwritten truce attached, but the possibilities were explosive. I recognized an acquaintance from high school named Jack, who was with the group of Barons.

The curiosity seekers in front of us moved at a faster pace and eventually spread apart and consolidated into the larger crowd. We were still about a hundred feet from them when a second group approached, moving toward us.

There were a dozen and they all wore black leather jackets of various styles, the seams along the shoulders and pockets adorned with silver studs. I braced myself for trouble. Some of them appeared to be the same age as us but most looked older. All of them looked a little more seasoned. I wondered for a moment if they were Imperials coming to challenge us for revenge over the movie theater fight.

They stopped a few feet from us. Kelly stopped and held his arm from his side in a halting gesture.

"How's it goin', *goombah*?" The lead guy of the group said. He had a modified Tony Curtis curl. He was taller but he was obviously related to Kelly. It was Benny and his boys.

The two leaders stepped forward, hugged and kissed each other on the cheek, then introduced as many of their people to each other before it became a mob scene of handshakes and guys calling out names to each other. Kelly and the officers finally broke away with Benny and a few of his aides, moving to a secluded corner of the park to discuss the alliance. I thought about Johnny and whether his input would be missed. Hell, maybe he didn't even want to be vice-president anymore.

The guys from the Heights who were left with us began moving on the Debs until they found out some of them were officer property. They backed off, probably forewarned by Benny. The consolidated group decided to move into the main audience that spread out from the stage. The general audience was beginning to get restless, and sporadic chants of "We want the show" and "Where's the band?" minced with shouts of boredom. A couple of guys shimmied up the light poles, causing the lamps to tremble even more in the wind. The front lines of the audience pulled down the flimsy chicken wire and strip wood fence that was meant to keep people away from the stage. The organizers of the event probably didn't count on this many people showing up, and I wondered if the cop who ticketed Eddie was just being a ball-buster or if a hurricane was really coming. Maybe that was the reason there was no activity on the stage.

I could see bits of the action around the foot of the stage. I huddled behind the wall of people in front of me using them as a windbreaker. I saw about three or four security guards - or maybe they were *parkies* - in brown uniforms finally wrest the twisted excuse for a fence away from the crowd. It was thrust into the air, bent into a spiral in several sections and then disappear behind the crowd. A guy in a dark suit carrying a bullhorn stepped onto the stage from one of the trailers.

"May I have your attention, please," his voice crackled through the bullhorn. "We have just been advised... National Weather... vice that a fast mov... icane is traveling up... coast."

"What?"

"We can't hear you."

The shouting became a roar and the guys on the lampposts rocked from side to side. The light beams created weird shadows across the distant playground and park building.

The man in the suit slapped the side of the bullhorn before bringing it up to his mouth again. He pointed to the guys on the light poles like Babe Ruth calling his home run. "Please stop that." He paused for a moment. "There is a hurricane moving up the East Coast and could strike our area within two to four hours. We must can... the show."

"What?"

"The show is cancelled. Please leave in an orderly manner." He turned and disappeared through a door in the trailer side.

A scuffle broke out at the foot of the stage while some of the more orderly factions of the crowd began to drift away. The lights fluttered, went off for a second, prompting a collective shout peppered with screams from the crowd, then blared on again. The pole climbers slid back to the ground.

As part of the crowd pushed toward the gateway behind us,

we were swept along. I was about ten feet from a parted opening when I realized the surge was caused by people moving aside to create a path. I saw the last few people move away from the gap just in front of a cop leading a guy stripped to the waist; his wrists pinned behind his back by handcuffs. A half dozen guys cursing and shouting insults at the cop followed them.

The six guys followed a few feet behind the cop and his prisoner. One of them slammed a cigarette off the cop's back. Another spat on him. I felt a twinge of pity for the cop, and then admiration. What a set of balls. He didn't turn. He just headed for the street, his captive in tow, his concentration on finishing what he had started.

As they reached the sidewalk, sirens came up in the distance like the cop had passed through an electric eye beam and activated an alarm. The park lighting flickered off again. Maybe it was the park staff controlling the lights from their building. Whatever was happening, the combination of the light tricks and the ever-growing loudness of the sirens caused a panic. People scattered for the sidewalks through every exit in the park. I saw people fall and sprawl into the street or against parked cars.

As I reached the opposite side of the street, I saw the red flashes accompanying the sirens. They were coming from every direction. I didn't look back and never found out how the lone cop made out.

I spotted Val and Freddy. They were a few yards ahead of me, along with a dozen or so other runners spread across the street and sidewalk. I followed them around the next corner away from the park just as one of the red flashing lights and screaming sirens overshot us. I thought I heard glass shattering then squealing tires. The flashing red, having vanished for a moment as it passed the corner building now threw its throbbing glow onto the block we were scrambling along. The siren fell silent with a loud whomp. Val and Freddy were on the opposite side of the street running slower than I was. Another group of teens rounded the corner an instant before the police car and passed Val and Freddy. I thought about crossing to join them, but I heard the throaty pitch of the patrol car's engine as it accelerated toward us.

I changed my direction and leaped down two concrete steps toward a passageway in the building. I stumbled, bounced off a wall, regained my balance and continued down a dark enclosed breezeway that headed to the rear courtyards of the apartment buildings. I heard the police car screech to a halt. Doors opened and shouts echoed down the breezeway. When I reached the rear steps, I started to turn my head and heard a gunshot. My peripheral vision caught the flash and what looked like sparks. They were shooting at us.

I twisted forward and tripped up three concrete steps, then broke into a trot. I had the presence of mind to know they hadn't fired at me. There was no way of a ricocheting bullet missing me in that cramped space. I cleared the two building wings that formed the courtyard and turned onto the common walk that connected the rear of the entire block of buildings. I wasn't going back to a cell - be it in a jail or in my house.

The only light came from low wattage bulbs mounted in metal shades on the rear of each building. I passed three of the lights before deciding to hop the waist-high wrought iron fence dividing the two street's courtyards. I dropped three feet onto the lower adjoining walk and found my way to another breezeway.

As soon as I stepped down into the breezeway the wind knocked me back. The passage was a wind tunnel. I leaned forward and fought my way to the street side. My straight long hair was leaping around, resembling a string of explosions in a haystack. I leaned out of the tunnel and scanned the street. It was empty.

I crossed the street to another breezeway. The wind howled through it but I leaped in and struggled to the other side. I continued the street hopping for three more blocks until I ran out of buildings and I was sure I was clear of any search area.

I zigzagged through the shopping area in the mid-Seventies and found myself on Roosevelt Avenue and Broadway. My stomach growled so I stopped at the Bickford's restaurant on the triangle and sat at the counter. I ordered a hamburger and coke and started to relax. *No crazy thoughts. No anger at the world.* You made it out of harm's way and you deserve a minute to clear your head. I pulled my comb from my back pocket and ran it through my mop, pushing at the front to form my usual wave.

"Please don't comb your hair at the counter," the waitress said as she placed the burger and coke in front of me.

I felt embarrassed being told about something I wasn't in the habit of doing. I put the comb back in my pocket. "Sorry."

"Okay. Ninety cents, please."

I pulled a single from my wallet and noted that I had only three more. I told her to keep the change. I hadn't been working after school for a couple of months and my cash was beginning to run out. I thought about volunteering for one of Shades' burglary jobs but quickly dropped the idea. It would be just my luck to get nailed the first time out. Trouble always had a way of finding me. I wasn't going to go looking for it and increase the odds. I would probably be able to pick up a part-time job around the holidays.

As I ate I thought about Sheila and what Johnny had said about finding someone I could communicate with. If only I could get myself out of this damn rut; get some balls and speak up. I had made a damn good start earlier in the evening. I knew she could be good for me. But then there was that lousy trip she was taking. She'd probably forget about me by the time she got back.

I glanced out the window and saw Val, Freddy and Speedo passing. I jumped from the stool, leaving the hamburger half-eaten, and ran to one of the glass doors.

"Hey, guys," I yelled.

They stopped and turned back.

"Man, what a fucking night," Freddy said.

"What happened?" I asked. "What was with the shooting?"

We moved away from the wind into an enclosed corridor behind Bickford's.

"The son of a bitch put a bullet right between me and Val," Freddy said, his hand pressed against his bare head. His hat was probably still stuffed inside his jacket. "Right into a tree between us, like he was target practicing."

"We just stopped dead and threw up our hands," Val said. "I almost shit in my pants."

"Why'd they do it?" I asked. "We weren't doing anything wrong."

"They said that somebody in the crowd that was running up the same block as us threw a bottle at their car."

"That's nuts. Why'd they pick on you?"

"We were the first ones they got to."

"Then they let you go? How come?"

"They jerked us around and tried to scare us, but they knew they didn't have anything on us," Val said. "And they probably knew that if they took us in, they'd have to explain why they shot at us."

"Yeah, but while our heads were screwed up over the shooting, they were asking all kinds of questions and searching us. They went through my wallet and found the newspaper clippings I had about the times we got picked up," Freddy said. "They had us shiting a brick until we regained our senses. They pulled out a folder with Vandals written across the front. They had names in there we didn't even know. They were checking the names in the articles they got from my wallet against the names on the list."

"I heard about those lists," Speedo said. "The reason it's so big is every time they grab someone who's already on the list and they're with someone who ain't, the guys who ain't get added whether they're a member or not."

"Guilt by association," I said.

"Use your fancy words to talk your way out'a a J.A.B. card when they call your house," Speedo said.

"What'a you mean?"

"Our buddies, here, gave us up when the cops ran down the list," Speedo said.

"What?" I looked at Val and Freddy, who sheepishly bowed their heads. "Why?"

"Every time they asked us a name they must'a watched our reactions. Like a lie detector test," Freddy said. "They kept pickin' out the names in the clippings and askin' us about each guy."

"That stinks, man," I said.

"We couldn't help it," Val said. "Before we could clear our heads and think about what was happening, they had already conned us. Then they wrote up cards on us and told us to beat it."

"Great. So if they call our homes and ask where we were to-night, we'll have to explain ourselves to our parents." My heart felt like it dropped into my stomach. That's all I needed. I decided right there that I was on my own. I couldn't go home until I could think up some kind of alibi. My old man would say I did something wrong whether I did or I didn't. *I was out for the night and that was it.*

"I guess that hurricane is coming," Speedo said.

"Yeah, I think I'll head for home," Freddy said.

"Me, too," Speedo said. "What the hell? I'm always in trouble at home. What's one more time?"

"Come on," I said. "Stay out. Let's do something."

"What can you do in this crap?" Speedo pointed toward the sky. "See ya tomorrow."

Freddy followed Speedo onto the sidewalk and across the street.

"What a bunch of humps," I said. "I thought I could depend on my friends."

"Look, man," Val said. "I'll stick with you for awhile. I mean, I owe you something for what I did."

I was always quick to hold a grudge, but was just as quick to lose it.

"Thanks, Val." I pulled a cigarette from my shirt pocket and lit it. I knew Val didn't smoke so I didn't have to pull out the pack and offer one to him. My thoughts drifted back to where they had left off when I was sitting in Bickford's.

"You know Tony Vellari pretty good, don't you?" I asked.

"Yeah, we're kind'a tight."

"You know if he still likes Sheila?"

"No, man. He dumped her."

"Why?"

"He says he couldn't get nothing," Val said.

"That's all he was interested in?"

"You know Tony. A broad's gotta give or - "He pointed thumbs down.

"Hell, man, she's a good kid. The kind you can really talk to," I said.

"Tony don't need no psychiatrist. A down-to-earth chick is good enough for him. I saw you talking to her at Bill's. You thinking of making a play for her?"

"Maybe. I don't know."

"She's the marrying kind. Don't expect anything until she's wearing a ring."

"So what? What's the big deal about bragging that you got laid."

"That's what they're for, man. Wake up. You can't spend the rest of your life jerking off."

"You saying you think I've never been laid?"

"I think it's a good guess from what I've seen of your score with chicks."

"Thanks a lot, you son of a bitch." My acceptance for Val's apology shattered. I felt a rush of blood to my head. Hate surged back into my mind. Sheila's face flashed before me and I felt as though I was protecting her and her virtues.

"Hey, fuck you, too." Val slapped a backhand off my chest. "I was trying to set you straight but you're nothing but a schmuck. Go bury your head in the sand. Guys like you can fuck up a wet dream."

Before I came out of my analysis of the moment, he was gone, following Freddy and Speedo into the haze of rain.

"Screw everyone," I shouted after him. "The hell with you. I don't need anyone."

An elderly couple had reached the head of the stairs that led from the subway. They stared at me in silent amazement.

I jerked my head back and my hair fell into place. "Sorry folks," I said. "I have this steel plate in my head." I tapped my temple. "Got hit with a grenade blast in Hungary. You know, the Freedom Fighters."

They stared for another few seconds and then shook their heads before shuffling onto the sidewalk and up the capped metal staircase next to Bickford's, heading for the elevated train line.

I couldn't get along with anyone for any reasonable period of time. I would probably wind up as a hermit. So what. Who cares? But what would I do with myself? I remembered a small movie theater a block away. It would be a good place to think and figure out my next move. I could get buried in a flick just to forget things.

The inner theater had a small orchestra section on ground level that was separated from the balcony by a wide aisle. The balcony rose on a steep angle to the rear wall. I climbed two rows into the elevated section and sat in an aisle seat. There weren't any more than five people in the section.

I hadn't noticed the names of the features playing when I entered and was surprised to find myself in the middle of "East Of Eden". I had seen the film before but had no problem seeing it again. James Dean. What a guy. He had that same inner conflict as me, and from what I had read, not only on screen but in his real life. It was too bad he was gone.

I settled back and forgot the rest of the world. Jimmy would speak for me. Jimmy for Jimmy. He knew how to get his point across.

I nodded toward the aisle and heard before I saw a woman in a flowered print dress pass me, heading for ground level. She was wearing high-heeled open back shoes that created the sharp rap on the concrete steps.

She disappeared into the lobby and I settled back into the movie for a couple of minutes before she returned holding a bag of popcorn. She started up the stairs, stopped next to me, feigning confusion, and then sat in the aisle seat across from me. My body went limp as I realized I was about to be picked up.

My eyes had adjusted to the darkness and I turned my head slightly, still appearing to be concentrating on the screen. Her hair was probably bleached; its reflective brightness was like a halo in the dark. She wore long crystal earrings that caught an occasional glint from the light of the screen. She had a nice shape with large breasts that punctuated the low cut top of her dress. Her bare legs were crossed and the shoe of the supported foot hung loose, bouncing with the movement of her foot.

"Excuse me, would you like some popcorn?" she asked. Her voice was husky and sensuous.

I turned to her and half-smiled. "Yeah, thanks." I reached across the aisle and plunked a few white kernels from the bag. My hand trembled as I drew them back to my mouth. I was calm, yet my hand shook. It was something new. It was always up to the guy to make the first move. But now all of the first effort was being taken care of.

"Well, that's it," she said.

"What?"

"The movie. It's over."

I looked at the screen and saw the credits rolling.

"Do you want anymore popcorn?" she asked.

"Yeah." I reached, then stopped. "Nah, that's okay."

"Well, I guess I'll head home. I hear there's a hurricane coming."

"Yeah, I heard that, too."

"Could I impose on you to walk me home? There's so much crime lately and I'm frightened to walk alone at night."

"I'd be happy to," I said, trying to sound a lot like Robert Taylor or Clark Gable.

She stood up and bounced down the three steps toward the ground level, the rapping sound from her stiletto heels deadened when she reached the carpeted surface. I followed and came alongside her as we passed an usher leaning against the glass concession stand. He tugged on the lapel of his maroon uniform and gave me a wink of confidence.

I returned the wink, still trying to emulate Robert Taylor or Clark Gable. After I did it, I felt foolish but maintained my cool, and held the door for her.

We stopped outside the string of glass doors and watched the downpour that had turned into a full raging storm. Jagged branches of lightning sliced through the darkness and crashes of thunder vibrated against the now empty ticket booth.

"I only live a block away," she said. "Thank goodness."

"Well, I guess we better dive in. Lead on."

She pulled a hot pink plastic hat from her handbag and tied the strap under her chin. She darted onto the sidewalk and hugged the walls of the buildings. She took short steps, her tight dress hindering her stride. I tried to compensate for her tiny steps but wound up bumping into her three times before we turned the next corner and entered the small lobby of a three-story apartment building.

Her apartment was on the ground floor. She turned on the light and took off the plastic hat.

I pulled out my comb and began stroking my hair. The dampness had turned it into a mess. I couldn't produce the wave and finally just combed it flat like Count Dracula.

"Thank you so much," she said moving back to me.

"What for?"

"For walking me home." She reached around me and I heard the door lock snap closed. "Stay awhile. It's much too nasty out for you to go anywhere."

I stared into her face and, in the light, I realized that she was a lot older than I first thought. The wrinkles in her face were visible under the heavy make up. The deep red lipstick stood out vividly against the paleness of the powder coating and seemed to give her the appearance of a clown. Her hair was bleached and the dark roots were evident. I began to second-guess my intentions, wondering if maybe she was somebody's mother. *What a stupid thing to think. Maybe the thought of Johnny and Pete's mother created the idea.*

Maybe I should suggest a similar relationship. Maybe I should just relax.

"Come on," she said, wrapping her arm in mine. "Let's have a drink."

I moved along with her to a black naugahide couch. I could smell the heavy scent of a perfume. *Was all this supposed to seduce a guy? Maybe she was a real lady of the night. Maybe I would have to pay for it. That would be embarrassing. Me with two bucks to my name. What do they get? Five bucks? Or maybe ten. Damn, maybe I should ask first. No, wait a minute. If she wanted any money, she would have asked a long time ago. She wouldn't waste her time on a kid with no bread.*

I took off my jacket, at her prompting, and hung it around the backrest of a matching naugahide chair. She sat me on the couch and walked into the kitchenette, then returned with two glasses and a half-empty bottle of Gilbey's.

"I don't really like gin," I said.

"It's all I got, honey. Come on, you'll get used to it." She poured two ounces into each glass and dropped ice cubes splashing into the tumblers. She sat down next to me and picked up one of the glasses. "Cheers, sweetie." I lifted the other and she clinked her glass against mine.

I sipped the gin and it tasted like I thought her perfume might taste. She swallowed half the gin in her glass in one tilt, then looked at me and my glass. "Come on, baby, drink up," she said.

I held my breath and chugged down. I tried not to shutter but it ran through my body as the ice cube clattered in the glass.

"See, you do like it." She downed the remainder of her gin and picked up the frosted rectangular bottle to pour refills.

"You have any beer?" I asked. "I'd rather have a beer."

"I'm sorry, I don't. You shouldn't mix anyway. It'll make you sick."

She finished pouring another quarter-tumbler of gin each and then stood up and moved to a record player on a lowboy in a corner of the room.

"Do you dance?" she asked.

"Not really."

"I don't mean that rock and roll stuff." The turntable buzzed as it started its rotation. "I mean slow dancing. I'm sure you do. A good-looking boy like you must get a lot of girls to slow dance at parties or on dates."

"Yeah, sometimes."

Frank Sinatra's voice floated from the two speakers in the corners facing the couch.

"Stereo. Sounds good."

"Come on." She held out her hands and tilted her head to one side. "This is your date for the evening. We'll have our own little party."

I felt a rush of blood to my head as I stood up and put my arm around her waist. I was a little clumsy as we swayed to the music. I let her lead. Her high-heels made her as tall as me, and she pressed her body against mine, her hips grinding slowly. My dungarees were damp and began to stick to my legs. I felt warm.

The first song on the album ended and she broke away, bending over to reach for her drink. "Recharge, honey," she said gulping the gin.

I picked up my glass to match her. I found myself following her lead in everything we did. We finished the second round of drinks and I started to feel a buzz. She poured the third round and then, glass in hand, moved to within a few inches of me.

"You're certainly the shy one, aren't you?" she said, staring into my eyes. "I hear the girls now'a days like that. The strong silent type." She sipped her drink, then tilted the glass to my lips.

I sipped from it and was struck by the sensation of a second taste. It was the lipstick on the rim of the glass. It tasted like the gin but more bitter. It was greasy and slick and the thought of lard passed through my mind. *What the hell was I doing here?*

She pulled the glass back to her mouth, downed the gin and let the tumbler drop to the carpeted floor. "Your shy days are over," she said. "I'm going to make you a man."

She slipped her arms around me and I returned the embrace. She kissed me on the lips and cheeks and it turned into a frenzy. She was smearing her lipstick all over my face. My taste buds picked up the sensation of lard again and my mind went as limp as my body. A buzz started in my ears.

"Just tell me you love me," she said between kisses. "You don't have to mean it. Just say it and you can do anything you want with me."

I started to say it. *I wouldn't mean it. So why should I say it?* Sinatra was starting into another ballad when a thumping overpowered his voice. I thought it was the record skipping or the lid of the player had fallen and bounced against the base. Then I realized the thumping was coming from the hall door.

"Mildred. Open the door!"

It sounded like what a gorilla might say if they spoke.

She released her grip on me and backed away, a look of dismay on her face. Her lipstick was smeared across her slack, drooped jaw.

"My God," she said. "It's Larry. My boyfriend."

"Boyfriend?"

"He's in the navy. He wasn't supposed to be home until Monday."

"Mildred. You there? I lost my key. Open up."

"Quick," she whispered. "Go through the bedroom and out the window." She snatched my jacket from the chair and threw it into my arms. "If he finds you here, he'll kill the both of us."

I followed her pointed finger to the bedroom as she shouted, "Just a minute, honey. I dozed off. I'll be right there."

I glanced back through the bedroom doorway as I slipped into my jacket and zippered up. Frank was still crooning, and Mildred was stuffing one of the glasses under the cushion of the couch. I hurried to the window and it slid open in one smooth flow. I was immediately struck with a wall of wind blown water. I heard her again answering an impatient Larry as I positioned myself on the

wide cement ledge facing the alley. I slid the window closed behind my back.

I pushed off the ledge and dropped into the alley below, landing in a crouch in the middle of a puddle. I sprang to my feet and
headed for the street. I splashed down the block until I found a
storefront with an enclosed entrance that could provide a temporary shelter. None of the stores were open. Their dark, uninhab-
ited windows were evidence of the turbulent night. What jerk
would be here under these circumstances and conditions if they
had somewhere else they could be? *Yep, it was me.*

There was a large white-faced clock in the store window, and
the black arrow tipped hands showed a few minutes until mid-
night. I looked at the street again. The rain was being driven in
sheets by the wind, traveling in continuous lines across the deserted street like a giant pulsating sprinkler system was controlling
it.

Now I wondered if I should risk going home and being yelled
at for not only my attitude in leaving the bar, but now an added
attraction of a phone call from the juvie cops telling them to bring
me to yet another hearing. And trying to explain that I again didn't
do anything wrong; my explanations falling on deaf ears. It was
pretty clear. I stuck with my earlier choice. I was on my own. *But
where would I go?*

III

I remembered the two blocks of condemned houses near Bill's.
We had set one up as a part-time clubhouse. The guys used the
rooms for a make-out spot, or to play cards, or to just hang out
when Bill's was closed or the cops were making it too hot for us at
the schoolyard. *If I was to be alone, it might as well be complete. Why
bother having robots whirl around me?* I doubted if anyone would be
there now. I lowered my head and sprinted for the graveyard of
deserted houses.

I reached the block and found that only one streetlight was

working. Fortunately, it was in the middle of the block across the street from my new home.

The front and rear doors had been nailed shut by the city or whoever condemned the houses. The buildings were not only an invitation to us or younger kids to play in but to a growing number of homeless that were beginning to drift away from their hangouts in back alleys of the business districts and under railroad trestles. It was probably easier for the city to try to button up everything than to guard the two blocks against a host of intruders until the politicians decided it was time to do something about the complaints from people living on adjoining streets.

I crawled through a break in the lower lattice of the front porch, along the slimy mud underside and to a cellar window. The street lamp gave off enough light to guide me through the narrow window and into the basement.

An inch or two of water covered the basement floor. There was a musty smell. I felt along the rough foundation lip until I found the box of candles that we kept for lighting the way through the dark house. I grabbed one and a handful of wooden matches from the long cardboard box. I lit the candle and found my way out of the flooded basement. I could hear the wind whistling through cracks in the outer wall as I climbed the stairs toward the second floor. The rain was pounding against the shingles, causing the interior walls to retain a chilling dampness. I shuddered from a sudden chill.

Every ghost story or horror movie I had ever seen began replaying in my mind. The candle flame flickered, the rain pounded and even the steps creaked. I was ready to turn around and get out of there. I stopped near the top of the staircase and froze. *Who or what might be waiting for me up there?*

I reached the second floor and stumbled over a chunk of plaster. The flame blew out from a sudden swirl of draft. I scratched the head of another wooden match against a door jam and lit the candle. I cupped my hand in front of the flame as I traveled the last few steps to the main bedroom.

The room was at the front of the house; its floor covered with a putrid pink oilcloth embedded with scores of black heel marks. The walls were surprisingly clean except for a large purple blotch over the rusted brass bed in the rear corner. An army blanket was crumpled in a ball at the foot of the bare mattress. Another corner of the room held a maroon couch; the two original lopsided cushions in its bed were flanked by a bright green replacement. Two maroon armchairs, a cracked full-length mirror and a flimsy card table completed the furnishings.

I was used to seeing the room when it was full of guys and sometimes girls. Seeing it empty made me depressed. I wanted to turn and run again, but this time to find someone. I wanted to talk to another person so I would know I wasn't the last human on earth.

I softened the bottom of the candle with another match and used the melted wax to hold it to the table, took off my jacket and fell backward onto the lumpy mattress. My dungarees clung to my legs like they were part of them. It was too uncomfortable. I looked at the open doorway to be sure no one was there, and then peeled the pants to my ankles, sat up and pulled off my loafers before removing the dungarees completely. My upper legs had a slight blue tint from the dye in the jeans. I settled back again and stared at the ceiling. A train whistle screamed in the distance and I thought I heard a kid crying. *Who would let a kid out on a night like this?* Then a rumble of thunder vibrated the windows for a long moment.

I was both mentally and physically drained. I concentrated on the smoke-stained ceiling. The movement of the flame made shadows dance across my view, their rhythm coordinated with the music of the pounding raindrops. It was really peaceful. The fury of the storm couldn't touch me. I closed my eyes and fell asleep.

A shattering explosion awoke me. I sat erect in the bed. There were jagged pieces of glass on the floor. My head was throbbing and the after-taste of gin pinched my dry tongue.

The candle had blown out leaving the room in semi-darkness.

A board was hanging by a few nails from the window frame allowing what light there was outside to filter into the room along with the rain and turmoil of the storm. It must have been morning.

I felt embarrassed about sitting there in my underwear - *like someone would come in and see me* - so I reached for my dungarees. They were still wet and felt heavy as I pulled them on. I slipped on my shoes and it felt like stepping into a mass of jelly.

I tried to push the loose board back into place but it became completely separated from the frame and dropped to the floor. The closet door was off its hinges and leaning against a wall. I carried it to the window and pushed one of the armchairs against it to hold it in place.

I lit the candle, flopped back on the bed and pulled out one of my last damp cigarettes as a reward for my deed. Sheila immediately entered my thoughts. I had to see her, if only to wish her well on her trip. I had to show her I cared, even if it was with some small gesture. She would at least remember that I was one of the last of the crowd to see her off.

I put on my jacket and snapped the candle from its anchor to the table. I walked down the two flights of stairs to the cellar window that opened under the front porch. My wet feet and thoughts of fighting through the storm again made me consider staying. *But what the hell could I accomplish here?* There had to be some reason for what I was doing.

I crawled through the window and was instantly drenched by the pounding rain that cascaded through every crack in the porch boards. I leaned against the force of the driving downpour and made a mad dash for Bill's.

The dawn was hidden behind the same pearl gray clouds that had been pushed across the sky the night before. The clouds were fused into a single continuity that seemed to encircle the earth like a dome of ashy charcoal.

The torrent lashed across my body, blurring my vision and even seemed to penetrate through the leather of my tightly zipped jacket. My lungs felt like they were going to explode when I reached

Bill's. I forced the door closed behind me and slumped against it. The store was quiet. It was the first time that I could remember not walking in and hearing the juke box playing.

"You okay, boy?" Bill was wiping his hands in a stained apron as he stepped from a small room next to the telephone booth.

"I'm okay. Anybody been around?" I thumbed through the Queens phone book and found Sheila's number.

"Nope. Nine o'clock and you're the only customer I had this morning. You must be nuts to be out on a day like this."

"Yeah." I stepped into the booth.

"You better get home and out of those wet clothes."

The phone rang twice before someone answered.

"Is Sheila there, please?"

"No, she isn't. This is her mother. Who's calling?"

"This is Jim Yadenik. I don't think you know me."

"Oh yes. I've heard Sheila mention you several times."

That's encouraging. "Do you expect her soon?"

"We're leaving on a trip tomorrow. Sheila is visiting her girl friends to say good-bye. I don't know exactly when she'll be back, but I'll tell her you called."

"Thanks, Mrs. Nelson. Bye." I hung up the receiver and sat in my puddle of water, a headache pounding against my temples and a mouth full of cotton. I probably wouldn't get to see her at all.

Bill probably felt sorry for me. He didn't complain about the river I was leaving behind as I sloshed through his store, and when I asked if he could sell me a couple of aspirins, he gave them to me with a tall glass of water. I slugged down half the glass of cool water before it penetrated the thick film of dryness in my mouth and I was able to taste the sweetness of refreshment.

I finished the glass of water and was about to ask for another when I thought otherwise. I never got pushy when I was given something for nothing. I thanked Bill and headed outdoors.

"Remember," Bill said, "Get home and out of those wet clothes before you get sick."

I sneezed.

"Gesundheit! Get home."

I waved a thank you and pushed onto the sidewalk. Dolores lived in an apartment house six blocks from Bill's, and I was a walking sponge when I reached it. This would be one of two places Sheila would be likely visiting. Once inside, I realized that I didn't know Dolores' last name or her apartment number. I decided on trial and error and pressed the first tiny black button above the line of mailboxes.

"Who is it?" a woman's voice asked from the speaker above the row of buttons.

"Is Dolores there?"

"Dolores? Dolores who?"

"Dolores Mfgabat." I mumbled the unknown last name.

"Who?"

"Never mind." I pushed the second button.

"Yeah?" Man, it sounded like Larry. I jumped back from the speaker, thinking somehow I had returned to Mildred's apartment house.

"Is Dolores home?" I asked.

"You got the wrong apartment, mac."

"Sorry." The third button offered no reply, and on the fourth, I figured I'd pull a switch. "Is Sheila there?"

"Sheila who?"

"Sheila Nelson."

"This is the Rosetti apartment. No Nelsoon is here."

"Sorry."

I was about to try number five when the inner door opened. The doorway was filled with a burly guy wearing a khaki under-shirt, the bottom stretched above his hairy beer belly.

"What'a ya want, mac?" It was the guy that sounded like Larry.

"I'm looking for Dolores."

"Dolores who?"

"Look, to tell you the truth, I don't know her last name but I know she lives here."

He waddled down two white steps leading from the door and

stood in front of me. "Why don't you get out'a here before I get mad?"

"Man, I'm not fooling around or anything."

"Beat it, mac." He shoved me.

"Thanks for your gracious help," I said.

"Get movin'." He kicked at my butt as I turned, the quick movement sending his slipper flying off his foot and out the door. I slammed the door behind me and gave the slipper a sharp boot. It bounced into the gutter and was washed down the block by the rushing waters. I could hear the guy shouting behind me as I charged through the rain. When I reached the corner, I looked back but couldn't see more than six feet, so I ducked into the lobby of another apartment building.

Maybe that'll learn you not to mess with Jim Yadenik, Fatso.

I laughed, took a minute to catch my breath and was back out into the rain for the millionth time. When I reached Fatso's building, I peeked through the wrought-iron swirls protecting the glass door. The lobby was empty so I started my little game again.

I pressed the fifth button and a voice scratched through the speaker. It was Dolores.

"Dolores, this is Jim Yadenik. Is Sheila there?"

"Yeah, she is. Come on up. Apartment 2A."

"Okay." I leaped the two white steps and grabbed the doorknob as the lock tripper buzzed. I took the inside steps three at a time and as I reached the second floor, a door opened below. I was sure it was Fatso and quickly ducked away from the railing.

"Hi, Jim."

"Hi, Dolores." I rushed into the apartment as the slopping of wet slippers moved up the staircase.

"Wow, are you soaked," Dolores said as she closed the door behind us. "Wait a minute, I'll get Sheila." She disappeared down the center hall.

I tried again to comb my straight hair into its usual wave but it fell flat like a deflated tire. I combed the sides back into the DA, the draining water rolling uncomfortably down my back.

"Hi, Jim."

Sheila was wearing snug tapered dungarees and a tight orange sweater. Her auburn hair was tied into a ponytail with a matching orange ribbon.

My pulse quickened and my ears felt warm. "Hi. How are you?"

"Fine. You?"

"A little wet. Man, you're one hard girl to find."

"You've got patience. I heard you were asking about me after I left last night. Val's sister is a friend of mine. She called me this morning and told me Val was ranting about an argument you got into with him over me. Then mother just called to tell me you were trying to reach me. I didn't think you thought so much about me."

"I don't say things to hear myself talk. How about you?"

"I was still hurting from Tony. I didn't want to get involved again so soon. But I've had some time to think. I let it sink in, and I realized that I must have been thinking of you and admiring you for some time to have noticed things about you."

"How about a nice long talk?"

"I'd like that very much. We can go to my house."

"Good." I squeezed her hand and then pulled back. "I'm sorry. I'm getting you wet."

"It's okay."

"I'm glad I didn't give up."

Sheila looked sweet in her yellow rain outfit. Like the Morton salt girl.

We said our good-byes to Dolores, who seemed confused about the two of us leaving together. I walked Sheila to the rear door on the ground floor and as I opened it, I heard a shuffling behind me.

"Hey you!"

I rushed Sheila into the courtyard, grabbed her hand and dragged her the two blocks to her house. After we caught our breath on her rear porch, I told her about my adventure with Fatso and we both had a good laugh. We entered the house and passed down a narrow flight of stairs to a playroom in the basement. While she left to check in with her mother, I pulled off my jacket and dried my hair with a bath towel she had given me.

I had the towel wrapped around my head when Sheila returned. "Want your palm read, lady?"

She laughed and extended her hand.

"You've just met a tall blond stranger. Watch out for him. He's a kook."

"A nice kook."

I unwound the towel. My hair fell into my eyes and I brushed it back. "But seriously, folks." We bumped noses as we kissed, then found the mark and clung together for a long moment.

"I need someone like you, Sheila. Don't turn me down."

"I won't."

We dropped back onto the sofa locked in embrace, until Sheila broke it off. I hoped she wasn't thinking I was trying to put the big move on her. I remembered Val's words about the reason for her break up with Tony.

She took my hands and stared into my eyes. "It doesn't seem fair that we have so short a time together. Stay with me as long as you can. You can borrow some of my brother's clothes. He's about your size and he's away at college. Get dry. Eat lunch with us. There's so much to say. Call your house and tell them the weather is too bad for you to start home." She hesitated. "What's wrong, Jimmy?"

"I haven't been home, or even called, since I saw you last night. I got into a hassle with them before I came to Bill's."

"Why don't you call to let them know you're okay?"

"They're probably hopping mad."

"They're probably very worried. Please call them. For me? I don't want anything to spoil this day with you."

"You don't know what it's like at my house. All the fighting and arguing and no one trying to understand my feelings. I don't have anyone to confide in. It's like this dream I have a lot, where

I'm on this dark street with nothing but blind people around me. I have to walk among the blind."

"I won't let you feel lonely again. Believe me. I have a feeling about you that I've never had for anyone before. You'll never have that dream again."

We kissed again.

"Give your parents another chance," she said. "Maybe they don't show their love like you want them to, but they must work hard and try to make a decent home for you, a better life than they had. Maybe it's the only way they know how to show that love. You, of all people should know people have different ways of showing their feelings."

"You make sense, Sheila." *I've been blaming them for not understanding me. Practice what you preach, man. You could have been Johnny, looking for someone who you'd never find and finally settling for a substitute. You have the real thing.* "Things could be worse," I said.

"Everything will be fine, Jim. You'll see. I'll help you in any way I can."

"I need that optimism." I thought of Johnny again. *This is what he told me to find. That different outlook. That someone to help change things around.*

I stood, still holding her hand. "I'm getting everything wet. Your parents will get mad if I stay."

"No they won't. They'll understand."

"There's that word again."

She stood with me. "Now it's your turn to understand. Call them, please."

"You're right. Where's the phone?"

"Next to the Ping-Pong table."

I dialed my number and mom answered. "This is Jim, mom."

"My God, what happened?" Her voice sounded teary. "Where've you been?"

"Thinking. I had some things to straighten out."

"I've been worried sick and dad was furious. Why didn't you

call? Where are you in the middle of this storm? What's wrong with you?"

"I'm okay. I'm at a friend's house. A very good friend." I smiled at Sheila, then remembered the incident at the park. "Did anyone call you about me?"

"No, no one. Why?"

I felt another release of pent-up anxiety. Maybe the cops had gotten enough names for their list. "I'll be home later, and we're going to sit down and talk - you, me and dad. Is he there?"

"He's sleeping. He had to work overtime and couldn't get home until this morning."

"He didn't ask you to check around for me before he sacked out - after he got *furious?*"

"He said you'd probably turn up sooner or later."

"Yeah, I guess he would." *Well, what the hell, I didn't expect things to change overnight.* "I couldn't get a call through because of the storm," I lied. It was a necessary lie and it seemed to calm her down. "I'm going to have lunch at my friend's house and then I'll be home. The weather should be cleared up by then. If dad stays home after he gets up, I'd like all of us to talk. It's about time we all took a good look at each other."

"Huh?"

"Later, mom. I'll see you later and explain."

I hung up and stared at Sheila. "Look and you shall see," I said.

CHAPTER 12

SONNY KRAUS – APRIL, 1957

Sonny and Blackie walked slowly along Woodside Avenue on their way to Bill's. There was no rush. It was dusk and the weather was still warm and perfect. So they took their time and enjoyed the view.

The girls had come out of winter hibernation in flocks. It always seemed to happen on the first warm day of the year. It was a ritual. Sure the Vandal Debs were always around no matter what season, but it was the new faces that caught the eye, especially the teasers in their short shorts. Their mothers had warned them about guys like this; hoods with DAs and gang jackets and guys who were out for only one thing.

Sonny had never taken any relationship with a girl seriously. Girls drifted in and out of the crowd as their interests changed. Some stayed to become members of the Vandal Debs, the female auxiliary. Some met guys from other neighborhoods at school and moved on to different turfs. Some just got tired of the scene and dropped out. He developed a corresponding attitude and had revolving door romances with anyone who was interested and who interested him. Serious was for suckers. If you got tied down to someone too long it would have an effect on your ambitions.

Sonny was war counselor of the Vandals. He had reached his first plateau of succession when Red Janek was arrested and eventually joined the army. Sonny's old job of secretary had been merged with the treasurer's position, giving Shades Gaglione the title of secretary-treasurer. Kelly had considered Jimmy Yadenik for the secretary job because it fit in with the Mad Russian's abilities to take accurate notes and keep a running record of Vandal happenings. But Jimmy had declined the offer. Since he was going out with Sheila, he started acting normal. His nickname was becoming a thing of the past. Just another poor schnook who couldn't think straight because of a chick.

An overwhelming vote had put Sonny into his new office. Blackie Chase had helped bring in the vote of the crazies - the restless, fighting faction of the gang. They had been itching for some action and Sonny and Blackie were ready to convince the old guard that it was time to spread out and start kicking ass to show that the Vandals were still a name to respect. The leadership was becoming too complacent. They were satisfied with the bulging treasury created by 'Shades' Raiders' and their burglary jobs and with the merger creating another chapter in Jackson Heights. They were beginning to forget that the Vandals were still a street gang who had to maintain their reputation as fighters or be stepped on by neighborhood gangs who were eager for turf.

Even his good friend, Johnny Sadinski, was becoming scarce. Sonny hoped it wasn't a chick. He liked Johnny a lot and didn't want to see the guy become a square over nothing more than a girl.

The top guys were becoming too soft for the hard core Vandals, and Sonny and his backers felt that the Vandals would fall into the same situation as the Madhatters found themselves when the Vandals were on their way up.

After blocks of casual girl-watching, they reached Bill's. Sonny was sure that he had enticed a duo of gigglers to visit the hangout. He knew they were young, but, like Val the lover said, you gotta set up a minor league before they can learn to hit in the majors.

A patrol car rolled slowly passed the corner. Bill's was on constant surveillance by the sector car and the rookies in gray uniforms that the mayor had pulled out of the police academy to augment the regular force. What a dope, Sonny thought. The only thing accomplished was to bolster the egos of the gangs whose territories had the extra patrols. The Vandals took the new measure with pride, and laughed at the youthful appearance of their proposed enforcers, many of them not much older than the kids they were ordered to control.

Sonny spat in the direction of the police car. He couldn't decide who he hated the most; cops or rival gang members. Neither could be tolerated by his drive to make a name for himself and the Vandals. He followed Blackie through the doorway, giving a quick backward glance at the green and white Plymouth. The occupants returned an equally hostile glare.

The place was jumping. Smoke clouded the store, Red Prysock's sax was pumping out the bridge of "Hand Clappin'", and from thirty to forty teenagers crowded the tables and aisles.

Sonny and Blackie pushed into the loud group of Vandals and Vandal Debs. They sidestepped through the front aisle to the rear area. A wild-haired boy in a black and aqua Vandal jacket was jostled into Sonny. He turned, laughing. "What's happenin'?"

"Nothing much, Tony. What's the occasion?"

"We're cuttin' down to the school dance, man," Tony said.

"Not that drag place."

"What the hell, nothin' to do here we ain't done before."

"Yeah, I guess so. I thought it was jackets and ties. How come nobody's dressed?" Sonny asked.

"They ain't been gettin' no big crowds lately so they're havin' a come as you are night."

"That's cool. Where's Kelly?"

"Over there," Tony shouted. He pointed over the crowd to a corner in the rear of the room where Kelly normally held court.

Sonny turned to find Blackie talking to one of the Debs a few feet away. He turned back and headed for officer's territory, pushing through the crowd and returning an occasional greeting. The white marble table was occupied by Kelly, Ginny - Kelly's girl - Shades and Johnny.

Kelly looked up. "How's it going, man?"

"Pretty good," Sonny said. He greeted the others before turning to Johnny in surprise. "Johnny, my man. I thought you said you weren't sure if you'd be around tonight."

"Change of plans," Johnny said. "I'm out for the weekend."

"Good deal."

"What's new?" Shades asked.

Sonny looked at the tinted glasses of the secretary-treasurer. He couldn't see his eyes and he didn't like it. He had developed that sixth sense about what people were really thinking, but he couldn't get a reading through the dark exterior that Shades seemed to hide behind. Shades was the one guy Sonny feared. He was too cool and calculating. He was money hungry and that was the type of guy that would do anything to anybody if a buck stood in the way. He had too much influence. And now, with his new title, he was the only record keeper of both what was earned and what was said.

At least Sonny didn't have to depend on Shades and his *Raiders* for a living. Sonny's father had died many years ago and had left a nice inheritance for his mother, who used it to keep her son out of any such activities. This, along with his Uncle Lou and his construction business money, kept Sonny very comfortable. But there was a trade-off. His mother was usually too busy shopping or traveling and Uncle Lou was too busy making money to spend time with Sonny. *But, what the hell.* The money helped him to buy companionship.

"I got an idea for you," Sonny said. "Kelly." He looked at Ginny and swung his head to the side.

"See you later, hon," Kelly said to Ginny.

She stood and walked to another table, and would probably complain to the other girls about the way the Debs, in general, were treated.

Sonny sat. "What about protection? We got muscle to do it, and you know a lot of people are scared shit of us already."

"No," Shades said.

"Why? A lot of gangs in Manhattan and the Bronx are into it.

They make a lot of bread. Johnny, you know that from the guys at school. Chinatown, Harlem, South Bronx."

"Our area is already covered by someone else," Shades said. "Someone who can't afford problems that could come out of a penny-ante shakedown operation."

Sonny hesitated for a moment to let Shades' statement sink in. "What'a you mean? Racket guys?"

"It doesn't concern us," Shades said. "Maybe in another year or two."

"But..."

"Drop it," Kelly said. "Thanks for your idea, but the subject is dead. We never shit in our own backyard before and we aren't about to start now. The time will come when we'll be able to operate bigger things without any problems."

"I know I'm only the war counselor, but it's tough to be in my spot without any wars to council. I thought I could make a useful suggestion."

"We appreciate it," Kelly said. "Don't worry about your job. We've been hearing some rumblings about the Sinners messing around with some of our girls. You might be going to work real soon."

"Good. I heard the same. I got a line on those guys. They're a bunch of young punks trying to make a name. There shouldn't be much of a problem."

"Don't take them too lightly," Kelly said. "They have older brothers and cousins on the Assassins. The Assassins aren't what they used to be, but between the two of them, we could run into some trouble. We'll see how far they push us before we move."

"I'll be ready," Sonny said. "And screw the Assassins. They stay holed up in their fortress on Roosevelt Avenue. They don't want anymore trouble with us."

"I'm counting on it," Kelly said.

"Okay," Sonny said. "This is what I wanna hear. We're back to what we're supposed to be. We're the Vandals."

"Okay." Kelly stood. "Now let's go have some fun."

"Hey, that's right," Sonny said. "I heard we were making it to the school dance."

"Yeah," Kelly said. "I figured we'd make the place to show it still belongs to us. Show the squares we're still in that part of town."

"When we cutting out?"

Kelly looked at his watch. "About five ticks."

"Life Is But A Dream" by the Harptones was the record playing when the hoard of teenagers moved out of the store. Kelly directed the movement and split the crowd into separate groups, traveling separate routes. It was becoming more difficult to put any sizeable amount of troops on the street.

The Junior High School was on the fringe of Vandal turf. A sampling of small, non-gang groups were now the majority of the Friday night crowd, and since most of the Vandals stopped going to the weekly event it had lost its charm and character. Some of the Vandals that occasionally spot-checked the dances reported that the thinned out population had started to request records by pop chart artists, a definite change from the core of rock and roll and rhythm and blues that were more to the Vandal's taste. The music business was beginning to shift back to the days before the beat encouraged the rebellious feeling that had changed teenage society. The attack against symbols such as the Vandals was coming from all directions, and the message was loud and clear: *This wave of disrespect and free spirit had to be crushed.*

There was a fifty-cent admission collected at the front door by a tall, very wide phys-ed teacher that doubled as the dance bouncer. The burly chaperone pointed the way through a tiled hallway, blocked off by a barricade of tables and portable desks forming a channel directly into the gym.

Retracted basketball backboards hung from the ceiling above the perimeter of the polished oak floor. The sides of the floor were lined with casually dressed teenagers milling about and waiting for the start of the music. A stereo record system, the turntable and racks of records on a long wooden table with fold-down metal legs, stood under the far backboard and was flanked by three-foot tall speakers set out six feet from each end of the table. Three more teacher-types stood chatting behind the table. One of them, a thin, white-haired woman in a gray suit and white high collar blouse, hovered over the spinning turntable, sliding a stack of 45s onto the cylindrical adapter.

Sonny scanned the crowd. Most of the faces were familiar. His gaze stopped on a group in the far corner. It was a large bunch and the way they grouped together, they were obviously a clique. No familiar faces. One of them turned his back and the gold script lettering on his jacket leaped out like a neon sign. Sinners. *What the hell are they doing here?*

"Look at this noise," Sonny said, turning to Kelly. "Who let them in?"

Kelly's answer was drowned out by the blast of Chuck Berry's "Maybellene" suddenly blaring through the speakers. Ginny tugged on Kelly's sleeve like a toddler asking to play. Kelly waved his hand in front of Sonny as though dismissing the situation turned and followed Ginny onto the dance floor.

The volume of the music dropped as the amateur disc jockey adjusted the knobs.

"There's those two chippies we was talkin' to before," Blackie said, pointing to the other side of the dance floor. "Let's go make some time."

"Later, man." Sonny looked at the group of Sinners and then back to Blackie. "You go keep them company. I'll be over in a little while."

"You think we'll get any trouble from them?" Blackie tilted his head toward the Sinners.

"Don't know, man. We can handle them. No sweat."

"Okay. I'll see you later." Blackie crossed the floor, bumping into dancers and continuing on without offering an apology.

Sonny was glad he could depend on a guy like Blackie to back him up if trouble started. His attention again focused on the Sinners. He counted fifteen guys and seven girls. There were two more black and gold jackets in the crowd. *What were they doing, advertising?* He didn't like it.

Sonny left the line of Vandals stretched along the edge of the dance floor and started moving slowly toward the Sinners. He sneered as he watched their antics. They had made their own dance floor in the far corner, off to the side of one of the speakers. They had formed a circle around two dancing couples and were clapping to the beat. *Friggen show-offs to boot.* His distaste for them grew with each step he took.

One of the girls standing outside the circle was watching him. She looked familiar, especially the raven hair. She was thin but buxom and the tight black sweater and half-slit skirt hugged her body nicely. Large gold earrings stood out against the dark outfit. She saw that she had attracted his attention and smiled.

Sonny stopped as she started toward him. The walk was very familiar. It was Sharon Norris.

"Sharon. How the hell are you?"

"Good, Sonny." She leaned up and pecked his cheek. She wore flat-heel shoes and was about two inches shorter than Sonny.

"I didn't recognize you," Sonny said. "You changed your hair or something."

"Yeah, shorter. Italian cut, they call it. Like Gina Lollabrigida. How's yourself?"

"Okay." Sonny's voice dropped as soon as the amenities were over. "You hanging around with those punks?"

"You got a problem with that?"

"As a matter of fact, I do. You used to be one of our Debs. Why the switch?"

"Come on, let's dance."

"I don't -."

Sharon hugged his muscular biceps with both hands and led him toward the dance floor. "Time to learn."

He gave into her persuasive charm, but justified it by his curiosity about her six-month absence.

The dance floor was crowded as "I Don't Stand A Ghost Of A

Chance" by the Solitaries drifted from the speakers. Even the squares were grinding, Sonny noticed. Sharon buried her head into his shoulder and they swayed and shuffled their feet to the smooth sound. He was about to continue his interrogation of Sharon when the music abruptly stopped with a loud click.

"Hey!" Someone in the crowd shouted.

"What's going on?" Sonny asked.

Most of the protests rose from the ranks of the Vandals, observing from the sidelines or in a clinch with their girls on the dance floor.

"I'm sorry but this record was not part of the suggested list," the gravel-voiced matron of the record player announced. She began flipping a switch, trying to drop the next record onto the turntable.

"What list?" Blackie shouted from the opposite side of the dance floor. He was still wrapped around one of the gigglers that he and Sonny had met earlier.

"Just be patient, please," she said as she fumbled with the switches. Another chaperone moved in to help her.

"This place has sure changed," Sharon said.

"You ain't kidding."

"It's getting hot in here. Let's go outside," Sharon said.

"Crazy."

They pushed through the crowd to the exit. Sonny received a pat on the back or a word of encouragement from the edge line of Vandals. Some of them thought he had picked up a new girl, not realizing she was one of their old Debs.

Sonny and Sharon were given crumpled pink slips left over from some long ago bingo game to use as re-entry passes. They wound their way through late arrivals, some of them from Bill's. Sharon was recognized by Roxie and Dolores, who greeted her with some apprehension.

The well-lit entrance steps were empty. Sonny stepped down to the sidewalk and leaned against the brick wall of the building, away from the glare of the four spotlights above the entrance.

He lit up a cigarette and smiled at Sharon. "Cooler?" he asked.

"A little too much." She nestled into him, then backed away and sat on the ledge of the lowest step. "Can I have one of them?"

Sonny flicked the pack with his wrist and Sharon took one. Sonny lit it for her.

She blew out a stream of smoke. "So I heard you're the war counselor of the Vandals now."

"You heard right." He looked at her suspiciously. "But how'd you hear?"

"It gets around. You're a famous guy."

"Stop the bullshit. You never answered my first question. What're you hanging out with those young punks for?"

"Hey." She pushed herself off the ledge and pointed at Sonny. "You ain't that much of a big shot to talk to me like that. I'll hang around with whoever I want."

"That's right, you can." Sonny flipped his cigarette into the gutter and swung around Sharon to the steps.

"Wait." She reached out and clutched his arm. "I'm sorry." She dropped her cigarette and nestled into him again. "It's because of my kid sister. She started hanging out with them and I gotta keep an eye on her."

"I didn't even know you had a sister."

"You didn't know a lot of things about me. How often did we every talk."

"True." Sonny relaxed and folded his arms around her. "So why didn't you say you were with the punks because of your sister when I asked you the first time?"

"Because I don't like being pressured. Mickey always pressured me. He was always asking me what I was doing when I wasn't with him. He even hit me a couple of times when he got those crazy ideas that I was two-timing him. I couldn't take it." She pressed tighter into Sonny's embrace. "I always wished that I could be with you instead of him."

"I've heard crap like that before," Sonny said.

Sharon rubbed her head against his shoulder.

"Weren't you with Mickey when he got grabbed in the stolen car?"

"Yes." She paused. "I didn't know it was stolen. My father hit me, too, when he picked me up at the police station. He called me a cheap tramp." Her body trembled with sobs. "Sonny, I couldn't take anymore."

He wouldn't buy it. No chick was going to sucker him. She could sob all she wanted. He wasn't going to give in.

"I couldn't come back to Bill's." She regained her composure. "There were too many bad memories. And when I found out about my sister, I had to protect her to make sure she didn't make the same mistakes I did. I didn't want my father calling her what he called me.

"I couldn't believe it when I saw you tonight," she said. "I saw the Vandal jackets and something inside of me felt good. Then there was you walking toward me." She pulled away and looked into his eyes. "I really couldn't believe it."

What was going on? *He wanted to kiss her.* He did. And she returned it with a passion he never experienced before on a first try. He squeezed her tighter.

"Don't screw around with me," he said. "You went out with other guys in the crowd. Don't tell me you always liked me. Why didn't you make a play before?"

"Because you were always too busy being a big shot. You didn't seem to be interested in anything but the Vandals. When you did go out with someone, I was going out with someone else. It was like something that wasn't meant to be." She gave Sonny a short kiss. "Until now."

Then came another long passionate kiss and Sonny felt himself becoming aroused. An excitement was rushing through his body. It had to be true. She couldn't make someone feel the way he did without meaning it.

One of the heavy school doors swung open and hissed as it reached the limit of the retaining piston. Sonny and Sharon, still holding each other, looked to the sound. The door bounced back and was slammed open again by the giant person standing in the doorway.

"Get your hands off'a her," he said. He wasn't wearing a Sinners jacket but Sonny had seen him in their circle. How could he have missed the guy? He stood out like a mountain in a desert. He was the Sinners' age, younger than Sonny.

"Get lost, Ralphy," Sharon said. "He's been trying to make me," she said turning to Sonny. "He's a real creep."

"Yeah, but a big one." Sonny pushed Sharon aside and faced him. Ralphy stepped forward allowing the door to close behind him with another hiss.

"You don't fuck around with one of our girls, pal." Ralphy started down the three steps toward Sonny. "You Vandals think you're hot shit, hah?"

Sonny saw the big hands, the meat hooks that could fold into massive fists. And then there was a whiff of booze. He had to put the guy down with the first shot or he was in trouble. He reached into his jacket pocket and wrapped his hand around a taped roll of nickels.

Sonny's fortified fist sprang from his pocket just as the Sinner reached the bottom step. The guy was big but inexperienced, probably getting away with intimidation in the past. Ralphy wasn't ready for the sledge hammer that smashed into his face. He sailed backward like a fast ball being driven off a bat. The points of the steps caught him along three parts of his body and he slumped into a ball that rolled to the sidewalk at Sonny's feet.

Sonny stepped back, ready for retaliation. The roll of coins had collapsed sideways in his hand, held together by the heavy electrical tape. He shoved it back into his pocket and looked down at Ralphy, who moaned, tried to straighten out, then slumped back to the sidewalk.

Sonny heard people scrambling behind the school doors. The three middle doors sprang open and unfamiliar faces filled the openings.

"Let's go, punks," he said, dropping into a fighter's crouch.

"Who's next?"

They stood frozen, looking at Ralphy lying semi-conscious on the ground. Sonny knew he would be backed up but it seemed like hours before Kelly, Johnny and Tony appeared in the crowd and pushed their way through. They rushed to Sonny's side, facing off against the still-paralyzed Sinners.

"You guys looking for trouble?" Kelly asked, pointing at the younger crowd.

"Us?" A tall, thin kid in a Sinners jacket stepped forward. "That's one of our guys on the floor."

"He started it," Sonny said, trying not to sound like he was whining. "You think I'd start something with an animal like him?"

"Okay, so he thought you were trying to make one of our girls."

"We heard the same thing about you guys," Blackie shouted from behind the Sinners.

The Sinners pushed forward, some of them stumbling. The four Vandals readied themselves, thinking for an instant that the Sinners were charging them. More Vandals streamed through the doorways, pushing aside Sinners. The pushing and shoving continued, the steps now alive with opponents jockeying for swinging room, until the phys-ed teacher bullied his way into the middle of the fray.

"Break it up," he shouted, shoving some of the combatants aside. "If you want me to call the police, I will."

"I already called them," the female gravel voice called from behind one of the doorways.

"Look, we were only trying to help this guy out," Kelly said. He moved to the step below the teacher. Ralphy was now sitting up but still stunned and oblivious to what was going on around him. "He fell down. I think he's intoxicated."

"Don't give me any of your crap, buster," the man said, shaking his finger in front of Kelly's face.

"Watch it," Kelly said, pushing the finger aside. "You can smell the booze on him from here."

"Don't give me no guff, you young hoodlum." The words had no force, no backbone. He was an adult version of Ralphy, trying to intimidate with his size.

"Get your clammy puss out'a my life." He pushed the teacher back onto the top landing. The action wouldn't change the situation - more than likely infuriate the chaperone staff - but, by Kelly's design, show the Sinners that no one, no matter what age group, could bully the Vandals into backing down.

"That's it." The flustered custodian turned and pushed his way through the crowd to the sanctuary of the doorway. He turned and announced, "You're all banned from this building."

"How can you do that?" one of the baby-faced Sinners asked. "We didn't do nothing."

"I don't care. I won't have this nonsense outside my building."

"How can you blame all of us?" Another Sinner said. "It was those guys that started it."

"Alright. Maybe I was too hasty." He pointed at the Vandals at the foot of the steps. "You older guys, I'm going to remember all your faces. Don't let me see you in here again."

"You're breaking our hearts. Who needs this crummy place?" Kelly turned away as the Debs and a few remaining Vandals filtered out of the school and through the Sinners' ranks. "Let's walk," Kelly said. "Split up."

"We'll see you guys another time," Blackie shouted at the Sinners, who were moving back inside the building. Two of them were supporting Ralphy. "Better keep your asses on the other side of Seventy-Sixth Street."

"Fuck you!"

"You son of a..." Blackie was up two steps before Sonny bearhugged him.

"Cool it," Sonny said. "We'll be meeting them again. Let's split before the cops get here."

Blackie shook Sonny off and followed him away from the school. "I'll beat the piss out'a the punk that said that. I'll kick his ass."

"You'll get your chance," Sonny said as he took Sharon's hand

and pulled her along. "You remember Sharon?"

Blackie scowled at the dark-hair girl on the other side of Sonny. "Yeah, I think so."

"I've got a few things to talk over with her. I'll see you later," Sonny said to Blackie. "Maybe we can figure some way to get the punks real soon."

"The sooner, the better." Blackie shook his fist. "I'll see you later."

Blackie crossed the street to join up with one of the groups of Vandals heading back to either Bill's or the schoolyard.

Sonny led Sharon three blocks to the setback entrance of a closed butcher shop. He wrapped his arms around her and leaned against the door, pulling her to him. "Where were we before we were so rudely interrupted?"

Sharon smiled and stretched to kiss him.

"Hey, wait. What about your sister? Maybe we better go back."

"She wasn't there tonight."

"How come you were?"

"Because she was supposed to be there. What's with all the questions?" She struggled to break free of his hold. "I told you I don't like being pressured. Let go."

"Wait." Sonny squeezed tighter. "I'm sorry. It's just the way you showed up out of the blue and all of a sudden here we are making time. It's only natural I'm curious." He thought of the browbeating from Mickey, the physical abuse from him and her father. He nodded his head in empathy. "Okay, no more questions. I promise."

They kissed and the rush of excitement raced through his body again.

"Sonny, I gotta go," Sharon said pulling her head back. "You were right, I should try to find my sister."

"I'll go with you," Sonny said. "You can't go walking in Sinners' turf alone after what just happened."

"Don't worry. They won't do anything. My sister is going out with one of their officers. I've got safe passage."

"What can you tell me about them?"

"Questions?" She stared into his eyes and half-smiled. "Didn't you promise?"

Sonny felt relieved that she was relaxed enough to joke about something that had upset her only seconds ago. "What time can you meet me tomorrow?" Sonny asked as he released his grip.

"Anytime you want."

"Ten okay?"

She nodded.

"Bill's?"

"I don't know." She shook her head slowly. "I'd rather not go back there right away."

"Schoolyard. Your block. You tell me."

"How about right here?"

"Yeah. Why not? It'll be like chapter two of a story, starting off right where tonight ended."

"You've become a poet in the last six months."

"Probably from hanging around with Johnny and the Mad Russian."

They kissed once more before she swayed away. Sonny watched her sensuous walk as she turned the corner and crossed the street. He slipped out of the doorway and kept her in sight until she disappeared down the next cross street.

What a night. A chance to take on the Sinners and meeting some-one that could be very interesting. Although he had known her for over a year, it had been like meeting her for the first time.

He crossed the street and headed toward Bill's. He wondered about the temperament of the guys after their run in with the Sinners. *Where they still up? Would Kelly be calling for a war?* As he drew closer to Bill's, the excitement of Sharon faded in favor of his need for fulfilling his duties.

CHAPTER 13

As he passed the schoolyard, he could hear the music loud and clear coming from the far side. The dark, least traveled side street entrance was reserved for night gatherings. He turned off Woodside Avenue and crossed the yard. He saw the large gathering of Vandals and Debs strung out along the back fence and the steps leading to the street as he was halfway to them.

The concrete patch had taken the place of the dance floor. Two portable radios were tuned into Alan Freed's Rock and Roll Party, the small plastic boxes placed at either end of the crowd. Someone had probably thought that a stereo effect could be simulated, not considering that the broadcast was in mono. Five couples were dancing to "Whispering Bells" by the Del Vikings. Some of the guys were bunched into the alcove next to the steps and were passing around a bottle. The others sat on the steps or spilled over onto the sidewalk of the back street.

Sonny knew that the rookie cops were only used on day patrol where the adults could see them. It was nothing but a con job by the politicians to make it appear that the neighborhood was getting extra protection. By this time of night, the normal beat cop and the sector car were concentrating along Roosevelt Avenue, protecting the more lucrative business district. They wouldn't scrutinize the schoolyard unless they became bored or had to respond to a complaint. And complaints had dropped over the years as the neighborhood adjusted to the presence of the Vandals.

The song ended as Sonny reached the fringe of dancers. The guys patted him on the back and shook his hand as he passed through the crowd. The group in the alcove passed the bottle of

Seagram's to him and he took a quick snort to celebrate his victory. He felt like a conquering hero.

"How many shots did it take you to deck him?" Johnny asked when Sonny reached the enclave of officers on the steps.

"Hey, I never need more than one."

A chorus of exaggerated cheer rose from those that heard his answer.

"Come on, the guy looked like a bull elephant."

"I ain't kidding you, man." Sonny pulled the collapsed roll of nickels from his pocket. "Me and a handful of Jeffersons."

Everyone laughed and then returned to what they were doing before. They would let the officers decide what to do about the Sinners.

Kelly and Shades leaned against Eddie Comanche's car parked under a street light. Sonny, Johnny and Blackie formed a semi-circle around them

"So what's the word?" Sonny asked.

"I think we should cool it," Kelly said.

"What? Why?"

"They're a bunch of kids," Kelly said. "We don't need to prove anything with them."

"They're getting pushy. You saw that tonight. You said that if they get pushy, we'd do something about it."

"It was just an incident. I think that what you did tonight and the rest of us backing them down proved our point. I don't think they'll be messing around again."

Sonny folded his arms and shook his head. "I don't think so. They're not gonna pack up and go out of business because of to-night. They're gonna be there." He pointed toward the Sinners' neighborhood. "Between us and Benny's turf until we put them out of business."

"Or we get put out of business," Shades said.

"By them?" Sonny's arms dropped to his side.

"By the cops," Shades said. "Things are too damn hot. We can't jeopardize my operations."

"Since when has the Vandals become your private operation?"

Kelly lifted his hand between Sonny and Shades. "He's right," Kelly said to Sonny. "We need the bread and we can't afford a bop to bring attention on us."

"I don't like that this guy is all of a sudden making the rules." Sonny folded his arms again and stared at the eyes he knew were behind the dark glasses. "By the way, where were you tonight when everyone came out to back me up?"

Shades' bland expression stayed frozen on his face. "I was convincing the old lady not to call the cops."

"But she said she did."

"Just to help break up the crowd. You see any cops show up? And while you guys were doing your act, I helped the treasury." Shades pulled a stack of folded bills from his pocket. "Thirty-two bucks. Nobody bothered to put away the night's receipts when the shit hit the fan."

"That's all this guy thinks about," Sonny said. He turned away in disgust.

"I left the change," Shades said.

"Alright, I think it's time to let you guys in on something important," Kelly said.

Shades looked at Kelly and then back to Sonny. "Yeah, why not," he said.

"What?"

"We already told Johnny before we left for the dance. It's only fair you two guys should know," Kelly said. "But one thing." He pointed at Sonny and Blackie. "No one but us five will know this. We've been socking every buck we can into the treasury because we need it to buy a future."

Sonny and Blackie stared blankly. It sounded like an opening for a television commercial.

"Benny has some connections who are willing to sell us some real operations - numbers, book, whatever else will make money - when the time comes. And they'll guarantee we can run it without any trouble. We'll have the full run of everything in our turf."

"We already do."

"Kid stuff," Shades said. "Real control. Not the peanuts we get now. We have to grow up."

"What are you going to do when you graduate in June?" Kelly asked Sonny.

"I don't know." Sonny shrugged. "I guess go into construction with my uncle's company."

"For how much a week? A hundred bucks?"

"Something like that. More with O.T."

"If our deal goes through, we can pull in three times that apiece for starters. And you won't have to bust your ass with overtime. You can work in a legit job to make things look good and still be making a bundle on the side."

"Sounds good to me," Blackie said. "High school drop-outs ain't exactly number one on anybody's hirin' list."

"It won't happen for a couple of years," Kelly said. "In the meantime, we can pick up a few bucks as runners or however they can use us. It'll give us a chance to learn the business."

"On-the-job training." Shades smiled.

Sonny stared into the night sky for a few seconds, then looked at Kelly and Shades. "It sounds too damn ify to me," he said. "And you make it sound too pat."

"It's there," Kelly said. He placed his fingertips on his chest. "Believe me. It'll happen in time."

"But who'll be in on it? All the Vandals? Just us?"

"As many as we can carry. You know most of these guys." Kelly gestured to the schoolyard. "They're going to be going their separate ways in another year or two. There won't be any Vandals as we know it now. As president, I have to plan for the guys who'll still be around. I made my decision. We cool it until it becomes absolutely necessary to protect our interests."

"Let's say everything you're telling us happens," Sonny said. "We still have a turf and rep to protect. If we let other cliques think we're gonna roll over, then we won't have the rep we'll needed in those couple of years from now. We have to stay tough now or we won't have a future."

"You're absolutely correct," Kelly said. "But hitting a bunch of kids isn't going to give us any bigger rep. Let it rest for now. If they start anything again, I'll reconsider."

"You're the boss," Sonny said. "If I could ask two things."

"What?"

"First, let me send a couple of guys to scout out our border with them. They can ask the squares whether the Sinners are getting comfortable on the blocks we claim as our turf. You know, like making it known who they are like they did at the dance tonight."

Kelly smiled. "You'd probably do it on your own, anyway. Okay, but not you. You're not too popular with them. What else?"

"I wanna check out the dance next week. I wanna see if they show up in force again."

"You heard that clown. He said he wouldn't let us in again."

"He can't remember all of us. Next week we'll have to go in suits. We can act repentant or whatever. Just a few of us to let the squares know we ain't backing down. If we get good reports tonight and none of them - or even a couple of them - show up next week, then I'll drop it."

"Okay. If you can get in, it'll make us look strong and hold that end of the turf together. But if they're there, don't start anything. Just let me know the situation. Remember, no trouble. Not tonight. Not next week. I can't let them push us into something we don't want."

"Good deal. I'll get on it right away." Sonny tapped Blackie with the back of his hand.

Sonny moved back to the steps with Blackie following.

Who could argue against making money? Who could stand up to an offer of large greens with only a counter proposal to stomp some kids. But there just might be a way to swing things in his direction, Sonny thought. If only the five officers knew about the future deal then there was a chance to convince enough of the

Vandals to back him and take on the Sinners. They weren't going to be fed any speeches about big dreams and a future of gold-paved streets, so all they still knew was that they had a turf and rep to protect.

"Do you believe those guys?" Sonny asked Blackie after they had found a quiet spot at the edge of the handball wall.

"What'a ya mean?"

"What kind of bullshit is that? There's no way in the world that Benny is that connected, that they can buy into some mob's business."

"Why not? I heard most of Benny's family is in the rackets. That's why he never has any trouble on his turf."

"It's just a rumor," Sonny said. "If people are made to believe it, then it's just as good as true."

"I don't know, man."

"Look, it all goes back to what I've been saying. They got a good thing going with the burglaries and car stripping. They don't want any action because it would blow apart their set up. Maybe some of the guys who bring in the bread would get nailed by the cops for a rumble and slip about the other stuff when they're being questioned. Their money-making operations would be broken up and they'd look like shit in front of the other Vandals."

"So, who wants that to happen?" Blackie asked. "I mean, I do okay by Shades on the jobs I pull."

"But anyone can run Shades' operation. What'a you need? Guys who are willing to make a few bucks and a good fence. It's no big deal."

"So what's your point?"

"I don't think they want me around," Sonny said. "And maybe not you either. Why did they wait until now to tell us about their plans?" Sonny tapped Blackie's chest with his index finger. "And the way Shades acted, we wouldn't have been told at all, if it was up to him. That guy has too much of Kelly's ear and he's gonna cause the downfall of the Vandals."

"I don't know, man."

"You say you do good by Shades on your jobs. How do you know you shouldn't do better. How do you know how much he gets from the fence? How do you know if you're getting the right cut? Where's this treasury they talk about? All we get is reports about how much they got. Never a look at the bread or a bankbook or something that shows there's actually money where they say it is."

"Kelly wouldn't fuck with us like that," Blackie said.

"Not Kelly. But Kelly might be getting snowed by Shades, same as everyone else. He might be showing Kelly a phony bankbook or something. Who knows?"

"So what'a we gotta do?"

"Force Shades out of the picture. If we can take over the Sinners' turf and link it up between Benny's neighborhood and us, we'd show Kelly we were right and Shades was wrong. We'll have a territory so big, we could write our own ticket. If Benny is connected, he'll be able to show his contacts that we know how to control turf. We'll make him and Kelly look good and they'll thank us for it."

"But Shades is too tight with Kelly. He's one of the originals."

"He can be replaced with someone we can control if we show him up."

"And Johnny?"

"He's my buddy. After everything goes down, I'll be able to convince him to throw in with us."

"I know the guys've been itchin' for a fight," Blackie said. "We gotta bust out sooner or later." He stroked his short silky hair. "Okay, what's the play?"

"You pick about four or five of the best guys and go into Sinners' turf. No jackets. Anybody you pick, trade off with somebody else for the night if they're wearing a Vandal jacket. You try to stay in the background. They might recognize you from the dance. See where they hang out. How many places. Where the most of them are concentrated. Where we would be able to hit with the most force and really hurt them."

"What if they jump us?"

"If you gotta defend yourself, what can you do? Right? That's why you gotta pick the best guys to go with you."

"Gotcha."

"I'll see you later. Or tomorrow," Sonny said. "I might split early."

Blackie waved then headed for the crowd. He faded among them and, five minutes later, emerged with his hand picked patrol. They crossed the schoolyard and turned in the direction of Sinners' turf. Sonny watched them shoving and jumping on each other. They were full of energy and ready to release it.

Sonny walked along the fence that overlooked the gradually descending back street and noticed that Kelly, Shades and Johnny were gone. Maybe they had gone off to plot against him. They were his friends but now with the idea of money driving a wedge between them, he wondered if there was still a friendship. It was a shame, but if that's the way they wanted it, he could forget about the friendship, too.

He decided to start campaigning. He would begin to build on his base of supporters. As far as the troops knew, they were close to some action with the Sinners, and Sonny would do nothing to change that assumption. He would try his best to fortify it. He would use his popularity to buttonhole as many guys as he could. He spent the rest of the evening joking, drinking and listening to Alan Freed retaliate against the Daily News for their articles blasting rock and roll. He would cheer with the rest of the crowd each time the DJ made a point. He would score points with whomever he could.

Neither Kelly nor Shades or Blackie's patrol returned. Sonny would have to wait until the following morning for both Blackie's report and to find if any repercussions might grow from the mission. And then there was part two with Sharon.

CHAPTER 14

Sonny overslept. Either the liquor or the satisfaction that he had scored with the troops the night before had put him into such a relaxed state that he didn't wake until nine-thirty. There was no hangover. He kept himself in good shape and it helped him to ward off any consequences that were associated with good times. He rolled over and stared at the round travel clock on the bed stand. It took him a few seconds before he related the time to the ten o'clock appointment with Sharon. He leaped up and stubbed his toe on the dumbbell that had rolled out of the corner overnight. He dressed quickly, cursing himself for not setting the alarm.

His mother had already departed for a day-trip and had left him a usual, substantial allowance on the kitchen table.

The weather was warm and perfect, and so was Sharon. The tight sleeveless aqua pullover and black toreador pants showed off her body warmly and perfectly. She wore the same gold crescent earrings she had on the night before.

"Hi," she said. "Right on time."

He took her hand and she pulled herself to him. She kissed him, then stepped back.

"You look great," Sonny said. "Nice combo. Vandal colors."

"Just for you. What're we gonna do?"

"Would you mind if we stop by Bill's? I've got something important to find out."

She took another step back. "I told you last night, I'd rather not go there right away."

"Why? I'm sure there's a lot of people who would like to see you again."

"I really didn't get along with some of the Debs. You know,

rivalries over the same guy. Stuff like that."

"Okay." Sonny raised his hands in front of him. "I won't push you."

"Thanks. I knew you'd be understanding."

"I haven't eaten since four o'clock yesterday. How about breakfast for starters?"

"Sounds good."

They found a diner on Broadway and reminisced about old times at Bill's while they ate. Sonny was cautious not to seem like he was pumping her for information. He wanted to see more of her and made things as pleasant as he could. He knew he could eventually extract her knowledge of the Sinners once they became more comfortable with each other.

"Did you find your sister last night?" Sonny asked as they left the diner.

"Yeah, the little brat was home all the while. She said she didn't feel good."

"So if you hadn't shown up looking for her at the dance, we wouldn't have met."

"That's right. Isn't it crazy how things work?"

"I guess it was destiny," he said.

"Definitely." She wrapped her arm around his waist and he draped his hand over her shoulder. "What's next?" she asked.

"You sure you don't want to go to Bill's?"

"I'm sure," she said.

"Okay, give me a minute to make a call." He broke away from her and stepped into the telephone booth at the curb. He got a busy signal, and hung up. He turned to leave the booth and bumped into Sharon.

"Hey, sorry," he said. "I didn't know you were right behind me."

She seemed tense for the moment but then stepped back and smiled. "I just wanted to stay close to you," she said. "No answer?"

"Busy. I'll try later."

"Why don't we go into the city," Sharon said.

"Manhattan?"

"Yeah. Times Square or Central Park."

"I go to school in Manhattan. And I was born there," he said.

"Come on. I haven't been in there for months. Please." She hugged him. "I need a change of scenery. Just me and you doing something different."

He thought about it and it didn't sound bad. It would be different to show her around.

"Let's go," Sonny said.

They caught the Flushing to Times Square express at Seventy-Fourth Street and were standing on the corner of Eight Avenue and Forty-Second Street by early afternoon. Sonny showed her the flea circus, wax museum, penny arcades and the novelty shops that flavored the district.

His old neighborhood was nearby and he took her on a tour of the blocks of tenements, pointing out landmarks that were historic to his life. He introduced her to an occasional acquaintance before the nostalgia wore off and he realized that the occasional acquaintance was all that was left. His old neighborhood had become a burial ground from crime, despair and a new sneaking menace, drugs. He wasn't a religious person but took a quick silent moment to thank God for his good life. He hoped that the Vandals could survive any spill over that would surely, with time, spread into their neighborhood.

"I should try Bill's again," Sonny said. His relationship with the Vandals suddenly loomed paramount after seeing, what was to him, the collapse of a civilization.

"I gotta find a phone," Sonny said as they crossed Thirty-Ninth Street back to Eighth Avenue.

"Can't it wait?" Sharon asked.

"No. I gotta know what happened last night."

"Last night?"

"Nothing much. Just some club business."

"I don't wanna share you today," she said. "I saw the look on your face when you found out all the things that happened to the people you used to know." She rubbed her head against his shoulder. "You care about people. You could love someone very easily."

"Like who?"

"Like me. I need someone like you. I want you." She stopped and turned to him. They kissed and clung together for minutes.

"I want all of you," Sharon said after they broke away. "Now."

"You wanna head for home?" he asked.

"That's too far away. Isn't there anywhere we can go now?"

"Nowhere around here. The closest place we can find some privacy is the park, but that's about a mile away."

"Closer than home."

Sonny looked into her eyes and he knew she was serious. He knew the look was special, something more than a passing moment. He put his arm around her and they headed north on Eighth Avenue.

It took twenty minutes to reach Columbus Circle. They passed the monument and entered the park. The spring day had brought out scores of strollers, ball players and other lovers. Sonny found a secluded grassy knoll hidden by a rock formation. He had remembered the spot and, luckily, no one else had discovered it today. Sonny had spent most of the day with his jacket hung loosely over one shoulder. He swung it off and spread it on the grass so he and Sharon could lean on it side by side. He unrolled the pack of Luckies from his T-shirt sleeve and they lit up. They finished their cigarettes and began fumbling with each other's clothes. In his impatience, Sonny groped with her bra and it snapped against her back. She yelped and they both looked over their shoulders, hoping that no one had heard. They laughed and then continued from where they had left off.

Their bodies intertwined in passion, and when they were both satisfied, they still clung together for a few lingering minutes. Even after they rearranged themselves, they lay silent and still, savoring the experience. Sonny knew that this was the girl for him. He didn't care that she wasn't a virgin. She had shown him that he was what mattered to her now. They small-talked for a half-hour and then left.

Sonny walked Sharon passed his high school before they decided to head back to Queens. He tried to use his school pass to enter the subway. He told the change booth clerk he had been in school on a Saturday for a special project. The clerk told him that the pass was only valid on weekdays, and made a special effort to watch Sonny deposit the correct change in the turnstile slot.

It was twilight when they reached their station in Queens.

"I have to show up at home for dinner," Sharon said. "I'll try to get out later."

"Try?" Sonny said. "It's Saturday night. You gotta get out."

"I don't know. My father's been a pain in the ass since mom died."

"I'll talk to him for you. Let me walk you home."

"Oh, God, no." She slid her hands inside his jacket and hugged him. "You'd get me into a pile of trouble."

"At least let me walk you home. I don't even know where you live."

She was silent for a moment. Her head was pressed against his chest. "Okay," she said. "But only to the beginning of the block. I can't risk him looking out the window and seeing you. He'd start trouble."

"You gotta try to get out. Sneak out if it's the only way. Tell him you're gonna keep an eye on your sister. *Anything*. I'll wait for you."

"I'll try. But it'll take awhile. If I can get out, I'll meet you by the butcher shop again."

"Jeez, I should get a job there," Sonny tried to joke. "Then I could have you waiting for me every time I got off work."

"How about nine o'clock?" Sharon asked.

"Yeah," he said. "I'll be there."

Her block consisted of similar apartment buildings. Sonny stood by his promise and planted himself out of sight near the corner. He watched Sharon disappear through the front entrance of a building in the middle of the block.

He lit up a cigarette and kept his focus on Sharon's building, thinking that she might reappear. Maybe she would get into a fight with her father and stomp out in anger. He continued his vigil until he finished the cigarette, all the time feeling uneasy. Something just didn't seem right. He wanted to be with her but he had to clear things in his mind. Then again, maybe he was becoming too suspicious, not only of Sharon but also of everyone.

"What the hell am I doing here?" he asked. He shook off the bad feeling and, after one last look at Sharon's building, headed toward his own neighborhood. There were too many things to find out at home base, too many things to work out.

CHAPTER 15

Sonny was back in Vandal territory in ten minutes. He didn't encounter a Sinner during his short trip along the back streets of their common border. Maybe something had happened during his absence. He was sure of it when he reached the schoolyard. *No music.* The silence lent a somber mood to the gathering of Vandals that hid themselves in the angles of darkness across the rear sector.

Sonny was halfway across the schoolyard when Blackie and Freddy The Hat broke from the crowd and approached him.

"Man, where you been?" Freddy asked.

"Buzz off," Blackie said. "I'll fill him in."

Freddy stopped as Blackie passed him and motioned for Sonny to turn around. Sonny fell into step with Blackie as they headed back toward the Woodside Avenue gate.

"The little bastards hit us this afternoon," Blackie said.

"What? How come?"

"Probably 'cause of last night."

"You mean because I decked that guy?"

"That and what happened later."

"Wait. Start from the beginning."

They passed through the gateway and crossed Woodside Avenue.

"Me and the guys were scoutin' Sinners' turf like you asked and we got a little too close to one of their candy stores."

"Yeah?"

"Two of them started smart-mouthin' us like we was regular citizens. When one'a them said Monk looked like a fruitcake, he popped the son of a bitch in the mouth. The other one ran in and got about six other guys. We held them off before they could get out the door.

"Then me and Crazy Lenny grabbed the guy that Monk decked and stomped his face into the sidewalk while Monk and the Looney Brothers held the rest inside with their garrison belts. We split before they could regroup. We headed to a movie to hide out in case the cops started lookin' for us."

"So what happened today?" Sonny asked. "Wait. How'd they know who you were? You didn't wear jackets, did you?"

"No. They didn't know who we was before stupid Monk used one'a the cards he made up in his printin' class in school. They say 'Compliments of the Vandals'. He stuffed one in the pocket of the kid we stomped. He didn't tell me 'til later."

"Oh great," Sonny said. "Advertisement." He had helped instigate an incident, but he wasn't going to take the credit. All he had to do to cover his tracks was to console Blackie for the poor judgement of one of his charges. "Well, what the hell can you do? It wasn't your fault."

"Anyway," Blackie said. "About twenty or thirty of the Sinners and Assassins come rollin' down the block this afternoon."

"The Assassins? Shit, I didn't think they'd get into it."

"They were there. They caught five of our guys in the schoolyard and swarmed all over them. They broke Johnny's leg."

"What? Damn, how is he?"

"Last we heard he was still at the hospital."

"How about the other guys?"

"Bloody noses. Split lips and stuff. Johnny got the worst. They hit and ran. Most of our guys were at Bill's when it happened. The punks were gone before we found out about it."

"So what's happening?" Sonny asked as they reached Bill's. He hadn't counted on problems with the Assassins. *And why the hell did something have to happen to Johnny?*

"Kelly'll tell ya." Blackie motioned to the library annex.

Kelly, Shades and four other Vandals were bunched into the

niche of the storefront. Kelly stepped out and waved for Sonny and Blackie to follow him to the corner.

"Remember that chick, Sharon, you was with, who used to hang out with us?" Blackie asked.

"Yeah?"

"I saw her in the Sinners' candy store."

"Nah, it couldn't be. It was probably her kid sister. She hangs out with them."

"Yeah, I guess. I only got a glimpse, but they sure look a lot alike."

The four officers formed a circle under the street light.

"You heard?" Kelly asked Sonny.

"Most of it. How's Johnny?"

"He's in a cast. He should be home by now. I had Eddie Comanche take him and stay with him until everything was taken care of."

"Where were you all day?" Shades asked.

"I had to go into Manhattan to take care of something," Sonny said. He wanted to ask what business it was of Shades' but held back.

"We didn't have time for formalities," Kelly said. "No war councils or declarations. I want this over with fast. I contacted Benny. He's sending three carloads of his Heights crew into Sinners' turf to clean house. When they see different faces and figure out we've got more troops then they thought, they should ask for a truce.

"In the meantime, our guys will visit the Assassins. I don't think they're as strong as they were or they would have kept coming this afternoon and hit Bill's after the schoolyard. From what I heard from Johnny and the other guys, the Assassins didn't take much part in the actual fighting. They were probably there for moral support."

"Looks like you did my job for me," Sonny said.

"Somebody had to," Shades said.

"That's uncalled for," Sonny said. "You know I'd been there if I could."

"Take a walk, Shades," Kelly said. "Blackie, you and Shades get everyone up to the schoolyard. Stay in the dark behind the handball wall. *And no noise.* I have some last minute things to talk over with Sonny."

Blackie and Shades called to the Vandals at the library annex and they followed toward the schoolyard.

"Forget about Shades," Kelly said. "He's a little edgy. He's scared that everything's gonna turn to shit if we let this get out of control. We know you'd have been there."

"Not only would I have been there, I'd have taken Johnny's broken leg for him. Who knew anything like that was gonna happen?"

"You didn't help things by what you did last night."

"What do you mean?"

"Sending Blackie was dangerous enough, but giving him Crazy Lenny, Monk and the Looney Brothers was asking for trouble."

"I'm sorry, I didn't know who he was taking with him."

Sonny stared down at Kelly, who was a head shorter than him. After a moment he knew he couldn't fool Kelly or himself any longer. But what did it matter? He was on the outs with Kelly and Shades already, and maybe even Johnny now.

"What's done is done," Kelly said after a long silence. "But we've got to finish it tonight. I don't have my diplomat to advise me so we may have to do it your way. What do you know about the Assassins?"

"Their hangout in good weather is in an alley behind a string of stores on Roosevelt Avenue," Sonny said. He had gathered intelligence on most of the gangs in Queens and could give a full report on any one. "One of their families owns a luncheonette that the alley is behind. The Assassins hang out in the luncheonette, the back room, where they got a pool table and stuff, or in the alley. They got outdoor lights and beach chairs, and I hear it's a constant private block party. The only outside entrance to the dead end alley is a locked heavy wooden gate. And the entrance to the back room and alley are always guarded."

"So surprise is out," Kelly said.

"Pretty much. And even if we got through, I hear they have a piece or two hidden in the back room."

Kelly was silent. He was putting together his strategy before turning over the job of tactics to Sonny.

"I know you were always against us having guns," Sonny said. "But if they have some, we won't have a chance. I could pick some up easy."

"Forget it," Kelly said. "No guns. They're trouble. We'd never get the cops off our backs." He hesitated. "The cops should start their rounds soon. We better get moving."

"I'll bet some of Benny's guys pack when they have to," Sonny said.

"He runs things his way over there." Kelly pointed both index fingers at the ground. "Here we stay clean."

"Okay. Sorry I mentioned it."

"Yeah." Kelly glanced through the glass front door of Bill's to be sure there were no stragglers, then headed for the schoolyard with Sonny at his side.

"A hit and run raid, like they pulled, isn't going to solve anything," Kelly said. "I gotta talk to Bruno, and convince him that we mean business. I don't think he even knew his guys were going to back up the Sinners. It was probably a few hot heads trying to protect their little brothers. He'll have to talk to his guys and the Sinners."

"But what about what they did to Johnny?"

"After Benny takes a tour of Sinners' turf, we'll be more than even."

"But all our guys are itching for action. They'll go ape shit if they don't let it out."

"They'll be on stand-by in case Bruno decides to back his guys and we need some hard convincing. If we don't need them against the Assassins, they can hit the Sinners and clean up after Benny."

"How do you wanna play it?"

"I'll take Shades and Blackie with me into the luncheonette." Kelly held up his hand in anticipation of Sonny's protest. "I need you as my field commander. I can't let Blackie lead forty guys. A guy like him can't control himself, no less an unruly mob. I need a guy like him to cover our ass in case I'm wrong."

"How am I gonna know what's going on?"

"A signal. You and the troops hide yourselves in doorways, down side streets, whatever. Once we're inside, I'll talk to Bruno. If he agrees to a truce, I'll send Blackie to the door. You take everyone and head for Sinners' turf. If Shades comes to the door, you line up everyone across the street and be ready to storm the place."

"You think he'll listen to reason?"

Kelly nodded. "I'll convince him."

"Too bad. We could probably take out the Assassins and the Sinners in one shot."

"Not necessary. I'll let Bruno know what's happening to the Sinners. He'll get the idea. I don't think he'll want to carry this on anymore than I do. He'll be our spokesman like he was one of us."

Sonny put together his own strategy. He would have control of the Vandals for most of the night. It was like Kelly was giving him a platform that would put Sonny in the limelight. Did Kelly finally slip? The only guy the Vandals would be listening to would be Sonny, *and with Kelly's wishes.*

When they reached the schoolyard, Kelly said, "Word is you have a thing going with Sharon Norris."

Sonny felt a shock travel through his body. "What's the problem?" he asked.

"She's trouble."

"Since when do we tell each other who we can go out with?"

"Since never. I just have a bad feeling about her. She screwed up a lot of guy's heads when she hung out with us. She disappears for six months and all of a sudden shows up with the Sinners." They stopped at the entrance to the schoolyard. "I know what she's like," Kelly said. "She'll give you grief."

"Bullshit." Sonny drew his body taller. "People don't understand what she's really like. She hangs out with the Sinners to look after her kid sister. She's had some bad breaks."

"I just don't want you getting screwed. Poor choice of words." Kelly looked at Sonny for a reaction. "You know what I mean. Just advice."

Sonny smiled, knowing he couldn't fence with Kelly. He would just break it off and leave Kelly with the impression that he was considering the advice. "Let me see what happens, okay?" he asked.

Kelly didn't answer. Sonny let it drop.

They joined the silent milling mob of Vandals hidden behind the fifteen-foot cement handball wall out of the view of Woodside Avenue.

There were no pep talks. Only cold calculations were needed. Sonny drew up a quick plan for the invasion. The standard procedure for movement was put into action. They moved out in groups of five at a few minute intervals. They were told to find scattered positions in stores or on side streets around the Assassin headquarters on Roosevelt Avenue and wait for the signal. They would get blood, either Assassin or Sinner, and everyone would be satisfied for the night.

Sonny took Jimmy and Speedo aside after the first groups had moved out.

"I want you two guys to scout into Sinners' turf," Sonny said. "You guys know how to keep your heads. Don't get into any hassles. Just look. Check out what's happening. Meet me at the corner of Roosevelt and Eighty-Third at nine sharp. Let me know where Benny's guys hit, how many Sinners are still around and where they're concentrated." He slapped them on their backs. "Be my eyes until I get there."

Jimmy and Speedo seemed relieved. They liked the stealth assignment. They wouldn't have to prove themselves in front of everyone, and from what had been said, Benny's crew was going to devastate Sinners' turf. There wouldn't be much left to do once Sonny and the others stormed into the area. They would have the glory of being the first of the Woodside Vandals in Sinners' territory that night without lifting a fist in anger. They could brag about this night for months to come.

CHAPTER 16

Sonny reached Roosevelt Avenue with the last group and, after he was certain everyone was positioned correctly, gave the signal to Kelly. He stationed himself with four Vandals inside the double glass doors of a Woolworth's store. It was on a diagonal corner from the luncheonette.

Kelly, Shades and Blackie talked their way passed the two Assassin guards at the front door. The guards' tunnel vision had no perception of the maneuvering taking place around them. The stores on their block and the adjacent streets had slowly filled with new customers, some wearing aqua and black jackets. *But why not?* It was Saturday night and a lot of people shopped on a Saturday night.

Sonny assumed that Bruno was inside or Kelly wouldn't have bothered entering. The Vandal officers sat at a rear booth with three Assassins and disappeared behind the lower blackout of the front windows and the high backs of the booth seats.

Sonny had to make this night count. He didn't feel comfortable with himself but he had to seize the moment. He had to fire up the troops and lead them into a battle that they would never forget. He didn't want it to happen this fast but there it was, dropped into his lap by a string of events. He was going to be the president of the Vandals or be nobody.

If Sonny could forsake friendship toward Kelly and Shades, he couldn't bring himself to do the same with Johnny. They were too close. They had known each other before there were Vandals. He would keep Johnny as vice-president - that went without saying - or maybe even ask him to share the top spot, like those South

American countries - a junta or something like that. The Vandals liked Johnny. He would be a definite asset to Sonny's plans.

The el train rumbled out of the Sixty-First Street station and began to pick up momentum as it passed above the stores. Falling sparks from the tracks broke through Sonny's deep calculating thoughts. For an instant he thought a gun had been fired across the street and his grip on the plastic puzzle in his hand tightened, snapping the corner.

"Why did you do that? You're going to have to pay for it."

"What?" Sonny turned his head to the saleswoman standing behind the counter, her owl-like brown eyes magnified by her thick horn-rimmed glasses.

"You'll have to pay for that." She pointed to the broken puzzle in Sonny's hand.

"This?" Sonny lifted the plastic game in front of him. "It's a piece of junk. It fell apart in my hand."

"I'll have to call the assistant manager."

Sonny glanced toward the luncheonette. Blackie was standing in front talking to the Assassin guards. It was as though he had appeared from nowhere within the few seconds Sonny's attention had been diverted. *Move out against the Sinners.* Blackie was the signal to get the Sinners.

Sonny pulled a half-dollar from his pocket and flipped it to the saleswoman.

"Keep the friggen change, lady." He waved to the four Vandals spotted around the store. They followed him out the door and toward the el station as planned. Within two blocks, there were sixteen Vandals trailing Sonny, spread along both sides of the street trying to appear like they weren't together.

The group met on a wide landing, one flight from the top of the stairs. The Looney Brothers - their real family name was Cloony - paid their way through the turnstile like good citizens. The others waited; leaning along the railings that overlooked the traffic in the street below.

Sonny surprised himself at his poise. Even with what was about to happen, he retained his patience and kept everyone in line with his soft-spoken encouragement and words of coming glory. Maybe he had the abilities of leadership all along.

Sonny heard the distant rumble of an approaching train. The vibrations on the tracks above them grew stronger as the train drew closer. A loud, shrill whistle rang from the platform above. It was the signal from the Looneys. It was their train, the local.

Everyone made ready and when the second whistle came, as the train roared into the station, they sprang forward. They slammed the wooden gates aside or leaped over the turnstiles, their assault so swift that the change-booth clerk shouted his protest only after the last Vandal had cleared the area and was on the steps leading to the train platform.

The Looneys were at two of the doorways of the steel-gray subway car, their bodies pressed against the open rubber stripped doors. The Vandals stormed into the cars and the Looneys let the doors slide closed. The train pulled out of the station with a hum before the clatter of its wheels overpowered the engine noise along the open rails.

Seventeen people for thirty cents. *Now that was thrifty. Let Shades top that.* Sonny laughed and joined in the slapping of backs and handshakes.

The Seventy-Fourth Street Station was the second stop. Everyone wished each other well as half the Vandals got off and headed for the stairs. Sonny was using Red's old pincer movement tactic. One strike was starting at Seventy-Forth Street and would sweep south of Roosevelt Avenue. The second would start at Eighty-Second and cover the north side. The last and largest group, which had started on foot when Blackie appeared in the luncheonette doorway, would spread out from several directions to cut off escape or be used as reserves.

The Eighty-Second Street station platform loomed ahead as soon as the train left its last stop. The doors slid open and the remaining nine Vandals were quickly on the street. Sonny led his team down Roosevelt Avenue and found Jimmy and Speedo waiting on Eighty-Third, ten minutes early.

"Man, what a massacre," Speedo shouted. "They clobbered 'em. There's nobody left to take care of."

"You're kidding," Sonny said. "There's gotta be somebody to hit."

"Nobody," Jimmy said. "Whoever didn't get caught must have spread the word. There isn't a Sinner left on the streets."

"There's gotta be," Sonny said. "Come on. I'll drag them out of their houses if I have to."

Sonny stomped up Eighty-Third Street. His followers tried to keep pace with him. "Fill me in on what you saw," he said to Jimmy and Speedo.

"We were two blocks from the Sinners' headquarters when a carload of Benny's guys goes by us," Speedo said. "When we caught up to them at the candy store, they had five Sinners lined up against the wall in the alley next to the store like they had 'em facing a firing squad.

"Another car pulls up and Benny and about six or seven other guys join in. We stood across the street and watched. Benny starts slappin' around the guys against the wall and then he takes one guy's head and starts smashin' it against the wall, all the time yellin' for the kid to tell him where the rest of the Sinners were.

"One of the kids mentions the schoolyard off Thirty-Seventh Avenue and another candy store on Broadway. Benny and his guys beat the piss out'a the five kids. They turned one guy upside down and bounced his head against the sidewalk until he passed out."

"When we got to the candy store on Broadway," Jimmy said, "Benny's guys had already been there. There was blood on the sidewalk. The only people we saw were two Sinners sitting on the curb, crying. We couldn't believe it.

"It was still only a little after eight, so we headed for the Sinners' schoolyard. When we got there, we saw one of Benny's cars on the sidewalk blocking the gate. It was too dark in the schoolyard for us to see anything so we found an apartment building across the street with the front door unlocked. We went up to the roof and we saw Benny's guys using baseball bats and pipes on about ten Sinners. Another of Benny's cars was blocking the gate on the far street."

"We stayed on the roof after Benny and his guys left," Speedo said. "We watched the Sinners stagger out of the schoolyard a couple at a time. You could tell they were hurtin'. Two of them had their Sinners' jackets slashed to shreds while they were still wearing them. The jackets were just strips hangin' on their backs. After the schoolyard cleared out, we headed for the meetin' with you. We didn't see anymore Sinners north of Roosevelt Avenue."

"There's gotta be some around," Sonny said. *Did Kelly know this was going to happen?* Did he send Sonny on this mission to make him look like a jerk? "What about the two cry babies?" Sonny asked. "We could find out from them if there's another hangout. Maybe there's some secret place they go to, like not one of their usual spots."

No one answered. From what Jimmy and Speedo had said, it sounded like Sonny had no chance of finding the Sinners. They would go along with Sonny but knew that the action was over for the night. Benny had shut them out of the game.

"That's the place we saw the kids cryin'," Speedo said pointing to a corner candy store.

Sonny flung open the front door. He glared at the tiny white-haired woman behind the counter before continuing along the long narrow bare wood-planked aisle between the racks of musty smelling magazines and the stool lined counter. There were three girls, in dungarees and colorful blouses, sitting at the rear of the counter. They seemed to range in age from fourteen to sixteen.

"You hang around with the Sinners?" Sonny asked.

"I don't want no more trouble in here tonight," the woman behind the counter shouted. "This time I call the police."

Sonny pushed aside his frustration and anger. He realized he had to shift to a new plan. If he couldn't find them, then he would take what they left behind.

"No trouble, ma'am," Sonny said holding his hands in front of him. "We're just here to talk." Sonny pulled a ten-dollar bill from his pocket and tossed it on the white countertop. "Buy everyone a soda." He gestured to the Vandals lined up single file behind him and then to the girls.

"Like I said, are you Sinners' girls?" he asked.

"We know them pretty good," The girl closest to Sonny said. She had blond hair tied back into a ponytail with a blue ribbon.

"Were you here when the trouble happened?" Sonny asked.

"No. When we got here only Pauly and Joe were around. They told us you guys came in and dragged them and two more of the guys outside."

"Not us guys," Sonny said. "They were from our clique, but we're here to see that it doesn't happen again."

"What'a you mean?"

"Well, we're taking over this store. This ain't the Sinners' turf anymore. That way we can protect anybody who hangs out here. Understand?"

"Who cares who hangs out here," the dark-haired girl closest to the wall said. "At least you guys ain't cheapskates."

Sonny smiled. "You got that right, honey. We got the bucks and we got the might." He spun on his stool to show them the back of his jacket, then spun back to face them. "Remember the name. Vandals. This is now Vandal turf."

"We saw you guys at the dance yesterday."

"Remember the big ape that got decked?" Sonny asked.

"Ralphy? Yeah, that was something."

"My name is Sonny and I was the guy who decked him."

"Wow."

The lady behind the counter placed two glasses of Coke in front of the girls.

"I'll have a cherry lime rickey," the blond ordered.

"Nothing for me," Sonny said waving the woman off. "You know where I can find any of the Sinners now?"

"Most of them hang out at Leo's candy store on Hampton

Street or at the schoolyard on Thirty-Seventh Avenue," the dark-haired girl said.

"Yeah, I know. But none of them are at those places now. Is there anywhere else I can find them?"

"That's about it," the blond said. "Not many of them even hang out here. They're mostly at the other two places."

"Can you girls do me a favor?" Sonny asked. "Can you pass the word through the neighborhood about us? Tell everyone that we took over this store. Anybody who wants to join up with us is welcome. No hassles. No problems. Okay?"

They all nodded. Sonny stood up as the woman returned with his change, placing a five-dollar bill, two singles and some coins onto the counter top. He folded the two singles and stuffed them into his pants pocket.

"Speedo. Listen, I want you and five of the guys to stick around here for awhile. Introduce yourself to the chicks. Use my change to butter up the old lady and the girls. Make yourselves at home. If any of the Sinners happen to show up, don't start with them. Just tell them we're claiming this part of their turf as ours. If they don't like it, tell them they'll get more of what happened tonight. Call Bill's if you think you'll have trouble. Got it?"

Speedo glanced at the money on the counter. "Sure. Who you leavin' with me?"

Sonny looked down the line of Vandals seated on the counter stools. "The Looneys, Vinny, Billy Ryan and Tony. I'll take the rest with me. See you later or tomorrow." He slapped Speedo on the arm. "Be cool. I don't think you'll have any problems."

"Not from what I seen tonight."

Sonny started for the door. Speedo called out the names of the Vandals who were to stay and directed the rest to follow Sonny. The crew still under Sonny's direct command followed the seemingly disoriented war counselor onto the sidewalk.

"You okay?" Jimmy asked.

"What? Oh. Yeah, I'm okay."

Sonny pointed. "This is our turf now, Jimmy. As far as we can see from this spot belongs to us. Write down what happened when you get home. This is the beginning of a new era for us. You can use what happened tonight in your book."

"That's great, man." Jimmy didn't want to appear patronizing. He knew what it was like to be confused. His gaze followed Sonny's sweeping arm and picked up the eight Vandals of the other half of the pincer. "Here comes Freddy The Hat's group," Jimmy said.

"Good. Maybe they found some Sinners."

"You get any of them?" Freddy asked.

"There aren't any around," Jimmy said.

"We didn't see any of them either," Freddy said.

"Let's check out their headquarters," Sonny said quietly. "If there isn't anyone there, we might as well head for home."

Jimmy briefed Freddy as they followed Sonny's now slower pace for the four-block walk to Leo's candy store. The store was empty except for a middle-aged couple at the counter. The confectionery cases and tiled floor was similar to the neat, scrubbed look of Bill's.

They linked up with the last two groups a block later. They were also thinned out when their search for the Sinners had proven fruitless. Not a sign of the Sinners, so most of the guys had headed home from boredom. The high they had built up from anticipation of battle was long gone.

A block later, two of the defectors, Monk and Chico, rounded the corner in a full trot. Sonny perked for a moment. Maybe they had found the elusive Sinners.

"Stay away from Woodside Avenue," Chico said. "There's cops all over the place. It's like they were expecting something to happen on our turf."

"Man, every cop in the hundred-tenth precinct must be there," Monk said.

"That's why there weren't any around here," Sonny said. "Not even a sector car. Not one bull. What the hell is going on tonight?"

"Maybe somebody tipped the cops," Chico said. "That's what

it looked like."

"But that don't make sense. Why would they tip them off about the wrong neighborhood?" Sonny hesitated, then answered his own question. "Unless it was to pull them away from where the action was really going down."

"I'll bet it was Benny," Freddy said.

"Or Kelly," Monk said.

"Whoever it was made sure whatever happened over here would go off as planned," Sonny said. "Nice of them to let us in on it. Did anyone see Kelly or Blackie after we left the Assassins' hang-out?"

"No," Chico said. "We saw them and Shades outside the place but they waved us on to head into Sinners' turf."

"I'd like to find out what happened at that meeting," Sonny said.

"Well, that kills the night," Freddy said. "Why don't we camp out at the Sinners' candy store?"

"It's our store," Sonny shouted. "It's our store and our turf. If there's any of them left they can have the other side of Eighty-Second Street south of Roosevelt. The rest is ours."

"Is that what Kelly wants?" Monk asked.

"It doesn't matter what Kelly wants," Sonny said. "He put me in charge of this operation and I'm claiming this territory even if I have to control it myself."

"But Benny is the one that beat them," Freddy said. "We didn't get to do shit."

"That was tonight. If we claim their turf, it'll force them to either come out and fight us to get it back or punk out." Sonny paused. "Look, you guys wanted action. You got cheated out of it. Maybe it was a coincidence or maybe Kelly planned it this way. But either way, you guys should have been part of this victory. You stick with me and we'll make our own victories even if we gatta do it on our own."

"I think we better check with Kelly first," Chico said.

"Fuck Kelly." Sonny even shocked himself at his outburst. "Hey,

I didn't mean it that way." Sonny waved his hand in front of him. "I mean he put me in charge of this show. I should be making the decisions to make it work." He bowed his head momentarily. "Look, we're a little disappointed. Why don't we call it a night? I left some of the guys at our new candy store. Why don't you go check the place out. There were some chicks there. Don't go in as a mob. You'll spook the old lady that owns the place."

"Sounds okay," Monk said.

"Sure, a change of scenery," Freddy said.

"Okay guys, have fun. I've got something to check out on my own."

Sonny waved and darted away, this time in retreat. His pace was a message that he wanted no company; no one to interfere with his thoughts.

It was probably too late, but he now thought of Sharon. Maybe she could bring him out of his misery. She had said nine o'clock and it was now ten-thirty. If she really loved him, she would wait forever. He hoped she was waiting, to comfort him, to make things better. *Hadn't he gone to bat for her with Kelly? Hadn't he stuck up for her because he knew what she was really like?*

The quiet street corner surrounding the butcher shop was empty. The street lamp cast a large circle of light along the sidewalk and curb, like it was emphasizing a point. *This was the spot you were supposed to be at nine o'clock.* But instead you blew it on a gamble to be a big shot. She said it was a reason you never got together with her in the past. Maybe it was time to re-evaluate things. It was the worst night of his life.

Suddenly, Sharon stepped from the dark recess of the butcher shop entrance and into the circle of light. His depression shattered. He needed her softness. He needed to wrap himself around her and be consumed by the tenderness.

"How long have you been here?" He asked as he slid into her open arms.

"About an hour," she whispered. "I was too scared to stay around my neighborhood when my sister told me what happened."

"They weren't from Bill's," Sonny said. "By the time we got there, it was over." He squeezed her tighter. "Nothing happened to you or your sister, did it?"

"No. She got away from the first place they hit and came home and told me about it. I didn't know what was going on. I mean, whether you were involved or what. It was terrible. The way she described it."

"Don't worry. It's over. They did what they had to and it's over. But I don't know if the Vandals won or Benny won. I got screwed."

"How?" Sharon pulled her upper body back from his grasp and looked into his eyes.

"I don't know if it was Kelly, Shades or Benny, but I was put in charge of a wild goose chase."

"Why don't you quit? You don't need Bill's. You can walk and take half the Vandals with you." Her eyes flashed and glinted in the street light. "The Sinners are through after tonight. My sister can set you up with what's left of them. Between them and the Vandals you take with you, you can form your own gang."

It was like she had read his mind. Like his game plan had been photographed by one of those tiny spy cameras and passed to her. She was on the ball, maybe more so than Sonny was. She was thinking the way he should be thinking.

"What do you think I should do?" He had been taken by her grasp of things. He relaxed and let her think for him. He tried to keep his own thoughts and maintain a limited feeling of control, but he would let her put the plan into words.

"The Sinners are going to be scattered for the next week. I'll ask my sister to arrange a meeting. How about at the dance next Friday?"

"Perfect. I was planning on going anyway to see if any of them showed up."

"Okay, I'll tell her tomorrow when I see her."

"I should have asked those girls at the candy store if they knew her."

"What girls? You were talking with another girl?" She asked.

"What're you kidding?" He smiled, thinking she was joking.

"I want you for myself," she said. "You and I are going places and only us."

"Wait a minute," Sonny said. "Maybe we think alike when it comes to going to the top, but don't think that because I happen to talk to another girl I'm trying to make her."

"I'm sorry," she said. "I love you and I want all of you."

"Love?" Sonny lifted her chin with his index finger. "Are you sure?"

"I am." The hard expression from a few seconds ago melted into the tenderness Sonny had first expected.

"Then I am, too." His words weren't strong. They didn't have the same ring as she had put into her vow.

"Are you *sure*?"

"You know I am. I love you and you alone." They kissed and that passion of the afternoon was back. He was hooked and he didn't care.

They found a new mowed patch of grass behind an unlighted house a block away from the butcher shop, and Sonny used his jacket as he had done that afternoon. Twice in one day. He had never heard anyone brag about an experience like that. Not even lover-boy Val had ever hinted of such a triumph. But this wasn't something Sonny would swill around with the boys. This was the foundation of their love.

He walked her to the corner of her block. They agreed to meet the following day and he watched her disappear through the apartment entrance in the middle of the block. He headed for home. The night, as it turned out, had not been the complete disaster it might have been. The mental and physical stress of the evening had been released in a half-hour. It was a lot easier falling asleep knowing he had at least one ally.

CHAPTER 17

Sonny had only met Johnny's foster mother once before and he found that her nasty attitude hadn't changed.

"What's with you bums?" She asked Sonny, the fat on her meaty arms dangling and swaying with the motion of her flaying hands. Her large frame was crammed into the doorway. "You get his leg broken for him and then come around like nothing happened."

"Nobody got his leg broken," Sonny said. "It was an accident."

"Yeah, sure." She folded the heavy arms in front of her. "Well accidents cost money. Who's gonna pay for the hospital and doctor? *You*?"

"If I have to. Yeah, me and the other bums. What happens to Johnny means more to us than money."

"Maybe you'll be paying when the state and social services investigates how this happened." She pointed at Sonny. "And if they don't do anything, our lawyer will."

"Does this mean I can't see him?" Sonny asked.

"Get out of here!" She stepped back through the doorway and slammed the door shut. The crocheted off-white curtain on the inside of the glass panes billowed and then fell flat.

That takes care of any advice or support from Johnny. The room he shared with the other male foster kids was on the second floor in the rear. The house was surrounded by a six-foot cyclone fence, and to climb it on a Sunday morning would make Sonny as obvious as if he were to climb a church steeple. They wouldn't allow any phone calls to Johnny so he was out of the action for now.

Sonny had tried to call Blackie earlier but his phone had been disconnected for the umpteenth time. Sonny had hoped to pump Blackie about the meeting and have some lead on what Kelly and Shades had pulled, but now he would have to move on and confront the pair on the blind.

Sonny had passed Bill's before trying to see Johnny. It had been closed, but was now open on his return trip. Bill's wife was behind the counter, a heavy-set woman with a slight German accent. After scolding him, as a representative of the Vandals, for the notoriety and bad image that had been cast on her store by a police visit, she returned to her normal calm manner and told Sonny that none of the guys had been there yet. She returned to her scolding, saying she was mad enough to throw them all out or put a limit on their numbers. Sonny apologized; putting the blame on a few *bad apples* who shouldn't be allowed to hang around there.

Dolores and Karen were the only customers. They sat at the first table in the rear. They hadn't seen anyone since Saturday afternoon. Even Ginny hadn't been around all weekend. Dolores was informed by the telephone grapevine that the neighborhood was still hot and might be for a few more days. Sonny was sure of that and told the girls to let Kelly or Blackie know he could be found at a candy store on Broadway and Seventy-Sixth Street.

Sonny apologized to Bill's wife again as he left the store. This wasn't the first time the cops had chastised the storeowners for allowing the Vandals to headquarter there. It would blow over just as in the past.

Sonny took Roosevelt Avenue rather than cutting through the neighborhood. He wasn't in the mood to be harassed by some overzealous cop on a beefed-up patrol. And he wasn't going to hide his identity by removing his Vandal jacket.

He walked slowly, knowing he had plenty of time before his noon meeting with Sharon, and reached the candy store at ten.

He expected to find either an empty store or a sea of angry, unfamiliar faces. He peered through the grimy, streaked window and saw Speedo, Monk, The Looneys - about ten of the guys, like they had spent the last twelve hours frozen in time. And there were five girls.

"Holy shit," Sonny said. "I can't believe it."

Speedo had spotted Sonny and stepped outside to meet him. He was smiling. "They like it here," Speedo said. "I think you found us a new home."

"This is great." Sonny stared through the glass door in amazement. "You mean they'd rather hang out here than Bill's?"

"That's what I been hearing. After you left last night, some of the other guys came by and we started getting friendly with the girls. They brought some of their friends with them today. The guys feel we owe you an apology."

"Why?"

"About a half hour after you left, Blackie showed up. He heard about the place from some of the guys heading for home. He told us he was pissed off at the way Kelly and Shades handled things with the Assassins."

"Like what?"

"Like, they wouldn't let him sit in on the meeting. They had him camp out on the other side of the room and he couldn't hear what they were saying. But he said Kelly used the pay phone once and it was near the door he was standing guard at. He overheard some of what Kelly said."

"And?"

"Blackie says that Kelly called Benny and he was pretty sure he heard something about tipping the cops."

"So it was them."

"Now that the guys have had time to think about it, they're beginning to feel you were right to be suspicious. Besides, they still want a crack at the Sinners. They like your idea of using this place to bust their balls and maybe draw them out to take us on."

"Not yet. We can't do anything until Friday," Sonny said. "I'm arranging a meeting with the Sinners at the dance. Maybe we can work something out with them. If not, we'll have them in the open." Sonny shook his fist. "Then we got 'em."

"We're with you," Speedo said. "However you wanna handle things, we'll back you."

"Thanks, buddy. Where's Blackie? Anybody seen him today?"

"He said he'd get here by late morning. There'll probably be some more of the guys with him. They say the cops are gonna be watching Bill's and the schoolyard for a couple of days so they figure it's safer here."

"This may be just a passing thing."

"I don't think so," Speedo said. "They think it was getting too boring there. They needed a change and last night pushed them into it."

"You know this might cause a split."

"They don't seem to care. The way Blackie was talking, it sounds like Kelly and Shades were planning on splitting us up anyway."

"I don't know. I mean, what good could it do for them?" Sonny asked. Now that he was on the verge of accomplishing his goal, he was beginning to doubt his own rhetoric. Kelly had always been the perfect leader. Why should he change now?

But why worry about it. The split was now evident, so why not take advantage of the situation? Sonny's chance for leadership was at its peak. Just another little push from him and a helping hand from Blackie and it would be there. He would wait until he could discuss everything with Blackie.

"How's the old lady taking to the new faces?" Sonny motioned to the store with his head.

"She sees bucks being spent. She's happy." Speedo reached into his pocket. "Here. I had a buck and some change left over from last night."

Sonny waved him off. "Forget it. Spend it on the chicks."

"Thanks, man."

"If the Sinners completely disband, we should try to take over their other store. The girls called it Leo's. It's got more class than here."

Sonny looked passed the advertisement stickers on the glass door at the narrow, cluttered aisle. There would be nowhere near enough space to house all of them. He caught the attention of Monk and Crazy Lenny, who waved to him. He waved back. "But for now, this is home."

"We gotta start somewhere."

"Yeah, I guess so. Look, I've got something to take care of," Sonny said turning back to Speedo. "If Blackie gets here before I get back, tell him to wait. I'll be back soon."

"Will do."

Sonny lit up a cigarette and started down Broadway. He had to see Sharon now. He had to tell her the good news. He reached her block in ten minutes. He hadn't been any closer to her building than the corner and wasn't sure of the exact building. They all had the same look. It had to be one of three in the middle of the block. He decided to check the mailboxes.

The name, Norris, wasn't on any of the small tags. He tried the other two buildings with the same results. Could they be living with someone else? Under a different name? No. How would they get their mail?

I don't understand. I brought her home twice yesterday. She went into one of these buildings and didn't come out. *What the hell was going on? What kind of game was she playing?* His stomach churned. Sure, she could've let herself into the building and then gone out the rear door without him knowing.

Every time he decided to trust her and feel comfortable with her, something would pop up to throw the relationship into turmoil. And this was only within a weekend.

Sonny headed back to the candy store. His stomach was still churning and beginning to ache. Too much had happened since Friday night.

Blackie was standing next to Speedo outside the store when Sonny turned the corner a block away. They met him at the curb as he crossed the street and Blackie shook his hand.

"You were right, man," Blackie said. "They're tryin' to pull some shit on us."

"I heard." Sonny tilted his head toward Speedo. "So what're we gonna do about it?"

"We're gonna say fuck 'em. There's fifteen guys here who are ready to back you. And they're the fightin' Vandals, the guys who want the action."

"Be cool," Sonny said. Nobody's gonna be fighting anybody just yet. We gotta see what we have to work with and we gotta organize. If we have to fight, we'll fight. But first we gotta be sure of our commitment."

"What'a you mean?" Speedo asked.

"Do we break away? Do we form our own clique? Or do we take the chance that our fifteen, sixteen votes are enough to get rid of Kelly and Shades?"

"Hey, who needs them?" Blackie said. "We got the strength of the Vandals right here. The ones that'll be left at Bill's will be nothin'. Some of them would probably wanna join us. Let's break away."

"I don't know," Speedo said. "I kind'a still like a lot of the guys that ain't here. I mean, we all get along okay. I like being a Vandal. It's our name and it still has a good rep behind it."

"How about we stay Vandals, but we form our own chapter?" Sonny asked. "We can be the Broadway Vandals. We stay on friendly terms with Kelly but we run things our way over here. This'll be our turf under our control."

"That sounds pretty good," Speedo said. "I like it. I think everybody would go for that."

"Blackie?" Sonny looked at the one member who could convince most of this crew of anything.

Blackie, head bowed as though in deep concentration, nodded in agreement.

"Good." The moment was anti-climatic. Sonny wasn't ecstatic. He had *known* he had won from the moment Speedo had told him about the attitude of the rebel Vandals. Blackie's loyalty and commitment had been a foregone conclusion. The only feeling he experienced was relief. There were still problems ahead, but at least he now stood on a solid foundation. Even the pain in his stomach had subsided. But there was no time to relax. The Sinners were still lurking somewhere out there.

He didn't have enough troops to go on an offensive or even to conduct a wide spread search for the Sinners. He would have to bank on the meeting that Sharon had suggested. He would have to rely on her even with the thoughts of deceit running through his head.

"I've got something important to take care of," Sonny said. "Once we meet with the Sinners next Friday, we'll know where we stand with them."

"What meeting?" Blackie asked.

"At the dance. I'm setting up a meeting with them so we can give them an ultimatum. Either they join us or we cream them."

"Join us? Why?"

"Because we need more than fifteen guys to run a turf the size we'll control."

"But they're only a bunch of little scumbags. We don't need 'em."

"I don't mean we take all of them. Only the ones we think are stand-up guys. We take a few of them and maybe find some small cliques willing to join us, like the original Vandals were formed, and we'll have a decent size crew."

Blackie shrugged.

"It'll work out," Sonny said. "One way or another we'll take all the Sinners' turf and whatever else is unclaimed around here. Then we'll be able to mix it up with anybody who wants to screw with us."

"What about pieces?" Blackie asked.

Sonny wasn't ready for Blackie's probe and had to make a quick, rash judgement. "I said we'd run things our way. It wouldn't hurt to have a few stashed in case of an emergency."

"I got a couple of zips I built," Blackie said. "I never brought them around 'cause of the way Kelly felt. I made them when I was helpin' my old man on some carpentry jobs."

"They'll do until we can pick up some real ones." Sonny half-smiled. "See that, we already have more firepower than the old crew. Just make sure you leave them where they are until we need them. I don't want the cops busting us on a Sullivan rap."

Blackie nodded.

"I gotta go," Sonny said. "I'll be back as soon as I can. You guys talk it up with the troops. Clue them in on what we put together so far."

"No sweat," Speedo said. "By the time you get back, we'll officially be the Broadway Vandals."

"Great." Sonny broke away and headed in the direction of the butcher shop. He glanced at his watch. Five to twelve. The morning had streaked by.

CHAPTER 18

"Hi, honey," Sharon said. "How'd you make out?"

"Pretty good," Sonny said after she kissed him. "I found out a lot of things I didn't know before."

"Oh?"

"I'll tell you later." His voice was neutral. "How'd you make out?"

"With the Sinners?"

"Yeah."

"They defiantly want a meeting." She spoke slowly. "The Friday night dance is okay with them."

"Anything I should know beforehand?"

"Like what?"

"Like, are they coming to talk or are they coming for a fight?"

"They wanna talk, as far as I know. They wanna straighten things out."

"How many of them are left?"

"Not many. There's only gonna be about seven or eight at the dance."

"Okay." *That's that.* "Did your sister tell you all of this?"

"Of course. She's the one who set everything up." Sharon backed away. "Why?"

"Because I don't think you have a sister."

"What are you talking about?"

"You don't have an apartment on Eighty-First Street. So if you lied about that, you're probably lying about everything."

Sharon took another step backward.

"What're you trying to pull?" Sonny stepped toward her.

"Don't hit me," she screamed, putting her hands in front of

her face.

"I wasn't gonna hit you." He dropped his arms to his sides. "I wouldn't do that."

"God, you looked like Mickey for a minute." Tears began to well in her eyes. "I can't take anything like that again."

"I don't hit girls, damn it." He reached out and grabbed her arms, thinking she might turn and run. "I only want some answers."

"Let me go. Don't hurt me."

"Stop trying to make a scene. You don't have an audience." He thought for a moment of releasing his grip, but his need for the truth overruled. "Just answer a couple of questions."

"I told you I can't take being questioned all the time. I thought you said you love me."

"You're not going to get away with that act this time." He told her about the visit to her block.

"Oh my God," she said. "You had the nerve to go to my house and risk making my father so furious that he'd make my life miserable?" Her body seemed to relax. The crying stopped, but left a streak of mascara on her cheek. She smiled. It was a cynical smile, and Sonny knew he had struck a nerve.

"My father does not love me." Her words were forced and spaced with hesitation. "He treats my sister as his only child. I do not exist in his eyes. I'm only a body who shares his home. She is the only one who counts." She glared into Sonny's eyes. "The only way I can live with him is to be her caretaker. I'm not loved by him, by her, by anyone. And now, not by you. I'll never find peace. I'll never be loved."

Christ, was she going over the edge? Had he pushed too much? "Why couldn't I find your name on the mailboxes? I checked three buildings and I couldn't find Norris in any of them."

"Okay, I'll answer your silly questions. My father, among his other evil ways, is a deadbeat. He can't hold a job and he skips out when he owes too much rent in any one place. We moved out six months ago, but we moved back to an apartment my aunt had in the same building. When my aunt moved, she felt sorry for us. Me and my sister. But he's so much in debt that he can't even use his real name. He kept my aunt's name on the mailbox to throw off people who are after him." Her smudged underlined eyes widened. "And, it seems, people like you."

"Wait a minute."

"You're a damn parasite! You wanted my love so you can screw me. Just like everyone else in my life screws me in one way or the other."

"Stop it," he said. "You can't say that. That's only part of our love."

"It's the only part you want. I'm sure of it now."

"Please don't say that. It's not true."

"*Sure it's not.* Okay, then let's go to my apartment. Let's go talk to my father. Maybe you and him can discuss our marriage plans." She laughed, tossing her head back. "Yeah, that's it. We'll discuss the dowry he'll put up for me. So you both can take advantage of me."

"Enough." Sonny shook her. It wasn't worth the satisfaction he could win if he proved her wrong. The doubts were still there, but confusing and diminished. "Nobody's gonna check anything out. What the hell good is it gonna do? I don't care what your family life is like. I want you no matter where or how you live."

"*Sure you do.* Like you did in Central Park and that backyard last night."

His fingers snapped loose from her arms like they had been jettisoned by heavy springs. He stepped back to show he no longer would hold her captive. He immediately noticed the dark red oval spots on her arms where his thumbs had dug into her flesh.

"I'm sorry," he said flicking his forefinger at the bruises. "I guess I did wind up hurting you after all. I didn't mean it."

"I guess there's nothing much more to say," Sharon said. "I can't put up with a relationship that has me getting hurt every time. I guess I'm not meant to love anyone. I might as well just die and make everyone happy."

"Don't say that." He spoke softly. "I think we still have a lot in common and we should still see each other."

"And what happens if you dig up some new evidence on me?" she asked. Her body straightened to a business-like stature. "What if someone gets your ear and convinces you I'm a conniving bitch? Do I stand there and take the humiliation to prove they're wrong or do I at least get a small benefit of the doubt from you?"

"Okay, maybe I was a little out of line," he said. "But I wasn't sneaking around or trying to find any *evidence* on you. I only wanted to tell you the great news. I guess I was getting a little paranoid."

"You guess?"

"Okay, *I know.* Do we go back to square one? Do we start fresh?"

"I need some time to think," she said. "You really hurt me. I don't mean my arms, I mean inside." She touched her chest. "I was scared. All the bad things that ever happened to me flashed through my mind."

"I'm really sorry," he said.

"What was the great news you wanted to tell me?"

Sonny told her about the formation of the new Vandal chapter, crediting her for her part in his rise to power. "I owe you a lot for your confidence in me," he said.

"Why don't we take a break," Sharon said, taking his hand in hers. "These last three days have made me so mixed up. I want to be yours and I'm glad that things worked out well for you with the Vandals. Why don't we stop seeing each other for the rest of the week? It'll give you time to concentrate on what you have to do. You'll be a great president. I know it. We'll meet at the dance on Friday. It's only five days. You'll have your new position set up, you'll meet with the Sinners and work out your differences, and you'll have me waiting for you to end the night. Everything will be glorious."

"Glorious? That's really pushing things."

"It'll be a night to remember."

"Fine." Sonny saw the logic in her words. "Until Friday."

They threw their arms around each other and kissed. The passion was still there, and more so, the heat of their conflict acting as an aphrodisiac. She broke away before they lost control.

"I'll meet you inside as soon as the dance starts," she said. "Until then." She turned and headed along the route she had taken Friday, passing from Sonny's view.

Sonny thought of running after her, to possibly have her find the Sinners now or to offer to walk her home or where ever she was heading, but thought again of the inference of his action. She might misconstrue it as suspicion and he wanted no more of what was just experienced.

Sonny was at his new headquarters within minutes. The Broadway Vandals had given up the musty surroundings of the store in favor of the spectacular weather outdoors. They had divided themselves into three groups, some sitting along the side wall, and two groups bunched on either side of the front door. There were now eight girls, most of them sitting with the side wall sunbathers. Sonny thought of the word Sharon had used. It looked glorious. He couldn't believe what he had accomplished in so short a time.

Blackie and Speedo led the way as the two groups at the front of the store converged and formed a semi-circle at the curb. Sonny crossed the street and stepped into the center of the crescent.

"Everything taken care of?" Blackie asked.

"All set," Sonny said.

"While you were gone," Blackie said, "We took our first vote. And you were unan-im-ously elected president of the Broadway Vandals."

A cheer rose from the group. It was, again, anti-climatic. Sonny knew he would be elected. But he still had to produce the reaction expected of him.

"I appreciate it, guys," he said and tried to seem humble. "I really do. We're gonna make the name of the Vandals feared again. We're gonna make sure that no one screws with us." He waited for another cheer to subside. "Whatever those Vandals -" He pointed toward Bill's. "Or those Vandals -" He pointed toward Jackson

Heights. "Think is best for the Vandals' name, then let them do it. But we'll be the guys that make sure we carry on our tradition."

Another cheer.

"But we don't want to fight among ourselves. We're all Vandals. We gotta make sure we live in peace. But we'll make sure these Vandals take care of anyone who doesn't want peace, no matter what Vandal chapter they mess with."

The next cheer turned into a demonstration; a curbside pep rally.

"Hold it, guys," Sonny shouted. "Cool it. I have one more thing to say. I want a vote on another officer before we break up the meeting."

A few shouts of "Blackie" came from the crowd.

Sonny laughed. "You guys are way ahead of me. Yeah, you got it. I want to nominate Blackie Chase as vice-president. All in favor."

"Yeas" rang from the mob.

"Against?"

Silence.

Sonny spun Blackie around and raised his hand in his for a triumphant salute. "It's unanimous," Sonny said. "Here's your V.P."

The enthusiasm was contagious. Sonny felt exalted. He saw himself on a balcony in a newsreel being lauded by throngs of admirers. "Business is suspended," Sonny said. "Drinks are on me."

They cheered once more and moved back into the store.

"Speedo, come're," Sonny said.

"Yo."

"Here." Sonny slipped a ten-dollar bill into Speedo's hand. "Take care of the tab."

"Sure." Speedo turned away.

"Hey, buddy," Sonny said grabbing Speedo's shoulder. "Don't think I won't remember your part in this."

Speedo nodded.

"You handle money real well. You'd make a good treasurer. A damn good treasurer," Sonny said.

Speedo smiled. "You think so?"

"I know so. Go ahead, spread the wealth. We'll talk later about some ideas I have to build up a treasury."

"Thanks, man." Speedo went into the store.

Sonny turned to Blackie, the only other person still outside. "Congratulations," he said.

"You, too."

"Thanks for your help. Now we can do what's right."

"You got it."

"How about we make this a real celebration?" Sonny said reaching into his pocket. "Since you're over eighteen, how about buying some beers? There's an alley behind the store where we can have some privacy." Sonny handed Blackie another ten -dollar bill. "I'm sure they'll dig something stronger than a coke."

"Now that's a president who knows what's good for his troops."

"Yeah. But I also know you're the guy who'll keep them in line. You and me, buddy."

The afternoon passed celebrating the founding of the Broadway Vandals. Nothing was heard from the main core at Bill's. Sonny was sure Kelly knew of the rebellion, but he wouldn't push for a showdown. The Sinners matter would have to be settled first. He would let Kelly stew until Sonny decided it was time for a meeting.

Sonny spent the daylight hours of the next week traveling to school, alone for the first time in four years, wishing that Johnny was with him. He missed his friend and made another futile attempt to talk with him, stonewalled again by his foster parents.

The late afternoons and evenings were spent at Selma's - She was the owner of the candy store - and a small triangular pocket park across Broadway. It was as though the other Vandals and the Sinners didn't exist. It was a waiting game that would hinge on Friday night.

CHAPTER 19

It was evident they were going to have problems getting into the dance. Sonny had sent the Looney Brothers through the admission line as a test. The Looneys were expert con-men who knew how to talk their way in or out of trouble. One problem was the electric blue suits and tall, blond figures. They couldn't hide among the moderately dressed crowd that waited on the admission line. The phys-ed teacher, wearing the same polo shirt, was at the ticket table. He directed the Looneys to step out of line and he questioned them about their part in the scuffle and robbery from the previous Friday. They played off each other, knowing how to confuse an issue, and frustrated the teacher during his grilling until he finally let them pass into the gym.

Sonny, watching through a window above the far eaves of the front steps, knew he would have to send everyone in separate, spaced intervals. It would be time-consuming but it would be the only way to get everyone inside.

Sonny had left six of his Vandals at Selma's - those that had no use for dances or meetings - to act as a garrison. The situation was still volatile and Sonny didn't want a Sinner waltzing into an unprotected headquarters to show they could take it back anytime they wanted.

Sonny would have preferred to strut into the dance as a group. It would be most impressive and more intimidating. It would now take at least twenty minutes to process everyone through, valuable time that could be spent in negotiation. He would have to find Sharon and rely on her to introduce the Sinners in authority.

The next four Vandals made it through with only long stares from the custodians. Sonny had thought about inviting some of the girls from Selma's to pair off with the guys. Less attention would be paid to couples. But he didn't want to rub it in the Sinners' faces - showing up at a peace conference with the spoils of a victory. And he didn't want to incite Sharon's jealousy and mis-understanding of his action.

Sonny watched Monk, Vandal number eight, shuffle through the checkpoint mixed among a group of squares. His checkered sport jacket and conservative white shirt and navy blue tie helped him blend. No one would ever suspect him of being one of the crazies.

Sonny couldn't wait the last five minutes of his schedule. He glanced down at Blackie leaning against the school wall a few feet below him. Blackie was quietly staring at the street, a cigarette dangling from his lips. He was dressed in a black suit, a black shirt and a white tie. His pointed French-toe shoes were highly pol-ished. *All he needed was George Raft's half dollar to flip.*

"Let's make a try," Sonny said. "I'm tired of this friggen wait-ing."

"Yeah, hang on a second." Blackie's attention remained on the street. "Something's wrong."

"What?"

"I though I saw people movin' around in that alley over there."

Sonny squinted through the darkness at the apartment house across the street. "I don't see anyone. Probably the janitor or some-body throwing out their garbage."

"Nah. I seen them more than once."

"So there's a lot of people with garbage. Come on, let's go in." Sonny pulled a pair of aviator sunglasses from the inside pocket of his charcoal gray Hollywood jacket. "Maybe they won't recognize us."

He put on the sunglasses and straightened his black tie. He smoothed the edges of the Mr. B collar on his pink shirt and closed the single low button of the jacket. He chuckled when he thought he might be mistaken for Shades. *Yeah, Shades with a wig. It was good not having to deal with that crumb anymore.*

Sonny followed Blackie into the entrance hall and heard "Peggy Sue" by Buddy Holly playing in the gym. Sonny was relieved to see another teacher had taken over as admission collector. The problem with timing had now turned in their favor.

Sonny dropped a dollar on the table. "That's for the both of us," he said removing the sunglasses. No need for a disguise if they weren't being scrutinized.

The lighting was dim along the edges of the gym, leaving only the dance floor as bright as the entrance hall. Sonny and Blackie tilted their heads from the teacher standing inside the doorway. They slipped passed him and found the Vandals strung out along the wall just passed the double doors.

Sonny gave a thumbs-up to the group, then turned to scan the room. "Anybody here we know?" he asked, still looking at the crowd, trying to pick out Sharon. *She should have been waiting for him at the door.*

"I thought I saw Chico and Roxie," Monk said pointing to the front of the gym.

"Nobody else from Bill's? Anybody recognize any Sinners from last week?"

"I saw the guy you decked," Crazy Lenny said. "His nose was all bandaged. You must'a broken it."

"What a schnook," Blackie said. "With a target like that to aim at, one shot and he's out'a the ball game."

"That's only if we gotta tangle," Sonny said. "We're supposed to be here to talk."

"I don't trust the little bastards," Blackie said.

"Relax," Sonny said calmly. "Let me go see if I can find my contact. Keep an eye out for Sharon, the girl I was with last week," Sonny told Blackie. "Her or her sister are supposed to introduce me to the Sinners' officers."

"Yeah, okay." Blackie seemed nervous, which was out of character.

Sonny circled the edge of the crowd. There were a hundred or more people, a good crowd compared to what Sonny had heard was showing up lately. Maybe the word had spread about the action last Friday. Even the music was improving.

Sonny stopped near the front of the audience and took a minute to watch the dancers bopping to "A Whole Lot'a Shakin' Goin' On" by Jerry Lee Lewis. He glanced at the phonograph table and saw that the same matronly woman was the D.J.

He had continued scanning the crowd on the opposite side of the dance floor when he picked out Ernie the Greek and Sal, two members of the Assassins. They were standing next to Ralphy and some of the Sinners he recognized. They were all staring at him. Ralphy's taped nose was flanked by black eyes. Sonny stared back for a few seconds, exchanging the customary hard looks.

Sonny broke eye contact and searched for Sharon in the vicinity of the Sinners. *No Sharon.* No females at all. He looked back to the Vandals and they started toward him. Blackie was the first to reach him.

"They got Assassins with them," Sonny said. "What the hell is going on?"

"I knew somethin' wasn't right."

"Keep the guys here," Sonny said. "I'll go talk to the Sinners and see what they're pulling. If they wanna start something, we'll do it outside."

Blackie nodded, then gave the order to the others. Sonny started across the dance floor as the song ended. He weaved among the couples that were leaving the floor and stopped in front of the Sinners' group.

"Who's doin' the talkin' tonight?" Sonny asked, putting on his street accent and staring at Ralphy.

"We are," Ernie the Greek said, motioning to Sal at his side.

Sonny's eyes shifted to Ernie. He was Sonny's height, thinner, with a large crop of curly black hair. "I thought you guys were Assassins."

"We were." Ernie smiled, showing a broken front tooth. "We decided the Sinners needed some better leadership. Where's Kelly?"

"He's got nothin' to do with this. I decided the Vandals needed some better leadership. I'm speakin' for my chapter of the Vandals. The one that took over your candy store and turf."

"That garbage dump?" Sal said. Sal was one of many who had adopted an Elvis Presley appearance, his high black pompadour accented with long sideburns. "Who needs it?"

"That's not the point. We took it away from you."

Ernie folded his arms. "So you must be the guys that put some of the Sinners in the hospital." His eyes flared and his fists dropped to his sides. "Like my kid brother, Spiro, and Sal's two cousins."

So that's their problem. This wasn't going to be a peace conference. "They weren't from our neighborhood. It was Kelly's cousin, Benny, from Jackson Heights." *If we're going to bring relatives into it, let's get everyone involved.*

"So you're saying our fight's with them, not you?"

"No one said anything about a fight. I figure there aren't too many Sinners left. You guys can't afford to go up against us. We want you to join us. Our chapter." Sonny felt his bluff and assumed advantage eroding but continued with his terms. "We'll break away from Kelly and Benny and if you join up with us, we could form a real solid clique."

"We should join up with you?" Ernie smiled and Sal chuckled. "And I suppose you'll be the boss and we'll go under the name of the Vandals."

"Of course." There was something wrong. Ernie's attitude was too blase. Sonny had to maintain his composure until he could figure out what was going on. "We've got the upper hand."

"Guess again. You ain't even gonna make it off this block." Ernie folded his arms again. "By the way, your girl friend ain't gonna make the scene tonight. She set you up for us."

"What?"

"Sharon. The one who's been pumping you for information for us."

Sonny felt his blood drain to his feet. "You're wrong. She used to be a Vandal Deb. Her sister is a Sinners girl."

"Her sister hasn't hung out with them for six months. Sharon took her place. And she hates the Vandals with a passion. Hey, don't believe me. Ask Ralphy."

"The broad you were with last week is a Sinners' girl." His words were robotic. "That's why I went after you. Maybe you think you cooled me good, but she sure cooled you even better. You're a real schmuck, man." He touched his patched nose. "And tonight I'm gonna get you even better."

Christ, was she that sinister? Could she have pulled off a bunch of lies and still have been as loving and passionate as the girl he fell for? That gnawing feeling in the pit of his stomach was back.

"Now we'll tell you what's gonna happen," Ernie said. "You're gonna get your asses kicked. We let you think you won. We let Sharon put you to sleep. We had her lead you by the nose right up to tonight.

"Just like you thought the Vandals were getting too soft," Ernie said, "Me and Sal and some of the other guys felt the same way about the Assassins. We decided to reorganize the Sinners into a better fighting clique."

"Yeah, it only took us a week to get them back in shape," Sal said. "And we're pissed at the Vandals. Any Vandals, whether they're from Kelly's crew or his cousin's or yours. We want somebody's ass and it looks like yours is the one that won the prize."

"With what?" Sonny asked. "A handful of little punks who cry when they get their asses whipped?"

"We'll see who cries this time," Ernie said with a sneer. "What'a you got, eight, ten guys? We got three times that waiting outside."

Blackie hadn't seen shadows or people putting out their garbage. Sonny had been suckered in and pulled everyone with him. Thanks to that treacherous bitch. *Why did she do it? The embraces. The love making. The vows. They were now all worth shit.* On second thought, he envied her tactics. He was the one who was going to use her to set up the Sinners. He choked back the defeat. He would track her down when this was over.

"So you got us outnumbered," Sonny said. "So you make a big

splash tonight and then you get fifty or sixty guys swarming over your turf tomorrow. You'll be back to zero."

"Think again," Ernie said, his smile now closed. "Kelly wrote you guys off. We heard that him and Bruno made a pact not to interfere in anything on Sinners' turf after last weekend."

Maybe Kelly didn't want anything to do with him. That's why he never tried to contact him and never tried to stop his plans.

"Okay," Sonny said. "You want us, you got us. I don't care how many guys you got. You want a bop, you got it."

"How long?" Ernie smiled. "You need time to get the six guys you left at Selma's?"

They must have been watching. They probably had an eye on the store all week, knowing each move he made, and every word he spoke through Sharon. "We don't need anyone else. Whenever you're ready."

"Good. 'Cause nobody's gonna get out'a here anyway. After we take care of you, we'll stroll over there and do to them what was done to ours." Ernie paused. "And we'll expect you to vacate that area permanently," he said.

"Gimme some time to talk to my guys." Sonny turned to the dance floor. A slow dance by a singer he didn't recognize was pulsating through the speakers.

"Hey," Sal said. "You wanna hear a good joke?"

Sonny turned back, his head cocked to one side in disgust, using his surface toughness to hide his internal doubts.

"It's been going around our crowd all week. What did the Vandal do with his first fifty-cent piece?" He paused, not expecting an answer. "He went steady with her."

The Sinner entourage burst into laughter.

He turned away again and bumped into Blackie who was leading the Vandals through the rows of dancers like they were moving through the stalks of a cornfield.

"Hold off." Sonny held his hands in front of him. "Back off. No problem. Let's talk."

The Vandals turned away and retraced their steps, picking up an escort of two male chaperones as they returned to their spot across the floor from the Sinners.

"I thought you guys looked familiar," one of the teachers said. "You're the trouble-makers from last week."

"No," Sonny said. "You got us mixed up with some other guys. We weren't here last week."

"Yes you were. And what was that little stroll onto the dance floor all about?"

"We were looking to cut in," Monk said. "We only wanted to dance."

"One more outburst and you're all out of here." The teacher and his aide moved away and settled against the edge of the phonograph table.

Sonny waved everyone into a circle and bent his head into the center like a quarterback in a huddle. "We got problems," he said. "They want a fight."

"I knew it," Blackie said. "I knew we couldn't trust the little bastards. Let's get 'em."

"It's not just these guys," Sonny said. "There's a lot more Assassins with them then we figured. They said they got about thirty guys outside."

"I told you I saw somethin' funny goin' on in that alley."

"I know. I know I was set up. But we gotta face it, we're outnumbered."

"Not with my two friends," Blackie said patting the sides of his jacket.

"You mean you brought them?" Sonny asked, feeling apprehension rather than relief.

Blackie opened his jacket and displayed the black taped handles and raw wooden butts of the zip gun in each pocket. "And ammo. I told you I had a bad feeling about tonight." He buttoned his jacket and looked around the circle. "Anybody wanna borrow one?"

The Vandals shook their heads. They were crazies, but somehow Kelly's long-standing edict on guns had influenced them.

"I got a blade," Crazy Lenny said.

"We got our garrison belts strapped under our shirts," one of the Looneys said.

"I don't want any weapons used unless it's absolutely necessary," Sonny said. "At least not the guns. I got an idea. It may be like begging or going back on what we started, but maybe we should find Chico and ask him to send Roxie to Bill's to get the rest of the guys."

"Fuck no," Blackie shouted, arousing the attention of their guards at the phonograph table.

"Keep it down," Sonny said. "If we get kicked out now, we won't be ready for them."

"I'm more than ready," Blackie said. "I'll go pump a couple'a slugs into those fuckers right here."

"Jesus, will you cool it?" Sonny glared at Blackie. "We have to think things out. We need help. Maybe we'll put up a good fight but there's just too many of them. If they beat us, we'll look like shit. Everybody'll say we bit off more than we can chew. If we get the other guys to help, we can win. Then we'll worry about what happens later."

They seemed hesitant. No one spoke. Sonny had been chosen as their leader. It was his decision and his embarrassment to absorb.

"Do it," one of the Looneys said.

"Yeah," Monk said.

"We're all Vandals. No matter where we hang out," Lenny said.

"Okay," Sonny said knowing he had just destroyed his dream. "Monk, go find Chico and Roxie and bring them here."

Monk darted off toward the front of the gym where he had seen the couple.

"Okay, guys, spread out," Sonny said. "Don't do anything stupid." He glanced at Blackie to be sure his vice-president knew the statement was directed at him.

His vice-president? For how much longer? And how long would he be calling himself president? There was no way Kelly would put up with someone using an equal title within the Vandal ranks once he bailed Sonny out of this spot. If he would even respond to Sonny's request.

Monk returned with only Chico. Sonny greeted Chico like a long lost brother.

"Listen, buddy." Sonny told him what was going on. "I'd like you to have Roxie go back to Bill's."

"Jeez, I don't know, Sonny." Chico fumbled with the corners of the blue handkerchief puffed out of his breast pocket. "I don't want Roxie getting into the middle of any trouble. Besides, I don't know if everyone's around. Some of them were going to a flick."

"She's gotta try," Sonny said. "The Sinners won't know where she's going. A chick alone, leaving a dance early. That isn't suspicious. But she's gotta do it quick while she can still catch most of the guys."

"I'll tell you the truth, I don't know if Kelly would help you out. I mean, you guys ain't hanging around Bill's anymore from what we heard."

"We're still Vandals, man. We kept the name no matter where we hang out. We just wanted to expand our turf. Once these guys roll over us, they're not gonna stop. They'll come after you guys next. They got to be stopped here and now."

"Who are they?"

"The kids from last week and some of the Assassins. Have Roxie tell that to Kelly. He talked peace with the Assassins and now they're breaking the treaty."

"I don't think Bruno would do anything like that," Chico said.

"They're not with Bruno. These guys split from him and joined the Sinners."

"You sure?"

"Yeah, look." Sonny pointed across the dance floor. "There's Ernie the Greek and Sal. You remember them from the Assassins?"

"Yeah."

"See, they're with that big gavone from the Sinners that I decked last week."

Chico nodded. "Okay, I'll tell Roxie to take her cousin with her and head for Bill's. I can't promise Kelly will back you, but you look like you could use another guy for now. I'll stick around with you."

"Thanks, buddy. We can use all the help we can get."

Chico returned to the front of the gym. He was back with the Vandals in five minutes to report that he had explained everything to Roxie and told her what to do. Now all they could do was wait for her to bring back Kelly's answer.

Most of the Vandals played wallflowers while they waited. "When You Dance" by the Turbans, a song with a cha-cha beat, was the next number to vibrate through the sound system - an internal cone damaged by the sound of the ragged tones. Blackie and Lenny, now full of pent-up nervous energy, had located two of the girls from Selma's and made sure they danced directly in front of the Sinners. Sonny, his stomach already quivering, was given another shock when one of the Sinners moved too far in his back step and scuffed Blackie's shoe. Blackie stared at the smudge and slowly reached into his jacket. Lenny saved the moment by grabbing Blackie's arm and holding him until Sonny could reach them and calm Blackie.

Ernie and Sal returned Sonny's visit after Sonny had rounded up his flock and settled them back in their corner of the gym. "Let's get this over with before something blows up in here," Ernie said. "What'a you stalling for? Let's go outside and do it."

"Okay, fellas, that's it," One of the teachers said as he and his partner were joined by the phys-ed teacher for support. They hovered behind Ernie and Sal.

"You're all out of here," the phys-ed teacher said. "Who the hell let you guys in here in the first place?"

"After you." Sonny swept his arm forward, gesturing for Ernie to be the first out of the building.

"Sure," Ernie said. "We'll meet ya outside."

Sonny couldn't stall any longer. Whether Roxie made it to Bill's, or whether Kelly would back them was irrelevant. Sonny had molded the events that led up to this moment. He would have to live with it.

Ernie and Sal crossed the dance floor to the two banks of double doors under the red lettered exit sign. All of the gym exit doors were open.

Roxie moved against the flow of the crowd, skirting the edge of the parade of Sinners on a narrow path between them and the spectators. She looked disheveled and harried.

Chico was the first to spot Roxie, and rushed to meet her. "What happened?"

"That bitch, Sharon, pointed me out to them."

"She's out there?" Sonny asked.

"Yeah, your little sweetheart is out there. With them. Man, what is her story?"

"You tell me," Sonny said. "I'm sorry."

"Me and my cousin, Judy, got a block away before ten of them surrounded us. They kept asking where we were going. And then she pops her puss in and says,'Yeah, she's a Vandal Deb, alright. She's probably going to get the rest of them'. She had this sneer on her face like she was getting me back for something I did to her."

"Who ripped your dress?" Chico asked. "I'll fucken kill them." He looked to the exit doors to see if he could catch up with the last of the departing Sinners.

"No, wait." Roxie grabbed his arm. "It wasn't any of them. She grabbed me and when I pulled away, the sleeve tore. Judy and I had to turn around and head back. We stopped at the deli down the block to catch our breath. I told Judy to wait five minutes after I left and go to Bill's. I told her what Kelly looked like and to tell him we were in trouble."

"Did she make it?" Sonny asked.

"I don't know. I bought a pack of cigarettes and left her there. Sharon didn't seem to be interested in Judy. The bitch probably knew Judy wasn't from Bill's so she didn't have anything against her.

"Some of them followed me back here, including Sharon. She

kept taunting me, trying to get me to fight her while they egged her on. I would've loved to get my hands into her hair and yanked it out by the roots but I thought it was more important to get back here to let you know what happened."

Chico hugged her. "You did good, baby. We'll take care of those mother.. And the bitch, too, if we can find her."

"No, man," Sonny said. "I was the one who made the mistake of trusting her. I'll get her for all of us. That's a promise."

"Let's hope your cousin made it to Bill's," Monk said. "Sounds like there's a lot of them out there."

"Yeah, there must have been twenty or thirty of them across the street," she said.

"We don't need anybody else," Blackie said. "Let's go get the mothers."

Sonny looked down the path through the crowd. The corps of teachers who had escorted the Sinners to the exit doors gestured and beckoned for the Vandals to leave.

"I guess it's time," Sonny said as he started down the path.

CHAPTER 20

Crazy Lenny, the last Vandal to leave the building, took his place alongside the ten Vandals stretched in a line along the wide landing. The door hissed shut behind them and the jarring sound of bolts slamming into place seemed to seal the atmosphere of immediacy. There was no retreat.

Chico had convinced Roxie to stay inside, and she watched from a window.

The Sinners were spread in thin echelons from the near curb and across the street to the opposite sidewalk. They were unusually quiet. The entire street was quiet. Ernie, Sal, Ralphy and the Sinners from the dance had removed their jackets. They comprised the front line. The remainder of Sinners and Assassins, dressed in dark street clothes, moved forward.

"I guess Roxie's cousin didn't make it," Lenny said as he hung his jacket on the handle of one of the doors and blew a kiss to a girl on the other side of the small window. A pair of brown suspenders supported his rust-colored pegged pants. He removed his gold-plated key chain from a belt loop and slipped it into his pocket.

Sonny elected to wear his jacket. It was loose enough for swinging room and could act as added padding against weapons. It wasn't enough protection, but it was at least another layer to ward off a glancing blow from a belt buckle or a knife slash. The only weapons made public by the Vandals were the Looneys' garrison belts.

Sonny looked over the heads of the waiting enemy. He squinted against the darkness and saw the glow of a cigarette dotting a familiar shapely silhouette in the alley that Blackie had been scrutinizing. *It was her. He was sure of it.*

Sonny took a deep breath and released it as he shouted, "Hit 'em in the middle." He was on the sidewalk in two leaps and, using Blackie's theory, aimed his first punch at Ralphy's nose. *Get the big guy first.* For the second time in a week, Ralphy reeled backward, this time a scream of pain followed him as he bounced off another Sinner and sprawled into the street.

Sonny turned to face off with another Sinner and was momentarily blinded by the glare of a car's headlights. A rush of bodies enveloped him and the Vandals. He was punched behind his ear and lurched forward. Another blow and a sharp pain in his ribs. He was on his knees, his upper body trying to remain parallel with the street. Someone careened off his back and he braced himself against the blacktop to keep from being flattened out and used as a stomping target. Sonny pushed off and stood, only to be driven backward, embroiled in a cascade of swinging arms and slamming, charging Sinners.

Sonny and his crew were forced into a line of ash cans at the mouth of the alley alongside the school building. He struck the cans with the back of his knees and was pushed into a sitting position. One of the Sinners landed across his lap like he was about to be spanked. Sonny judo-chopped the Sinner across the back of his neck and flung the dazed teen headfirst into the school wall. The headlights were back, turned and aimed in his direction, casting elongated shadows on the brick wall. He turned and looked to the side of the glare, trying to shade his view with an outstretched hand. He could make out the front of Eddie's Oldsmobile bouncing to a stop, straddling the curb. The doors flung open. Sonny was again smothered by a crush of bodies.

He was bumped from behind and tumbled over the ash cans, two lids flying into the air along with a cloud of pulverized white ash. The cans acted as a temporary barrier between Sonny and the fight. He used the few seconds of reprieve to roll to his feet and look passed the now empty Oldsmobile. The main body of rescuers were a half-block away, sprinting toward the battle. Sonny felt something stir inside him. He didn't know if it was pride or relief.

Or maybe it was remorse for trying to destroy the unity that was now being demonstrated.

Sonny scooped up one of the lids and used it as a shield while he charged around the cans and through the clusters of skirmishes, butting and prodding Sinners with the steel cover. A sharp crack snapped off ahead of him. A space cleared among the struggle and he saw Blackie standing spread-legged, one arm straight and extended, his hand holding a zip gun, his other arm coming up from his side about to bring the other single-shot gun into a firing position. A woosh rushed passed Sonny's ear. He spun around and saw a Sinner in a motorcycle jacket bringing his arm back to swing a length of chain at Sonny for a second time. Sonny swung his shield around, deflected the chain and snapped his wrist sideways. The lid smashed into the side of the Sinners' face. The motorcycle jacket crumbled and dropped to the street just as Blackie's second zip gun fired.

The hollow crack was overpowered by a booming roar. And another. Someone had a real gun. A mad scramble of teens burst from the area of the shots like they were being forced forward by a shock wave. Sonny turned to join the retreat before he could be swallowed by the wave and driven back to the ground. He dropped the lid, as he became one of the scurrying mob. Another shot. Then the sound of sirens.

Sonny thought he had tripped, but as he skidded along the sidewalk, the heels of his hands rasping and tearing on the concrete, he felt the weight of another person bounce off him. He rolled over in time to see Sal scrambling to his feet next to him.

"You ain't goin' nowhere," Sal shouted. "We ain't done with you."

Sonny managed to sit up before Sal planted the point of his shoe in Sonny's back. He lost his breath momentarily and tried to twist his body toward his assailant, lifting his hands for protection. Sal's kick missed and continued high into the air as though he was falling backward. Sonny looked up and saw Sal being restrained from behind in a chokehold by someone he didn't recognize.

"I'll take care of this punk," Shades said.

Shades was saving Sonny's butt. Sonny realized it was the first time he had seen Shades without his sunglasses. Sonny was numb with pain, both physically and mentally. *What was going on?*

Sonny hustled to his feet sending pangs of pain through his rib and back muscles. The pain seared as he slammed his fist into Sal's stomach. Sal doubled over carrying Shades with him into a heap. The sirens were deafening. The block was splashed with red lights. He was caught in the panic.

"Let's get out of here," Sonny said to Shades as he turned and ran.

Sonny passed the ash cans and was at the rear of the school alley. A spiked iron-bar gate blocked his escape. It was locked. *He had to get away.* A cement wall separated the alley from the rear courtyard of an adjacent apartment building. He scaled it, the pain racking his every movement. He teetered on the brick inlaid apex for a moment. He scanned the alley and realized Shades had not followed him. He was the only one to choose this escape route. He dropped to the opposite base of the wall and ran to a passageway that led to another block.

Sonny scampered across the back street, through more alleys and yards, and finally, after circling the area of the fight, found his way to his apartment building. His home would be a temporary haven. Throughout his membership with the Vandals, he had never been arrested or detained. It would be hours before his name, if at all, was associated with the rumble.

He was tired, drained, and unable to travel any farther. Fatigue settled into him. The pain of his injuries was returning in stages like a succession of hot lights being turned on; the ribs; the back; then the back of his neck. He touched his neck and felt a lump below one ear. He stared at the heels and palms of his hands and saw dried blood. He had to rest and plan his next move.

He limped as he climbed the three flights to the top floor. He would change clothes, maybe rest for a short time, and then scout around for news.

He found the apartment empty. A note on the refrigerator door advised him that his mother was having dinner with Uncle Lou. A twenty-dollar bill was scotch-taped to the note. Sonny was relieved. He could hide his suit until he could make a secret trip to the tailor instead of having to explain its torn and battered condition.

He stripped and took a shower. The jets of hot water massaged his aching back and neck. He found dark bruises along the skin of his rib cage and knees. The pain slowly diminished to occasional annoying pangs by the time he stepped from the shower.

He dressed and slumped into an easy chair in the living room. He though about turning on the television, but instead floated off into a nap.

When he awoke, he slapped together a sandwich of assorted cold cuts and was headed back to the streets. He wore a black windbreaker instead of the attention-seeking Vandal jacket. This was not the night to advertise.

It was now a couple of hours since his escape. He had calmly put the thoughts of an aftermath out of his mind. If he didn't think about it, then nothing was there. But the sequence of events was still clicking through his mind like he was watching a slide projector. He saw his desperation in the blind alley and the last glimpse toward the street before clearing the wall. There had been no one behind him. Not Shades, as he had anticipated. Not any of the Vandals. Not any of the Sinners. He wondered if he was the only one that got away.

The only faction not touched by the evening's events were the guys at Selma's. That is, if the fight hadn't spilled over to them like promised by Ernie. Speedo and the other five Broadway Vandals may still be camped out at Selma's.

Sonny used the same skirting maneuver along Roosevelt Avenue as he had been deploying through the week. He felt less conspicuous in street clothes than if he was still in his disheveled suit. As he crossed onto Broadway, a Daily News truck had just dumped a bound stack of its evening edition onto the sidewalk outside the entrance to the subway arcade. He looked at the headlines.

TEEN KILLED IN SCHOOL DANCE FIGHT
42 ARRESTED, MANY INJURED

Under the bold headline was a picture of a blurred dark shape laying face down in the middle of the street, his blood running into the gutter. The caption below the photo read:

VINCENT 'BLACKIE' CHASE
SLAIN IN GANG FIGHT

"Blackie!" Sonny blurted. *He's dead?* Sonny crouched and tore the top of the front page away from the metal band around the stack. Page three displayed a long distance photograph of the Junior High School and the street; Blackie's body covered with a white sheet and only a dot in the middle of an assemblage of police cars, ambulances and spectators. Sonny skipped over the half-exposed story to the list of names in the second column. Lenny. Chico. A dozen or so of familiar names. Cloony. And Cloony - both of them. And Kelly. And - *Oh, hell* - Anthony Gaglione. *They got him instead of me.* He wasn't sure if he felt guilty about Shades taking his place or if he still disliked the guy and now owed him a favor.

Sonny's muscles began to tighten and ache again and he felt like he had aged twenty years as he slowly rose to his feet. He stood slightly hunched, favoring his stiff back and unable to turn from the stack of papers. *Blackie is dead.* He remembered Blackie always bragging about the dozen times his name had appeared in the papers. Unlucky thirteen would be his obituary.

Sonny felt like busting out laughing. *What the hell was going on?* Then he remembered his Uncle Lou telling him about his war experiences, and how a guy wanted to laugh in spite of a buddy being killed. It was a natural emotion, Uncle Lou had been told by the head-shrinkers. You were glad you were alive before you could mourn for the dead.

Yeah, he would mourn for Blackie. Not only because he had been a buddy, but also because Sonny was responsible. He never really thought that guns would be used. Sure, he had told Blackie not to take the zips out of hiding, but he wasn't strong. He didn't insist upon it. He all but prompted Blackie to carry them, like he had prompted Blackie not to start trouble on that first raid. He should have realized that Blackie needed more guidance than he had provided. He should have done a lot of things differently than he had done.

Sonny knew he had not only ruined his own life but the lives of many. And if he couldn't justify his actions, how could others? He would have as hard a time facing the Vandals as he was facing himself. He wasn't worth saving. Except for one purpose. To bring down the person who helped him in his deeds. He had promised to get Sharon, and he would do it. She would have to pay for what she had done to him and his.

All of the neighborhoods would be swarming and devastated by police. Vandals, Sinners, whoever they suspected, would be taken in. There would be no more turfs. The streets would be owned by the police, by the adults again, like they were meant to be. Anyone under twenty would be scrutinized, hustled off the corners, their IDs checked like they were under an occupation force. If Sonny were to find her, it would have to be tonight while they were still off-balanced; still investigating; before the daylight brought the sanctions.

Sonny tore himself away from the stack of newspapers and continued down Broadway. He fantasized about finding the same warm surprise he had experienced the Saturday before when he had found his new crew waiting for him to take command. But the evening was deteriorating beyond his control and his needs. Selma's was closed, unusually early for a Friday night. *But why not?*

There should be no one to buy drinks for, no troops to rally around him and applaud him.

Maybe the cops had grabbed them. Maybe Ernie had also survived and completed his threats. And maybe Sharon was with him. He had to do it himself. He was sure he had been spared for a reason.

He needed something to flush her out in case he found her with what was left of the Sinners. Guns had brought everything to this point. They might as well end it. He remembered Uncle Lou's construction site he had worked at near the recently built Elmhurst General Hospital. He had seen the pistol in the foreman's office. It might still be there.

A rough wooden fence surrounded the carved out corner of land. The foreman's shack was a few yards from the corner, flush with the fence-line and accessible from the sidewalk. It was dark and unoccupied. He climbed the three crude wooden steps and found the door double padlocked. He wrapped a handkerchief around his fist, leaned across the banister, and jabbed at the screened window. The glass shattered with a muffled thud and a patter of clinks. He yanked on the chicken-wire screen and tore it from the fastenings around the frame. He unlocked the window, crawled inside, and began feeling his way in the dark.

The desk was in the far corner. He stabbed around in the drawers until he found the gun. He placed it in his jacket pocket and snapped the flap closed. A rush of excitement pulsed through him. He slipped while climbing out the window, but his anxiety drove him onto the alley behind Selma's.

If only he knew where Sharon really lived. She would probably be hiding just like everyone. *The butcher shop.* She was always there early every time they met. It was his only lead. He would have to try it.

CHAPTER 21

After snaking his way through the maze of alleys and courtyards, he stood in the darkness of a driveway between two private homes and scanned the windows above the corner butcher shop and the remainder of the block. There were only two lighted windows, one with its shade drawn. He turned his attention to the street that eventually led to the Junior High School. Only a few windows showed life.

He had picked the best vantage point possible. He had an unobstructed view of every entrance door within blocks of the butcher shop. He leaned against the brick house but soon grew tired and settled into a sitting position. The weight of the pistol in his pocket pulled on the light fabric of his windbreaker and sat heavily against his hip. He tried not to think about why it was in his pocket, what he intended to use it for, why it had come to this. Somewhere in his shifting thoughts he was sure he had decided to use the gun on Sharon.

The only thing he knew clearly was that what he was about to do wasn't spawned by hatred. He thought he knew how to hate and he knew that what he felt wasn't hatred. He didn't even hate himself.

He hoped it wasn't pity. *Damn, that would be too much.* How could you pity someone who ruined your life? No, he would rather hate Sharon. He would rather hate himself than have self-pity. He would rather pull out the pistol and put it to his own head than sink to self-pity. *Jesus, why should anyone else have to die?*

Would it bring Blackie back? Would it help the guys sitting in jail? Maybe everyone would think better of him than they surely do now. But then what? Would he be forever absolved? And what would that do for him? He was becoming disenchanted with the heavy piece of iron hanging at his side. *To hell with it.* He'd bring the gun back to the shack. It was over. Only Blackie would die this night.

He stood, feeling the stiffness again, and shuffled out of the driveway. But something tugged at his sleeve. It was only a few blocks away. He could see the school from where he stood. There didn't appear to be anyone there.

He was cautious, yet impetuous to see the battleground once more. He rambled through the confinements of obstructions behind the blocks of buildings and found himself in the breezeway where he thought he had spotted Sharon before the fight had begun. The school building was dark and strangely calm. Black and white wooden horses with 'Police Dept.' stenciled on the horizontal bars had been placed along the block, midway into the street and to either side of the school building. There was a sign on the middle door of the school, but Sonny couldn't read it through the darkness.

He stared at the site that should have generated more vivid pictures but there was nothing more than an empty street. He had blanked it out of his mind. He would try never to recall this night again.

He began to turn to find an exit when he saw the shadow blink across a rear corner of the building. *Cops?* Were they staking out the place to get some jerk like him who was obsessed with returning to the scene of the crime. *Screw it.* They got him. He wasn't going to fight it. Let the night finally end.

He didn't know if he should raise his arms in surrender or wait until they ordered it. Shit, the gun. Don't reach toward your pocket or they'll burn you on the spot. He stood frozen, staring at the grayish strip created by a distant light, running parallel to the building wall, across the mouth of the courtyard and ending at his feet.

"You bastard. How the hell did you find me?"

Sharon stepped from the edge of the building and stood rigid and firm. He could only make out her imposing shape, a shadow pressed against the dim gray ribbon of light, but he knew she was sneering.

"It wasn't easy," Sonny said.

"But I never came directly here. I always turned before this block."

"So you could double back and come in the rear entrance like you're doing now," he said.

"So you're not as stupid as I thought you were."

She wasn't making things easy. "I thought you really did know me. If you think I was stupid, then I misjudged you. You might try gullible or naive."

"Okay. I'll give you that. You sure fell for a load of shit. Mr. Big Shot, melting like a snowball in hell."

"Hell? Someplace you know a lot about, hah?"

"That's right. I know it because of the people who put me there. The bastards at Bill's. And their snobby bitches. Those fucking little tramps had the nerve to talk about me behind my back. *Well, I got you all.* I brought everyone down to hell with me. How do you like it here?"

"You did all of this for revenge? You too? For some stupid petty bullshit? You're one nutty broad."

"You're calling me crazy?" She stepped toward Sonny with such ferocity that he backed away, bumping the wall behind him. "Just like that friggen old man of mine. Just like those bastards at the hospital. But I got away from them. I got away so I could get all of you."

She kept coming. He felt a rush of terror. It embarrassed him for a moment, but then, he had never confronted her in this state of mind. The fear guided his hand to the pistol in his pocket.

Sonny unsnapped the pocket flap, drew the revolver and straight-armed it into Sharon's face. She took two more steps before stopping, not threatened by the gun. Her thin smile was a crack spread across her lower face.

"What're you gonna do with that?" she asked.

"I'll blow your goddamn head off for what you did."

"You?" She chuckled softly. "You don't have the balls. I don't know how many times I wanted to bust out laughing when you were making your plans to be a big leader. You have to be strong. You have to be ruthless to be a leader. I was the only one who made you strong. You were nothing without me. I made you and I made the Sinners. I was the one who controlled this war. You just ain't got it, little boy."

Sonny's hand trembled. The pistol felt like one of his exercise barbells and the tendons in his wrist strained to keep the weapon pointed straight. He couldn't bring his finger to move the last millimeter and complete what he originally started out to do. All his bravado about bringing guns into the gang was bullshit. He probably knew it all along but hid behind a facade. And now it was in the open. *She was forcing him to face himself.*

"I don't need this to handle you," he said, giving way to the weakness in his wrist. He dropped his arm for an instant to relieve the pressure, then brought it forward, hurling the pistol toward the dark corner of the courtyard. It bounced off something and clattered around on the concrete before coming to rest somewhere in the blackness.

"So what're you gonna do now, punch me around? Get your frustrations out and be able to tell everyone how you made things right."

"I don't know. I don't know what I wanna do with you."

"Maybe we can start again where we left off." She inched closer to him. "I think you still love me."

"What?"

"If you didn't care for me, you would've shot me." She stood before him, her hand moving to his arm. "You know, that Friday night we met, I really did go for you. That's no lie. No matter what I've already said, I mean that. That's why I made you take me to Manhattan the next morning. To keep you out of danger. I knew they were gonna raid your schoolyard. I helped them plan it. But there was something about you. I wish we could've lived that Friday and Saturday forever."

He believed her. Even knowing how she could lie and twist words, something rang true in her tone.

"I felt bad, at first, about using you, but I needed to do it. I needed so much to get them back. And besides, you are one of them. But we were destined to survive, so maybe we were destined to be together." She wrapped her arms around his, mesmerizing Sonny. "You got what you wanted. You helped to destroy the Sinners. And I got to destroy the Vandals. We're even."

Sonny pulled from her grasp and slammed into the wall behind him. "You crazy bitch! I didn't want things to happen like this. How can you say..."

He felt her soft body crush him into the wall and heard the sharp click. The rush of terror that had embarrassed him earlier was now more than a passing sensation as Sharon drove the knife into his side. The pain raced through his body and overwhelmed the minor aches of his previous injuries.

He blindly threw a fist and he saw Sharon back-peddle, stumble and fall into a sitting position. He saw the knife in her clenched hand, held tightly like it was her only possession in the world.

"Jesus Christ, why do I keep trusting you?" he yelled.

"Because you're a soft-hearted jerk," Sharon said as she rose to her feet, the knife still clutched in her hand. "You should be the leader of the squares at the Friday night dance. You can't make it in the real world." She was moving toward him again. "You don't know what it's like scrounging on the streets, to have nowhere to go, no one to turn to."

"I know what it's like to be alone. That's why I trusted you. We both needed someone."

Sonny wanted to retract his plea. It was pity. Something that she could use to twist his guts into tighter knots.

He watched Sharon limp slowly toward him. His rib muscles screamed in agony and he clutched at the pain. He felt the sticky fluid that had soaked through his jacket. He wondered if he was dying. He wondered if he had the strength and time to finish what he should have done when he had the means in his hand. He reached back with his free hand and hurled it forward. His fist smashed into Sharon's face and she was on the concrete again, first sitting, then sprawled backward into a spread-eagle position.

He pressed his hand against his side and stretched his other hand in front of him. He stumbled into the darkness of the inner courtyard.

"You won't get away through there," Sharon said. "You won't get away at all." She propped herself up. "One of us has to die tonight. You know that, don't you?"

He looked back as he passed from the grayish light into complete darkness. *God, she still had the friggen knife in her hand like it was glued in her fist.* He hadn't hit her as hard as he could. Something inside him had pulled his punch. He cursed himself for his indecision. She was trying to stand again. He saw what he thought was a smear of blood below her nose and across her cheek. It was a black stain, about the same color as her hair, and her skin was gray from the distant light. He watched her, like she was a character in a slow motion black-and-white film, as she finally pushed herself to her feet.

He knew he couldn't bend over. He knew he would pass out from the pain if he moved the wrong way. He began kicking with each step, trying desperately to make contact with the pistol.

"I know what you're doing," she shouted. Her voice was loud and echoed off the many walls of the enclosure. "But I'm gonna get you before you find it. You're the one who's gonna die, little boy."

Sonny's outstretched hand jammed against a wall and like the robotic impulse of a mechanical toy turned him around. He was heading back toward the light on a collision course with Sharon; her knife poised straight at him. He continued his kicking, shuffling motion, trying not to pass out, his brain grasping to remain alert.

Thud! *Oh shit, that was it.* The metal surface crackled as it slid along the rough cement. *Where'd it go?* She was close; the knife now leveled horizontally like a bayonet. *It's got to be in front of him.* He dove forward and landed like he had taken a belly-wop into the Sunnyside Pool. The pistol squirted out from under his body, a tiddlywink pinching off the cement and landing alongside his probing hand. He thought he blacked out for a second but regained his alertness. He steadied the gun. He had no apprehension about squeezing the trigger. No need to think about it this time. No reason to be reasonable.

The explosion reverberated over and over - *Had he fired that many shots?* No, he only squeezed the trigger once. They were echoes bouncing through the canyons of courtyards, still resounding as Sharon flew backward. She landed in a fetal position.

"Thanks, sucker," she said. Then silence.

Sonny wondered if he had been conned one last time. *Had she planned her own death?* Did he put her out of her misery and be made to pay for it? Did she help to destroy his life, at first slowly over the last two weeks, and now completely as a finale of her warped plan?

He lost consciousness before the last echo faded into the night.

At first, only a few windows lighted the dark walls of the courtyard, the glow producing fuzzy-edge squares of brightness on the gray and black patch of cement. Then the illumination came in quick sequence until the patchwork of squares fused together to highlight the two still figures below.

Sonny gained consciousness and heard Sharon moan. She was still alive. He knew she was too tough to die. But so was he. He had to stay alive. It would be the only way he could finally beat her and make this night come to an end.

CHAPTER 22

SHADES GAGLIONE – NOVEMBER, 1958

Shades Gaglione crossed Queens Boulevard and followed the slope of Sixty-Ninth Street on its incline toward Woodside Avenue. It had been a year and a half since he had traveled this route. *Eighteen months in prison.* But it would have taken a lot longer to forget the inbred routine practiced every night before his arrest.

A year and a half. Shades snugged the tinted horn-rimmed glasses back against his forehead. The new, more powerful prescription lenses had been replaced while he was in the first of two reformatories, and the new frame never did sit as tightly as the original. His weakening vision was running a close second to his thinning hair. His front hairline was even with his sideburns, which made him look thirty-five instead of his actual nineteen years. His mother had blamed the deterioration of his sight and rapid aging to both his confinement and the death of his father. She had tried to get an early release for her only son, now her only source of support. But the parole board was unconvinced. They facetiously explained that such an arrangement was only applicable to someone serving their country in the military, not a convicted criminal. They did allow him to attend his father's funeral.

The neighborhood hadn't changed much. The same stores, same buildings, the funeral home where the letters said Blackie was waked. Shades reached Woodside Avenue, turned the corner and crossed the street. There was a sudden chill in the evening air. He buttoned the front of his blue woolen overcoat and hurried toward the door of Bill's candy store. He skirted around a gray-primer customized Mercury parked at the curb and gave a fast once-over to the store windows before pushing open the glass door. He saw the same cardboard Coke and Chesterfield signs adorned the yellowing plastic-covered glass facade.

Shades couldn't remember the place being this placid. One customer, his back to Shades, stood in the rear of the store looking at the juke box. The short, curly-headed teen was wearing one of the old Vandal jackets, a dark clean outline on the back highlighted where the script lettering had been. No one was behind the counter.

Shades sat at one of the counter stools and it squeaked. The boy in the rear of the store turned.

"Speedo."

"Shades," the youth shouted. "Shades, man. How've you been?" He strutted quickly toward his friend, his hand outstretched.

"Good to see you." Shades smiled as he shook Speedo's hand.

"Man, I wouldn't have recognized you if it wasn't for the shades."

"Yeah, I got a little more forehead than the last time you saw me."

Speedo chuckled. "It's been a long time, man."

"You're telling me. Where is everyone?"

"Probably down the Connecting Highway, dragging."

"What?"

"The Connecting Highway. Remember the old houses they were supposed to tear down? They finally used some of that land to build a highway between Astoria and the B.Q.E. Cars come from all over to use it as a drag strip. Hot cars and racing are the big kicks now."

"Is that your car outside?"

"Yeah. A 'fifty Merc. Remember when we used to steal them with tin foil?"

Shades chuckled. He remembered how easy it had been to hot-wire the old Mercurys. His wheelmen on burglary jobs would collect the tin foil from cigarette and gum wrappers, pealing the shinny foil from the paper backing and molding the residue into a ball. They would jam the ball between the three ignition contact points under the dashboard and have instant start-up.

"Remember the night Mickey couldn't keep his heap going because the wad was so small that it kept falling out and the engine would cut off?"

"Sure," Speedo said. "I had to crawl under the dash and try to hold it in place until we finally gave up and left it in the middle of Queens Boulevard."

They both laughed.

"So, who else is left?" Shades asked.

"Me, Val, Tony and Jimmy. The rest of the guys are either in the service or going their own ways. Johnny lives somewhere in Jackson Heights and hangs out with Benny's crew. And, of course, some of them are still locked up."

"Yeah, locked up. I was going crazy. They should of let Sonny die instead of putting him away for so long."

"You think Blackie is better off?"

"That's right."

"He was only eighteen when he got it. He had his whole life ahead of him."

"Let's drop it," Shades said. "I mean, it was because of Sonny and Blackie that everything we built came crashing down. At first I was pissed at Sonny for what he did to everyone. What he did to me. If we hadn't felt obligated to bail his ass out nothing would have happened. Kelly could've turned his back on the guy like he originally intended and we could've saved our deal. We would've been in damn good shape by now. All of us would be. Instead, we had to spend the whole damn treasury on friggen lawyers who didn't do shit for us."

"I liked Sonny," Speedo said. "If me and some of the other guys hadn't been left behind that night, we would've been nailed along with everyone else. I don't know if it was a coincidence, but I feel obligated for it. Not only that, he had some good ideas. Maybe not in breaking us up. I never had my heart into splitting from Bill's, but I still liked him. He wanted to keep our name on top."

"What name?" Shades asked. "I don't see any name on your back. You call that keeping our name on top?"

"We had to take the name off the jackets. The cops were always on our ass."

"That's what I'm saying. He destroyed the Vandals. He destroyed what we could've had. Him and that broad. Too bad she didn't die. Anybody hear anything about her?"

"Nah. Who the hell cares about that nutty bitch?"

"What about Johnny? He's hanging out with Benny?"

"Yeah, once he turned eighteen, he left his foster home and went on his own. Rumors say he's living with that kid, Pete's mother. You know, the guy who shot Dave."

"Yeah, I met Pete at the reformatory before they transferred me. He's really grown up in those four years. They should be letting him out soon." He shrugged. "Well, I gotta hook up with Benny and Johnny. We gotta pick up where we left off. I hear Benny's doing okay. And if Johnny is with him and Kelly ready to get out in a couple of months, we can really get things shaking again, like we had planned."

Speedo restlessly shifted his stance, starring at the white tiled floor. "The few guys that are still left here at Bill's are kind of happy with what we're doing," he said. "We got jobs and we got our cars. We ain't really interested in getting involved with Benny's crew."

"You're not interested in making a good buck?"

"Not that way."

Shades remembered how Kelly had predicted that most of the Vandals would drop out when it came time to make the big decision on a future. Shades couldn't fault the dropouts if they wanted to stay straight, although he couldn't understand why.

"You got it, pal." Shades extended his hand and Speedo shook it. "Whatever, we're still the Vandals."

"Forever."

"How about a ride to the Heights?" Shades asked. "So I don't have to find a cab."

"Yeah, sure."

As they stepped out the front door, Shades realized that no one had ever appeared behind the counter. He wondered if Bill was still the owner. He was about to ask Speedo when his thoughts were distracted by the dechromed, primered two-door Mercury sitting at the curb. The rear of the low slung vehicle was dropped even closer to the street by shackles on the rear coil springs. He had always liked this model car, not only for its use in his burglary jobs, but also for the style of swiftness and power it seemed to depict even when it was motionless. And now, with the modifications Speedo had performed on its body, its lines were even more flowing.

He reached for the door handle and found there was none. He stepped back in amazement, staring at Speedo for an explanation.

"Electric doors," Speedo said. "I took off the handles, welded plates under the holes, covered it with body filler and installed lock trippers." Speedo pushed down on an angled antenna mounted on the rear quarter panel. Both doors popped open.

Shades pulled on the lip of the door and dropped into the black rolled and pleated bucket seat.

The engine roared to life when Speedo pressed the starter button on the dash panel. The radio speaker blurted a string of static before the middle of "One Summer Night" by the Danleers followed.

"I still have the original flathead engine with a special cam, lifters and three pots," Speedo said.

"Pots?"

"Carbs. Carburetors. I have two extra. More power. I might drop a bigger engine in some day. And maybe chop the roof to make the body look lower."

"It's cool, man," Shades said. "I really don't know what you're talking about."

Speedo pulled on the large plastic ball atop the floor mounted shift lever and released the clutch. The Mercury leaped forward with a squeal from the rear tires. Shades' ill-fitting glasses slipped off the bridge of his nose as Speedo spun the steering wheel and headed for Roosevelt Avenue.

"Peal out," Speedo said. "This is how we make ourselves known now."

Speedo ran through the next two gears before they reached Roosevelt Avenue and downshifted to second as they swung right toward Jackson Heights.

"I can't open it up around here," Speedo shouted above the music and rumble from the dual glass-pak Hollywood mufflers. "I'll take you for a spin on the Connecting Highway later."

"Yeah, sure. You know how to get to Benny's place?"

"I only been there once but I think I can find it again. It's on Roosevelt Avenue somewhere around Eighty-Ninth Street."

The Mercury negotiated the light evening traffic under the elevated train tracks, out-racing a Main Street bound express before being passed by the clattering line of cars when stopped for a red light at Eighty-Second Street. Speedo guided the car to a stop at a stretch of curb six blocks later.

"That's it over there," Speedo said pointing to a line of stores across the street. "It's somewhere in the middle of the block, in the basement."

"Basement?"

"Yeah," Speedo said as they pushed out of the low seats and slammed the doors shut. "It takes up most of the space under the stores. It's a combination bowling alley, pool hall and bar. Benny's father probably owns the place. He's usually behind the bar."

"Aren't you scared somebody's gonna steal the car? Like we used to?" Shades asked.

"No way. I put a plate over the contacts and a kill switch under my seat. See, you didn't even see me throw the switch before I hit the starter button. They would have to break a window, crawl in and then try to start it. They can press that starter button all night and nothing'll happen."

"Takes a thief to know a thief, hah?"

Speedo laughed. "I guess so."

Shades felt a rush of excitement as they crossed the street. He was about to have a second birth of freedom, this time with the backing of age and experience.

Speedo led Shades down a flight of concrete steps below a red neon sign that advertised: BO LING. BILLIARDS. COCKTAIL LOUNGE. Speedo pushed open the solid wooden door at the foot of the steps and they stepped in, taking a moment for their vision to become accustomed to the dimmer light.

Shades had to blink his eyes a few times before the room came into focus. Speedo had already descended the one step inside landing and was near the narrow bar, its surface illuminated by hidden red and blue lights behind a wall cornice. There was no one in the room.

Red cushioned, chrome leg barstools were randomly scattered in an uneven zigzag placement. The vertical panel of the bar was covered with red vinyl, cushioned and tufted with rows of red vinyl buttons. Tiers of liquor bottles on glass shelves were mounted to a mirrored wall behind the bar and below the light cornice.

A bit gaudy, Shades thought, but if it attracted customers that's all that mattered. He stepped down from the landing and his glasses slipped along the bridge of his nose again when he looked down. He pushed them back into place and followed Speedo along the red tile floor of the barroom to an archway that opened into a brightly-lit room and three pool tables on a bare-wood floor. Three people - two sharply attired in sport jackets, one in his twenties, the other a teen, and a burly, middle-aged man in a polo shirt - were standing around one of the tables with pool cues in their hands.

The older man rose from his hunched stance at the end of the table, the tip of his stick still resting on the green felt in the middle of a smattering of multi-colored balls. The younger pool shooters turned to Shades and Speedo.

The older man brushed a hand through his salt-and-pepper

hair. "Hi'ya, fellas," he greeted with a hint of mistrust in his voice. "Pool or bowlin'?"

One of the younger players dropped his cue from a military port arms stance into a more relaxed posture. "Shades?"

"What'a you say, Al," Shades said.

"Relax, Mr. Petrillo," Al said. "These are our buddies from Woodside. This is the guy Benny's been waiting for. Him and Johnny the gimp were Kelly's number two guys."

A smile spread across Mr. Petrillo's face. "Any friends of my nephew are welcome here."

"This is Benny's father," Al said moving toward Shades. "And Paulie. He was with the old Sinners clique."

"*Sinners?*" Shades asked with a flush of disdain as he shook Al's hand.

"Yeah," Al said. "We made peace with them after the last blow-up. How's it going, Speedo?" Al nodded, his sloped, thick-lid cold eyes staring at Shades' partner.

"I don't know," Speedo said. "I didn't hear about any peace with those mothers."

"How about a drink, fellas?" Mr. Petrillo asked. "On the house."

"Sure," Shades said as he shook hands with Mr. Petrillo. "You remind me of Johnny. He always knew how to defuse a bomb."

"Yeah, he's a good boy. He has wisdom beyond his years." Mr. Petrillo slapped Shades on the back and beckoned everyone toward the bar.

"Why did you call him Johnny the gimp?" Shades asked Al.

"'Cause of his leg. When he got it broken that time."

"You mean that time the Sinners broke it?" Speedo asked.

"Come on, man," Al said. "Paulie's okay. Let by-gones be by-gones."

"Relax," Shades said to Speedo. "So what happened?" He asked turning back to Al.

"He got a real quack that set the bone wrong. Johnny wound up with a limp after the cast came off."

Shades shook his head. He glanced over his shoulder at the

bowling lanes, two steps down from the pool hall. He remembered working as a pin setter in a bowling alley when he was young. "You still use pin boys?" Shades asked Mr. Petrillo as they passed through the archway.

"We put in automatic machines as soon as they came out." He slid behind the bar and began placing ice filled glasses in front of them.

Shades ordered scotch on the rocks and was given the top-shelf choice of Johnny Walker Black. He was apprehensive about its effect after a two-year abstinence.

Everyone seemed to relax, except for Paulie, the outcast of the group, who further alienated himself by sitting three stools away from the trio of Vandals. Neither Shades nor Speedo had offered him their handshake.

"So, tell me what's been happening," Shades said.

"We're doing pretty good," Al said, smoothing down the collar of his black silk shirt. "Benny's been waiting for you and Kelly to get out so we can expand. He knows you guys can get things rolling even better."

"Where is he?" Shades asked, purposely sipping at his scotch but still feeling a slight rush.

"He's never here in the middle of the week. He's taking care of business. Taking names and kicking asses."

"And Johnny?"

"He's kind of a part-timer. He handles some of the bookkeeping. I think he's even going to school for accounting. He knows his shit."

"That's Johnny," Shades said. "Everyone always thought Sonny was my main competition because he was outward and aggressive. But it's always the quiet guy you gotta watch out for." He stared at Paulie, who was silently monitoring the conversation. "Ain't that right?"

Paulie shrugged and turned away, cupping his drink and staring at the mirror.

"Don't get me wrong," Shades said turning back, and taking a full swig of the scotch. "I love Johnny. We're no more competitive than Benny and Kelly are. We're more like partners. That's the way it was supposed to be. Partners. Brothers. Kelly, Johnny and me."

"Have another," Mr. Petrillo said while pouring a stream of scotch into Shades' glass. The fresh ice cubes crackled as the scotch flowed over them. He filled the other glasses, except for Paulie who waved off the offer.

Shades was feeling very relaxed and began taking larger gulps. "We're gonna have a lot of guys getting out in the next six months. Some of them are gonna want jobs. I gotta get together with Benny and Johnny to work out some details."

"I know they wanna see you," Al said. "But they're hard to get hold of during the week. Right, Mr. Petrillo?"

Mr. Petrillo nodded. "Since he's had his own apartment, I hardly see him," he said. "Sometimes him and the boys drift in unexpected. Friday is your best bet. This place is packed."

"Okay," Shades said, slugging the rest of his drink. "That's when I'll be back. Can I have a pencil and paper?"

Benny's father slid them across the bar to Shades.

"If anyone makes contact before then," Shades said as he scrawled a telephone number on the pad, "Ask them to give me a buzz."

"I'll do that," Mr. Petrillo said, tearing off the slip and placing it in his pocket.

"Thank you, sir." Shades offered his hand.

"How about one for the road?" Mr. Petrillo asked pushing Shades' hand aside.

"I don't know. I'm starting to feel it." Shades turned to Speedo. "Unless you do."

Speedo tilted his head to show interest and Mr. Petrillo poured another round. Paulie nursed his original drink. After awhile the topics were exhausted. Everyone had tried to avoid controversy, especially the old rivalry with the Sinners.

"This is a nice place you got," Speedo said, trying to stimulate the dialogue. "A lot better than the candy store."

"Candy store?" Al laughed. "You don't still hang around at Bill's?"

"Just to meet at. We go cruising after. Why, something wrong with Bill's?" Speedo pointed at Al, feeling a surge of courage from the drinks. "That place used to be the best damn hangout around."

"Even Paulie and his guys graduated out of candy stores," Al said. "And they're just barely old enough to drink legally."

"What're you looking for trouble?" Speedo asked. "Why're you sticking up for some punks who were the cause of one Vandal getting killed and half of them going to the can?"

Al stood and Speedo followed. Shades sprang up between them.

"That's it," Mr. Petrillo shouted. "We have a rule here. Trouble-makers have to leave."

"I'll take care of him," Shades said. "We should be going any-way." He had pushed the two apart and held them at a comfort-able distance. His glasses had slipped forward and he cursed under his breath. He was sure the exchange of words was only the booze talking.

"Come on." Shades adjusted his glasses, put his arm around Speedo and walked him to the door landing. He glanced back and gave a reassuring gesture to Mr. Petrillo. "Thanks again. See you Friday."

Mr. Petrillo pointed at Speedo and shook his head.

Shades nodded, acknowledging the exchange. Speedo stumbled on the first concrete step outside the door as he tried to turn to thank his host. Shades turned him forward and up the steps.

"I wanted to thank Benny's father," Speedo said as they stepped onto the sidewalk.

"Don't worry about it," Shades said. "He knows you appreci-ate it." The cold air started a buzz in Shades' head. "Damn, I don't know which one of us is in worse shape. Can you drive?"

"Sure." Speedo broke free of Shades and staggered off the curb before straightening out. He walked to the rear antenna of his car and unlocked it. The doors popped open and Speedo bowed and swept his arm forward. "But I'm gonna let you drive anyway."

"Come on. It's been a couple of years since I drove," Shades said crossing the street. "I never even had a license."

"So what? One more ticket and I loose mine." Speedo laughed and slumped against the car. "We can take back streets. Come on, you gotta get behind a wheel sooner or later."

"Yeah, it would feel good again." Shades felt uninhibited. He only hesitated for a moment before throwing away caution. "Okay, let's go."

CHAPTER 23

Shades held his glasses in place as he slid behind the steering wheel and closed the door. "I gotta get these friggen glasses fixed," Shades said as he familiarized himself with the driver's area. "How's this floor shift work?"

"The same three speed 'H' pattern as a column shift," Speedo said as he reached under the driver's seat. "Don't worry, I'm not getting familiar. I just turning off the kill switch." He sat up. "Okay, clutch it and hit the starter."

Shades followed the directions and the loud rumble of the mufflers vibrated beneath his seat. The radio static disappeared in a few seconds. "The Closer You Are" by the Channels replaced it. Shades shifted into first, released the clutch and stalled the engine.

"Do it again," Speedo said. "It'll come back to you."

The rumble vibrated again and the Mercury swung slowly into the unoccupied traffic lane. Shades turned the next corner after shifting to second. Speedo gave directions for the least vulnerable route back to their neighborhood.

"Can you believe those guys?" Speedo asked.

"Man, when you told me you didn't wanna get involved with Benny's crew, I thought it was because of the business end," Shades said.

"It is," Speedo said. "But now I got an even better reason. I don't want anything to do with guys who team up with our old enemies."

"There's gotta be more to it. It's probably a business arrangement," Shades said. "Johnny would never go along with anything less and Benny wouldn't deal with the guys that helped put Kelly away without a very good reason."

"You make it sound okay," Speedo said as he lit up a cigarette. "But I still don't trust them. Especially guys like Al."

"Guys like him don't bother me. I've learned how to deal with all kinds of people while I was away. Him and the punk from the Sinners are just little cogs in the wheel. They're needed to keep things going. Like Blackie and the crazies. They serve a purpose."

"What?" Speedo gyrated in his seat and his hand struck the dashboard. His cigarette flew passed Shades' face. "Oh shit."

"Get it, man." Shades looked at the glow on the black shag carpeting and his glasses slid to the tip of his nose.

"I see it." Speedo bent forward and twisted around the shift lever, reaching for the cigarette.

Shades felt a jolt. The car had struck something. He jerked his head up and the glasses sailed off. They bounced off the windshield and fell to the dashboard. He felt the panic of an unfamiliar situation and stomped on the gas pedal. The steering wheel became loose in his hands and the car swerved into the opposite lane before he gained control. He rammed his foot on the brake, bringing the Mercury to a screeching halt. Speedo careened off the dash and was thrown back into his seat. The engine stalled and the car sat across the width of the street.

The block of two story homes was dark, the streetlamps hidden behind and dimmed by the line of robust oak trees flanking the length of the street, their autumn leaves still clinging to the branches. The Mercury had settled a few car lengths from the corner, about a half-block from where Shades had panicked.

Speedo twisted in his seat and squinted through the fogged rear window as Shades fumbled for his glasses.

"Shit, there's someone laying in the street next to a truck," Speedo said. "And there's a guy walking up the block waving his arms."

"What?" Shades jammed his glasses into place and turned in his seat. He could only make out the red, clouded tint of the taillights through the rear window. He rolled his door window down halfway and heard shouting.

"Get out'a here," Speedo yelled. He reached for the starter button. "Put the clutch in and shift it back to first."

"Are you sure it was a person?" Shades asked, his voice unintentionally calm.

"It sure as hell looks like it." Speedo poked at the starter button. "We can't stick around to find out. Go. Get out'a here before this guy gets close enough to get my plate number."

Shades' knee trembled as he released the clutch pedal. "A hit and run," he shouted as he slammed the shift lever into second, the gears grinding when his foot slipped off the pedal. "If it was a person, they'll get me for hit and run."

The Mercury continued through the intersection and down a hill.

"I gotta stop, man," Shades said.

"Not here. Put some more distance behind us and then I'll take over."

"I don't want you to take the rap."

"Nobody's gonna take a rap," Speedo said. "I can't afford it anymore than you. We'll find the other guys. Maybe they'll alibi for us. They can say we were with them all night."

"No," Shades said. He leaned his head back to steady his glasses and stared along his nose. "We can't let anyone else know about it."

"Hey, it's my car. Somebody's gonna see the dent. Look, the headlight is out on my side. How am I gonna explain that?"

"You were teaching me how to, or refreshing me on how to drive and I hit a pole or something. It makes sense."

"Damn, this stinks." Speedo pointed to the next corner. "Pull into that A&P parking lot."

Shades maneuvered to a stop in the small blacktop lot and turned off the lights and ignition. They jumped from the car and went to the damaged front.

"Shit," Speedo said. "All the work I put into that frenched

headlight."

A gaping hole where the extended, molded custom headlight bezel and assembly had been was accompanied by a large flat dent on the edge of the fender. A small piece of the seal beam, still attached to its wiring, hung from the opening.

"Shit," Speedo said again. He turned to the other cars in the lot, then looked back to the damage. "I can't run around with a light out or the cops will pull me over."

Shades felt useless. But, at least Speedo was now sober and able to plot some kind of strategy.

Speedo reached through the open passenger window and, with a dull pop, the trunk lid rose. "The lid lock's electric, too," he said in passing as he moved to the rear of the car. "Keep a lookout for me, Shades. I'll be right back."

A screwdriver and hammer in hand, Speedo walked quickly to the front of another Mercury parked facing the building wall. Shades moved to the corner of the lot and scanned the adjoining blocks. He heard a hammered bang behind him, followed by the sound of metal clattering on the blacktop. Two minutes later, Speedo squatted in front of his damaged fender.

"Couple'a more minutes and we're out'a here," Speedo said.

Shades scanned toward the side entrance of the supermarket and saw the battered metal framed glass door swing open. He gave a shrill, short whistle, the old Vandal lookout warning. Speedo looked up and then continued with his effort when he saw the couple that had emerged from the store stop their rattling shopping cart next to a DeSoto.

Shades returned to his vigil and took the minutes offered by Speedo to try to put the last fifteen minutes of fast moving stressful events into perspective. He was still calm. His only concerns were self-preservation and a big money future. If some jerk decided to step in front of the car he was driving, then *tough titty* for the jerk.

A thought flashed through his mind. How could they prove who was driving the car? *It was his word against Speedo's.* No witnesses. The car belongs to Speedo, who would be naturally driving it. Why would a guy just out of the can, on parole, with no license be stupid enough to be driving a car? No one he had met in his lifetime had ever considered Shades as stupid. He would be very home free if the hammer ever dropped.

There was just one very important factor. Speedo was a Vandal. If Shades had once stuck his neck out for a guy who was bent on destroying him just because the guy was a Vandal, then there was no way Shades could consider anything but sticking it out with Speedo. *You and yours.* And the yours was the Vandals, be they then or now.

He heard the Mercury's engine start and for a fleeting moment thought that Speedo was leaving him behind. He spun around and saw Speedo jump out of the car and check the now operating headlight.

"Let's get out'a here," Speedo said as he climbed back into the car.

Shades hustled to the passenger seat and the Mercury headed for the driveway cutout. The DeSoto suddenly pulled into their path and Speedo jammed on the brakes.

"Hey, don't blow it now," Shades said.

"Yeah, okay." Speedo waved the DeSoto on and then followed it into the street.

They were both silent as Speedo manipulated the Mercury through back streets, eventually reaching the brightly-lit main thoroughfare of Northern Boulevard.

"Shades, I'm scared," Speedo said. "I didn't have time to think about it before but what if they got my plate? What if they find a part of my car they can trace back to me?"

"Just keep calm. We don't know if it was a person. It could've been anything. And if it was a person, maybe he just got bruised and will forget about it because he's lucky to be alive."

"And what if - "

"Don't think about that. It's not easy to get killed by a car unless you hit someone dead center. Look, find the guys and act as though nothing happened."

Speedo let out a long breath. "Okay, I'll try."

The Mercury traveled slowly. Speedo avoided weaving through traffic and gave extra attention to traffic signals. While they were stopped, waiting for a red light to change, a police car streaked by, heading in the opposite direction, its siren blaring. Speedo turned pale.

"They look like they're in a hurry," Speedo said, sitting straight in the seat and facing forward.

"Relax. They weren't interested in you," Shades said.

"Sure, not now. They're probably on their way to check out the hit and run accident."

"Come on, man. Snap out of it. I was driving, not you. You see me shiting in my pants?"

"I can't help it. It's the way I am."

The light turned green and they continued. The car turned onto the entrance ramp of a highway and swayed slightly as it negotiated a small interval of slick bricks around a curve in the normally blacktop roadway. The highway dipped and then leveled out below the streets.

Two vehicles were racing ahead of them. Speedo let them distance themselves from him before he accelerated, pressing Shades against his backrest.

Shades looked at the metal railing that lined the service road above them. Clusters of people leaned against the barricade with a ringside view of the illegal drag races.

Speedo's coupe ran the stretch of blacktop and concrete in twenty seconds, spewing a rapid popping from its exhaust as it decelerated under a looming overpass.

"It's about a quarter of a mile between bridges," Speedo said as he steered into a curve then accelerated again. "That's the normal distance of a drag strip track." The curve of the road led to a quick radical cut-off and the Mercury exited, jerking to a stop at the foot of the ramp.

Shades straight-armed the dash to keep steady. "You sure look like you're back into the swing of things," he said.

"Yeah, I guess so." The coupe made a series of turns and found its way to a street that overlooked the highway. "Speed is like booze to me. It takes away all my troubles."

They cruised slowly along the groups of people Shades had seen while on the highway. A variety of customized and straight cars lined the curb on the opposite side of the narrow service road.

"When I'm dragging somebody and all these people are watching me, man, what a high. Especially if I win."

"A lot bigger crowd than you and Val and the Emeral-Tones got when you were singing," Shades said. "Not that you guys weren't half bad."

Speedo laughed. "Yeah, but those days are over, too. This crowd is nothing, though. They're thinned out this time of year. You should see it during the summer. There's hundreds of people, three deep along the rail, three cars at a time dragging in both directions below. What a charge, man"

The Mercury swung around a corner as it passed the last group of spectators and stopped midway up the block.

"That's them," Speedo said as he shut everything down. "I'm gonna park over here so they don't see the fender."

"Good thinking," Shades said, now fairly confident Speedo had cleared his troubled mind. "But don't say anything to them about what happened."

"Don't worry about it."

They moved toward the group. Jimmy and Val were facing them, leaning against the railing. Tony stood on the bottom rung of the structure, stretched over the top to get a better view of the action below.

"Holy shit, that's Shades with him," Jimmy shouted.

They met in the middle of the street, shaking hands. Tony hugged Shades after leaving his railing perch. Shades dropped back a step after the greetings and scanned their faces. None of them had changed much. Val was still as handsome as ever, even more so with maturity. Tony still had that crazy uneven look that made someone think twice about even talking to him. Like Speedo, he was wearing the old Vandal jacket stripped of its name. Jimmy, although smiling still had that brooding pouted lower lip. Shades wondered if Jimmy had reverted back to his old antics as the Mad Russian.

"What'a you think about Speedo's rig?" Val asked.

"Tough, man. Real tough," Shades said.

"Hey, wait'll you see mine," Val said, jerking his head toward the two cars parked along the opposite curb.

They turned to a black, '58 Chevrolet Impala convertible, the top up, sitting in front of a maroon '53 Oldsmobile, the word "Ruby" scripted in white behind the wheel opening of the fender. Chrome side pipes ran along its rocker panels.

Shades walked around the Impala, showing as much enthusiasm as he could muster, wishing Val well with the car. Tony was quick to claim ownership of the Oldsmobile. Jimmy didn't own a car and made a comment about how everyone thought more about machines than people, but qualified his remarks by saying he was saving to buy one.

Val had slipped behind the steering wheel of the convertible and turned on the radio. "I think music stinks since that Payola crap," Val said. "That's why I rigged up this little beauty." He pointed out a small phonograph player mounted to a shelf under the glove box. "I can't use it while I'm driving, but if I don't like what's on the radio while I'm parked, I can throw on some of my old 45s. Especially if I want the right mood while I'm trying to make some chick."

They hung around the two cars, mixing conversation rehashing old times and the enthusiasm with racing. Shades was relieved to see that Speedo had engrossed himself in the discussions. Shades tried to transfer his thoughts to Speedo. *It's over and everything is cool. You're among friends. It never happened.*

The normal national and international news drifted through the radio - President Eisenhower's illness, the cold war with the

Soviet Union, problems in Southeast Asia - until the local news events caught the attention of Shades and Speedo.

"In Queens, the fourth hit and run accident in two weeks occurred less than an hour ago," the announcer said. "The victim was killed instantly when an unidentified car struck him down in front of his home at..."

"Let's get some tunes on," Val said. He spun the knob and jumbled words and musical tones jumped through the speakers until "At The Hop" by Danny and the Juniors was settled on by Val. "You can't find too many colored groups anymore. It's like they've been cut out of the picture," he said. "I guess they don't have the bread to pay off the D.J.s."

Shades looked at Speedo and saw his face was as pale as when the police car had passed them. He looked like he would get sick at any moment. Speedo turned to Shades, his gaze glassy and frightened.

"Hey, Speedo," Shades said, "I think I lost my wallet in your car. Give me the keys so I can look for it."

"You may have trouble with it. I'll open it."

"Be right back," Shades said as he followed Speedo to the Mercury.

"We gotta get out'a here," Speedo said. "You heard that radio. The guy got killed." He stopped next to the car.

"Where can we go?" Shades asked.

"I don't know." Speedo fumbled the key around the antenna lock cylinder. "I just know I gotta go."

"You can't run. It'll be too suspicious. Sit tight. I'm sure Benny or somebody knows a guy who can do the bodywork. I'll pay for it."

"You'll pay for it?" Speedo asked drawing back the key. "And who's gonna pay for me not sleeping at night?"

"I did it," Shades shouted. He looked around to see if any of the others had heard his outburst. None of them were looking his way. "It was me who was driving," he said. "And I don't give a crap. Can you dig that? I killed the guy and I - don't - give a crap. Why should you?"

"But it was my car. I'm involved."

"I told you I'm not going back to the can. And I'm not. If you keep up this crap, you're gonna put me there."

Shades was reluctant to threaten but needed a means to jolt Speedo out of his attitude. He grabbed Speedo by the shoulders and held him firmly. "If I go up again, it's gonna throw off the plans of a lot of people. If Benny found out you were the guy that put me away and he wound up loosing a lot of bucks because of it, then you'd be as dead as the guy I hit."

"I don't believe it. You'd have me knocked off over this?"

"Not me. Get this straight. They would. I'm a needed commodity. I know how to make bread and they need me. They would be the guys who would be highly pissed off."

"But you'd put in a good word for me."

"You still don't understand." Shades shook him. "It wouldn't be up to me. I could make you sound like my brother and they wouldn't care."

"But I wouldn't squeal. You know that. I'm a Vandal. I don't squeal."

"Okay, that's it. You gotta keep thinking that way. I know you'd never squeal, but you gotta get tough. You gotta make like this never happened so if the cops check you out - and that's far from happening - then you can brush them off in a way that they'd never be able to pin anything on you, or us."

"Okay, man, I'll straighten out." Speedo relaxed and Shades released his grip. "I'm a fucking rock."

"Hey, remember what they used to say when we were kids?" Shades slapped Speedo on the arm. "We piss on rocks."

"Not this one." Speedo turned and followed Shades back to the other Vandals.

Val had put on the 45 player. "Church Bells May Ring" by the Willows was playing.

"We decided to make a run into Rockaway," Val said when the

duo reached the Impala. "It's dead here. Maybe we can catch some action along the way on Cross Bay Boulevard."

"Jeez, it's getting late," Speedo said. "Tomorrow's a work day."

"Fuck it," Tony said. "Call in sick. We gotta celebrate Shades being home again. Even Jimmy's coming."

"Come on, rock," Shades said. He wasn't overly enthusiastic about the Rockaway run but needed to keep an eye on Speedo for a few more hours. "I'll bet it's been awhile since you called in sick."

Speedo nodded. "Yeah, it has been. Okay, let's roll."

Speedo was behind the steering wheel of the Mercury again, Shades in the passenger seat. The engine rumbled to life and the car made a three-point turn at the next intersection, heading back toward the service road. Speedo reached out and silenced the radio. The Impala and Oldsmobile had left their parking spaces and disappeared.

"Those fucking guys never wait for anybody," Speedo said as he rammed the shift lever into second. He maneuvered around winding turns through a bleak factory district and was again on Northern Boulevard heading back along their earlier route. "I lost them. They expect people to read their minds. They must be going to Tony's house first," Speedo said. "He lives in Elmhurst. That's too damn close to where it happened. I better take another route."

The Mercury swung off the boulevard at the next intersection and wound through sidestreets until Speedo slowed to a cruise on a block of apartment buildings.

"Shit, they ain't here," Speedo said. "This happens all the time. They screw around and change their minds and then change them back again until we wind up either doing nothing or spending the night back at the Connecting. "

"Calm down, man," Shades said. "Go back to the highway. If they aren't there, then you can drive me home and we'll have a couple of beers at my place and call it a night."

"I guess so." Speedo began another succession of turns out of the area. "I don't know why I put up with them. Not so much Jimmy. He cares more than the other two. They only care about themselves and what they wanna do when the urge hits them. Maybe after some of the other guys get out of the army - and even some of the guys from jail - we can start getting the old crowd back together. Then I won't have to depend on those two. But that won't be for awhile. I don't know. Everything just stinks."

"Hey, there's no reason why you and Jimmy and whoever else can't check out Benny's place - as my guest - without getting involved in the action." Shades remembered Mr. Petrillo's gesture. "As long as you behave yourselves and keep your cool. You can hang out with us and still do what you're doing now."

"Ahh, what the hell for?" Speedo asked. "Goddamn it, what's this all about?"

A wooden barricade painted white to reflect approaching headlights blocked the next street, STREET CLOSED - CONSTRUCTION stenciled in black across the horizontal beam.

Speedo picked his way through an unfamiliar maze of disjointed one-way streets. Shades began to feel Speedo's frustration as the steering wheel snapped in its revolutions and the gearshift lever was constantly snapped and yanked through its positions. Speedo finally found a road that extended for more than three blocks in a straight line. He rammed into the power gear and accelerated, generating a quick yelp from the rear tires, the frustration vanishing in a burst of speed.

"Oh no," Speedo said. The Mercury jerked as Speedo and Shades lurched forward and the engine groaned in protest. "This looks like the block."

"They all look the same around here," Shades said. "Just get out of this neighborhood."

"*It is,*" Speedo yelled. "That's the same truck that was parked there before." Speedo shifted into second gear and the engine regained its spirit, propelling the Mercury passed the moving van. "They saw us," Speedo said. "There was someone looking out the window of the house."

Shades held his glasses in place and jerked his head to look at the window. He couldn't see any movement.

The Mercury was halfway through the intersection and the other car was in as much a hurry. It lightly grazed the end of the Mercury's rear bumper, but with enough force to tear the chrome bar from its brackets. The distorted hunk of metal bounced and skimmed along the street surface, traveling perpendicular to the fleeing Mercury.

Speedo had no trouble correcting the relatively minor fishtail from the impact. He had become an expert wheelman in his dedicated years of driving and had pulled out of worst jams in the past. He avoided the row of parked cars and was down the small hill and a block away before he saw the flash of red in his rear view mirror.

"Oh shit. Cops." Speedo shifted again and drove through the continuous intersections, daring anyone in his way.

The traffic light was green when he reached Northern Boulevard and he was sure that if he reached it, and made his way to the highway, he could loose the cops on the makeshift drag strip where he had crushed a host of takers in the past. The Mercury cornered onto the boulevard, moaning and straining against the pressure on the springs and suspension. Another gearshift as the car regained its stability and a burst of power from the second carburetor kicking in rocketed the vehicle as it straightened into a lane. The rear dipped like a giant hand had pushed down on the trunk lid.

Speedo heard the distant siren scream as he swung around the Impala convertible and maroon Oldsmobile trawling along the boulevard.

Shades, as pale as Speedo had been when he heard the broadcast, and clinging to the sides of his seat, confirmed what Speedo had seen. "It's them. It's Val and Tony."

"Slow 'em down, man. Cut 'em off," Speedo yelled, giving directions to deaf ears now two blocks behind. "That's what I'd have done for you."

"Rotten bastards," Speedo said as he watched the red flashing light swing around Val and Tony in his rear view mirror. "I should've guessed those guys would screw me again." He was on the verge of tears. *Those guys were no longer Vandals.* He would see to it when the others came home and could be told of Val and Tony and their indifference. And he would have Shades Gaglione as his witness.

Speedo down-shifted and swung wide into the opposite lane to catch the angle needed to put the Mercury into a straight line through the confines of the entrance ramp. An approaching car veered away and bounced over a curb before stopping on the sidewalk.

Shades saw a cement wall coming at them and bellowed, but the rear of the Mercury swung back into line and pushed them toward a curve in the road. He clung to the bottom of his seat with one hand while keeping his glasses in place with the other. If anything was going to happen, he wanted to see it coming. *Don't let them catch us.* Shades didn't want to put his words of uncharacteristic emotion into speech. There was suddenly no fear of physical injury. The cement wall was behind them. If they had hit it, he would have been more concerned over his ability to drag himself to freedom than about the broken bones or ripped skin he could have suffered. He sank deeper into his seat as Speedo twisted the steering wheel into the first curve, rambling across stretches of slick brick and pothole gouged blacktop, heading for the smooth strip of highway that led toward the Triborough Bridge. They were jolted by a staccato of vertical vibrations and Shades was pressed against the door through the curve.

The Mercury slithered down the dip in the road and Speedo's enthusiastic shout was reassuring as the third carburetor boosted the power.

Shades glanced at the speedometer. The needle was about to touch 90. He clung to his glasses and swung around in his seat. The patrol car was slipping and swaying across the patch of bricks. Shades was now positive that Speedo would win.

Shades reluctantly looked at the speedometer again. The needle was buried at 100. *Maybe faster with the modifications on the engine.*

He felt a mixture of anxiety while still awed by Speedo's abilities. "You got them," he shouted. "You're gonna loose them."

The second overpass whizzed by in a blur and the next curve loomed a few yards ahead. A line of multi-shaped red lights was suddenly strung across the lanes ahead of them. The last drag racers of the evening, hidden from view by the bend in the road, had slowed to a crawl after their contest. Speedo spun the Mercury into a right angle turn toward the exit that he knew was somewhere in the immediate area.

The brake lights flashed momentarily before they were darkened by the impact that severed every wiring system of the vehicle. The Mercury smashed into the curb of the ramp and twisted skyward. It completed a double somersault, throwing off its two front wheels and mangled suspension parts before slamming back to the ground, bouncing and twisting three times before settling against a light pole. The pole tilted, then partial straightened before its light extinguished from the pressure.

The pursuing patrol car was a full minute behind and slid to a halt behind the crumpled wreck.

"Crazy damn fools," the cop surveying the wreckage said. He walked back to the patrol car in a state of nausea. He saw a black convertible streak by and then an older maroon Oldsmobile pull onto a triangle of grass at the head of the exit ramp.

"What do you guys want?" he shouted, propelling his flashlight beam into the faces of the two kids who had stepped out of the Oldsmobile. "There's nothing here you want to see."

"We think we know the guys in that car," Jimmy said. "Are they..."

"Yeah, they're dead. Damn it!" The cop stopped midway between the two cars and studied the kid's faces. One of them looked like he belonged in a carnival sideshow but the other had a worried seemingly concerned baby face. "And for no damn reason. All we wanted to do was tell them some people moving furniture wanted to talk to them. No mistaking the description of the car. It was the one hit by a statue that fell off the tailgate of a moving van.

The people who reported it were worried about the damage they caused. What the hell did he run for?"

"They don't trust cops," Tony said.

"A lot of good it did them." The cop rubbed his eyes. "I don't know why I'm telling you this. You really know them?"

Jimmy and Tony nodded.

"You guys stick around. I want to talk to you." He dropped the flashlight beam off them and thrust himself into the door opening of the patrol car to confer with his partner.

"Well, at least we got that other son of a bitch," the cop said as he stood up.

Jimmy and Tony stared at him blankly.

"The hit and run driver from a couple of hours ago. They caught the bastard."

CHAPTER 24

THE WILSON FAMILY – FEBRUARY, 1959

Johnny sat at the kitchen table staring at the half-eaten food on his plate. Madge Wilson was puttering around in the overhead cabinets, seemingly stalling for time before starting into her compulsive diatribe about her son, Pete. The kid had been home for a month. *Kid?* Johnny corrected himself. Pete was only a year and a half younger than him.

Johnny hadn't been pleased about accepting another favor from Benny. He was becoming more entangled, more prone to indebtedness to the acting-president of the Vandals. But he had reluctantly given in when Benny offered to have one of his limousines chauffeur Johnny and Madge to Elmira. Like most of Benny's previous generosities, this was for the benefit of Johnny's surrogate mother, the woman he had adopted three years ago. Her real son had been released from the reformatory and she needed a way to get him home.

Pete was in awe when he saw the long black Cadillac that his mother and Johnny Sadinski had arrived in. He had not only been surprised by the limo - he revealed to Johnny later that day - but also the elegant appearance of his mother. He had noticed changes in her hair, clothing and mannerisms through the years, but that day she looked extra special. She was petite and her hair was now a soft brown with a few strands of gray highlighting the subdued bouffant style. Her face was even more angelic with the elimination of the heavy make-up that had hidden her true beauty. She had worn a blue pants suit, the color accenting her equally blue eyes.

He had also scrutinized Johnny, one of his oldest friends, who had become more and more part of his life in the past year, accompanying Pete's mother on most of her visits to Elmira, as though his presence encouraged her to take the long train and bus trips. Johnny was still tall and lanky but with broader shoulders and a mature fullness in his face. His dark brown hair was medium length, straight and slicked back, a third change in style since Pete had known him.

But while Pete had been familiarizing himself with them, Madge and Johnny had also pondered the changes in him. The fourteen-year-old boy who had entered Elmira was now a young adult. He had started shaving, showing a slight shadow and stubble below his lower lip. His dirty-blond hair was in need of a trim, and worry lines across his forehead and circles beneath the eyes completed the transformation.

Johnny had told Pete about Shades during the trip home and Pete took the news hard. He remembered how Shades had looked him up when he passed through Elmira and told Pete how good things would be when they all returned to the old neighborhood. Pete was convinced that the limousine he rode in was part of the legacy vaunted by Shades. The ten- dollar tip he saw Johnny slip to the driver and the classy building they arrived at fortified his dream.

Johnny gave Pete a tour of the spacious apartment before stopping at one of the two bedrooms. "And this is yours," he had said. He allowed Pete to enter the neat room ahead of him. "I officially turn it over to you."

"Turn it over?" Pete asked, pressing on the bed mattress to test its flexibility.

"Yeah, I've been looking out for it until you got home."

"You've been living in my mother's apartment?"

"It belonged to both of us," Madge said. "Johnny was sharing it with me until you got home."

"How's that?" Pete's voice raised slightly and his fists clenched. *"What the hell's been going on?"*

"Watch what you're thinking," Johnny said. "And get rid of that hothead attitude. You're not on the street or in Elmira. You're in your mother's home."

"And so are you. Don't talk to me like you're my old man."

"Petie. Stop it this instant." Madge slapped the door jam. "If it wasn't for Johnny I'd still be living in that dump we were in when you left. I wouldn't have the job I need to afford this place. I wouldn't have anything if it wasn't for him." Tears welled in her eyes.

Pete and Johnny moved to her. Pete looked suspiciously at Johnny before turning his mother away and hugging her.

"I'm sorry, mom," Pete said. "I know I told you before, but I'm sorry for everything I put you through."

Madge wrapped her arms around Pete and planted a sharp slap on his back. "I don't want you two fighting. Johnny has been my protector while you were gone and I want you to treat him with respect." She tapped his back. *"Understand?"*

"Okay, mom." He released his grip and stepped back, turning to Johnny. "I'm sorry. I just didn't know what to think."

"Forget it. Your mom deserves the apology. And like I said, this is now your room." Johnny pointed to a set of matched luggage sitting next to the dresser. "I'm moving into my girl's place so I can help her pay the rent. I expect you to take care of this room the same way I did," he said in a jokingly stern tone before realizing he sounded too patronizing.

Pete grimaced as he nodded. Johnny saw that Pete was embarrassed about his outburst and detected a hint of continued confusion and doubt.

Johnny became convinced of Pete's suspicions as the month unfolded. Johnny wanted to discuss the last three years in detail, to show him the closeness they should share because of their central interest, but *the kid* had avoided him. Not even Madge could bring her son to the negotiation table.

"…The limo. And the apartment," Madge was saying. Johnny was back in the kitchen of the once-shared apartment.

"Mom, please," Johnny said holding up his hand. He only called her mom when they were alone. "I told you I was taking care of everything. You know I've managed to keep out of the rackets. Benny has allowed me that. He knows I want no part of it. All I want is enough bread to put myself through college and live halfway decently. Now, if I can do that for myself, I can do it for Pete."

"But he's still vulnerable," Madge said. "It doesn't matter what you and I tell him. I've got to do something about it. I've got to change his way of thinking or get away from what's making him think the way he is. We'll have to move away."

"To where? Or more importantly, to what?" This was a new twist. She had never suggested packing up and getting out. Johnny knew she was comfortable in these surroundings. But he knew she would gladly return to the drudgery of the earlier years if it would protect and insulate Pete. "You can't step back. We can't. All three of us would be back were we started. We need the money we're making to build a future."

"What kind of a future? To wonder if Pete or you might someday be snuffed out of my life? Then I'd be back to nowhere. No more start. No more life…"

Johnny let her trail off into her thoughts, unable to counter her assessment. She was right, of course. But he had prepared himself for what was to come. Benny was constantly on him to become involved in the real organization. He had hoped it would never come to this, but he would gladly sacrifice himself to save all that had been gained. It wouldn't matter if he were the one snuffed out of her life, as long as she and her real child came out of it intact.

"Benny's a reasonable guy," Johnny said. "What about the limo?" He held up his hands again in anticipation of her protest. "There was no way we were gonna take two trains and a bus each way to get Pete home. I accepted Benny's offer for the convenience. And besides, you know Pete heard about Benny's operations from both Shades and the grapevine. Pete expected to see what he saw. We'll steer him in the right direction, back to school, and I'll see what I can do about getting him a legit job."

Madge rose and moved to Johnny's side. "I'm very lucky to have two sons." She bent and kissed his cheek. "I always knew you'd look out for him. But you can only try. It's becoming frustrating. Like tonight. Why didn't he show up for dinner?"

"Probably because I was invited," Johnny said as he slipped his arm around her waist and hugged Madge. "He still can't get it out of his head, you know, about us sharing this apartment before he came home."

"Maybe you should've started calling me mom in front of him right away."

"Not really. His head was still screwed up without someone else claiming you as his mother. Like we discussed, if I ever get to talk to him, I'll try to make everything look like it was a business arrangement rather than Platonic as it is."

"Oh my, I've got myself a college boy with fancy words," she said with a smile.

"You'll have two of them," Johnny said, hugging her. "As soon as we get him through high school. And that's a promise."

"I won't accept that promise from you." She tapped his shoulder. "Every time you promise something, you go out of your way to make sure it happens. That's something only Petie can make happen."

"He'll do it. And I'll help. No matter what."

"I love you. And I cherish that day that you knocked on my apartment door." Her eyes welled with tears as they had done so many times in the past month. "You changed my life so much."

"And you changed mine. We're more than even." He released his grip. "Okay, I gotta go. I've gotta see Benny and then find Pete so I can get his butt home to you."

"I'll wring his neck for not showing up," she said. "He better show more respect for you."

"Don't worry about it," Johnny said pushing out of the seat.

"He'll come around sooner or later. After all, he is your son."

Madge smiled again and hugged Johnny before he donned his overcoat and limped through the living room to the hallway door. He waved and softly closed the door behind him.

She stood staring at the door for a minute. She knew he was taking too much on his shoulders. She knew she was the one who should be bearing the burden.

CHAPTER 25

Johnny passed through the lobby and out the double glass entrance doors ornately trimmed in gold leaf swirls and address numbers. It was twilight and the rows of apartment buildings cast long
shadows across the street.

He knew what he had to do. There was no way his mother
would ever have to suffer through what she had experienced four
years ago. He would try to wrest control of - *his brother?* Damn, he
never thought of him that way. That would be a lot to ask. But
Pete was the linchpin that held them together.

Johnny had developed a cynicism from his dealings with Benny
and it helped justify his deception of Madge. He had lied about a
girl friend and moving to her apartment. He had slept at Benny's
office until another apartment was found. It was best for him to
have moved. It helped to dispel any lingering doubts Pete may
have had. *At least, he hoped it had.* And if Madge had known the
truth, she wouldn't have let Johnny leave.

Johnny also knew Benny was targeting Pete as one of the replacements for the troublesome kids recruited from the Sinners'
ranks. This was the second lie he continually spouted, now by
rote, to ease Madge's mind. *No, Pete is in no danger of being recruited by Benny.* Now, he would have to trade himself for her son.
What the hell! It would mean more money, and money was the
surface reason for what they were doing. Under the surface, it would
be the noble thing to do. At least he would retain that principle.

Johnny hobbled down the concrete steps to the basement
grotto, swinging open the heavy wooden door under the red neon
sign with the malfunctioning W in 'Bowling'.

Benny's father was tending bar at the narrow red and blue

tinted mahogany counter. Johnny saw Al, Paulie and a girl he didn't recognize sitting at the far end in front of the archway leading into the pool room. Mr. Petrillo read a newspaper, the tabloid spread across the bar surface.

Johnny swung his stiff leg down from the inside landing.

Mr. Petrillo looked up from his paper and smiled. "How's it goin', Johnny?"

"Okay, Mr. P. Has Pete been here today?"

"I don't know." He shrugged. "We were busy earlier. He may have slipped in and out without me noticin'." He returned to his paper.

Johnny nodded, not wanting to press the issue. He had asked Benny's father not to let Pete hang around the club. Pete had found his way there by the second night of his freedom and Johnny had tried to use his influence to have the kid banned. But once Benny had met Pete, he had countered Johnny's request. Mr. Petrillo was caught in the middle and Johnny, knowing whose influence would prevail, had compromised. Pete was allowed in when Benny was there and not allowed when Johnny was there. Johnny was not going to embarrass the man for siding with his son. Nor would he for any reason, knowing Mr. P was more than the bartender.

Al and Paulie glanced at Johnny before returning their attention to the girl.

And fuck you, too, Johnny thought as he crossed through the archway toward a door at the far end of the poolroom, flicking greetings to the players alongside the tables. He took off his overcoat and then rapped the secret knock on the solid door.

"Hi'ya, Frankie." Johnny gave a handshake to the large brute who guarded the inside of the doorway. "Nice going on your last fight."

"T'anks. Louie, my manager says I might get a shot at Sunnyside Gardens next," Frankie said in a deep baritone. "You guys can make a nice piece'a change if ya bet on me."

"Sure thing, man." Johnny stepped inside and Frankie closed the door behind him.

Johnny never failed to delight in the atmosphere Benny had created. The door guard; the secret knock; the typical smoke-filled room. The clinking of poker chips and the murmur of players asking for replacement cards in their poker game was the only sound in the room. The scene was something only a mind that had absorbed every chronicle about Al Capone, Bugsy Segal, the Purple Gang, and whoever and had seen every Humphrey Bogart and James Cagney gangster movie could create.

"Hey, Johnny babe." Benny was the dominant figure of the seven card players. His black curly hair was combed forward into a Tony Curtis curl - much like Kelly - and the thin mustache could have been plucked from the upper lip of Clark Gable. He was twenty-three, going on seventeen. Benny Petrillo was tough and smart but was living a second childhood.

"Ready for me?" Johnny asked after greeting everyone at the table.

"Yep." Benny spread his cards across the green fuzzy surface of the tabletop. "Three queens, gentlemen."

A smattering of good-natured grumbles tripped through the group. Benny stood, reached to the center of the table and picked up the money.

"Keep my seat warm," Benny said to Rocco, one of three spectators hovering behind him. Benny dropped ten twenty-dollar bills on the table and stuffed the remainder of his winnings into the pocket of his pinstriped charcoal gray pants. "Make sure I got more than that when I get back," Benny said pointing at the bills. He laughed. "Or you pay the difference."

Rocco shrugged, then slid into the vacant seat as Benny headed for another door on the far side of the room. Johnny followed.

They entered an office and Johnny closed the door behind them. He glanced at the closed Venetian blind covering the large window that overlooked the six bowling lanes and tossed his overcoat on the backrest of a black leather couch.

"No hot shots on the alleys today?" Johnny asked as he pulled an envelope from the inside pocket of his tan cashmere sport jacket.

"Nah." Benny reached for the envelope. "There should be some money games going tomorrow."

Benny slipped the folded papers from inside the envelope, unfolded them and began reading, flipping each under the ream as he was finished. "Looks good," he said after reviewing the final sheet. "How's things look on the books?"

"Your limo company and towing outfit are loosing money and your father's bar, the pool hall and bowling alley are just about breaking even," Johnny said.

Benny laughed as he unlocked a drawer in his desk with a key from a set attached to a gold chain on one of his belt loops. "Maybe we'll get a refund from Uncle Sam this year 'cause I'm doing so bad."

Johnny smiled. "Why not? The government is only gonna piss it away if they keep it."

Benny locked the desk drawer and dropped the keys into his pocket, the gold chain draping into place along his pant leg.

"So when are you gonna help me with the rest of the business? I mean, I got a good handle on things but I need an honest guy…" They both laughed. "…Like you to make sure everybody's doing right by me."

"Hey, stop already." Johnny held up his hands. "We agreed I take care of the books on the legit businesses only." Although he had conceded to himself to surrender, he was still geared to playing the game. Maybe there was still an outside chance to save both him and Pete. "How many times are you gonna push me?"

Benny pointed a joking finger at Johnny. "When my father turned over the limo business to me, it was doing bad - for real. Now it's making as much as two of those guys out there bring in." He shifted the finger over Johnny's shoulder toward the door. "And mainly because you know how to make things happen on paper."

"Sorry, buddy, a deal's a deal."

"I can make you do it," Benny said. Johnny had never seen him go beyond a joust during their conferences. "I'm your boss. I can do anything I want."

"My boss? Show me that on paper. You deduct for income taxes or social security? Or do I get paid in cash? I don't even officially exist. My name on all documents is John Wilson. Even my college tuition is paid through Madge under that name. And didn't I let you jump over me in rank? I let you become president of the Vandals because I knew what it meant to you."

Benny threw his head back and laughed. "You bum," he shouted, still laughing. "How the hell can I win with you? I had ya going though, hah?"

"A little," Johnny said. "Look, when Kelly gets back, you'll have someone ten times better than me to look out for you."

"But I need help now." Benny's face was serious. "They're fucking around Kelly and the other guys. We can't get anyone to pull the right strings. They're gonna be serving their full terms. It'll be another three months before they hit the streets. Shades getting out early was a fluke. And then we lost him." He bowed his head momentarily. "You know, I didn't even get to see him before it happened. When we lost him, it set things back for maybe six months."

"Why?"

"Sit down, Johnny." Benny held an outstretched palm toward the leather sofa. It had once been Johnny's temporary bed and he was used to its plush softness. He eased into the low cushions, stretching his bad leg in front of him. Benny leaned back into his chair.

"You know we're a small crew for now," Benny said. "My cousins, Ciro and Nick, got the real power. I work for them. That's why I'm telling you, it's no sweat if you get involved. You would never have to deal with them. Only me. Just you and I would know. They let me use my own people as long as everything stays cool."

Johnny nodded. *Maybe a different deal could be worked out here*

"I gotta admit I was wrong." Benny pointed at Johnny again. "That's between you and me."

"There's another marker I just worked off," Johnny said.

"You know I gotta get rid of those fucking kids. I should'a never let Al talk me into taking them on."

"Everyone knew that. They had no place with us."

"Hey." Benny wiggled his finger. "You know I needed them in the beginning. I needed their neighborhood to increase the profits and show my cousins I could produce. They were temporary replacements for the guys who were sent up. Their asses would be bounced the minute Kelly and the guys walked through that door. You know it's the only reason. And I apologize for using them in view of what they did to you and the rest of the Vandals."

"So what's the problem?" Johnny asked.

"You know they've been giving me grief. They're smoking marijuana and really going off the wall. Now I hear they're pulling small time heists on their own. They're turning into two-bit stick-up artists who can't control themselves. They're not concentrating on my business and I got my suspicions that they're skimming from me. I gotta dump them before they wipe the shit on their shoes on my doormat. One of them even brought a sixteen-year-old chippie into my father's bar. She was all dolled up, looking like she was of age. My old man figured she was okay 'cause she was with them and didn't proof her. It's a good thing he knew the beat cop who checked her out when she got outside. He could'a lost his liquor license and we'd be up the creek."

"Okay, so dump them," Johnny said.

"Not so easy. They're out'a here for sure, but they do all the legwork. The only guy left to cover their turf would be Al, and I'm not too happy with him. He was one of my most trustworthy guys until he got involved with them. It was his idea to take them on to help me expand. It was his operation and I let him control them and their turf. But he got too involved and now he goes for those young babes and smoking that shit."

"Yeah, he's had a bug up his ass lately. He acts like I'm trying to cut in on his action."

"That's not too far from the truth," Benny said.

"Meaning what?"

"I need you, Johnny. You and the kid."

"Pete?"

"Yeah."

"I thought we had an agreement. He doesn't get involved. No discussion."

"Johnny." Benny straightened in his seat. "I kept my word. I didn't offer. He volunteered."

"So what? You knew he would. You knew he wanted in and it was only a matter of time before you two cooked up a scheme to get around me."

"There's more to it," Benny said.

Johnny's silence was enough to extract the rest of Benny's thoughts.

"Don't ever tell him what I'm telling you now." Benny's finger pointed again and the ceiling light glinted off the diamond in his pinky ring. "He likes you. No matter what kind of a front he puts on when you're around, he thinks a lot about you."

"Come on. How'd you get him to tell you that?"

"He didn't tell me. I know. By the way he talks to me. He knows what you did for his mother. He didn't say it but it was almost like he was volunteering himself in place of you."

Johnny slumped against the backrest of the sofa. *He was putting on an act all this time? He was protecting me?* I don't believe this. It had to be mom. She must have finally gotten through to him. About me, anyway. But not about him staying out of this.

"Look," Benny said, "I can't ask my cousins for some guys to fill in. They'll think I bit off more than I can chew - like I can't handle things - and they'll leave their guys with me permanently. I only want *us* controlling things here. *No more outsiders.* Just Vandals, like it should've been."

"You can't stretch your other guys out to help cover Al's operation?"

"No way. I'm spread thin already. I could shift one or two guys over but it wouldn't be enough."

"This isn't some elaborate scheme to suck me in, is it?" Johnny asked.

"No, my man. If I don't get rid of those kids now, I'm gonna hear about it one way or another. And when I do cut them loose, I'll be just as much in the shithouse as if I didn't. You see my problem?"

"Okay," Johnny said.

"Okay? That's it?"

"Yeah. I'll do it." Johnny poked his fingers into a V. "On two conditions."

"I knew it was too easy."

"Hey, I don't come cheap," Johnny said. "I do it only until the rest of the guys get back and can take over."

"Agreed," Benny said.

"And I do whatever share of the work that two guys would do so you don't have to use Pete."

"Johnny, what'll I tell the kid? He's always hanging around my door, waiting for me to take him in. I'll bet he's out there right now 'cause he doesn't see you in the place."

"Leave him to me. Between Madge and me, we'll talk him out of it."

"I need all the help I can get. I'll give him the same time period as you. You're both off the hook in three, four months," Benny said.

"No way. I can't take the chance he'll be picked up on some petty rap and sent back up because of his record. It would kill Madge. It's me or neither of us."

"Why can't I ever win with you?" Benny flicked his hand. "I believe in family. And I know what it was like for you to get a family." He hesitated. "Okay, I agree. But now for my condition."

"Why can't I ever win with you?"

Benny laughed. "I want you to do the books on the central collections. You're too good to be nothing but a small-time collec-tor. I want you to control the receipts, in my place. I'll clue you in on all the sources and what we should be seeing every week. Every-thing you would have to know to make sure I'm getting what I should. I told you before that I need an honest guy to watch out for me. I got some plans I gotta spend time on. With you doing that part of my job, I'll be able to concentrate on expanding my operations before Kelly and the other guys make the scene. You won't have to answer to nobody but me."

"Which means I'll know your business. *All of it*," Johnny said. "Then I'm into it up to my ears."

"So what? So, what're you scared you're gonna have to squeal on me someday?"

Johnny scowled. *But maybe something like that was what had been bothering him.* The reason why he had resisted so long. The reason why he didn't want to know the other end of Benny's operations. Maybe his basic honesty had been holding him back. Maybe he was incapable of doing anything that could put him in a compromising situation. *Maybe he was afraid of himself.*

"So?" Benny asked. "You really think you'd do that? Or I'd risk putting you in a spot where you could if I thought you might?"

Johnny always needed to justify his actions to himself. *Red Janek had managed to juggle his dedication between two worlds and Jimmy Yadenik had decided that no matter how he perceived his family, they were still his family.* Those were foundations for his philosophy. *He was a member of this family before he had become a Wilson and he was in both families to stay, with the duty to assert as much devotion as he could to both.*

"Agreed," Johnny said.

Benny rose and moved around the desk, his hand extended. "Agreed."

They shook hands and Johnny felt unexplainably relieved, even though the knowledge he would soon gain would never release him from Benny's grasp. He would become a dedicated, unimpeachable member of the inner circle for life.

"But I'm holding you to your offer of doing two guys' work. You still keep your job doing your regular legit bookkeeping duties."

"But what about..." *College*, Johnny finished in his thoughts.

He was only in his second year. He would have to become a full-time employee to handle both jobs. There would be no time to study. But once Kelly and the other guys got there he could be freed up to finish school at night. He was sure Benny would agree. Why not have a full-fledged CPA working for the organization? There was still plenty of time to combine the two worlds.

"What about what?"

"Nothing."

"Look, man," Benny said, "Don't worry about anything. I'm sure you know we're only into making book, numbers and loan sharking. The local cops are taken care of, my cousins got a real sharp lawyer on retainer and there ain't anything we're into that's gonna get any special attention." Benny sat on the edge of the desk. "The guys running dope and peddling whores usually get the spotlight. So far, my cousins don't ask anymore of me. I've got a few ideas for scams and major heists, but strictly my business. Nothing involving you. I only want you to do what you do the best."

"And you got it," Johnny said. "We shook on it and that's it. Just one more small request. It's very important to me that Pete doesn't know about this. Or Madge. I want her and Pete to think everything is status quo."

"Status quo? As is, right? You got it. On my honor." Benny held his fist to his chest. "You won't regret what you're doing. You just got yourself a fat raise, buddy."

And why not? I just sold you my life. Ahh, stop the shit. It was for sale all the while. I just didn't know it until now.

"Thanks," Johnny said. "Now, when are you gonna get rid of our problem?"

"Our problem?"

"The Sinners. They're as much my problem now."

"I told Al to get them all together tonight. To tell you the truth, I didn't think you'd come around this fast, but I was still gonna dump them no matter what."

"You sure they won't turn into a real problem?"

"No way. They're little punks on the bottom of the ladder. The only thing they know about is the collections they make. They report to Al only, and make their drops to him. Al makes sure their receipts are right and gives the collector his cut on the spot. They couldn't testify to anything passed him. I'm gonna talk to Al next. He's gonna be the one who actually fires them. That way, there's still no connection between them and me."

"So if there's a problem with skimming, like you suspect, then Al's gotta be involved?"

"Don't concern yourself. I'll take care of it before you start your new job."

"You're the boss."

Benny stretched out a supporting hand but Johnny had swiveled his hip and pushed off, standing without help. He had become adept at compensating for the limited use of his leg.

"If I could, I'd give you a shot at getting them back for that," Benny said pointing to Johnny's leg.

"Just knowing I won't have to deal with them will be enough. Once their smug faces disappear, I'll be happy." Johnny followed Benny through the doorway and back into the smoke-filled poker room.

Benny passed Rocco, waving at him to continue playing.

Johnny limped slowly behind Benny as they passed into the poolroom. Pete was standing in front of an old Wurlitzer juke box tucked into an alcove at the other end of the room. His back was to them, his head bowed toward the selection chart of the machine.

CHAPTER 26

"You still like what you see, kid?" Benny asked as he reached Pete.

Pete turned, bringing his fists up from his sides. "Hi'ya, Benny," Pete said, dropping his hands. "How's it going?" He ignored Johnny.

Benny shook Pete's hand. "You still like my little corner, hah?"

"It's great," Pete said. He visited the alcove several times a week. "These records are real cool. They came out around the time I went away. It makes me feel like I never left. And the pictures. There's Johnny when he was a real beanpole..." Pete pointed at the gallery of framed photos behind the juke box before realizing he had given recognition to someone he was trying to ignore. "And the old Vandal jacket framed and hangin' there. Fabulous. Really way out."

"Hey, I still need a nice big picture of you," Benny said, placing his hand on Pete's shoulder. "I wanna put it right in the middle of them all, where one of the original seven belongs."

"Yeah, but I can't find one, and my mother won't look through her old stuff. But, man, I'd dig that. It wouldn't make up for everything I missed, but at least I'd be up there with everybody, like I did belong."

"Don't let anybody tell you that you don't belong." Benny tapped Pete's shoulder. "You're one of us."

Johnny cleared his throat to enforce the deal he and Benny had just struck. Johnny knew it was difficult to control Benny's enthusiasm when he found someone who appreciated his shrine. He became a kid again and could talk for hours.

Benny slid a quarter into the juke box slot. "You got six selections, champ. Use 'em up." Benny turned to Johnny and waved his hand. "Relax." He lowered his voice. "I still like him. He's a good kid." He turned and headed for the bar.

Johnny limped after Benny, hoping he could talk with Pete, but more interested in what would be the opening shots in the demise of the Sinners. There were now two more members of the younger crowd at the bar, bookends to Al, Paulie and the girl.

"How's it going, fellas?" Benny asked. "Hey, you old enough to be in a bar?" he asked the girl.

"I'm eighteen," she said.

"You got proof?" Benny asked.

"I... Not with me."

"Al, ask your friends to leave." Benny pointed to the door. "Pop, how many times you gonna let this happen?" he asked, turning to his father.

"Al said she was okay," Mr. Petrillo said.

"Okay, that's the last time this is gonna happen. Out! The whole bunch."

"What's this all about?" Al asked.

"About shit," Benny shouted. *"Don't question me."*

Al motioned for his crew to leave. They moved slowly to the landing.

"Tell them to meet you down the block in an hour," Benny instructed Al in a low voice when the Sinners reached the door. "I got some things to discuss with you."

"Meet me at the coffee shop on the next corner in an hour," Al passed on to the Sinners.

Paulie turned and retraced his steps, gliding toward the telephone booth just inside the archway of the poolroom. Benny glared at him before nodding to the four billiards patrons who were filing passed him to tally-up with Benny's father. They were regular customers and had sensed enough trouble from Benny's shouting to know it was time to leave.

"Benny, you're loosing business," Mr. Petrillo said as the door closed behind the last person.

"They'll be back, pop." Benny waved his hand. "They need a

break." He turned to Johnny. "Wait here," he said.

Johnny still hoped to talk with Pete at the apartment, to lure him there where he could double-team him with Madge. *But this had to be taken care of first.*

"What's the scoop?" Johnny asked, bowing to Benny's agenda.

"Distance, man. Distance. As far as the punks know, they were tossed out for breaking the rules of the bar. Now I sit down with Al and tell him what their marching orders are." Benny tapped Johnny's chest with a backhand. "You'll like Al's expression when he leaves my meeting with him."

Johnny smiled and nodded an acknowledgment toward Benny's attempt to satisfy a small taste of revenge for him. It was a feeble gesture but he meant well.

Benny turned and passed through the archway toward Al, who had stationed himself outside the telephone booth being used by Paulie.

"What's he doing?" Benny asked. "I told him to split."

"He was gonna call his girl, but I told him to call the other guys to meet us later," Al said. "I figured what you wanted to tell me involved all of them."

"Yeah, you're right. But I told you to get rid of them."

Benny pounded on the slim glass panes of the telephone booth, collapsing the accordion doors into each other. The edge of the door struck Paulie's arm as he hunched in the booth.

"What're you doing?" Benny asked.

"Calling the other guys," Paulie said.

"Do it someplace else. Come on, get the fuck out'a here."

Paulie hung up the receiver and made his way to the door.

"Pop, no more customers after the bowlers leave, okay?" Benny spun around and headed for the back rooms. Al followed him through the open doorway and Frankie closed the door behind them.

Johnny slid onto one of the red cushioned bar stools. "Can I have a vodka on the rocks, Mr. P?" He looked at the poolroom as Pete poked his head around the edge of the telephone booth.

"What's he mad about?" Pete asked.

"None of your business. Come here, I'll buy you a drink."

"You don't want me to split?"

"We've got things to talk over." Johnny wiggled his finger, beckoning Pete to join him. "Show Mr. Petrillo your proof."

"I ain't got none."

"You're eighteen, aren't you?"

"Yeah, you know I turned eighteen last month." Pete dropped onto the stool next to Johnny. "Why?"

"That's something else we've gotta take care of. You have to register for the draft. You use the draft card as proof of age."

"Okay."

"He's okay, Mr. P," Johnny said, turning to his pony of vodka. "Give him what he usually has."

"Come on, Johnny, you ain't tryin' to trick an old man, are you?" Mr. Petrillo smiled as he dropped Johnny's change next to the drink. "You seen how Benny gets when I serve youngsters." He motioned toward Pete with his head. "And you asked me not to let him hang around here."

Johnny returned the smile, then turned to Pete. "Tell Mr. P what you want."

"Schaefer draft."

"Mom's g... Your mother's gonna smell beer on your breath." Johnny held up his glass of vodka before sipping at it. "This stuff is practically odorless."

"Well, that's two helpful hints you gave me so far. Is that what you wanted to talk to me about? How you're gonna take me under your wing and be my big brother?"

"If you want me to," Johnny said. "That's up to you."

Mr. Petrillo placed the mug of beer in front of Pete, took some coins from Johnny's change, and then settled back into his newspaper at the other end of the bar.

"I don't know what you're trying to pull, man," Pete said.

Johnny was pleased at the maturity hinted in Pete's action. He didn't burst into a loud, abrasive condemnation, as he might have. He was now fairly sure Benny's assessment of Pete was correct.

Pete took a swig from the mug, leaving a trace of white foam above his upper lip. "You're always acting like I can't think for myself," Pete said. "You try to get everybody around here to treat me like I'm some nobody kid. Everybody but Benny. He knows what I can do. He wants me to work for him. He's the boss and he'll overrule you."

"Don't bet on it," Johnny said.

"Yeah? Well, we'll see."

"Let me ask you one thing," Johnny said. "Who do you want to make happy? Who do you want to be proud of you, Benny or your mother?"

Pete was silent. He took another drink of his beer, washing away the mustache. "*What kind'a question is that?*" He took another swig. "It's two different things. I can make my mother happy by being somebody, and Benny'll..."

"Benny isn't the answer. You'll be somebody by going back to school and staying straight like your mother expects of you."

"Bullshit." Pete finished the beer and tapped the mug on the cardboard coaster in front of him.

"Don't be a smart ass," Johnny said. "Don't sink down to the level of the punks that usually sit here. You're better than them."

Mr. Petrillo hovered in front of them.

"Excuse him," Johnny said. "Give him another brew."

Pete reached into his pant's pocket.

"His money's no good." Johnny touched the bills and coins on the bar. "On me."

They were both silent during the refill until Mr. P was again back at his newspaper.

"Y'know, you keep telling me I gotta stay out'a things," Pete said. "What about you? How come it's okay for you? How come you wanna make big bucks but leave me out'a the action?"

"My bucks come from legit means. I've got nothing to do with the other end of Benny's business," Johnny said. "I'm sure you know that from what you've heard around here. And the reason I'm in a position to stay legit and still stay on the fringe of everything is because I made sure I went back to school and learned what I need to control my own living. And I'm gonna keep going until I'm an expert. I learned what it takes to keep us one step above..."

"Us?" Pete sneered as he gulped at the beer mug.

"Yeah, us. Your mother and me. You said *bullshit* before. Well, let's cut out the bullshit once and for all. You know I care for your mother, and you know in what way. The same as you. We both have the same reason to be thankful. It's her. Whatever we do is for her. So let's be sure we do the right thing."

"Yeah, you're so smart. I knew that. I knew that a long time ago. I guess I just didn't wanna share her with you. You know she's all I got. All that kept me going while I was away. Since that night, I knew I had to make things right." He stopped, his eyes clouding. "I was protecting her honor, sticking up for her when I got into that thing with Dave. I knew from that moment on, it was her and me."

"Forget about that night." Johnny squeezed Pete's arm and was relieved he didn't shake it off. "That part of your life is over and done with. Your new life started a month ago. Let Benny and whoever live in the past if they want to. You gotta think about the future. You told your mother you were sorry for everything you put her through. You made your amends to her. She knows you're sincere and you'd never put yourself into anything like that again. Well, now you have the chance to prove that."

"I never wanted anyone to see me like this." Pete rubbed at his eyes. "I never wanted to show I wasn't a Vandal."

"It's been done before. By Vandals. *The real Vandals.* The guys who cared."

"But what about you?" Pete asked. "I know she thinks of you like..." He nodded. "I guess like me."

"No. You're special, man. You're the one she brought into this world. You're the one she struggled for. I was only a substitute. I'm thankful for that. That's why I wanted you to know how things really were, and somehow repay her for helping me turn my life around."

"I know all that. I meant, what about you keeping out of Benny's rackets. You're a lot closer to getting involved than I am, and she doesn't want you getting into it any more than me. I figured if I stepped up, Benny would lay off you."

"Don't worry about anything," Johnny said. "Benny and I had our talk and everything is cool. I'm keeping the same dull job I have now. Neither you or me is getting involved." Johnny sipped at his drink. "And you're heading for home before your mother comes looking for you. You know, she was pissed that you didn't show up for dinner."

Pete turned on his stool and looked at the empty poolroom. "Didn't Benny tell us to wait? What's going on?"

"Just some business. He only wanted me to wait. Your mother really wanted you home to talk with her."

"Come on, Johnny. I opened up to you. I let you know how I really feel. Isn't that worth letting me hang around a little bit longer?"

Johnny felt a warm surge of comfort. He had accomplished more than he had set out to do. "Sure, why not?" He stood. "I'll call your mother and tell her that I'm treating you to dinner. Which we will do later. Okay?"

"Sure." Pete lifted the beer mug and toasted Johnny. "On you."

"You got it." Johnny headed for the telephone booth, passing the group of bowlers heading for the bar.

Johnny crouched into the booth and dialed Madge's number. He let ten rings pass before hanging up in puzzlement. He slid out of the booth and returned to Pete.

"Your mom didn't answer." Johnny sipped at the vodka. "Was she supposed to work tonight?"

"I don't know. Yeah, maybe. I think that's why she wanted to have dinner early."

"But you're not sure?"

"Yeah, pretty sure. I think she was supposed to work a couple of Fridays in a row. Why?"

"I don't know. I just had a strange feeling that she might be on her way here, looking for us to finish what she wanted to do at dinner."

"You mean jump on my ass again?" Pete sipped at his beer.

"Come on, you know she means well."

"I guess so. I guess we can talk to her tomorrow. We can tell her what we worked out tonight."

"She'll love it," Johnny said. "She'll be in her glory."

"I'm glad. Like you said, that's what it's all about." Pete studied his beer mug for a moment. "Before, when you said I shouldn't be like those guys that Benny kicked out, I didn't say anything." He shrugged. "But I'd like you to know I'd never think of being like them. I seen their kind at Elmira. *All talk, no balls.* All they got is a line of bullshit. Shades had told me how him and the other guys went up because of the rumble with them. I knew what kind of shit they were, and I never tried to get in with them. I knew Benny was using them for a reason; that he needed them, or he would've never let them hang around here. So I kept my distance from them, hoping someday he'd kick their asses out for good. And I didn't wanna get into any scrapes with them and blow things for you and me.

"There was this one time, though, that I came close to popping one of them. It was my second time here. They were talking loud enough for me to hear, but still ignoring me. They were bragging about how good they thought they were; how I would have to prove myself to be able to hang around in *their* bar, when one of them says something about me being a *momma's boy* and how Benny got a job for her 'cause him and you...'"

"Those fucking little bastards," Johnny said.

"No, wait." Pete held his hand up. "I don't know how, but I kept my cool. I said, *'I killed the last guy who said something like that'.* They didn't say another word after that. Maybe they heard about the reason I was sent up. I told them to ask Benny about it and walked away."

Johnny was again stunned by Pete's candor.

"It worked," Pete said. "I never had to become like them." Pete sipped at his beer, and Johnny knew Pete had the same intentions as he and Madge. "I guess I learned to be my own man; to think for myself. That's all I want people to know about me."

Johnny had let Pete work out of his confusion on his own, but couldn't resist the need to wash everything clean. "Was it hard for you to - You know, to bring up that night again?"

"I don't remember many details. The only real thing that came back to me when I think about it is how guys like these losers remind me of Dave. *Like kind of a symbol.* I only wanted them to leave me alone; to let my mother out of it; to let me be myself and stop trying to make me be like them."

"They're still around," Johnny said. "Those same people are still around and your mother and me became part of them. *They're called society.*"

"No you're not," Pete said. "*Don't say that.* My mother meant well back then, but she was ruled by the same people that I hated. So maybe now she's got things a little better, but it's you and her who's thinking about me as a person, not 'cause what I can do to help you make more money or put you on top. You care, man. Like you said before, the real Vandals are the guys who cared for each other. Guys like Shades and Red. And you."

Johnny would never refer to him as a kid again. "Welcome home, man."

The door to the back room opened and the din of conversations drifted from within.

Benny and Al emerged and the door closed. They passed through the poolroom. Al was in front, his posture drooped. He stopped in front of Mr. P.

"Give him one on me," Benny called to his father before stopping in front of Johnny. "Good to see you guys are still here."

Benny slapped Johnny on the arm. "I wanted to let Pete know about his new job."

Johnny's head jerked furiously toward Benny. He felt a stab of deceit. *"What?"*

"Dispatcher for my limo service," Benny said in stride, pleased that his poke had penetrated Johnny's defenses. "It seems that the present dispatcher has been promoted to another position."

Johnny relaxed and turned on the stool to face Benny. "I'll get you for that." He pointed at Benny with a smile, then offered his hand to Pete. "Congratulations."

Pete shook their hands, and, seeing Johnny's smile was genuine, turned back to his beer.

"Fill 'em up, pop. All around, on me," Benny said before signaling Johnny to follow him into the poolroom. He stopped near the entrance to the bowling lanes and turned to Johnny. "What a look on your face," he said.

"Don't fuck around like that, man. I thought you were going back on your word."

"You think I'd do that?"

Johnny jokingly nodded a few times to relieve his sudden tension. "You know I don't. What's going on?"

"You know Gary, the guy I got dispatching during the day? I think he can handle a collector's job, so I figured I'd hire Pete as his replacement. Pete's a smart kid and I know he needs the work. It's a bonus to you and Madge from our deal."

Johnny thought about the offer. Pete would have a legit job and Johnny could look in on him during his frequent visits to the business. It sounded good and he accepted.

"What happened with Al?" Johnny asked.

"I explained the situation to him, in private, and he *agreed* with me," Benny said. "How'd you like the expression on his face?"

"I'd rather see the collective expressions on all of them, but his will do."

"Hey, you can't have everything." Benny smiled. "I told Al to meet the punks and pay them off for the last time. I threw in a bonus to help ease the pain. He knows enough to make it a clean break. He's still got his own ass to worry about." Benny looked away for a moment. "Everything's gonna be okay," he said.

"Change the shifts around at the limo shop so Pete can have time to go back to school and study during the dead time," Johnny said.

"Man, I don't see what you college boys see in school. You wind up making a helluva lot less than us but you still gotta try to show you're smarter."

"That's the way we are."

"Work it out with Jean," Benny said, referring to the limousine office manager.

Johnny headed back to the bar while Benny disappeared into the back room.

"Everything's cool," Johnny said as he squeezed Pete's shoulder.

"So, the *momma's boys* won out," Al said, placing his empty glass on the bar.

"Relax," Johnny said as he grabbed Pete's arm. "Just steam."

"Yeah, relax, pal," Al said. "No offense. You should be proud of the title. Your mother has more pull around here than me. I just lost my crew but you guys are doing okay." He raised his glass. *"A'salute.* " He tipped his glass and sucked in the watered-down remnant from the bottom. "More power to you." He slammed the glass to the bar surface, turned and plodded up the landing. He unlocked the door and left.

Mr. P was a few steps behind, locking the door again. "He'll get over it." He returned to the bar. "Maybe he'll loose that smart-guy attitude now that he's had some wind knocked out of his sails."

Johnny didn't comment. *Mr. P knew everything that was said behind the closed door of Benny's office.*

Johnny only hoped that Benny's actions wouldn't force Al into some rash retaliation. Benny had made a bold stroke but may have created a potential hazard. Maybe the guy could be ordered to deal with Johnny for business purposes but that wouldn't eliminate the seething undercurrents. Al's mild reaction was acted out too obviously. Johnny would have preferred to see a blow-up. He would have to watch his back.

Johnny decided to delay the dinner plan. He would wait until the time he knew it would take Al to disband his crew. He visualized them meeting at the coffee shop and Al trying to make the event seem like a corporate downsizing. He would tell them he couldn't use them anymore. *Good luck on your future endeavors*, with the emphasis on *'I can't use you'* rather than *'we can't use you'*. Out of the half dozen or so, one of them would resort to vengeance, having to give up their plush positions. Johnny sympathized with his rival, but only that far. He could never empathize with a person who couldn't see passed his own nose.

Johnny let the hour pass, switching to club soda to keep his composure, and having Pete drink coke. They played pool and Johnny tried another fruitless call to Madge. They were now sure she was managing the dinner shift at the restaurant. An occasional card player left the back room to use the public men's room when the private john was occupied.

When Johnny was sure the time was right, he decided to leave. They were both hungry; even though munching on the bar snacks, he had still heard Pete's stomach grumble as they paced around the pool table.

"See you tomorrow, Mr. P," Johnny said as they left. "Tell Benny I'll be here first thing in the morning."

The lock snapped shut behind them as they climbed the cement steps. The Flushing-bound el train roared passed above them. The sidewalk was empty. Only a handful of pedestrians on the other side of the street. It was safe. They headed for Corona. Johnny would surprise Madge. He and Pete would walk in unannounced and see the look on her face when he asked to see the manager like they were strangers off the street. They would all smile when she saw them and she would know everything was okay. Then they would be given a choice out of the way table reserved for only the best customers.

CHAPTER 27

Madge was hidden in the shadows behind the distant el pillars. She had been there for an hour, once taking a break at the coffee shop to warm herself, returning to her vigil only minutes before the mob of hyper teenagers had been guided to the corner cafe by the guy she knew as Al, barely escaping recognition. She wasn't adept at stealth operations and had only avoided detection by shear luck. There was no reason for this ruse; no reason to be isolated in the cold of the evening; to be in this self-imposed holding area. She had set up the meeting with Benny through her boss, Ciro, and could have just strolled to the meeting on time, or late if she preferred. She was early because she wanted to at least get a glimpse of them, those two wonderful guys she would do anything for. She had hoped they were at the club, and there they were. And they were together. It was what she had only dreamed. It was more than them leaving together. She was sure they had shared the evening, that they had become close, by the way they walked, the way they shared a conversation, the way they seemed to be watching out for each other. They were like brothers. She was on the verge of tears, but she would hold back and keep the moment as a memory she could dwell on in the future.

Benny was alone when he climbed to the sidewalk. He tugged on the velvet lapels of his gray overcoat, looked up and down the block, and then headed for the opposite corner from the coffee shop. Madge left her perch behind the el pillar after Benny turned the corner. She crossed the street toward him.

The black Cadillac convertible had white exhaust billowing from under the rear bumper, parked a few yards from the corner, its white top shimmering in the street light from a film of evening dew. Madge opened the passenger door and turned to sit on the leather seat illuminated by the dim interior lights. She slammed the door closed, extinguishing the light, and the car swung away from the curb.

"Hi'ya, Madge. How've you been?"

"Fine, thank you. Ciro sends his regards," she said as the Cadillac crossed Thirty-Seventh Avenue.

"Yes, I spoke with him earlier." Benny was cordial. "He tells me you have a proposition for me."

"Yes, I do." Madge pulled her skirt forward and across her knees, adjusting for the shifting of the material when she angled into the seat. "Ciro wants you to know that he hasn't changed his policy. He will not interfere with your operation." Her words were exact, to the point, verbatim from her boss's diction, used as he coached her earlier in the evening - after her desperate visit to him. "He's only asking you to consider my proposal as a favor to me and to him."

"I understand."

"First, I'd like you to know I have never asked Ciro for any favors since I've worked for him. This is the first time we've even acknowledged I know about anything other than his restaurant business."

The Cadillac stopped for a red light on Northern Boulevard. A thin coating of moisture had spread across the windshield. Benny adjusted the heater switch to defrost.

"I'd bet on that. You and Johnny have that same opinion about what you feel is right and wrong." He smiled. "You sure he's not really your son?"

"He's been my son for three years. And we've made sure things went well for us in that time. Up until now." She saw Benny's puzzled look and tried to match his smile but returned to the purpose of her mission. "Which is why I'm here."

The traffic light turned green and the convertible crossed the intersection.

"I want to make a trade," Madge said. "My management skills

for Johnny. I know enough about what's going on. Don't think Johnny has been talking about your business with me. I just know from bits and pieces I hear from him and around the restaurant that you had trouble with those little punks you hired."

"Okay, that's common knowledge. But Ciro doesn't think I can't..."

"Ciro knows you're going to do what you have to, and maybe my idea will help. I have a plan for a new operation so you won't feel the sting when you get rid of them."

"Yes?"

"I'm sure Ciro will confirm my ability to manage a business. He's even paid for my training courses. And if a person knows how to manage, it doesn't matter what the product or service is. The same principles apply to most everything."

"That's true. And Ciro's thanked me many times for recommending you to him. I have no doubts about your abilities."

She nodded. "My plan involves an arrangement I've worked out. I befriended a girl who's become a regular at the restaurant. She's actually the one who proposed this. She's a little strange, but somehow down to earth and very analytical. I don't know where in our relationship it came up, but she proposed a call girl service."

"Hookers?"

"No, not the garden variety street walkers. *I can't believe I'm saying this or that I'm about to get involved.* Well, her idea is to hire real class girls and set them up in exclusive apartments under the guise of an escort service."

"Ciro would never get involved in pimping. It's too risky."

"This is different. There are services like this all over Manhattan. It's in the papers almost every day. Why not here? Near La Guardia Airport where hundreds of out-of-town businessmen and diplomats and other people of means are coming to mix pleasure with their business. We could rent luxury apartments away from the glare and notoriety of Manhattan. We could cater to high-class patrons who would be more relaxed about not being subjected to the danger of exposure in Manhattan. They could use our services when they get here, before their business, or on their way home. We charge heavy fees for class girls and for the anonymity of the setting."

"Classy word."

"For a classy operation. And what works for the customer, works for us. Low exposure. If they don't want anyone knowing what they're doing, they're not going to let anyone know about us. Except for some highly recommended referrals. This girl has almost everything worked out in her head, like a telephone contact system and moving the places of operation from time to time to avoid someone picking up our routine."

"Ciro likes this idea?"

"He does. And he asks that you test the idea for him. He feels that if it works, it'll help both his and your profits. He's warned me of all the pitfalls involved and that if anything goes wrong, I'm on my own, and I fully accept those consequences. Ciro feels you should consider this proposal."

"You know, then, that I must accept. What's next?"

"I'll need - Ciro called it seed money - to start, but I'll take care of setting up the organization. My assistant will do the hiring. She assures me she can find the right girls for the job, but I'll double check and oversee everything. I don't like dealing in this kind of business, but I'll be sure the girls are treated with respect. They'll be employees, not someone to be looked down on. And I'm sure they'll respond in kind."

"I know you'll handle things well. We'll work out the details and the money arrangement tomorrow." Benny guided the Cadillac to the curb alongside a small Italian restaurant in East Elmhurst. "How about some dinner?" He flicked his index finger at her. "Don't let Ciro know I eat in anyplace other than his joint."

"I think he eats here, too," she said.

Benny switched off the ignition and turned to open the door.

"I want to finish our conversation here, in private," Madge said, touching his arm.

"There's more?"

"Do you think you were getting all of this for nothing?" She pinched into the sleeve of his overcoat and he flinched. "I'm giving you a chance to trade off a bad situation for something that could lead to a big opportunity and you give me a blase attitude? I told you I was here for a trade."

"I'm sorry, Madge." He pulled his arm away from her furor. *She was an emissary of his superior and was entitled to the same respect.* "I thought we were gonna finish up inside. Please continue."

"I want two things in exchange for my services to you." Her inflections returned to the imitation of her boss. "I want you to never let Pete or Johnny become involved in any of your operations. And number two, you will never let either of them know what I'm about to do."

Madge glared at Benny and he felt the furor again, but quickly regained his poise. He would follow orders. He was bound by the chain of command. But there were things that only he knew; things that he would use to his advantage. He had sworn to Johnny never to reveal their arrangement. He would keep that oath.

"I swear that no one, not only Pete or Johnny, but anyone you don't want to know, will ever find out what was discussed tonight." He held his fist to his chest in the same salute he had given Johnny. "As far as I'm concerned, everything will remain status quo." Benny smiled. "That's a term I heard from your Johnny. He also wants things to stay as they are, and I promise that everything will stay just as it is at this moment in time."

"Thank you." Madge's body seemed to collapse in her seat, followed by a long exhale. "God, I'm glad that's over."

"You did good," Benny said. "You and I are gonna have a good relationship."

Benny was also relieved, sure that she had heard his words the way he wanted her to hear them, and sure that she would carry that same impression back to Ciro. He had just gained the services of two valuable people during this day of transition and for the cut-rate price of not letting either of them know what the other was doing. All they had managed to do was save Pete, who didn't need saving. Pete would have never fit in. He was too sensible for what Benny had intended for him, performing menial tasks on a temporary basis. Those four years at Elmira had only added surface callousness. *But why not use him, too?*

"To show you I mean well, I'm gonna hire Pete as a dispatcher at my limo place. I'll arrange his shifts so he can go back to school and still be able to study during the quiet periods."

"Thanks. I appreciate that." Madge smiled. "To be honest, I wasn't sure I could do this. I'm a little embarrassed about what I'm getting myself into, but I'd do anything to -no offense -but to keep Pete and Johnny out of your clutches." Her smile widened to show her remarks weren't hostile.

"So instead, you're in my clutches," Benny said. "By the terms of our agreement, you're my underling."

Madge wasn't sure whether he was still playing off their conversation or if he was implying that she might be involved... *He better not be thinking that!*

"Yes, but also Ciro's," she said. "Under the terms of our agreement, I only manage things. So you can just call me 'Madam Manager'." She laughed to break the deadlock and a few seconds later Benny joined her after grasping the pun.

"Actually, the real madam is going to be the girl who started this idea," Madge said. "The ironic thing about this is that she says she even knows some of the Sinners. She used to live in their neighborhood. Imagine coming up with the very idea that eliminates them? Her name is Sharon. Sharon Norman or Norish. She gives me a different pronunciation each time I talk to her. I guess she wants to hide something in her past. But, no problem. I'll keep her hidden from everyone. All she has to do is produce.

"She's a voluptuous girl, with stark black hair. Like Gina Lolabridgida. I just hope all the other girls she brings in are as glamorous. We'll have a lot of pleased clients - and a good income."

"Hey, the way you describe her, I'd like to meet her."

"In good time. But strictly business. I don't want anyone other than our clients to sample the wares."

"Sure, I agree." *For now.* "Ready for dinner?"

"I could use a stiff drink first."

"You got it."

They stepped onto the sidewalk and headed for the restaurant, both silently congratulating themselves on their victory, but only one knowing he had truly won. *But why not?* He was more responsible for the future than Johnny or Madge. And from where he stood, the future looked very good.

EPILOGUE

Excerpt from the journal of Jim Yadenik
DECEMBER 2, 1959

The bar was in the same neighborhood that had been original Vandal turf. I was the first of the other than regular frequenters to stroll into the corner tavern. Val, Tony and Mickey probably spotted the blue uniform before recognizing me as the guy wearing it, since I had filled out from my skinny kid image in the last year. It was a year since I joined the Air Force and I was still proud enough to wear the uniform rather than civies when home on leave. They greeted me with a chorus of "Wild Blue Yonder" and bought me a beer.

"I gotta go," Val said as soon as I settled onto a cushioned stool. "Sorry I couldn't stick around to see Red. Say hello for me." He gathered his change from the counter, bid everyone good-bye and hurried out the door.

"What's up?" I asked.

"He's married," Tony said.

"Val? The lover who would never be tied down?" I asked.

"And his wife is a bitch," Mickey said. "If he doesn't get home on time she'll come here looking for him."

I laughed. "Anybody else coming?"

"Yeah," Tony said. "Some of the old crowd might drift in. The word was passed around about you and Red being home together."

"Here comes Freddy The Hat," Mickey said.

Freddy was decked out in a black beret and goatee, looking

very much like one of those beatniks that hung out in The Village.

"Hey, man, cool threads," Freddy said. "Where can I get me a set?"

"Agree to work for Uncle Sam for four years," I said.

"No thanks, man."

Chico and Roxie, still inseparable, were the next to arrive. "We were on our way to another party, but we just had to come by," Roxie said.

Roxie had her camera and began shooting pictures of the group. Thank goodness for the girls that had hung around with us, and their penchant for taking pictures. Most of the photos in my album came from that source.

"I can buy film for the other party when we leave," Roxie said. "This is more important to preserve."

"You guys married yet?" I asked.

"We're kind of planning to get engaged," Chico said. He smiled and Roxie slapped his arm.

"It better be soon," she said.

Red finally arrived, a half-hour late. He was still slow and easygoing despite the variety of rugged special training courses I knew he had completed through his military career. He, too, wore his uniform, adorned with three gold chevrons, a paratrooper badge and red good conduct ribbon.

We saluted each other before shaking hands.

"A good conduct medal," I said. *"You?"*

"Not only that, I'm going to officer's candidate school," Red said.

Someone from our circle had found a sprinkling of leftover tunes from our past among the juke box menu, and for the rest of the evening we heard "Earth Angel", "Love Is Strange", and "Let The Good Times Roll" so many times they became an inconspicuous backdrop to our party.

The old mob of crazies came roaring in like the Vandals of old. Roxie squealed with delight as he hugged them one by one; Monk, the Looney Brothers and Crazy Lenny.

"This is becoming a regular reunion," Roxie said as we moved from the bar to a group of empty tables, chairs and booths in the rear area.

"We can't stay long," Monk said. "As soon as Kelly and Johnny get here, we gotta split."

"Ahh, how come?" Roxie asked. "We've got other things to do but we're staying."

"We got some business to take care of," Monk said. "We gotta talk to our lawyer about a bum rap they're trying to pin on us." Monk's breath told anyone close to him that he had a few drinks before and he was loose enough to share some low priority information with his old crowd. "The cops are pretty sure one of the old Sinners killed Al over money problems, but the D.A. keeps trying to pin it on Benny and us. His office will do anything to bust balls."

"Let's shoot some shuffleboard bowling," Lenny said looking directly at Monk. "Twenty bucks each. Winner takes all."

"Sounds good," one of the Looneys said, and they strolled into the bar area. Lenny grasped Monk's shoulder so hard that *I even* winced. He whispered something into Monk's ear before they dropped their quarters into the slot of the bowling game.

"What happened with you and Sheila?" Roxie asked.

I shrugged. "You know, conflicts over stupid things. Her parents wanted me to think their way. If I wouldn't do it for mine, I wasn't going to do it for them."

"Ahh, you'll find somebody," Roxie said. "It takes time." She looked at Chico. "Sometimes a long time."

"Come on, baby," Chico said. "I got the ring all picked out."

We all snickered, and the conversation drifted into reminiscence.

The crazies managed to drive out most of the other customers within an hour. They took over the games, betting heavily among themselves; throwing money around like it was from a monopoly game.

Crazy Lenny was a big looser on the bowling game and when

he blew a spare, he hurled the puck at the back glass. It bounced off the wooden trim and the ricocheting disk just missed the forehead of an old man sitting at the bar. A chunk of wood followed the puck and landed on the bar surface.

The old man downed his beer and headed for the door, joined by a few other regulars. Harry, the bartender, tried to come around from behind the bar but was blocked by Tony and Mickey.

"Don't worry about them," Mickey told him. "They're only staying for a little while. They'll be leaving soon."

"What's your fucking problem?" Lenny shouted when he saw Harry being restrained.

"Relax, man," Tony said. "Be cool."

"Don't tell me, man. Don't tell me nothing," Lenny shouted.

The Looneys stepped in front of Lenny and spoke to him in low tones. Monk stepped in front of Harry and tossed two twenty-dollar bills on the bar.

"That should cover the damage," Monk said.

Harry looked at the bills.

"Put 'em in your pocket," Monk said. "Your boss won't know how the damage happened."

Harry slipped the twenties into his tip glass near the cash register and moved to the other end of the bar.

"Let's get the fuck out'a here," Lenny said.

"We gotta wait for Kelly and Johnny," Monk said.

"So, we can meet 'em at the club."

"You think Mr. P would put up with this shit?" Monk asked.

Lenny was silenced. He dropped another quarter into the slot. The others followed.

The place now belonged entirely to us. The Crazies bounced between the bowling machine, the bumper pool table and reminiscing with the rest of us.

Kelly and Johnny wore three-piece pinstripe suits and silk ties, their dress a symbol of authority compared to Pete's scaled-down, but still fashionable casual clothes. They seemed to cast a spell over the crazies as they nodded to their crew before strolling to our party in the rear area.

"Hi, buddy," Johnny said as we embraced. "You look great," he said. "If I wasn't 4F, I would've picked the Air Force."

"So, who've you been hashing things out with lately?" I asked.

"Just me," he said turning to the crowd. He pushed pass me and greeted the others at the party.

I expected him to come back to talk with me but he drifted from person to person, shaking hands and giving stock responses.

"Hi prez," I said to Kelly. Kelly waved a greeting and he and Johnny moved back to the bar area where the crazies were assembled.

I watched as Kelly and Johnny tossed twenties and once a fifty on the bar and bought rounds for everyone. I watched and I still didn't learn that the only way to survive in this world was to have those never-ending twenties and fifties. Johnny had learned. I guess I had been influenced by different circumstances, unable to attain the education - both formal and street-wise - that he received after we separated. But then, maybe greed wasn't in my blood, and that would keep me anchored to where I was.

I shook off my depression and rejoined the party before some-one became reminded of my old moniker, The Mad Russian.

Billy Ryan and a total stranger drifted through the front door. Everyone greeted Billy, while giving sidelong glances to his com-panion, a weird, disheveled guy with stringy, shoulder-length blond hair and beard. Billy was too involved with greeting everyone and didn't introduce his companion. The stranger, who looked to be our age under all the hair, took it upon himself to single out Pete.

"Remember me?" he asked Pete.

Pete shook his head. Then said, "My God. *Timmy?*"

It was Timmy Ryan, Dave's brother, and a second cousin of Billy. He hadn't been heard from for five years.

Timmy hugged Pete. "I was just visiting Billy's family when we heard about your get-together," Timmy said. "I can't believe all you guys are here."

"This is great," Pete said. "I've always wanted to get in touch with you."

"Don't feel like you have to apologize or anything," Timmy said. "I have no problem about what happened. We all have to forgive and forget." Timmy seemed saintly as he held his hand, palm open, in front of him. "We all must seek peace of mind."

"We're splitting," Kelly said. "Great to see you all again." He shook hands with Red and me and waved to the rest of the crowd.

"I'm sticking around," Pete said, and Johnny waved an okay to him.

"Call for one of the limos if you need it," Johnny said.

"Wait," Roxie said. "I want a picture of the originals." She shot several pictures of the five surviving founders.

Kelly, Johnny and the crazies filed out the door, a draft of cold air left behind.

Timmy hugged Pete after a few minutes of conversation and left with Billy.

I was sitting alone at one of the tables and Pete approached me. "I know you don't know me," Pete said. "But from what Johnny told me about you, I do know you."

"Thanks, man," I said. "That's good of you to say."

"You were disappointed in Johnny tonight, right?"

I shrugged. "Yeah, I guess so."

"More than guess so. He told me how close you guys were."

"Yeah, we were."

"Well, in his new position, he's expected to carry a hard, unemotional shell." Pete nodded. "He's not one of them..." He touched his chest. "In here, but he has to act the part. He's still a good man. He's helped my mother and me a lot. She's in Florida now, running a chain of restaurants. And I'm going to CCNY. It was him that did it all for us."

"I'm sure," I said. "He always thought of others."

"And he still does. I know he would want to tell you this, and he would have if he were alone with you." Pete nodded again to reassure me. "He still speaks of you often, and you hold a special place in his thoughts."

"Thanks for telling me that," I said. "It means a lot to me."

"You deserve to know it. And I apologize for him not telling you himself."

"It's good to know there's someone to speak for him; to think the same way he did."

"*Hey*, he's my brother," Pete said.

I glanced at the front door when it swung open and saw a woman in black sit at the front corner of the empty bar. I thought at first she was going to join us, as she hesitated before sitting. She was mysterious, with a black shawl wrapped around her head and neck and sunglasses covering a large portion of her pale face.

Harry served her a drink and then moved to our end of the bar. "Mickey," he said. "Keep an eye on things for me. I gotta go downstairs and tap a keg."

"Okay," Mickey said.

"We drove by the school yard you guys hung out at," Pete said. "There's a new group of kids hanging out. Kelly stopped and asked them if they ever heard of the Vandals. Some hadn't and the ones who did only knew the name from when they played in the school yard during their elementary school days."

"How fleeting fame is," I said.

"Yeah," Pete said. "Sometimes you wonder what it was all for."

I was about to comment when I saw the mystery woman leave her drink and walk toward us. She stopped at the booth where Mickey, Red, Chico and Roxie sat.

"I got a message from your friend, Benny," she said. "He says *'ouch'*." She laughed. "Just like you will." She reached into her handbag and pulled out a knife. Everyone sat dumbfounded as she jerked the knife over her shoulder. Mickey slid from the booth seat as she slashed the blade across his arm, her aim spoiled by his sudden movement.

She drew the knife back again as Mickey sat on the floor clutching his arm. Everyone leaped to their feet and Red's judo chop shot forward smashing into the sunglasses. An ear piece of the black plastic frame snapped as the woman reeled backward into the bumper pool table. She swiped her hand across her face and the broken frame fell to the floor. The shawl pushed back off her head. Sharon Norris stood glaring at us, rubbing her temple where Red's blow had glanced off.

Everyone moved toward her.

"Stay back," she shouted, the knife extended in front of her. "I came here to get him." She pointed at Mickey. "But I'll take out as many of you Vandal bastards as you want."

She looked behind her, forward, and then edged along the pool table to the wall. *You see this?* She reached inside her unbuttoned coat and lifted her blouse to show a circular scar on the side of her stomach. "I got this from a Vandal bastard with a gun. Before him, it was that son of a bitch hitting me all the time." She pointed at Mickey. "And *them* isolating me." She pointed to Roxie. "But I forgot about it. I was willing to wait it out, to let the past be, until tonight when that pig, Benny, tried to rape me. I showed him. He won't think about trying that on anybody again. Yeah, I heard about your little party through the grapevine. Now you'll all pay."

She pushed off the wall and headed for Mickey, who was still sitting on the floor. She ignored everyone else for the moment and we all rushed forward. Chico and Freddy grabbed her and Red squeezed the knife from her hand. I expected her to kick and fight, but she gave up as soon as the knife left her hand.

"You nutty bitch," Mickey said as Tony helped him to stand. "What you need is a good beating to straighten you out."

"You touch her and I'll kick you in the nuts," Roxie said.

"You taking her side?" Mickey asked.

"I think she's had enough abuse from you," Roxie said. "I'm no fan of her's, but I sure as hell don't have any sympathy for somebody like you."

"That goes for me," Chico said.

"But look what she did to me," Mickey said, looking at the slashed sleeve of his coat.

Red spread the edges of the slice and looked at the wound.

"Like they say in the movies, it's only a scratch," Red said. He pulled out a handkerchief, folded it and tucked it inside the coat over the cut. "Put some pressure on it with your other hand and go to an emergency room for a tetanus shot. You'll be okay."

"Well, I'm calling the cops," Mickey said. "She's a looney and needs to be locked up."

"I didn't see anything," Pete said. He looked at me. "My mother said she liked her."

"I was talking to Pete," I said. "I didn't see anything either."

Chico and Freddy released their grip on Sharon.

"I think you better split before we change our minds," Chico said.

"No, wait," Mickey said. "You can't do this."

"You better visit the hospital and get that tetanus shot for the cut you got when you fell off your seat," Red said. "Funny how some cuts happen."

"You know she was the cause of all the shit two years ago," Tony said. "How do you know she won't come back after Mickey, or any of us, again?"

"What about that, sister?" Freddy asked.

"I can't promise," Sharon said. "What I did back then only helped to speed up the inevitable. Sonny was going to have his war with the Sinners, no matter what. But I see something different here. You aren't the people I hated." She looked at Mickey. "Well, most of you. I'm sorry so many of you became involved."

"And you don't seem like the person we hated. Let's call it a draw," Roxie said. "Let's finally put it to rest."

"How can you let her off the hook like this? If the crazies were still here, they'd put a bullet in her," Mickey said. "She got Blackie killed."

"Blackie got himself killed," Freddy said. "And you weren't even there, so don't try to sound like a martyr or something."

"You'll be sorry," Mickey said as he watched Sharon walk to the front door. "Pete, what about Benny? He's you're boss. You gonna let her go? She may've killed your boss."

"I doubt it," Pete said. "He's a tough guy. He can take care of himself. If he wants to, he can track her down himself. I don't know anything."

Sharon waved. "My aim wasn't so good with Benny, either." She tried to smile. "I'll remember this." And then she was gone.

"What if she waits for me outside?" Mickey asked.

"I got the knife," Red said holding up the closed pearl-handle switchblade. "Here." He tossed it to Mickey, who caught it with his good hand. "Now you can protect yourself," Red said.

"You guys suck," Mickey said as he stomped passed the bar and out the front door.

"I better give him a ride," Tony said. "Take it easy everybody." He followed Mickey.

We all stared at each other for a moment until Harry broke the silence closing the cellar door.

"Where the hell is Mickey?" Harry asked. "You can't trust that guy to do anything."

"He had someplace else to be," I said. "We kept an eye on things for you."

"Thanks," Harry said. "How about a round on the house?"

"No, thanks," Roxie said. "We still have that other party to go to."

"Yeah," Pete said. "I don't think there's much more we can do here."

We stopped on the sidewalk outside the door and wished each other well. Roxie promised to mail copies of the pictures she had taken to Red and me.

"Maybe someday we can have a real reunion," Roxie said as she and Chico climbed onto the bus that stopped at the corner. "I'll work on it."

The bus pulled away and the four of us who remained decided to end the night at the diner we had frequented when we were younger.

"The real Vandals," Pete said, as him and I paired off.

"What?"

"Something Johnny said once. The real Vandals are the guys who cared. There were still some here tonight."

When I got home that evening, I sat down and wrote the words that were swirling through my head:

They had been memories
Only faces staring at me from the pages of a photo album
The escapades of our youth had become dimmer with the years
But then, on a night of nights, they were there
And although their faces were more mature than those in the album,
    it was them
They spoke of those days from our past
They carried on like they did in our past
They laughed, they marveled, they revealed
It was a night to remember, but it came to an end
And in a fleeting moment they were gone
Another memory in the pages of a photo album.